# THE GIFT OF SAMUEL

*Grey Dawn*

## PAUL PADRÓN

In Libras Libertas LLC

Publisher's Cataloging-In-Publication Data
(Prepared by The Donohue Group, Inc.)
Names: Padrón, Paul, author.
Title: The Gift of Samuel : Grey Dawn / Paul Padrón.
Description: Wheaton, Illinois : In Libras Libertas LLC, [2021]
Identifiers: ISBN 9780578853406 (paperback) | ISBN 9780578863276 (ebook)
Subjects: LCSH: Teenage boys--Fiction. | Dystopias--Fiction. | Survival--Fiction. | Spirituality--Fiction. | LCGFT: Dystopian fiction. | Bildungsromans.
Classification: LCC PS3616.A3362 G54 2021 (print) | LCC PS3616.A3362 (ebook) | DDC 813/.6--dc23

Library of Congress Control Number: 2021903525

**To What End**
Words and Music by Dustin Kensrue, Edward Breckenridge, James Breckenridge and Teppei Teranishi
Copyright (c) 2003 Sceptor Of Malice
All Rights Administered by Universal Music - MBG Songs
International Copyright Secured All Rights Reserved
*Reprinted by Permission of Hal Leonard LLC*

Selected Thrice lyrics included from the songs "Only Us," "Beyond the Pines," "Everything Belongs," "The Grey," and "The Long Defeat," reprinted by permission of Wixen Music Publishing, Inc. and Thrice.

Front Cover Design and Artwork by David Fuerst.

Printed in the United State of America.

Published by: In Libras Libertas, LLC, 101 Tennyson Drive, Wheaton, Illinois 60189

www.thegiftofsamuel.com

# CONTENTS

# DEDICATION

*For Mary Blomquist*
*One of the kindest souls I've ever known*

# ACKNOWLEDGMENTS

The gifts of love and support allow one to experience hope and achieve seemingly unreachable goals. The Gift of Samuel would never have come to fruition without the love and support I received from countless individuals. My most heartfelt gratitude begins with my mom, Carol, my dad, Lorenzo, my godmother, Mary, my stepmother, Susan, my father-in-law, Dan, and my mother-in-law, Pat. It all starts with parents, and I couldn't have asked for better ones.

To my wife, Rachel, who not only supported this dream, but also provided crucial feedback after reluctantly agreeing to be one of the book's final content editors. My two boys, Andrew and Sam, who allowed me to know true unconditional love. And to all the rest of my family and friends— every time I gave you a hug and told you that I loved you, I meant it.

To those who willingly volunteered to read early drafts: Jessica Wenzel, Matthew & Cristina Croft, Gene Bechen, Erik Mennecke and the Mennecke family, Sean Leonard, Dave Cooper, Rachel Legorreta and Amy Teeling. The fact that you showed interest, in and of itself, inspired me to press on. To those who read early drafts and were generous enough to provide written feedback: Germán Diaz, James Ryan, John Beavers, and Kathy Ryan. The comments you provided were more vital than you realize. Finally, to Adam Sleper, a professional writer and editor who was kind enough to take on a content edit between gigs.

On the technical side, Sergio Oliveros, doubling as the world's greatest cousin and web manager. Attorneys George Xamples, Allen Hoover and Travis Life, who helped an old friend maneuver publishing's legal landscape, pro bono. Lisa M. Lilly, founder of WritingAsASecondCareer.com, for her time and sage advice. To Dan Houle, for his help with Audible. To Tripp Fuller, Ken O'Leary, Wixen Music Publishing and Hal Leonard for the assist on licenses for Thrice lyrics, and Dustin Kensrue, Riley & Eddie Breckenridge, and Teppei Teranishi of Thrice for their music and inspiration. To Judy Conner, humbly the best grammatical editor on Earth. Finally, to Lydia Janacek, the first person to request a signed copy of this novel, and Dave Fuerst, who took my jumbled thoughts and transformed them into the perfect front cover.

A very special thank you to Joseph Neil Connelly and Denise Santomauro. Neil edited the first draft of this book, and carried me through the dreaded first revision, always encouraging me to keep my chin up. At the other end, Denise took the last draft and gave me a meticulous edit, while never losing the human side of the thoughts and emotions I wanted to convey. Without Neil's unwavering reassurance, I would have thrown in the towel at the onset. Without Denise's remarkable direction, I would have never crossed the finish line. They are simply magnificent.

Lastly, and most importantly, I thank you, the individual reading these words at this very moment. I wrote this book to share a message of hope with anyone willing to listen. We all falter, question our worth, and often fall short of the mark.

There's no shame in this aspect of life. Just don't give up. Instead, find strength in your weakness and rise to face the challenge again. I hope you enjoy this story, find inspiration in its words, and then share the tale with anyone willing to listen.

# EPIGRAPH

"I know not with what weapons World War III will be fought, but World War IV will be fought with sticks and stones."

– Albert Einstein

# PREFACE

The following narrative originated from a series of dreams I had beginning in 1999, containing recurrent themes and characters. The final storyline was then developed and completed through meditation and prayer. I never would have written this novel, were it not for the dreams, meditation and prayer I experienced.

# PROLOGUE

**W**illiam pressed the palm of his hand firmly against his forehead. His eyes were shut tight and his face red. Despite several attempts to end the conversation amicably, Theresa would not quit until she had the answer she wanted. They had been sitting across from each other, arguing, for over an hour, while the rest of Hartland slept.

"What they are proposing is not the answer, William, and you know it. There are better alternatives. Why won't you listen to me?"

William dropped his hand, his wrinkled and weathered skin revealed by the single lit candle between them.

"I've been listening to you, Theresa, for your entire life. That's the problem. I've been too lenient with you. I shouldn't have let the tragedy of your father's death affect me as it did. I should have used more discipline in raising you. It's my fault that you've forgotten your place in our Commune. We shouldn't even be having this conversation."

Theresa leaned forward, her head tilted, her eyebrows scrunched, mustering every ounce of emotion she could to gain William's attention. "And yet, here we are, having this conversation because deep down, you know what the others are about to set in motion is not the right course of action."

William shook his head from side to side before abruptly shifting his torso sideways in his chair. He stretched out his long legs and adjusted his seat.

Theresa reached out and took his hand. "Please, William. You know who I am and you know my heart. We want the same thing for the people of Hartland. But what they have proposed is not going to help bring our population back."

William pulled his hand away. "What would you have me do? This is not my proposal. This is a decision reached by our leaders after countless hours of debate and discussion. We have done everything we can think of to raise our numbers, but they continue to dwindle. Desperate times call for desperate measures. If we don't take this final step now, there will be no Hartland tomorrow. Our leaders understand the difficulty of what we're about to do. It's going to be hard for all of us, not just for you and your son. But it's our last option and we have to take it."

"It is not our last option! Please, William. Our leaders trust you. You must convince them to *leave* Hartland. Every man, woman, and child must leave this place. We need to find another Commune, outside these walls."

"Leaving Hartland is suicide."

"You don't know if that's true. There have got to be other Communes out there that have survived for as long as we have. What's more, we don't know what these other Communes have discovered in that time."

"Theresa—"

"I know the thought of leaving Hartland is scary. I understand that Hartland is all we have ever known. But for all we know, there could be another Commune out there that has already found the answer to what we are so desperately searching for."

"The last time we sent a party to explore what's out there, it never returned."

"That party was dispatched decades before you were even born. Think of how much time has passed since then. We don't know how the rest of humanity has managed in its fight against Grey Dawn. If we stay here and proceed with the plan our leaders have devised—that's the real suicide."

William stood up from the table where they sat and crossed the room to a four-pane window overlooking Round Lake. The wood floor underneath him creaked with each step he took, the sound echoing in the silence between him and Theresa. He folded his arms against his chest and stared out into the darkness. From the reflection in the glass, he could see Theresa's wide eyes staring at him. Her brown hair, half up in a bun, half down and draped over her shoulder, reminded him of when she was a little girl. She was just as stubborn then. William hung his head.

After several seconds, Theresa broke the silence. "I haven't changed your mind, have I?"

William turned to face her. "No, you haven't. We cannot leave Hartland. This Commune is our foundation. We must move forward with the new plan. It's the best option we have to save ourselves, to save humanity."

Theresa knew it was a long shot that William would agree to convince their leaders to have everyone evacuate Hartland, but she had to try. Desperate times call for desperate measures, indeed. It was time to put her alternate plan into effect. She pushed herself up and rushed to the door, flinging it open. The brisk night air swept into the room, causing the candlelight to flicker. With one foot out the door, she stopped and turned back to William. "You can do whatever you want. But there is no way in hell Joshua and I are following this ludicrous plan."

Theresa slammed the door behind her. The tears she'd held back during their discussion began falling in streaks down her face. She tried to regain her composure, reminding herself that this was the most likely outcome. She took a deep breath and wiped at her cheeks, but it was no use. She began crying even harder, realizing she had just seen her surrogate father for the last time and never told him how much she loved him.

## GREY DAWN

The rain beat down hard on Joshua as he trudged south along the cracked pavement of what used to be U.S. Route 23. He'd been on this stretch for over thirty days and nights. That's what he estimated, anyway. He usually kept a better record of the passing time, but counting the days now seemed pointless. His frail body and mind were consumed with the constant chills and hunger pains that coursed through him. He was slight, weighing one hundred pounds, at most, but the lack of food had left him gaunt. Ever since his mother, Theresa, told him that they were making this voyage, Joshua's thoughts were fixated on his pain and the uneasiness of his unknown future.

"Wake up," she'd whispered to him the night they'd left. Her voice that night was seared into his memory.

"What? What time is it?"

"Shhh," she said, brushing his brown, stringy bangs aside and tucking them behind his ears. "Everything is okay, but I need you to be quiet. Take a moment to wipe the sleep from your eyes and gather your wits. I've laid out some clothes for you. Quickly."

He still wore the same clothes, despite how they'd changed since leaving Hartland. His grey, long-sleeved cotton shirt and his jeans had become black from nights sleeping on the earth's floor. And his shoes, the soles cut from car tire rubber and stitched together with a heavy, water-resistant cloth, were coming apart at the seams.

"Where are we going?" He had asked her the night of their escape. "What's going on?"

"I'll explain everything when we're on the road. Just trust me and do exactly as I say. There's a backpack for each of us, full of supplies. I'll lead the way. You follow close behind. Let's go."

"But—"

"Joshua, please. I promise I'll explain everything soon. Right now, I need you to shut up, get dressed, grab your pack and follow me."

Dressed and on the move, Joshua didn't say another word. Growing up in Hartland, he learned the importance of following orders and not making any waves. It was expected of him. But more than that, Joshua would do whatever it took to avoid the tension he observed between his mother and William. The arguments between them were epic, especially when Joshua was a child. William was like a grandfather to him, even though they weren't blood related. The fighting had toned down over the past few years, but he still heard the occasional shouting between his mom and William, followed by a thrown object or a door slamming.

Aside from the uncomfortable fights between his mom and William, Joshua had lived a good life in Hartland. At least, he had considered it a good life. He didn't have anything to compare it to.

Until now.

Before that night, Joshua had spent every single day of his fifteen and a half years inside his Commune. In the time before Grey Dawn, Hartland was a small, rural town in the state of Michigan with a population of just over sixteen thousand. In the months that followed Grey Dawn's arrival, nearly half of those people left in search of loved ones and answers. The remaining citizens built a barrier around four small, clustered lakes: Long, Round, Handy, and Maxfield. That's where the Hartland Commune existed ever since.

The citizens knew how to farm the land and produce enough food to survive, even if they were always hungry. And they were skilled enough with their hands to build a secure perimeter and shelters, even if they were always cold. The environment was as safe as one could imagine, given the circumstances.

From what Joshua could piece together about the time before Grey Dawn, people of the entire world communicated via computers, some so small they fit in the palm of your hand. Bigger versions sat on desks or tables. Hartland had some of these devices, but they didn't work. Any abilities these computers possessed were vanquished with Grey Dawn.

For generations, the physically strongest and healthiest males ruled Hartland. But before Grey Dawn, the ranks in society were determined by small, distinct, and elaborately detailed pieces of paper called currency. The more currency someone had, the higher their status, and the more power they wielded, regardless of their physical stature. Given the importance of currency and its unique ability to establish order, the citizens of Hartland referred to the time before Grey Dawn as the Paper Era.

Like its computers, some currency had survived the fall of the Paper Era. A few pieces had been encased in hard, clear plastic to preserve their shape and act as a memento of humanity's history. The rest served as kindling to start fires long ago.

As appealing as computers and currency sounded to

Joshua, both paled in comparison to the Paper Era's alleged greatest gift: the sun. According to the now dead, founding members of the Hartland Commune, people of the Paper Era felt the warmth of direct sunlight on their skin. Not that it was sunny every day at that time, but the sky wasn't *always* grey, and the rainfall wasn't nearly as persistent as it was now. Today, people had to go through extraordinary measures to get any kind of vitamin D.

"Boys! It's almost noon! Shirts off! Remember Robbie Williams!" Theresa had shouted from a distance to Joshua and his two best friends, Jamie and Neil, the day before Theresa and Joshua made their escape.

"Like we need the reminder." Jamie said as the three boys removed their shirts. "We've only been doing this our whole lives."

The boys were pale and skinny enough to count ribs.

"Good Lord, I'm freezing." Neil said. "Isn't it torture enough being forced to constantly eat mushrooms? Is it really necessary to be shirtless when it's this cold out?

"Work faster," Joshua said, rubbing at the goosebumps along his arms. "The faster we move, the sooner we'll warm up."

After a few minutes, Neil spoke up. "This is pointless. Robbie choked down mushrooms and froze his ass off just like us, and he still killed himself. It doesn't matter what we do. Grey Dawn is going to end us all eventually."

"Stop it," Joshua said. "We have to stay positive if we're going to beat Grey Dawn."

"Beat Grey Dawn?" Jamie asked. "How are we going to get the sun back when we don't even know what caused it to go away in the first place?"

No one answered. They just put their heads down and continued working.

Some thought Grey Dawn was the result of a bottom quark bomb war. Others believed an asteroid or comet hit the earth. However, the prevailing belief in Hartland was that Grey Dawn was an act of God meant to punish humanity for its evil and sin. Despite the numerous blessings present during the Paper Era, its people were never satisfied with what they had, always wanting more. Greed and self-indulgence came to rule the day, and God corrected that with Grey Dawn.

Myths and personal beliefs aside, the fact was that air filled with cloud one morning, and the sky dimmed. With it, the great technologies of the world no longer functioned. Currency became nothing more than worthless pieces of paper. And with Grey Dawn's arrival, Joshua's ancestors banded together to survive.

After the Commune was settled, a dozen men left Hartland with three months' worth of supplies. Their mission was to find out what had happened and report back. They never returned. The failed mission and the uncertainty of what caused Grey Dawn led to more than just conflicting theories of its origin. Hartland suffered from a lingering and unmistakable sense of fear.

The people were scared. Always scared.

Several generations passed before Joshua was born. By that time, no one was sure how long it had been since the rise of Grey Dawn. Now, exact dates didn't matter. In the time since he left the Commune, all that mattered to Joshua was knowing what he was and where he was: a fifteen-year-old boy headed south on U.S. Route 23.

Joshua came to an overpass and decided to take shelter from the rain.

"I can't believe this," he said out loud as he threw his pack down. "What am I doing walking on this God-forsaken highway?"

He heard nothing but silence in return, aside from the falling rain.

"Damn it, Mom! Why did you make us leave Hartland?"

Again, silence.

Joshua picked up several stones and began throwing them as hard as he could, one at a time, out into the downpour.

"Mom!" He screamed at the top of his lungs before falling to the ground.

As Joshua laid there, he pictured the last time he saw his mother. None of this was her fault. She was only doing what she thought was best.

"I'm sorry, Mom. I'm so sorry," he whispered, wishing she was still there with him.

## ❧ 2 ❧

## U.S. ROUTE 23

During the day, Joshua would walk as far as his physical body would let him. Constant showers allowed him to maintain an ample water supply, but food was scarce. Joshua was starving. His eyes were constantly scanning the terrain for anything to eat.

He still had the small waterproof backpack his mother gave him when they departed with the essentials: a pouch to hold water, a pocketknife, a slingshot, a bow and spindle with a hand block to start fires, and a blanket no bigger than a few square feet. When it rained, he would collect as much water as he could. When it wasn't raining, he would start a fire, especially if he had a rabbit or squirrel to eat. But he would eat anything edible, from weeds to plants, small critters to insects—literally anything. At night, he would find as comfortable and safe a spot as possible and curl up in a ball with his blanket. It wasn't long before sleep washed over his exhausted mind and body. Joshua's dreams were always detailed and vivid but often made no sense.

When his mother started them on this journey, their goal was simple: walk south on Route 23 until they reached another Commune or the ocean. Given that neither one of them had ever been outside of Hartland, they didn't know what to expect on the highway. They only had Hartland's folklore of savages and gangs of cannibals who wandered the earth wreaking havoc upon anything they encountered. Women were raped. Men were tortured and killed. Children were forced into slavery, eventually becoming a cannibal and member of the gang themselves, if they wanted to survive. The highway was the last place anyone would want to be, especially a scrawny, fifteen-year-old boy and his middle-aged mother.

Yet, despite the danger that was allegedly outside Hartland, Joshua's mother took the chance and forced them to leave. Once outside of their Commune and on the road, Joshua's head was on a swivel as he constantly scanned his surroundings with his heart pounding. He continued following his mom with his eyes wide and mouth shut until he couldn't stand it any longer.

"Mom, I understand that we don't want to make any noise, but will you please tell me what the hell is going on? Why are we walking outside of Hartland in the middle of the night?" Joshua's tone was urgent, but he spoke just loud enough for his mother to hear him. He didn't want to gain anyone else's attention. "This is dangerous. You know what goes on outside of Hartland. We're going to die out here!"

Theresa was not easily rattled, though. More importantly, she was smart and perceptive. Their Commune hadn't been attacked in over a century. Joshua's mother knew better than to believe the old folklore.

"Don't be ridiculous." She did not use the same quiet tone as Joshua. "You sound just as paranoid as the others. There's no danger out here, at least, from other people. You should know better than to believe the hysteria. We've been on the move for what, over an hour? Have you seen any savages ready to throw us into a stew?"

She was right. They had not seen a soul since leaving Hartland.

"But what about when we get further south?" Joshua asked, still speaking in an anxious whisper. "How do we know there aren't a bunch of cannibalistic barbarians waiting to kill us at the end of this highway?"

"Joshua, get real. There's no one else out here. If there were others this close to Hartland, we'd know about them. As we get further south, we'll need to be more cautious, sure, but there's no need to get all worked up. If you see something, alert me immediately, and vice versa. We'll stay sharp and keep the chatter to a minimum. I *always* walk lead and you follow close behind. And we won't wander off Route 23 to investigate anything unless it's obvious that it's an active Commune. You understand? We stay on the highway.

"Then, we use common sense, like no fires at night or during the day. If we need to start a fire, we do it at twilight only, and we keep it small. If we encounter someone on the road, you let *me* do the talking. As long as we use our heads, we'll find another Commune in no time. We will be fine. Settle down before you start making me nervous."

"Settle down? You want me to settle down?" Joshua was no longer quiet. "Why don't you tell me why we're out here in the first place! Were you in some kind of trouble? *What's going on?*"

"We were both in trouble. All of Hartland is in terrible trouble. We didn't have a choice; we had to leave. We're going to head south on Route 23 and find another Commune where the people in charge have more sense than those in Hartland."

By the time day broke, Joshua had realized his mom was right—the stories about the outside were erroneous. The days that immediately followed were more of the same. Joshua and his mother weren't scattering from one hiding spot to the next, avoiding constant violence and brutality. The outside was a barren wasteland. There were no gangs, no savages, and no cannibals. There was no one.

They did encounter small wildlife along the way, though. Joshua was easily the best slingshot in Hartland, so when it wasn't raining, he would arm his slingshot and be ready to hit anything that came within striking distance. Though he was skinny as a rail, his quick reflexes and accuracy made his shots deadly.

A week into their trip, Joshua and his mom encountered a cluster of tall buildings unlike anything they had ever seen, some so tall they touched the grey sky. For every building that still stood, there were five others that had collapsed. Joshua wanted to explore them. He wanted to get off the road and see what else he could discover in these structures and the rubble. However, Theresa wouldn't have it. From what they could see, the structures still standing were void of life. She insisted that they stay on the move. They were only to leave the highway's path for sleep or in the case of an emergency.

With each uneventful day, Joshua worried less about being attacked by others. However, when night arrived, the thought of there being no one else alive became more frightening than the thought of the brutes Joshua had originally envisioned. Hartland could be all that remained of humanity and he left it. At least he had his mom. She had a way of calming him down and reassuring him that everything would be fine. But that comfort would soon come to an abrupt and catastrophic end.

## ❧ 3 ❧

## THE SICKNESS

"**A**re we ever going to find another Commune?" It was a question Joshua asked his mother daily, usually when they were on the move. "We've been walking for nearly two weeks and have nothing to show for it. How do we even know there's another Commune out here?" Joshua aimlessly flung a stone into the open air with his sling shot, ahead of his mother. She pretended not to notice.

"Joshua, you have to stay positive. The power of thought is more controlling than you realize. It has the ability to alter the physical world around us. If you keep telling yourself we're not going to find another Commune, that negative energy is going to manifest into our reality. We will find another Commune."

"Fine. Let's say we find another Commune. How do we know they are going to allow us inside? What happens then?" Joshua extended his sling shot to fire another stone. Theresa stopped and turned around, grabbing his hand and forcing Joshua to disarm the weapon.

"Joshua, please." Theresa coughed hard before continuing. "Everything that happens during your life is either a blessing or a curse. Which one it's going to be is up to you alone. You keep on thinking harmful thoughts and we're finished. Don't curse your own life with negativity. Save your stones for the next rabbit we see." Theresa turned back around and continued walking.

Joshua stood motionless, looking down at the pavement, before catching up. "I don't know," he muttered under his breath. "And, your cough is getting worse, by the way. Do you consider that a blessing or a curse?"

Theresa turned her head and threw Joshua a sideways glance from the corner of her eye. "Don't change the subject. If you keep a positive attitude, positive things will happen. We are going to find a Commune. And when we do, they are going to allow us entry. It's not like they are going to turn away two Chosen."

Within a few years of Grey Dawn's arrival, a handful of Hartland's children exhibited a small skin abnormality. It would start as a bumpy, discolored rash that would appear anywhere on the body. With some of these children, the rash would grow, sometimes becoming so severe, it would deform the muscle and tissue of the infected area. It was something no one had ever seen. With half of those infected, the ailment would suddenly stop. These children would grow to adulthood, marked with the abnormality for life, but have no other side effects.

For the others, the rash continued to grow and consumed nearly their entire body. Fever and difficulty breathing followed. In a matter of days, they were dead. This disease became known as the Sickness.

Despite years of study, the citizens of Hartland never determined its origin or its cure. However, once a child hit puberty, they appeared to be no longer susceptible to the disease. Hartland had no recorded case of an adult acquiring the Sickness.

Since its inception, the number of children at Hartland acquiring the Sickness, and those dying of the disease, rose every year. By the time Theresa was born, the disease was rampant. Hartland's population was down to just a few thousand, with most of its adult citizens marked with the Sickness. Children hitting puberty without showing signs of the skin deformity became a rarity. Eventually, the minority who made it to adulthood untouched by the Sickness became known as Chosen. Chosen became coveted and were seen as the last chance for survival of the human race.

"Yeah, so what? We're Chosen—big deal. Say we find a Commune that has already discovered a cure. You really think they are going to let in a couple more mouths to feed?" Joshua refused to let go of his fear without a fight. Again, Theresa stopped and turned to face her son.

"Your negative thoughts and energy end here. When we find a Commune, we *hope* they have the cure. The Sickness not only takes life from the living, it also forces a harsh way of life onto the living. Hartland is so obsessed with Chosen that they structured their entire society around them. Don't get me wrong. I am forever grateful for having you as my child. But it was extremely difficult to be forced to procreate with your father just because he was Chosen."

All of Hartland's Chosen were required to procreate only with other Chosen in an attempt to build a race of humans immune to the Sickness. Unfortunately, the plan wasn't working. By the time Joshua was born, of the few thousand that lived at Hartland, the number of Chosen totaled just a few hundred.

"I begged William to convince Hartland's leaders to venture out to search for the cure," Theresa continued, "but he's just like the rest of them: too fearful of the unknown to leave. They think they're so smart, coming up with their new plan. They fail to realize it's nothing more than a death sentence. That's why we had to leave."

Joshua wondered if his mom would have made the same decision had she known leaving their Commune would be her death sentence.

## ❧ 4 ❧

## THE DREAM

Whatever slight hope Joshua had of finding another Commune had nearly vanished. He'd been walking for over a month and was convinced Route 23 led nowhere. The fatigue and constant scavenging for anything to eat were taking their final toll. His feet grew heavier with each step. He never felt refreshed, even after a long night's sleep. And the loneliness was agonizing. Joshua knew it was only a matter of time before he would be dead.

"Why'd we have to leave, Mom?" Joshua said to the empty road. "You'd still be alive if we had just stayed. Is this really what you wanted? You really wanted us to die out here?"

Joshua took shelter under a dying tree next to the highway and closed his eyes.

"I should have turned back. *We* should have turned back. Now it's too late. You're dead and I'm too far south. There's no way I can make it back to Hartland, even if I tried."

Evening was upon Joshua, and he had come to a fork in the road: the entrance ramp to U.S. Route 441 was within his sight. He had stayed on U.S. Route 23 as his mother instructed. It had brought him nothing but misery. Maybe it was time to break the rule.

Then again, maybe none of it mattered. Maybe he was going to die soon regardless of which route he chose.

Too defeated to think about the next day's direction of travel, instead Joshua thought of William, Jamie, Neil and others that he'd left behind at Hartland. People that he loved that he'd never see again. Were they thinking of him? Was the new plan working? Did Theresa die for nothing?

Joshua covered himself and curled up into a ball. Hugging his knees, he began to cry softly. "I can't do this anymore. I'm so alone. I'm in so much pain. Please take it away. Please make it stop." The thought of waking up and facing another day of loneliness was too much to bear. "I just want it to be over. I just want to die. Please, let me die."

As Joshua's mind moved towards the realm of his dreams, he thought about his wish. Perhaps death would be like dreaming; a blissful release. It had to be better than walking Route 23. With his last conscious thought before falling completely asleep, Joshua made up his mind. He was not going to choose a path of travel in the morning. If God would not grant him his wish in his sleep, Joshua would find a way to end the isolation and pain himself. He would take his own life.

Once he'd reached this decision, his breath became deep and even, and light surrounded him. He was asleep and he knew it. He frequently believed his dreams were reality while he was having them, but this time he was conscious of the fact that his mind had taken him somewhere else. In this place, he did not want for a single thing. He felt no pain, no sadness, no loneliness or isolation. He was safe, content, and overcome with the feeling of being fully and unconditionally loved.

The sensation of timelessness enveloped him. Past,

present, and future still existed but were compressed. Linear time was replaced by one, singular moment that expanded into eternity. He never wanted to wake and leave this place.

As he floated through timelessness, Joshua became aware of other people. They were joyous and filled with a vibrancy to a degree he'd never known. A warmth of acceptance and compassion glowed around them. They communicated with each other, and even with Joshua, through shared thought alone. Each individual existed as his or her own entity, but the group possessed a collective consciousness, making misunderstandings impossible.

With an awestruck, childlike wonder, Joshua approached one of the other beings and asked where he was and how everyone could be so wholesome and complete in this place. The answer came as the question was asked: this place was his home and allowed for all beings to control the living organisms around them through thought alone.

A single wilted pink carnation appeared before him. As Joshua took in its features, he found himself moving inside the flower, becoming one with its essence. Its simplicity, matched only by its complexity, stunned him, and a deep and inspired love for this pink carnation seized him. As he basked in its aura, the wilted petals sprung to life, and the flower suddenly radiated with the same vibrancy and glow as the beings around him. As Joshua separated from the carnation, he knew his love for the flower had brought it back to life.

Once Joshua faced those who surrounded him, upon separating from the carnation, he understood these beings enjoyed perfect health by curing any illness through the power of their thought. The sky illuminated with swirls of bright white and pastel blue instead of grey, and the light that surrounded them emitted a love for everything that it touched. This place radiated overwhelming joy and a universal sense of peace and prosperity.

As Joshua continued scanning the scene, one face looked upon him with an exceptional love. It didn't take long for him to recognize her face.

Theresa.

She was no longer tired and weak from hunger. Her lips were full, and her cheeks flushed. The wrinkles along her forehead had smoothed out, and her long brown hair flowed with slight curls. Her wide, crystal blue eyes captured Joshua and filled his soul with love.

"I love you, Joshua," her voice rang clear and crisp in his head. "My love for you will never die. I will remain with you, always. You must press on in this life. You still have many important things you need to accomplish. Know that I am right by your side at every moment, encouraging you. I will never leave you. Do not lose hope, son. Never lose hope."

With Theresa's last word, Joshua was abruptly jarred out of his sleep and he sat up straight, wide-awake. His mother's voice and the word "hope," echoed in his head. She had been right there, in front of him. It couldn't end that quickly. He wanted so desperately to fall back asleep, to be back in that place. He laid back down, closed his eyes and tried to picture the heaven he just experienced, but it was pointless. The moment was over.

Joshua hugged his knees into his chest and cried harder than before. He cried as hard as he had on the day his mom died. He cried until he fell asleep again. But this time, his sleep took him to a great, empty void. He slept a hard, yet restful sleep, but didn't have another dream.

## 5

# CROSSROADS

J oshua woke early the next morning and for the first
time in a long time, he felt optimistic. While his
stomach was still empty, the hunger pains were gone.
After his mother's visit, he felt like he had his
companion back at his side. The dream was a sign. If he could
just continue to carry on for a little longer, things would turn
around. He had to persevere.

Joshua thought of the Route 23 rule as he stood at the
Route 441 crossroad. He was to stay on U.S. Route 23 until he
reached another Commune or the ocean, whichever came
first. But last night's dream couldn't have been a coincidence.
It must have been a sign from his mom to take the crossroad.
Route 23 had been nothing but a disaster since he first
stepped foot on the abandoned highway. Joshua decided
Route 441 would bring him better fortune.

After walking a good seven hours in his new direction,
Joshua came upon a small, deserted town and an entrance
ramp to another major highway, Interstate 85. As Joshua
stood there, debating whether or not to take another new
route, the temperature plummeted, and massive storm clouds

rolled in. He gathered as much dead wood as he could carry and took shelter under the open roof of an old gas station. Leaves and other debris had accumulated between two barren gas pumps, making it a good place to rest and wait for the storm to pass.

Joshua fumbled with some receptacles to try and capture the rain and fill his water pouch. After a couple of hours of staring into nothingness, Joshua cursed under his breath as he spilled most of the water from some hard, rounded plastic. As he poured the little that remained into his pouch, he couldn't stop his hands and arms from shaking from the cold. He cursed out loud, barely transferring a sip into his pouch. He threw the plastic out into the rain, "worthless piece of junk," he muttered, securing the cap to his water pouch before slamming it on the ground. "Some change of fortune," he said to himself as he wrapped his blanket around his shoulders and sat on the hard concrete.

Joshua watched in disbelief as the rain kept on until dusk. He thought about his friends back at Hartland, dry inside their homes. His chest heaved as he itemized all the things that were wrong with his situation. He had to get away from this nauseating gas station, but the thick clouds and heavy thunder made it too ominous to venture. Joshua shivered uncontrollably as the post-rain cold set in. It was the coldest he had been while on this journey. He had to start a fire.

As he sat and stared into the fire's glow, the cold abandoning his body, Joshua recalled his mother's warning to avoid a fire at night. But he'd just gotten warm. He couldn't bear the thought of putting it out. If he kept the fire burning through the night, he'd probably get a good night's sleep, and he'd need it to make up for lost time from the storm. It would draw attention to him, true, but he'd been in this wasteland for weeks and still hadn't seen anyone. A shiver went down his spine thinking of sleeping without the fire. He knew it was worth the risk to avoid enduring a night of icy breezes.

As the sky turned from grey to a solid black, Joshua gathered anything that would burn. With a sizable fire and warmth encircling his body, he closed his eyes and his mind wandered off. As he stood on the cusp of the realms of dreams, Joshua mumbled, "I must be the only one left."

Up to that point, his fires hadn't drawn anyone's attention. That was all about to change.

## ❧ 6 ❧

## SAVAGES

"Wake up, you stupid fuck."

With a startle, Joshua snapped awake. His blazing fire illuminated a group of twenty-five to thirty people, mostly male, based on their size and builds, standing in a circle around him.

Joshua jumped to his feet, ready to run, but as he turned around, he realized he was completely surrounded. There was nowhere for him to escape. The group hurled insults and vicious laughter at him.

Their attire was almost entirely black, with one glaring exception. The biggest and tallest man Joshua had ever seen was covered with what appeared to be shiny, silver-coated sequins that shimmered from the light of the jumping fire. This behemoth wore a helmet that covered his entire head, with slits cut out where Joshua could see only daunting, malice-filled eyes. Large, sharp teeth were enmeshed into the surface of the mask where this person's mouth should be. It was exactly what Joshua envisioned people outside of Hartland would look like when he began this journey. Joshua's insides trembled with uncontrolled fear.

The masked leader raised his hand, and everyone in the circle went silent. The only sound was the occasional crackle from the fire. Slowly, the leader moved his hands towards his head and lifted his mask. Joshua had seen plenty of people with the Sickness before, but when he saw what lay underneath, he thought he was going to be sick.

Instead of hair, the man's entire head was covered with large, uneven bumps, separated by thick veins that protruded through the skin. The surface of the deformity glistened with some type of moisture. Whether it was sweat or puss, Joshua couldn't tell, but it was wet. His nose was flattened to a slight degree and showed the same deformity as the man's head, while his mouth angled to the man's left side and downward, causing saliva to run out of its corner. If this man had ears, Joshua couldn't make them out in the firelight; they blended in perfectly with the raised and veiny surface that covered his scalp. The only portions of this man's face free of the Sickness were his eyes, which remained steadfast on Joshua. The leader's stare was sharp and calculating. He had the eyes of a predator.

He handed his helmet to the person standing to his right and took one step toward the center of the circle. Joshua was mortified. He didn't know what to do, so he just stood there as this menacing presence glared at him. Joshua's spatial perception expanded, and he began to feel lightheaded. He took a slow, deep breath to right himself.

"Take off your clothes." The leader said, with a deep, rasping voice.

"What?"

"Take off your clothes!"

With the command, the encircling gang laughed and hollered at Joshua once again.

"Quiet," the leader said.

Everyone went silent. Joshua just stood there, hoping this

really wasn't happening. The leader took another step toward him.

"Take off your clothes right now, or we will remove them for you. And, I can assure you, it will be done in the most painful way possible."

Joshua looked around at the staring faces and back at the leader's daunting eyes. His chest heaved with each breath. His hands clenched into fists, forcing the defined and massive muscles in his arms to flex. Joshua put his head down, removed his shoes, his shirt, and finally his pants.

As Joshua stood there, completely naked, he closed his eyes and brought his hands together in front of him to cover himself as best he could. His onlookers whistled and made other noises adding to Joshua's embarrassment. To his surprise, Joshua felt a sudden calmness. The calls of his captors ringing in his ears faded. Joshua understood that he would soon be dead, and he was at peace with the realization. He surrendered to his vulnerability and moved his hands to his sides. He asked silently in his mind that his death be quick and without pain.

Joshua waited with his eyes closed. He expected to be rushed by the savages around him. Yet, the only thing that grabbed Joshua was the quiet surrounding him. He opened his eyes to discover that the sneering grins and self-possessed faces morphed into shock and amazement. Even their leader seemed taken aback.

"I don't believe it," one of the onlookers said. Soon, the whispers expressing doubt multiplied. Joshua slowly scanned his head to his left and then his right. He had no idea what was happening.

Again, their leader screamed, "Quiet!" and everyone went silent.

"How old are you?" the deformed leader asked Joshua.

"Fifteen."

"Where did you come from?"

"I've been walking south on 23, and then I hit 441, which brought me here."

"How long did you walk south on 23?"

"I don't know. I've lost count of the days and nights. I think it's been over a month."

The leader relaxed his balled-up fists and turned his stare toward the sky. He looked back at Joshua and wiped the saliva from the corner of his mouth with his forearm.

"My name is Leon, and, as you can see, I'm the leader here. I don't care what your name was before now. From this point forth, you are simply my prize. You belong to me and will obey my every command."

Leon extended his right hand out to his side. The man holding Leon's helmet immediately gave it back to his master. "We'll stay here for the night. Nuri, secure my new prize and make sure he's properly bound. Build up that fire and keep it going until dawn. I want my prize near the flame. I don't want him getting ill from the cold. Aside from his bindings, leave him as he is so he remembers who's in charge."

Leon put his helmet back on and turned to the rest of the group. "I don't want *anyone* touching my prize. Understand? Nuri and I are the only ones that can touch him. If any of you disobey, you'll be the main course at our next meal. Is that clear?"

A collective grunt came from the crowd.

Leon turned to Joshua and with three quick, colossal steps, covered a space that Joshua might have been able to cover in six. It seemed impossible that Leon's large frame could move so swiftly. But his long and muscular legs allowed him a strength and agility that astonished Joshua. Two feet away from Joshua, Leon raised his right arm and gripped Joshua's chin. He turned Joshua's face left and right, examining him while saying nothing.

He let go of Joshua's face and in a voice only Joshua could hear, he said, "And you, my new prize, better stay in this condition until we reach Caulfield. If you disappoint me and begin showing signs of the Sickness—you'll wish you'd have never been born."

## 7

### MORE THAN A TRADE

"Wake up, Prize!" Nuri shouted as he gave Joshua a hard kick to his side. "We don't have time to waste. Leon wants us back at Caulfield as soon as possible, so you better be ready for some traveling today."

Joshua pushed at the ground with the side of his face. He wanted to rub his ribs where he had just been kicked, but his wrists were tied together behind his back. His ankles were also bound, loose enough that he could take small steps, but not enough to where he could get on his own two feet. He squirmed in a vain attempt to stand up, but it was impossible. Nuri crossed his arms and watched Joshua struggle. Quickly bored with the sight, Nuri grabbed Joshua at his armpits and pulled him up to his feet in one swift motion.

Joshua surveyed his surroundings and noted all the eyes upon him. He hated being naked in front of these strangers and wished they would allow him to put his clothes back on. Yet, he didn't say a word. He knew it would only encourage his captors to make such a request. Instead, Joshua pretended to be at ease with the situation and stared off into the distance as Nuri disappeared around the corner.

To Joshua's relief, his perceived indifference paid off when Nuri reappeared with a large cloth containing a hole in its center and Joshua's shoes. Nuri placed the large hoodless poncho over Joshua's head, covering him from his neck to his knees. Then, Nuri took a length of rope and tied it around Joshua's waist. His wrists were still bound behind his back and under the poncho, but at least his body was covered. Finally, he put on the shoes that Nuri had thrown to Joshua's feet.

"If there's one thing that Leon hates, it's the smell of human waste. So, you better tell me when you need to go or hold it, cause if that cover smells with foulness, Leon will be most displeased." Then Nuri placed a leash around Joshua's neck, secured another length of rope to the leash, and turned to one of the few females in the group.

"Carol," Nuri said, "You're going to hold the end of this rope and walk with Leon's prize as we make our way toward Caulfield. Make yourself useful for a change."

Carol approached the prisoner, took the rope's end from Nuri, and stared straight at Joshua's face to the point that he felt uncomfortable. She had long, grey hair that hung disheveled around her unassuming face. Her eyes were empty and hollow, like she was either lost in thought or unable to have one. Joshua couldn't decide if she was the most frightening or most harmless woman he'd ever met.

"Remember what Leon said, Carol. Don't touch his prize. You'll be leading the group, so if you have any problems, we'll see. Should be a simple enough task for an idiot like you."

Carol nodded and began walking, without uttering a word.

As they started down Route 441, a sense of excitement buzzed about the gang that trailed Carol and Joshua. He overheard them talking about what Leon was going to get for such a bounty. Possibilities from large quantities of food to medical supplies were discussed. He even thought he heard something about getting some artillery, so they could finally launch another attack on Caulfield.

There had been so much chaos surrounding Joshua since he had been captured, it wasn't until now that he grasped what was happening: they were in route to a Commune! If his captors were speaking the truth, Caulfield had resources and supplies equaling, and maybe even surpassing, Hartland's. Those resources were going to lead to his salvation, if Leon really was going to use Joshua for barter. He wanted to shout with delight at the prospect, but he kept his head down and his excitement contained. If they knew he could overhear their conversations, it could turn the whole plan upside down. He had to stay calm, especially with Carol often looking back at him.

Most of the time, she just faced forward with her head down. However, she'd regularly turn and gaze directly into Joshua's eyes with a look so penetrating it made him uneasy. By mid-day, her repetitive glances had turned ominous. Every time she'd turn and stare, Joshua feared the stare was going to turn into action. Other members of the gang occasionally shouted commands or insults at her. She would obey the commands without comment. Whatever was going on with this woman, Joshua wanted no part of it.

As evening fell, Nuri joined Carol and Joshua at the front.

"We're going to take shelter tonight at North Base," Nuri said to Carol. "Do you remember the marker?"

Carol simply nodded. Shortly thereafter, Carol took a hard right off Route 441 and into the dense foliage. She snaked through trees until they came upon a small pond and a trail beyond it. The path led to a clearing where a large, one-story brick building sat atop a small hill.

After walking the entire day, Joshua could barely stand. His body felt like it weighed a thousand pounds. If he did not get off his feet soon, he was going to collapse. Outside, the gang gathered dead tree branches and started a fire in a large fireplace in the building's foyer. They then spread out amongst the inside of the building. Once everyone was settled, portions of some type of root were distributed. Leon got the biggest portion by far. Joshua's portion was merely a few bites, but he felt lucky to have anything to eat. Soon, the fire was roaring, and the gang gathered in the foyer, taking their places for the night's rest.

Joshua, still bound, laid against the far wall, opposite the fire, closest to the front door. Carol laid next to him. Leon grabbed Nuri and took him outside the front door. Neither man closed the door behind them, allowing Joshua to over-hear their conversation as he fell asleep.

"What is it, Master?" Nuri asked.

"The last time we attempted a trade with Caulfield, those arrogant fools insulted me to an intolerable degree. They offered me a pittance."

"I remember it well."

"This time, however, we have a bounty that far exceeds anything we've ever been able to barter—a Chosen." Leon's eyes widened as he said the word. "Lorrick and the rest of Caulfield have worshipped these people for decades, and what has it brought them? Have their numbers increased? Have they found a cure for the Sickness or an escape from Grey Dawn?

"In exchange for this Chosen, I will command the highest price. Food, clothing, and supplies, but above all else, I want weapons. No fewer than a dozen firearms of my choosing. Caulfield is so obsessed with Chosen, they will have no choice but to accept."

"Master, Lorrick is still Caulfield's leader. He was the one that insulted you at our last exchange. Do you think he will give you firearms?"

Leon stood to his full height, his finger pointed at Nuri's

chest. "When we reach Caulfield, I want you to put my prize down on his knees and stand behind him with a knife at his throat. If Lorrick refuses to give me what I want, if they do not accept my demands, I will slaughter their precious Chosen right there before their very eyes. They will never allow a Chosen to die in such fashion.

"Here, Nuri, it is crucial that you carry out my order without hesitation. If Lorrick refuses to give me what I want, I will signal you, and upon my signal, slit the Chosen's throat. Let him bleed to his death before their very eyes. Then, we will start a fire at the front gate of Caulfield and roast their cherished Chosen on their doorstep before we feast on his flesh."

Nuri licked his lips.

"As you wish, Master."

## ❧ 8 ❧

## CAROL

Joshua awoke confused and disoriented to someone pressing their hand over his mouth. It was not yet morning, but the fire had burned down to merely ash and a few embers. It was Carol's hand covering his mouth. With her other hand, she pressed her index finger to her mouth. Joshua could barely breathe as he was sure she was about to do something terrible. Carol bent to his side and whispered at a level he could barely comprehend.

"Listen to me. Be absolutely still and do not make a sound." Instead of feeling fear with her command, Joshua instead was reminded of his mother waking him in a similar fashion the night they escaped Hartland. "If you make the slightest noise, they will wake, and we will both pay a heavy price. Nod if you understand so I can take my hand away from your mouth."

Joshua nodded, and Carol removed her hand. Then, to Joshua's astonishment, Carol began untying his bindings. As silently as she could, she freed the knots from his ankles, then his wrists. She stood and motioned for Joshua to stand up. Once standing, she barely whispered again in Joshua's ear. "I will lead. Step exactly where I step."

Carol crept toward the front door with deliberate and slow steps. Joshua followed, making sure to step on the exact spots that Carol used. At the front door, Joshua watched several sleeping bodies that laid just feet from them as Carol placed her hand on the latch to release the dead bolt. Joshua held his hand over his mouth and nose. His breathing was too loud. If they woke anyone up, Leon would surely kill them both. Carol turned the latch and managed to release the dead bolt with the softest click. The click was as loud as a clap of thunder to Joshua. They were doomed. But it was only in his mind. He watched as not a single sleeping body stirred.

Carol moved her hand to the doorknob and slowly wrapped her fingers around the knob, turning it counter-clockwise. Again, Joshua heard a click that, to him, was loud enough to wake the entire house. But as Carol opened the door, Joshua could see everyone was still fast asleep. Joshua exited first. Carol followed, closing the door silently behind them. She turned to Joshua and softly began speaking.

"Make your way down to the trail from where we came, back to 441. Go the same direction we were headed yesterday. Go left at the first street that intersects 441, and after a few minutes you will come upon a small grey building with a blue door. At that building, take a soft left, onto the bigger street. You understand? At the grey building with a blue door, take a soft left, onto the bigger street. You will take that road all the way to Caulfield. You'll know you're at Caulfield when you see the guard tower. Repeat to me what I just said."

Joshua stuttered his way through Carol's instructions accurately, and she continued.

"Do not stop, no matter what. It will take you an hour or two to get to Caulfield, depending on how quickly you move. You need to run if you can. When you cannot run, walk, but never stop. Once Leon realizes you are gone, he will come after you with reckless abandon. Do you understand?"

Joshua's torso shook with adrenaline and cold. The early morning air wrapped its chill around Joshua's body, even the parts covered by cloth. He was lost for words. He had a million questions to ask her, but only questioned, "why?"

With her left hand, Carol brushed the brown, stringy bangs along the right side of Joshua's head and tucked them behind his ear. "I had a son like you once. You remind me of him very much." A single tear ran down her right cheek. "Now go."

Joshua looked hurriedly toward the direction of the trail, then back to Carol. He couldn't delay. "Come with me," he said.

"If I leave with you, Leon will know we're headed to Caulfield and he'll catch us. I need to send Leon looking for you in another direction. Besides, by setting you free, I will have made amends for losing my son, and I can move onto the next life, where I will join him. Leon will take care of that for me. Now, please go. Hurry."

Joshua's head told him run, but his heart said something else. For the second time in just over a month, a woman was sacrificing herself to get him out of danger. He grabbed Carol and embraced her tightly. She returned the hug.

"Thank you," he said. "I will never forget what you've done for me."

Carol released Joshua from her arms and smiled at him as a second tear ran down her cheek.

Joshua smiled back at her before taking off for the trail in the distance. He feared tripping over the terrain, so he cautiously moved through the trial and woods until getting to 441. Once back on the road, Joshua broke into a full sprint. The air rushed past his face and ears, turning his cheeks to a deep red and filling his head with waves of sound.

After a few minutes, Joshua felt discomfort at his heels, where the skin was being rubbed raw. The homemade shoes he had from Hartland were not made for running. But he didn't have time to deal with the issue. Minutes later, Joshua felt his chest tighten and the twitch of a cramp develop at the bottom of his left ribcage. He breathed hard through his mouth as he tried to disregard the pain. He thought of Leon and Nuri for inspiration, as the cramp grew larger and his heels became more irritated. Then another shot of pain struck him sharply in his right ribcage; it was a second cramp. With every breath, it felt like an icepick was being plunged into each lung. With each stride, his exposed, skinless heels began to bleed. Joshua tried to run through the pain, but it was too overbearing. He had to slow to a walk and became discouraged, realizing he hadn't even made it to the grey house with the blue door.

Joshua kept moving and spread his arms wide, trying to stretch out his ribs to resolve his cramps. He thought of Carol and her sacrifice. She willingly gave her life to save him. He wondered how he could ever repay this debt. He had to make it to Caulfield. If he ended up getting caught before reaching Caulfield, they'd both be dead, and her sacrifice would be for nothing. His cramps had not subsided and is heels still burned, but the thought of Carol wasting her life for Joshua only to be recaptured was enough to get him running again.

This time, Joshua tried to pace himself so he could run a little longer. After a minute, his cramps were raging strong again. He was tired and weak. He wanted to stop and rest, but the image of Leon and thought of Carol pushed Joshua to carry on.

When he reached the grey house with the blue door, Joshua thought he was going to be sick. He told himself he was fine, until he wasn't. Joshua leaned against the grey house and threw up what little he had in his stomach. To his surprise, it made him feel better. He took the soft left on the bigger road and began jogging again. Unfortunately, his newfound energy was short-lived, and it wasn't long before Joshua knew he was going to be sick again. With nothing in his stomach, this time, he dry heaved. This pattern of jogging with intermittent dry heaves continued as he made his way closer to Caulfield. Each time his stomach convulsed, he saw stars and felt lightheaded.

As the sun began to rise behind him, Joshua could see a tall watchtower in the distance. As he got closer, a large complex, surrounded by a wall at least five times taller than he stood, came into view. Around the wall were two layers of tall chain-link fence, topped off with barbed wire.

Joshua had found Caulfield.

## 🜲 9 🜲

## CAULFIELD

Joshua could hear people shouting from the other side of the wall. Something moved at the top of the watch-tower, and a single bright light shone down on him. A loud horn blew from inside the massive walls. Joshua instinctively raised his hand to block the light, but he was still blinded.

"Who are you? What is your business here?" Someone shouted from inside.

Joshua tried to yell back, but he lacked the strength to shout with any force. With all his might, he took a deep breath and spoke out as loud as he could.

"My name is Joshua. I'm trying to escape from Leon."

A few seconds of silence followed, then a litany of people shouted inside the watchtower. Joshua couldn't make out what was said, but he was desperate and needed to get inside. A wave of dizziness swept over Joshua. If they refused him entry, there was no way he would have the strength to get away from Leon and his gang. He would be recaptured, and Nuri would slash his throat, just as Leon had instructed Nuri to do the previous night. Carol's sacrifice would be for nothing. Joshua's failure would be his reality.

"Please . . ." he said, in such a soft tone, he didn't think anyone is the watchtower heard him.

"Take off your clothes, put your hands in the air, and turn all the way around *slowly*."

The embarrassment of being naked in public that Joshua felt the first time doing this drill was gone. The sheer exhaustion and threat of recapture weighed heavily on Joshua, making the decision an easy one. It took him only a few seconds to untie the rope around his waist and lift the one-piece cloth over his head. Then, he kicked the bloody shoes off his feet. Joshua slowly turned around and faced the watchtower, with his hands at his sides. Again, he heard muffled chatter, but couldn't make out what was being said. He wasn't sure how much longer he would be able to stand there. He desperately needed to rest.

"Put your clothes back on and walk toward the main entrance. You will be escorted inside by a guard. We are armed! If at any time we sense anything suspicious, we will open fire. Do you understand?"

It took everything within Joshua to get out a barely audible, "Yes."

The blowing horn inside Caulfield silenced, and a portion of the outer gate slid open, exposing an enclosed area inside the main gate that had the same fence and barbed wire. As Joshua walked inside, the main gate behind him slowly crept to a close.

A man deformed from the Sickness exited the watchtower and stood on the other side of the inner gate from Joshua. The inner gate slid open just far enough to allow the Caulfield man to walk through and join Joshua inside the enclosed area.

Despite being on the verge of collapsing, Joshua immediately noticed the man's smile, which gave off an extreme sense of peace and welcome. Joshua also noticed multiple armed guards in the watchtower pointing assault rifles down at him through an open window.

"Don't mind them," the man said, following Joshua's gaze. "My name is Andrew. Follow me."

The two walked through the inner gate, Andrew first, followed by Joshua. Once inside Caulfield, two guards exited the watchtower and pointed their assault rifles at Joshua. Andrew gave an irritated look.

"Really, guys? I don't think that's necessary."

"You can think whatever you want, Andrew. The truth is we couldn't care less if he took you out. But if he does us that favor, it will be the last thing he ever does. Chosen or not."

Joshua was too tired to speak, so he nodded his head, acknowledging the guard's threat. Joshua and Andrew walked on, followed by the two guards, their guns still pointed at Joshua. As they moved away from the tower, other people inside the complex either stared outright or glanced over their shoulders, pretending to be doing something else when they were really watching him. Joshua's body felt like cement. Even though he was dragging his feet and could barely keep his head up, he needed to gain his bearings the best he could.

The first thing Joshua noticed was that Caulfield appeared to be just as big as Hartland, if not bigger. In front of Joshua were two large buildings with a road between them that led into another building, creating a t-intersection. The building on the left was three stories, made of yellow stone, while the building on his right was two stories, made of red brick. Directly in front of him, at the end of the road, was a white building that had only a ground floor. They were similar to structures that Joshua had only seen while walking Route 23; Hartland had nothing of their equal.

Joshua was led down the wide road before him, toward the white building, where more people stood off to both sides and stared at him. When he got to the t-intersection, Joshua looked to his hard left and saw a huge open space, filled with black mirrors, angled toward the shaded sun. To his soft left, approximately four hundred feet north of the black mirrors, Joshua could see a group of four buildings encircling a large yard, with people milling about. To his soft right, over the roof line of the long white building before him, two large water towers loomed in the far distance.

Andrew turned right at the t-intersection, and Joshua followed. As they walked along the length of the white building, Joshua took in more eyes glaring upon him. Opposite the white building was a long row, where multiple shops with glass storefronts sat behind wooden pillars, spaced out every twenty feet, holding up a slanted overhang that went the length of the porch. Underneath the overhang, the people coming in and out of these shops froze in their tracks. Joshua paid little attention to what was displayed in the windows. Instead, he moved his gaze from one set of eyes to another, where Joshua was always met with a hard stare. Everyone was fixed on him.

Finally, Joshua came to a man who didn't stop to stare. This man walked just a few feet ahead of Joshua, in the same direction. He had long, brown hair, and wore a white shirt over his broad shoulders, with blue shorts. As Joshua got closer, he noticed this man wore no shoes and carried a large box covered with a cloth. Every inch of his legs was covered with Sickness and he was so severely bow legged that he waddled as he walked. Each of his steps accentuated the visible veins in his calves, and when a foot met the ground, his toes swelled as if about to burst.

Joshua didn't know if it was the shock of seeing this man's

legs, the intense exhaustion, or a combination of both, but a wave of dizziness distorted his vision and he felt his body begin to shut down and give way to gravity. Blackness over-took him as he hit the ground, unconscious.

## ❦ 10 ❧

## WORTH A FIGHT

Two men sat in silence, sitting just feet from one another, at their own respective tables. Both men were Chosen. However, this was the only feature they shared. At nineteen, the younger of the two had broad shoulders that extended down to his strong, folded hands. Sitting with his back straight as a board, his muscular build was matched only by his striking square jaw and piercing blue eyes. His full head of sandy blond hair appeared messy, and at the same time, impeccably manicured.

To his right, sat a man with a look of quiet distinction, much older and not nearly as muscular. He was handsome in his own right, but nowhere near as attractive as his adversary. He had short, white-grey hair, with a slender and slightly wrinkled face. His forgiving brown eyes gave him a fatherly quality, like he would give the shirt off his back to a stranger. He was not openly nervous but buried underneath that look of distinction sat a subtle hint of concern.

In front of them, a much longer, slightly curved table held nine empty seats, the middle seat noticeably taller, bordered by long curtains. Behind them, a few random people sat in wooden pews, but there were plenty of empty seats. Five men and three women in black robes, carrying themselves with a stern manner, emerged from behind the curtain and moved to their places behind the eight shorter chairs. Everyone in the room stood up and bowed their heads. One by one, the eight individuals sat, leaving only the middle, higher chair unoccupied.

"Please state your names for the record," said one of the women.

The younger man spoke first. "Seth Blackmore, Your Honor. I am the Petitioner in this emergency matter."

The older gentleman followed suit. "Lorrick Wilton, Respondent."

"You may be seated." The two men promptly sat back down at their respective tables, followed by the individuals in the benches behind them.

"Mr. Blackmore, what is the nature of this Emergency Petition before the Council this morning?" said the same woman who had instructed them to state their names.

"May it please the Council," Seth began, with his nose high in the air. "As we are all aware, a young man named Joshua Barratt found his way to our Commune yesterday. He is Chosen and currently recuperating in our infirmary. All indications are that he will be fine. As we also know, despite the plentiful yields of nourishment and protections that Caulfield provides, the rate of death from the Sickness or old age continues to rise, while the number of children born, let alone Chosen children, dwindles." Seth pushed his right index finger hard against the table, as if squishing a bug. "We need to take advantage of having a new Chosen join us.

"Once Joshua is released from the infirmary, he will need a place to live, and he'll need a mentor. That mentor will need

47

to be strong, someone that Joshua can look up to and aspire to be like, someone who will do whatever is necessary to ensure the survival of our Commune. That is why I am before you this morning. I need to be that mentor."

"I see," said one of the male Council members. He turned to Lorrick. "And what is your response?"

Lorrick was calm and deliberate in his response. "With all due respect to Petitioner, he has never taken on the responsibility of caring for another. It is true: Joshua could be a great asset to Caulfield, but first and foremost, he must be given the choice of whether he wants to join our Commune. If he chooses to stay, we will have to contemplate the capacity in which Joshua will serve Caulfield. Furthermore, we will eventually have to arrange for a proper Chosen marriage." Lorrick rose from his seat, moved to the space between his table and the Council, and began to methodically pace back and forth as he continued.

"For a multitude of reasons, we have been unable to find a suitable apprentice for our Head Farmer. Joshua has been in and out of consciousness since arriving, but from what he's indicated, it appears he is from a small, rural Commune in Michigan and has been farming his whole life. If I were to adopt Joshua, it would allow him to spend the most time with our Head Farmer, given that Samuel lives under my roof. I don't think anyone here would argue over the importance of maintaining Caulfield's harvests." Lorrick paused, looking across the row of the eight Councils before him. "I only need reference the Law of the Red Circles and we are all instantly reminded of the harvests' significance and the reason the Law was enacted in the first place." Lorrick began pacing once again. "Samuel needs a protégé for maintaining our crops and Joshua could be just the person to take on such a role."

Seth rolled his eyes and looked off into the distance, mumbling something under his breath. Lorrick glanced at his opponent briefly, turned back to the Council, raised his index finger into the air, and continued.

"Furthermore, if Joshua were to live with my family and me, we could foster and nurture a relationship between him and my Chosen daughter, Adin. In this way, Joshua would be in the best position to form two bonds that could greatly affect the future of Caulfield. Therefore, when taking all factors into account, I believe the Commune's best interests would be served by having Joshua join my family. Thank you, Council Campbell, and the other members of the panel." Lorrick sat down and gave a slight nod of his head.

One of the female Council members turned back to Seth. "Any reply, Mr. Blackmore?"

Seth stood up from his seat and paced the floor in a similar manner as his opponent. "I'm glad that Lorrick—ah, please forgive me—*Head Council Wilton* brought up his son Samuel. We all know what happened all those years ago when Samuel appeared at Caulfield's doorstep. Eerily similar to the circumstances of Joshua's arrival: a single, Chosen boy, like a discovered treasure, seemingly belonging to no one, ready to assist Caulfield in our endeavor. There was considerable debate at the time over which family would adopt Samuel," Seth turned and stared at Lorrick. "Despite sufficient and reasonable objection, Head Council Wilton was given that right." Seth turned back to the panel, shrugging his shoulders. "And, look how well that turned out. Samuel remains the only case in our history of a young man at that age unexpectedly stricken with the Sickness."

Seth resumed pacing in front of the panel. "The only benefit that came of Samuel's arrival was his eventual appointment as Head Farmer. But was this something that came from Head Council Wilton's tutelage or instruction? Of course not. Head Council Wilton was just as clueless as the rest of us when it came to why our crops were failing. The fact is Samuel had those farming abilities well before he came to Caulfield. Accordingly, it's fair to conclude that no good came of Samuel joining Head Council Wilton's family over a decade ago.

"Now, we have a chance to get it right!" Seth exclaimed, clinching both hands into fists. "If Joshua ends up working with Samuel to become his apprentice maintaining our crops, so be it. In fact, I encourage it. However, having Joshua live with Samuel will not in any way improve Joshua's ability to perform his duties. And Joshua can be paired with any other Chosen female in Caulfield. I understand that Adin is close in age to Joshua, but there are other Chosen females that would be just as suitable to be paired with him. Joshua needs to come with me. Thank you." Seth said as he sat down, smiling and maintaining eye contact with the panel.

"Is that all from the parties?" Asked one of the male Councils.

"I have nothing further," Lorrick stated.

"Mr. Blackmore?" Asked the same male Council.

"Actually, there is one more thing. While it's not the official reason for our meeting this morning, the issue of Caulfield's numbers dwindling is obviously pressing. Sooner or later, we are going to have to change the archaic and outdated rule of one Chosen male to one Chosen female. If we are really going to beat the Sickness, we are going to have to allow the strongest Chosen males to breed with as many Chosen females as—"

"That is enough, Mr. Blackmore," one of the female Councils interrupted.

"Of course. My apologies, Council Campbell." Seth said with a smirk.

Council Campbell gave Seth a watchful eye and continued. "The Council will take into consideration everything both parties have said and will issue a ruling before Mr.

Barratt is released from the infirmary. I will remind you that since Head Council Wilton is one of the parties before us, I will be acting as Head of the Council for ruling on this issue and will make the final decision should the Council come to an impasse. You are both dismissed."

The entire room stood and bowed as the eight Council members exited the room. The gallery behind Lorrick and Seth followed. The two men stood and looked at each other without saying a word. As Lorrick went to exit via the lane between the wooden pews, Seth suddenly darted in front of Lorrick, nearly knocking him over. As he regained his footing, Lorrick thought he heard Seth laughing.

"Real mature, Seth," Lorrick said.

"We'll talk outside," Seth said, not looking back.

Outside the building, three young men waited for Seth, while one young man waited separately for Lorrick. Before joining his three comrades, Seth turned to Lorrick with a look of disgust.

"What promises have you made to your friend, Council Campbell, to have the Council rule in your favor? Maybe some of those exotic foods or plants that Samuel hides from the rest of us?"

"Don't be ridiculous, Seth. The Council will make its ruling based on the merits alone."

"Just be thankful that you have those mysterious things to give to your friends on the Council. Otherwise, there is no way they would rule in your favor and let you ruin another Chosen. Everybody knows the best thing for Caulfield is to have Joshua with me." Seth scoffed before joining his friends and heading out of sight.

The young man that was left was stout, with a round face and short brown hair. His lower right arm and wrist displayed signs of the Sickness, with his right hand being badly deformed. Around his right wrist, he played with a thick, braided bracelet that was worn, but still colorful. He spoke up as Lorrick approached. "I still don't understand why you're fighting this fight, Dad. Joshua is going to be part of our Commune. He's got nowhere else to go. What difference does it make if he lives with Seth or with us? It seems like an awful lot of trouble for one Chosen."

"Gabe, this is an issue more pressing than you realize. Come on, I'll walk you to the guard headquarters." Lorrick leaned into Gabe as they began walking side by side. "Seth won't give Joshua the choice to stay or leave. If Joshua is going to be of any benefit to the people of Caulfield, he must be here on his own free will. To force him to stay would be a mistake. You understand?"

"I don't know, Dad." Gabe continued fussing with his bracelet, looking down at the ground in front of them as they walked. "Joshua isn't going to leave here. There's nowhere for him to go. The minute he stepped outside these walls, Leon would him eat alive—literally."

"We have to give Joshua the choice, Gabe. Joshua is not from here and he doesn't know our ways. If he becomes part of this Commune, it must be by his own doing, not ours." Lorrick leaned closer into Gabe, so passersby could not hear. "Furthermore, remember who we're dealing with here. Seth would rule over Joshua with an iron fist. Joshua appears to be of good intentions with a kind heart. If Seth got a hold of him, he would crush that kindness and twist Joshua into another one of his lost minions."

Gabe leaned back into his dad, finally leaving the bracelet alone. "Don't get me wrong: Seth is hardly my favorite person." Gabe then quickly scanned the area and lowered his voice to a whisper. "But it's just a matter of time before he's appointed to the Council, regardless of what you've tried to do to avoid it. I know he's gruff, but I can see why people want him in a role of leadership. He does emanate a sense of power and confidence. He's a natural born leader, whether for good or ill, and people know it."

"Don't be fooled like the rest." Lorrick said firmly, not caring who heard him. "Seth's only interest is his own ascension of power. He talks about the greater good of our Commune and the future of a Chosen race of humans prevailing over the Sickness, but those are all deceitful lies to hide his true intentions. His only desire is to gain as much power as possible. Mark my words, if he has his way, the Council will eventually be abolished, and Seth would be a dictator. Maybe God sent Joshua here to help us avoid that future. Regardless, we have to protect Joshua from Seth."

Lorrick and Gabe continued weaving their way through the citizens of Caulfield, everyone moving with a purpose. Lorrick had administrative matters to attend to, and Gabe had to get back to his security post.

"All right, Dad, I'll see you tonight—"

Before Gabe could finish, the same loud horn that signaled Joshua's arrival rang through the Commune.

"What now?" Lorrick said as people around him either bee-lined for Caulfield's front gate or for their respective homes. Lorrick and Gabe exchanged a worried look before joining those running toward the main entrance watchtower.

"This month's offering isn't for another couple of weeks," Gabe said, jumbling the words while running.

Lorrick picked up his pace, pushing past the people in his way.

As they approached, Lorrick saw that Seth and another individual were already at the top of the watchtower with rifles pointed out the window at whoever or whatever was outside the gate. Lorrick ran up the stairs of the watchtower with Gabe at his heels. When they got to the top, they came up beside Seth.

"I was beginning to wonder if you were ever going to join us," Seth said, never taking his eyes off his target.

"Damn it," Lorrick said under his breath as he took in what had sounded the alarm. He reached down and flipped the switch to silence the loud horn.

"Good morning, Lorrick," Leon said through his mask. Nuri stood beside him, looking around as though bored. "I'm sure you realize it's another two and a half weeks until the next offering. But I'm not here for that. I'm here because I believe you have something of mine."

"Something of yours?" Lorrick asked.

"Don't pretend like you have no idea what I'm talking about. I'm here for that young Chosen male you've recently acquired. Did he not tell you that he belongs to me?"

"I haven't had much of a chance to properly interrogate him. What little he did mention, he never said anything about belonging to you. He indicated only that he was part of a small farming Commune in Michigan."

"Where the boy came from is of no concern. The fact is I found him, and he was mine until a former member of my group decided to let him go without my permission. She led us on a bit of a wild goose chase, or I would have been here sooner. I never authorized his release, so he's still my property."

Lorrick ground his teeth and flexed the muscles in his jaw. "What do you want?"

"I want a separate, special offering right now, double in size. And a dozen firearms. Once I get what I rightfully deserve, I'll leave Caulfield in peace and will not return until it's time for my regularly scheduled, monthly offering, in another two and a half weeks."

"*He wants firearms?*" Seth exclaimed to Lorrick, still concentrating on his target. "Leon and these ludicrous offerings are Caulfield's greatest detriment. As long as he's alive he's a threat to all of us. I have a clear head shot on Leon and Darin has a kill shot on Nuri. Let us take these two savages out right now. Caulfield will be safer with both of them dead."

"Besides, they deserve to die." Darin added coldly.

"No," Lorrick said. "Do not fire. That is an order. Keep your targets in sight, but do not fire."

Sweat ran down Lorrick's forehead. A robust smell of body odor lingered in the watchtower.

"Dad?" Gabe whispered.

"Leon," Lorrick shouted, "you will have to wait a few moments; give me some time to gather what I can."

Leon gave no response.

"What?" Darin said. "You're actually going to give in to his demands? You can't be serious!"

Seth interjected. "Lorrick, think logically. If we give in now, his demands will continue to grow and will become more frequent. We can't let that happen. We already give him and his people too much. Let us kill Leon and Nuri right now. Send a message to the rest of their gang that we can be just as vicious as these savages."

"Dad—" Gabe started, but Lorrick stopped him in his tracks.

"We've had nine years of peace since the offerings began. I'm not about to start spilling Caulfield's blood again when it can be avoided at such a small cost." Lorrick turned to Gabe.

"Go help Samuel prepare a double offering."

"What about the firearms?" Gabe asked.

"That is not your concern. Just get a double offering together with Samuel, immediately. Go!"

Without another word, Gabe took off running.

From the corner of his eye, Darin looked at Lorrick. "You're making a huge mistake, Lorrick. We need to kill these bastards right now."

"That's enough, Darin. You forget your place and rank. I

don't want to hear another word from you. Just keep Nuri in your sights and do not fire unless I give the order."

"What about the firearms?" Seth asked.

"We're going to give Leon everything he wants, except for the weapons. Let's just hope the food and supplies are enough to get him out of here without any violence." Lorrick looked up at the sky. "And, you're wrong about Caulfield's greatest detriment. It's not Leon or his gang or the offerings. It's the Sickness and Grey Dawn. Those two realities are everyone's greatest detriment, not just to those of us in Caulfield. The sooner you realize we're all in this together, Seth, the better."

Seth gave a snicker. "I just hope Leon tries something, so you have no choice but to order me to shoot the son of bitch. You don't realize how dangerous this man is to our people, to our way of life. You endanger all of Caulfield's citizens by allowing this man to live."

Once the materials were gathered, Gabe and a dozen farmworkers arrived at the inner gate entrance, each carrying a box of food and supplies. Lorrick opened the inner gate just enough to let Gabe and the workers inside one by one, where they left the offering. Once Gabe and the others were back inside the main premises, Lorrick closed the inner gate and opened the outer gate, again just enough to let one person inside at a time. Leon stepped aside, and Nuri walked in to inspect the merchandise.

"It's a double offering, but there are no firearms," Nuri shouted.

"I thought we had a deal," Leon said.

"I never agreed to your demand." Lorrick answered.

"Lorrick, I grow tired of you continuously taking advantage of my services."

Lorrick wiped the sweat from his brow. "The way I see it, Joshua was free when he showed up here alone. I'm not giving you firearms in exchange for something that was not yours when Caulfield acquired it. Consider this double offering a show of good faith on Caulfield's part."

"The last time we had an exchange like this, I delivered priceless seeds to add to your farming collection, and you gave me next to nothing in return."

"I gave you medical supplies that you indicated you were in desperate need of. You accepted the supplies, Leon, and the trade was completed. We're well past the point of negotiating that deal. However, as far as this deal goes, my counteroffer here is more than fair."

"I want firearms!" Leon shouted up at the tower.

"Why do you need guns, Leon? Don't tell me it's for protection because we all know we're the only ones around these parts. Our respective people have enjoyed peace for nearly a decade, and I intend to keep it that way. Besides, if you truly desired protection, you would dispose of that silly mask and join us. The offer for you and your people to join Caulfield stands and will continue to stand as long as I'm around."

Leon brought his head down, put his hand under his mask, and whistled loudly. Behind him was a small cemetery, with headstones, large cement monuments, and significantly overgrown vegetation. Hidden behind the headstones, monuments, trees, and bushes, twelve of Leon's tribe members suddenly appeared and gathered around their master.

"All of you," Leon ordered, "help Nuri gather the double offering." He turned back to the tower. "As for you, Lorrick, my people will never join Caulfield. What good have your rules brought you? I know for a fact that your irrational obsession and worship of Chosen has not solved any of your problems. I know your numbers are declining. A time will come when my strength will surpass all of Caulfield. When that time comes, mark my words, there will be no more peace."

Leon and his gang were soon out of sight with their newly acquired food and supplies.

Seth lowered his weapon and gave Lorrick a long, cold stare. "Not if, but *when* Leon attacks Caulfield," Seth said through gritted teeth, "I hope you remember this day."

## ❧ 11 ❧

## LORRICK

Several people surrounded Joshua as he regained consciousness.

"What...where the hell am I?" Joshua said in a low whisper.

From the crowd, an older gentleman stepped forward and kneeled at Joshua's side. He did not appear to have the Sickness, but what caught his attention more was the heavy, serious look in the man's eyes. Oddly, it reminded Joshua of looking into Leon's eyes. There was a sense of responsibility and fierce determination. People depended on this man to lead and protect them. Yet, there was a kindness behind the stern glare. In a strange way, this man was Leon's mirror image, and, at the same time, his exact opposite.

"My name is Lorrick. You've been in and out of consciousness for the past couple of days. You've had some brief discussions with my medical staff, but I'm told you continue to be disoriented. I'm the Head of the Council here in Caulfield. That's where you are right now. Do you remember arriving in Caulfield?"

Joshua's whole body ached. He tried to ignore the discomfort and, instead, concentrate on the fact that he was alive. "I remember walking through the gate, but that's about it. I recognize some of you, but I can't say that I recall anything we've discussed." Joshua's head throbbed with pain. He closed his eyes and raised his hand to his head to rub his temples.

"That's fine. Just know that you are safe and can continue to rest here for as long as you need. However, you are extremely dehydrated and malnourished. You must continue to eat and drink. The head of our medical staff, Mary, and her assistant, Andrew, will help you. Do as they say until you are well. Do you understand?"

Joshua couldn't believe the words he had just heard: safe, rest, eat, and drink. He had escaped Leon and found another Commune. He felt his throat choke up, but he was not going to cry in front of these strangers. "Yes, I understand."

"Good. Now, except for our medical staff, we're all going to leave you so you can recuperate. I'm sure we both have many questions to ask each other. We will get to those soon enough."

Lorrick stood and left, everyone following him except for Mary and Andrew. Mary walked with a cane as the Sickness plagued one of her legs. But she had a pleasant, easygoing nature that made Joshua immediately feel like he was in good hands.

Over the next couple of weeks, Joshua's days became routine as Mary and Andrew nursed him back to health. Most of the time Joshua slept, but it was mandatory to eat three meals a day, which he always did with enthusiasm. What unsettled Joshua was the half hour daily requirement of sitting underneath a light bulb. It was the first time Joshua had ever encountered a light bulb, as the only artificial light they had at Hartland was candlelight.

"What are you doing?" Joshua asked Mary with trepidation, the first time he was instructed to sit under the light. "Why do I have to do this? Is this going to hurt me?"

Mary gave a slight chuckle before answering. "Of course not, dear. Haven't you ever seen a full spectrum lightbulb?"

Joshua answered in fast, blurted out, spurts. "Never. What is it? I don't need it if it's the cure for the Sickness. I'm Chosen, can't you see? Is this the cure for the Sickness?"

Again, Mary laughed before giving a response. "No, Joshua. Please, relax. This light is not the cure for the Sickness. I wish it were! And, I know that you're Chosen. Since you are going to be stuck inside for a while, this light will help give your body what it needs to recuperate."

"Am I just supposed to sit here?"

"Yes, but don't look directly into the light." Mary positioned the light at an angle, to Joshua's two o'clock. "I want you to look straight ahead, keeping the light in your peripheral vision. You can blink regularly but keep your eyes open. I'll be back in thirty minutes."

"Wait! Can't you stay and tell me about Caulfield as I sit here?"

"I'm sorry dear, but I have rounds to make and I'm under strict orders from the Head Council himself. I am not to discuss anything about Caulfield with you. My only job is to nurse you back to health. Once you are discharged, I'm sure everything will be explained." Mary gave Joshua a reassuring smile. "Don't worry. Caulfield is a nice place and all your questions will be answered soon enough."

When he wasn't sleeping, eating, or sitting under his artificial light, Joshua would look out of as many windows as he could find, trying to get a layout of Caulfield. The problem was there weren't that many windows to look out of, and the building only had a ground floor, so the windows didn't give him much of a perspective.

From what he could see and from what Mary shared, the

infirmary was in the southeast corner of the compound, with dense foliage beyond the boundary of the wall and double fence to the east and the south. The windows to the west revealed the red, two-story building that Joshua saw when he first entered Caulfield. A single window facing north held the most interesting view: a giant field where people tended to assorted crops. The only crop Joshua could distinctly make out were corn stalks. He had grown plenty of corn during his time at Hartland. The remainder, he could not make out from the infirmary. What appeared to sit in the middle of the crops was a large, brick, four-story building. There were windows on the top floors, but the building appeared to be abandoned, as Joshua never saw anyone moving around inside it.

Finally, the morning arrived when Mary informed Joshua right after breakfast that he would be picked up by the Head Council later that afternoon and be formally discharged from the infirmary. When Joshua was served lunch that day, it was the first time he did not devour every morsel put down in front of him. He didn't take a single bite. Instead, he sat in deep concentration, mumbling to himself, and rehearsing what he was going to say to the Head Council and how he was going to say it. He thought of the things he learned at Hartland that could make him an asset to Caulfield, such as growing corn. He also went over the questions he'd been compiling in his head about Caulfield since his arrival. He didn't want to appear anxious to stay, but, at the same time, he quivered at the thought of leaving this place. He had to make a good impression and come across as a competent, but not overly confident, young man. He closed his eyes, centered himself, and prepared his dialogue one more time.

That afternoon, as the Head Council walked into the room, all the confidence Joshua had built up during the day suddenly evaporated. The detailed script in Joshua's head went blank and his palms filled with sweat. He tried his best to inconspicuously wipe his hands on his pants and hoped the Head Council wouldn't shake his hand.

"Hi Joshua," the Head Council said, while extending his hand for a handshake. "Mary told you I was coming to get you today, yes? I'm sure you have all sorts of questions."

Joshua reluctantly stuck out his cold, wet hand. "Not really," was all he could muster in response.

"Well I have a few things I need to discuss with you. Come on, let's go for a little stroll around Caulfield while we talk."

Upon exiting the infirmary from the main door facing west, they headed south about one hundred feet on a paved road until the street turned ninety degrees west. They followed the turn and continued west, walking along the south wall of Caulfield towards the front gate. There weren't many people on that stretch as they walked, but the ones that they did encounter stopped and stared. Joshua avoided eye contact with others as much as possible and kept looking around. The Head Council could tell Joshua was avoiding the stares while also trying to piece together the puzzle of Caulfield that he had seen from the infirmary windows.

"Mary told me you've been looking out any window you could find to try and get a lay of the land," Lorrick said, smiling. "Do you know where we are?"

"I know this Commune is named Caulfield, and I know the infirmary is in the southwest corner of your Commune. I also know you grow corn and a bunch of other stuff, north of the infirmary, but that's about it."

"Impressive." Lorrick said. Joshua made no reaction to the statement, but he was definitely keeping score in his head, and he had just earned himself a point.

"During the Paper Era," Lorrick continued, "this facility

was one of the largest high-security prisons in what was formally known as the United States."

"You turned a prison into a Commune?"

"My ancestors did, yes. Once Grey Dawn arrived, the people who worked at the prison went out and gathered as many friends, family and supplies as they could and brought everyone here. Regrettably, the resident inmates of the prison at the time were exiled. A place that protected the public on the outside by keeping the criminals inside was inverted. Leon and his crew are the offspring of the criminals that were evicted from the prison at the end of the Paper Era."

When they got to the watchtower, they turned right and headed down the same street Joshua walked down upon his arrival.

"This stretch is known as Orchard Lane. Both of these buildings to our left and right serve as living quarters for our community. To the left is what everyone calls 'Gold Castle,' but it looks more yellow to me, so I've never understood why it's not called 'Yellow Castle.' Most of our older residents live there. To our right is Mistrik Manor, occupied mostly by Chosen. Straight ahead is the Hyde Center, where most of our administrative matters are handled, including all hearings and voting issues. Our classrooms and library are also located in that building."

"Who is in charge here at Caulfield?" Joshua asked.

"I'll get to that at the end of our walk." Lorrick answered.

At the t-intersection, they turned left, toward the field of black mirrors. Upon reaching the mirrors, the road continued forward, but there was another road intersecting to their right, which they took. As they walked along the paved street with the mirrors to their left, a large round building, with a domed roof, appeared on their right.

"This is Halsted Street. It's the longest, paved street in Caulfield running north-south, approximately three-quarters of a mile. Most of what you've seen so far was here before Grey Dawn. The infirmary, Mistrik Manor, Gold Castle, and the Hyde Center, were all here when the prison was first built. Fortunately, the solar panels to our left were installed just before the end of the Paper Era. At the time, they were state of the art. They capture the light from the sun, which is then used to power our equipment. However, with the lack of unfiltered sunlight that came with Grey Dawn, the panels, alone, were not enough to power our Commune."

"But you have power here, at Caulfield. How is that possible with the lack of sunlight?"

"We had to get creative. Prior to the installation of the solar panels, the prison was powered by diesel generators, which we still had on the premises after the panels were installed, thank God. The problem was we didn't have any diesel fuel to power the generators. So, we began growing soybeans."

"Soybeans?" Joshua asked.

"Soybeans can be converted into a biodiesel fuel that can run any diesel engine. We built the biodome to convert our soybeans into biodiesel fuel and reinstalled the diesel generators. Between the solar panels and our engines running on biofuel, we generate enough power to keep Caulfield running."

"Amazing. We didn't have electric power at Hartland, where I'm from."

Lorrick nodded his head but didn't ask a follow up question. Joshua wondered why Lorrick wasn't asking him about his former Commune.

"Would you like to know about Hartland?" Joshua asked.

"Not right now, maybe later." Joshua's point was erased from the board in his head. Once they were north of the solar panels and biodome, there was another street that intersected to their right, but they continued walking forward while Lorrick picked up the conversation.

"To our right is our Security Headquarters. All our guards and security work out of that building. To our left is Hopkins Court, surrounded by four buildings, Taft, Snyder, Garner and Weston. They have all been converted to living quarters." Lorrick pointed to his two o'clock. "You see those twin towers in the distance? Those also serve as living quarters for our residents. Between Mistrik Manor, Gold Castle, Hopkins Court and the Twin Towers, all of our citizens have their own, individual residences."

"Which one do you live in?" Joshua asked.

"I was just about to get to that. Let me show you."

Lorrick and Joshua continued north, passing a large field on their left and another small building on their right. Lorrick made no mention of either. They passed a dirt road intersecting on their right but continued walking forward. Finally, they reached the end of the road where their only option was to turn left and head down a dead end road. They were now approaching the north west corner of Caulfield where a row of nine houses sat along the north wall. The first house was larger than the other eight.

Lorrick stopped in front of the first, larger house, turned to Joshua, and continued, "This is known as Elders Row. Our Commune is led by a group of nine individuals known as the Council, sometimes also referred to as the Elders. Of the nine, one is the Head of the Council. That is my position. The nine members of the Council and their families live in these homes. This first house in the row, that is where the Head of the Council lives, where *I* live, with my family. This could be your new home."

"My new *home?*"

"Well, that's assuming you want to stay. Do you think you might want to stay and live here in Caulfield?"

"Absolutely. There's nothing for me out there, besides Leon."

"You are certainly welcome, but if you choose to stay, you have to live by our rules and follow the laws of Caulfield. You need to hear everything I have to say before you make up your mind"

Joshua nodded as Lorrick gripped Joshua's left shoulder.

"One of our rules is that you cannot leave our Commune if you are Chosen. Since you were not born here, I am going to give you this one chance to leave freely. Once you hear everything I have to say, if you want to leave, no one will stop you. On the other hand, should you choose to stay, you can never leave, unless the Council permits it. Do you understand?"

Without blinking an eye, Joshua answered, "Yeah, I get it, I can't leave. Like I said, there is nothing for me out there."

"Great." Lorrick took a deep breath. "That's great to hear. Now, as I indicated, should you choose to stay, the Council has decided that you would become my adopted son. That means you would have to obey the rules in my house, as well as those of Caulfield. You would have a list of daily chores that will be completed without delay or complaint, and you will be expected to respect and get along with my wife and our four other children, one of whom is also adopted. Can you do that?"

"Yes, sir." Joshua said, sternly, although he wondered what kind of chores he would have to do, and he wondered what the rest of Lorrick's family was like.

"Caulfield has a very simple but strict way of life. Like I said, we are ruled by the nine-person Council, and I am Head Council. But I don't rule over the other eight Councils like a dictator. All issues are brought before the Council and decided by majority vote. The only exception is when we don't have time to conduct a hearing. In those instances, what I command is to be obeyed by all. We are run very much like the military. There is a clear rank, and rules must be followed and enforced. Caulfield nearly came to an end ten years ago. It shook us to the very core. Caulfield's near demise reminded us that there must be order. Without it, we cease to be human. Therefore, as you will see, rules here are simple, but must be strictly adhered to."

"I'll follow the rules," Joshua said, although the offer began to sound less appealing the more Lorrick revealed.

"There is one more major thing. Apart from Leon and our offerings, which I will explain later, we've had no communication with anyone outside of this Commune. From what you've told Mary which she relayed to me, it sounds like Hartland was dying. Coming here all the way from Michigan and seeing no one besides Leon..." Lorrick went silent and looked off into the distance for a couple of seconds before continuing.

Lorrick grabbed Joshua's other shoulder and looked him in the eye. "Caulfield could very well be humanity's last hope of surviving. Given that you are Chosen, you will be paired for marriage with a Chosen female within the next few years. Your spouse will be selected by the Council; you will have no say in the matter. The Council does not care what the two of you think of each other or if you're even attracted to each other. The pairing is made only in the interest of Caulfield and humanity's future, not your happiness. It will be your responsibility to have as many offspring as possible with your partner, and to dedicate your life to raising these children, in hopes of replenishing our Commune with Chosen."

Joshua's eyes went wide, and his head fell, his mind taking in more than it could process.

Lorrick continued. "The family unit is your number one priority. It is strictly forbidden to have sexual relations with anyone outside of wedlock. All must abstain until the Council makes a pairing and the wedding is performed. Once you are married, your wife is your one and only partner for life and everything comes second, including your own interests, to procreating Chosen children and caring for them until they can care for themselves. This law is absolute and must be followed."

Joshua felt a wave of nausea sweep over his stomach.

Lorrick took Joshua's chin with his right hand and lifted it gently. "Joshua, this is our most important rule in Caulfield. We tried to extend an invitation to Leon and his people to become citizens of Caulfield and end the conflict between our people, but Leon would not make his people follow our procreation law. He argued that a person should always have the freedom to choose who they wanted to marry, and be free to have consensual sex, married or not. He doesn't see the importance of Chosen like we do, hence why Leon and his gang continue to live outside these walls. Peace has been reached between these two groups, but tensions are on the rise, and Leon is not happy that you escaped him and made it here."

Lorrick let go of Joshua and watched him. Joshua let out a deep sigh and ran his fingers through his hair. He looked down at the ground again and remained silent for several seconds, thinking of his mom and her caution of putting Chosen in an elite and elevated class. Lorrick tilted his head, angling to look into Joshua's eyes for a response, but Joshua was frozen.

"Joshua, I know this is a lot to take in," Lorrick finally continued, "but our race is dying, and for reasons we may never know, a select handful of people, including you, are immune to the very thing that is destroying us. If we want to have any chance of surviving Grey Dawn, we must adhere to this plan."

Joshua looked up at Lorrick, looked at the house, and then back at Lorrick. "I get it."

Lorrick gave a slight smile and put his right hand back on Joshua's shoulder. "My hope is that you were sent to us for a reason, Joshua. However, I cannot force you to be a part of our Commune and live by our rules. So, I ask you for the last and final time, will you stay here in Caulfield, making it your home and swearing to live by its laws?"

Joshua reflected back on the loneliness and desperation he felt on Route 23. He shivered at the thought of being cold, wet, and starving, and at the sheer terror of being captured by Leon again. Despite the heavy burden laid upon him with Caulfield's rules, despite his mother's thoughts and warning on worshipping Chosen, Joshua knew he had no choice.

"Like I said, Lorrick, there's nothing for me out there. I will stay here and live by Caulfield's rules."

Lorrick's slight smile blossomed into a wide and welcoming one.

"Good. Now, let's go inside so you can meet your new family."

## ❧ 12 ❧

## SAMUEL

When Joshua entered the home, he was hit with the smell of something delicious. Not that the food at the infirmary was bad; that food was incredible compared to the insects, roots, critters, and plants that he ate while on the road. But this smell made his nostrils open wide and his mouth salivate. He was hungrier than he realized after skipping lunch that day. The ruckus of footsteps and play echoed on the floor above him. As Lorrick led the way further inside the home, a child's voice screamed out, "Dad's home!"

Lorrick turned the corner only to be embraced by a skinny boy with short brown hair. The two hugged for a couple seconds, and then Lorrick turned to Joshua.

"Asher, this is your new brother, Joshua. He's fifteen. Say hello."

With his head down and eyes up, Asher said, "Hello."

"Hi, Asher. It's nice to meet you."

"Nice to meet you too," Asher said flatly before taking off, clearly not interested in conversing with his new family member.

Two other children about Joshua's age appeared.

"Gabe, Adin," Lorrick said, "this is your new brother, the young boy that I was telling you would hopefully be joining our family. Joshua, these are my middle two, Gabe, who is eighteen, and Adin, who is your age."

Gabe reached out his left hand toward Joshua. "Nice to meet you. Welcome to our family."

"Thanks," Joshua said, noticing the firm strength of Gabe's handshake. Joshua turned to Adin, who was cute and gave off the impression of being a tomboy, with long sandy blond hair and blue eyes. She had no signs of the Sickness. Joshua reached out his other hand towards Adin.

"Hi, Adin. It's nice to meet you."

Adin shook Joshua's hand but didn't say a word.

A woman about Lorrick's age with a cold stare walked in. With her salt and pepper hair pulled up in a bun and a flat expression on her face, she couldn't have looked more serious. Like Lorrick, she was Chosen.

"Joshua, this is my wife, Mariam."

"It's nice to meet you, Ma'am," Joshua said, smiling at her.

Mariam took his hand, shook it once, and dropped it, as if Joshua were too insignificant for a real handshake. Mariam turned to Lorrick and with a stern voice said, "you didn't tell me you were bringing him home tonight. I thought the Council was still deciding. Can I speak with you in private?" Mariam walked up the stairs and into one of the nearby rooms.

Lorrick turned to Joshua. "She's just stressed upon knowing that there's an extra mouth to feed, but she'll warm up to you eventually. I'll be right back." Lorrick followed Mariam, closing the door behind him. It was just seconds before Mariam's shouting rang through the house.

Adin grabbed Asher, and the two ran into another room, leaving Joshua alone with Gabe.

"Don't worry about Mom," Gabe said. "Dad's right: she's just letting off some steam. She'll get over it." It was awkward for Joshua to hear Lorrick and Mariam referred to as 'Mom' and 'Dad.' It was going to take some time before he got used to that. He felt terrible for being the reason that Lorrick was getting an earful.

"I had nothing to do with this adoption. Lorrick just told me I was coming here."

"Dad didn't tell you about the controversy surrounding your adoption?" Gabe asked.

"No. He only mentioned that if I stayed, I couldn't leave, and that, in a couple years, I would be paired with another Chosen to have offspring hopefully immune to the Sickness."

"That's strange," Gabe said, starring off, playing with his bracelet.

"Is there something I should know?"

Gabe snapped out of his daze and stopped fidgeting at his wrist. "About ten years ago, a boy appeared at Caulfield's front gate out of nowhere. It was nearly identical to how you arrived. You must understand, this is extremely rare. The fact that it has happened twice is...Anyway, that boy's name was Samuel. He was the same age as you are today and appeared to be Chosen. In fact, we were all amazed at how healthy he appeared, given that he was coming from the outside."

"Where is Samuel now?"

"He's working, tending to our crops, but should be home any minute. He turned out to be an amazing farmer and eventually became our Head Farmer. What was odd was that he had a serious case of amnesia when he arrived. We asked him about his parents, friends, anyone he knew before arriving to our Commune, but he just shrugged his shoulders and said his only memory was approaching the gate. Given that he was Chosen, he was a very valuable commodity. Our Elders were anxious for him to join a Caulfield family and eventually be paired with a Chosen female. Some even whispered that he was a gift from God sent to Caulfield to conquer the Sickness and bring humanity back from the brink of extinction. At the time, Caulfield was going through a terrible famine, the worst in our history. Having another Chosen in our group gave people a small glimmer of hope."

Joshua felt his hands getting sweaty once again and understood why Mariam was so upset. He rubbed his hands against his shirt, trying to absorb the moisture. He hated being the center of attention and suddenly felt a tremendous amount of pressure as the newly adopted, Chosen son of Caulfield's Head Council, and brother of Caulfield's Head Farmer. Joshua was a good farmer, but he was far short of amazing. He hoped he wasn't adopted under the same expectation that he'd be a master farmer. "How was it that Samuel came to be adopted by your family? Did you know about his farming skills?"

"No. when Samuel arrived, the Council wanted to give him the best chance of pairing with a Chosen female. At the time, I was only eight, Adin five, and Asher wasn't even born. I had two older sisters, both Chosen. Hannah, who was seventeen, and Alessia, who was twenty. Alessia had already been paired, but Hannah hadn't yet. She was so close to Samuel's age, the Council decided that we would adopt Samuel. We had no idea about his farming skills."

Joshua felt a bit of relief, but still listened to Gabe with anticipation.

"When Samuel joined the family, we were all excited for the potential pairing with Hannah, but also because of Samuel in general. He became one of the family instantaneously, and as far as the rest of Caulfield was concerned, he made a positive difference straightaway. Dad had him at the farm just days after his arrival, and whatever Samuel did before he got here, one thing was certain: he knew how to work the land. Our yield made a miraculous turnaround. And while no one was acting on it or saying anything, it was clear that Samuel and Hannah were falling in love. We were all very happy and excited."

Gabe paused and looked down. Joshua could tell Gabe was troubled with what he was about to share.

"We felt that the announcement of Samuel and Hannah's pairing was around the corner—" Gabe went silent and began playing with his bracelet once again.

"Somehow, Leon knew about the yield turnaround and was able to sneak one of his men into our Commune. From inside, he helped Leon and the rest of his gang launch a surprise attack on Caulfield in the middle of the night. We were eventually able to suppress the attack, but Leon got away and both Hannah and Alessia were killed. Then, just days later, Samuel woke up with the Sickness on his hip. He wasn't Chosen after all."

A few seconds of awkward silence passed before Gabe continued, raising his right wrist.

"Hannah made me this bracelet before she died. It's been tough for all of us, but especially mom. She has never been the same since losing Hannah and Alessia. Don't get me wrong. She has her good days. But, no matter how good a day she's having, there is still a feeling that she's never fully accepted the altercation that took my two sisters' lives. I think when you walked in, it just brought back all the memories of having Samuel join the family and the happiness that was taken from us. Mom will be ok, just give her some time to warm up and, in the meantime, help out around here as much as you can."

Joshua nodded his head. "Thanks Gabe. I will follow your advice. And I'm sorry what happened with Hannah and Alessia."

Lorrick walked back into the room, with Mariam trailing

behind, still visibly upset, but at least she wasn't yelling anymore. "Let's sit down for dinner, guys." Lorrick said. "I saw Samuel approaching from upstairs."

# FAMILY DINNER

Everyone gathered in the small, cozy kitchen. The mouthwatering smell of Mariam's dinner filled the air, and Joshua's stomach growled. The kids were busy setting the table while Joshua asked what he could do to help. Mariam simply looked at him and went back to the dinner she was preparing.

After a few uncomfortable moments, Gabe finally asked what was on everyone's mind.

"So, Joshua, tell us about yourself and how you ended up here."

Joshua looked around. Everyone staring at him, including Lorrick. He wasn't sure where to begin.

"My mom and I were part of a Commune in Hartland, Michigan, where I learned how to farm and live off the land. It was all I ever knew. My mom and I left when things started getting...worse. Our population numbers were down, and our Chosen numbers had dwindled to a few hundred. Our leaders weren't sure how to beat the Sickness. They were desperate, grasping at straws. My mom didn't agree with the ideas they had come up with, and she was sure we'd find another

Commune. Both of us were Chosen, so she figured we would be granted entry wherever we ended up."

"What happened to your mom?" Lorrick asked, softly.

"A couple weeks after we left, she developed a violent cough. She was so determined to make it to another Commune that she pushed herself to stay on the move. A week after that, she got a fever and came to the point where she could barely even breathe..." Joshua's eyes began to water. "She died a few days later. I didn't know what to do, so I just kept walking. I was eventually captured by Leon."

At the mention of Leon, he noticed the alarmed look on everyone's faces. Joshua continued. "When I first saw him, I thought for sure he would kill me right there and then. But when he saw I was Chosen, he started calling me his 'prize' and planned on bringing me here, to trade me. I overheard him say that if you refused to give him what he wanted, he was going to kill me at Caulfield's gate. Before that could happen, though, one of the members of his group freed me and helped me escape." Joshua stared at the table in front of him. "I don't even want to think about what happened to her." Joshua looked back at Lorrick. "Once I got away, I pushed myself harder than I thought possible to get here, away from Leon."

Gabe had started to say something when the back door opened. Asher jumped up and screamed, "Samuel!"

In walked a man with thick, shoulder-length brown hair, crystal brown eyes, and a smile that had no equal. His muscular arms carried a box filled with different types of fruits and vegetables. From Joshua's vantage point, he could only see Samuel from the waist up.

"Hey, everyone," Samuel said as he put the box down on a side table. "You guys are going to *love* this ration." Joshua had never seen many of the ripe and delicious looking fruits and vegetables that were revealed inside. As the group inspected the contents of the box, uttering sounds of anticipation and excitement, there was a noticeable shift in the energy in the room. It was not only the food that Samuel had brought, but his presence made everyone smile and line up to give him a hug, even Mariam.

Lorrick put his hand on Joshua's shoulder. "Samuel, I'd like you to meet the newest member of our family, Joshua Barratt." When their eyes met for the first time, Joshua understood why everyone was so happy to see Samuel. There was something about him, something about the way his gaze seemed to envelop you with unconditional love and acceptance.

Samuel walked around the table to shake hands. As Samuel approached, his legs finally came into Joshua's view. The degree of Sickness to Samuel's legs was dreadful. He also walked with a waddle due to his legs being severely bowed. It was then that Joshua's last memory of entering Caulfield erupted and he realized he was about to shake hands with the man whose deformed legs were the last thing he saw before he collapsed. As the two shook hands, Joshua felt his soul leap with inspiration. Despite whatever challenges Samuel had with his legs and the Sickness, Samuel exuded an aura of gratitude and genuine happiness. Joshua instantaneously knew that they were going to be friends.

"Lorrick told me you would be joining us. It's nice to finally meet you, Joshua."

"Thanks, it's nice to finally meet you as well," Joshua said as he leaned over Samuel's shoulder, trying to get a closer look at the contents in the box.

"I have some great stuff here for the family, and I brought a little something extra for you. A small token to welcome you into this wonderful household." Samuel reached into the box and pulled out a handful of bright yellow daffodils sitting in a petite vase with water. The deep colors of the flower captured Joshua's attention and reminded him of the dream he had of his mother when he was on the road. Maybe it was a sign from his mom, a reminder that she's looking down on him, protecting him. Or, perhaps it was just coincidence.

"They're beautiful. Thank you," Joshua said.

"We grow anything and everything we can here. Not just fruits and vegetables, but plants and flowers as well. They have such great value. Flowers can help you mentally, help put you in a positive mood. I thought a few daffodils seemed especially appropriate given your arrival and the meaning of the flowers."

"Their...meaning?" Joshua asked.

"Throughout history, humanity has associated all types of symbology to flowers. A daffodil symbolizes a new beginning. May your new beginning here in Caulfield be a blessed one, Joshua," Samuel said with a reassuring smile.

Joshua stared at the daffodils. He wished his mom had made it to Caulfield. Joshua wanted to ask Samuel the meaning of a pink carnation, but it didn't seem appropriate at the time. It was Joshua's first night with his new family, so he was going to stay away from asking strange questions like the meaning of a pink carnation. Joshua hung his head at the thought of his mom.

Samuel leaned down and spoke softly in Joshua's ear, "It's ok, Joshua. You're safe. New beginnings are always difficult, but that's how life works—it is forever changing. Embrace every new road, every new chapter in your life with optimism. Think of it as an adventure. I promise you're exactly where you're supposed to be. Trust me. Plus, I guarantee you've never had a meal like the one you are about to experience tonight."

Samuel stood up straight and raised his voice. "Now, I don't know about the rest of you folks, but I'm starving, and whatever mom's cooking smells delicious. Let's eat!"

As everyone sat down and began dinner, Joshua's tension gave way to his hunger. Samuel was right. The meal that Mariam had prepared was the best meal that Joshua could remember. Gabe, Adin and Asher bantered amongst themselves while Lorrick engaged Samuel about his day.

"That's quite a nice variety of food that I see," Lorrick said, pointing to the box on the side table.

"What can I say? I've been fortunate to grow what the Commune needs."

Asher, sitting closest to the box, sat up to look inside the box one more time. "Is this really all for us?"

"These are the rationed portions for our family. Just because Dad is Head Council doesn't mean we get special privileges."

Lorrick turned to Joshua. "Samuel is the best farmer I have ever known. His gift is, quite simply, beyond comprehension. Before he came, no one could produce half the yield that Samuel can produce on his own. I'd hate to think where we'd all be without him."

"It's no big deal," Samuel said with a shrug of the shoulders. "You give me so much credit when the ones you should be thanking are my farmhands and the bees pollinating everything. They've made the difference more than anything."

"Bees?" Joshua asked.

"Our bees do the heavy lifting," Samuel said, scooping another helping onto his plate. "I just try to stay patient, let them do their job. We're also fortunate that the Commune came into possession of the seeds needed to grow these things. It's allowed me to grow the plants and flowers we produce, which are the main ingredients for all our tonics and medicines.

"We also have some special, seasonal fruits that are very difficult to grow, but feasible. I've been successful, but I can only produce them in small portions. We rotate the yield between everyone, and it's our turn to receive these special items." Asher stared back at Samuel with a big smile on his face as Samuel rubbed Asher's hair into a mess. Adin and Mariam discussed different recipes they could make from the special items Samuel had brought. Gabe and Lorrick mentioned some names of people they wanted to introduce to Joshua in the coming days. Everyone was content consuming their dinner and conversing. Joshua could not believe his good fortune in joining Caulfield and his new family.

## ❧ 14 ❧

### NEIGHBORS

As Adin and Gabe finished cleaning up dinner in the kitchen, the rest of the family gathered in the living room where there was a soft knock at the front door. Asher jumped up, ran to the door, and opened it. A handsome young man with the Sickness in his shoulder and a young Chosen woman, maybe a year or two older than Joshua, stood on the other side. The young woman was, without question, the most beautiful girl Joshua had ever seen, with dark, wavy hair falling past her shoulders and a face that seemed, to him at least, impeccable. She had dark brown eyes, healthy skin, and like the contour of her face, the shape of her body was flawless.

"Ian and Belinda, come in and meet our new family member," Lorrick said as he waved them in. Ian smiled and nodded as the two individuals walked into the home and closed the door behind them.

"This is Joshua Barratt. Joshua, this is brother and sister Ian and Belinda Lillith. They are twins, in fact. They live in Mistrik Manor, near the front gate. You remember the building, yes?"

Joshua nodded yes and tried not to stare at Belinda, but he was failing miserably. Joshua and Ian gave each other the usual pleasantries. But, when it was time to shake Belinda's hand, Joshua felt the same sensation he had felt just before passing out. Waves of dizziness made his balance uneasy as his palms and forehead began to sweat. Joshua shook her hand as she said hello, but he couldn't get out any words in response. He forced himself to look down at the ground and pulled his hand away quickly.

Samuel laughed and nudged Joshua. "You okay?"

Joshua looked up at Samuel, startled. "Huh? What? Oh! Me? Yeah. I mean...are you talking to me? Yeah. I'm fine. Just, ah, yeah, just...no, I'm good. You're talking to me, right?"

Everyone had a quiet laugh at Joshua stuttering all over himself as Ian and Belinda sat down and joined the conversation.

"We live in Mistrik Manor, for now," Belinda said, "but that should be changing in the very near future, right Lorrick? You do realize it's my half birthday next week. In just another six months, I'll be seventeen. Are you really going to make me wait until then before I'm paired with another Chosen? Someone strong, tall and handsome? You know who I mean."

Joshua's eyes opened wide at the news that Belinda was not paired, despite the fact that he was neither strong, tall nor handsome.

"We know who you mean, and never mind that it will be my birthday as well," Ian added. "Not to mention that when you're paired, I'll be kicked out of Mistrik Manor and forced to live at Hopkins Court or the Twin Towers, cause there's no way I'm getting into Gold Castle."

"Oh, Ian," Belinda huffed, "you know I appreciate that it's your birthday too. I can't help it if only Chosen are supposed to live at Mistrik Manor and citizens of higher rank live in

Gold Castle. Maybe Lorrick can bring the matter to the Council and they'll let you stay in Mistrik Manor after all, make an exception for you just like when Mom and Dad died."

"Everything will work out in good time, Belinda," Lorrick interjected. "I've brought *both* of your names up to the Council for pairing, but they voted it down. I have to wait until our next quarterly adjournment to raise the issue again. Once you guys are paired, living quarters will be addressed."

"But everyone knows that our Chosen numbers are down," Belinda protested. "Shouldn't I be paired with another Chosen sooner rather than later?"

"Lor, can't you do something?" Mariam asked, as Adin and Gabe joined the group in the living room. "They're like our own children. It's bad enough they lost their parents a year ago. Now, we're going to make them wait to be paired? This should be an easy matter to remedy as Head Council."

Everyone sat in silence, staring at Lorrick.

"Give me a break, guys. I'm doing what I can. Both Ian and Belinda's names were in consideration for pairings at the last quarterly, and they were both voted down. They will be up for consideration again next time."

Another knocking came at the door, this time louder and violent, as if someone was kicking the door with their foot. Asher ran to Lorrick and took shelter at his side while Adin lost all the coloring in her otherwise pink cheeks. It was a far cry from how easy-going Adin had been at dinner and how anxious Asher was to answer the door when Ian and Belinda arrived.

Gabe scanned the room, waiting for someone else to answer the door, but no one was getting up. Again, a loud pounding thrashed against the door. Shouting soon followed.

"Open up! I know you're in there. I saw the Lillith twins

walk in a few minutes ago. Open the door!" Gabe took a deep breath, walked to the door, and opened it slowly.

Without invitation, four young men pushed their way past Gabe and into the home. The first to enter was striking with strong arms and a chiseled jaw. There was no doubt he was Chosen. His blond hair was slicked back, and his sharp, blue eyes surveyed the room. The thing that caught Joshua's attention most, though, was the sinister, malicious grin on his face. A terrified shiver run down Joshua's spine. The grin reminded him of Leon.

The other three men looked just as devious, although not quite as calculating. The second man was also Chosen, but not nearly as good-looking or strong as the first. His hair was bright red and disheveled. Of the four, the look in this one's eyes was the most aggressive; he had an evil aura about him that made it clear he was looking for trouble. The third man had visible Sickness to his left ear and was skinny. He appeared aloof, same as the fourth man, who walked with a slight limp, and was short and pudgy. There was not a single thing that Joshua liked about any of them.

"So, it's true!" the first one boasted. "Caulfield's new Chosen, Joshua Barratt, is out of the infirmary and into his new home. I still can't believe your ridiculous arguments actually convinced the Council to let you take in the young man. Either that, or you worked an arrangement on the side with Council Campbell to keep Joshua away from me. It's no matter. It is all just further proof that they are a bunch of sympathetic fools that have no idea what the hell they are doing." The other three men snickered.

The first man turned to Joshua and approached him slowly, looking him up and down, sizing him up. The closer he got, the more Joshua was taken aback by the veins covering his powerful arms, his thick neck, and his broad shoulders. At least two feet taller than Joshua, the man probably outweighed him by a hundred pounds.

"Let's hope you get hit with a heavy dose of testosterone and amount to something in the upcoming years," the stranger said, backhanding Joshua on the chest and bringing on more laughter from his posse. "I'm Seth Blackmore, Head of Security here in Caulfield, and therefore responsible to assure that the citizens of this great Commune follow the laws of Caulfield, down to the very letter. These three men are my most trusted staff. The redhead is Darin Brown, followed by the very serious Keegan Stone, and finally, our chubby, but oh so lovable, Cade Grissom." Keegan and Cade began exchanging shoves, until Seth gave them one look, immediately ending the shenanigans.

Seth turned to Joshua and continued. "In case you didn't already know, we're also the ones who will be running this entire operation in the very near future. I mean, we essentially already do, as Caulfield's law enforcement. Wouldn't you agree, Lorrick?"

Lorrick rolled his eyes and shook his head in response.

"You see, Joshua, while I'm sure Lorrick told you about the Council, I guarantee he failed to mention their old age and their tendency to make foolish decisions, like the one to have you live with this family, instead of with me, for example. Thankfully, it's just a matter of time before I'm on the Council. Then, we'll really set things straight in Caulfield."

"Take it easy, Seth," Lorrick said, "The Council has more knowledge and wisdom than you realize. They thought long and hard about the situation and concluded that it was best for the Commune to have Joshua adopted by Mariam and me."

"And why is that? So you two can take in another Chosen and screw it up like you did with Samuel? You've already had your chance, and you failed."

Seth turned to Adin and Belinda, standing together, and stalked toward them. "Sooner or later, you'll realize that if you really want this Commune to survive, all the Chosen females in Caulfield should be paired with me. It just makes the most sense. Wouldn't you agree, Adin?" Seth gently put his hand to Adin's chin and lifted her face toward him. She couldn't even fake a smile and, instead, closed her eyes to avoid eye contact.

"I thought maybe you'd like to be paired with me," Belinda said with a coy, yet flirty, tone.

Seth dropped his hand and looked to Belinda. "Everyone knows you're the most beautiful woman in Caulfield. Should we continue with the current, obsolete pairing laws, there is no doubt you'll be my bride. But the reality is this Commune needs the seed of the strongest male Chosen spread among all the Chosen females. Unless you people prefer extinction..."

"That might be a better alternative," Gabe said under his breath.

"What was that, Gabe? Speak up!" Seth shouted.

"Nothing."

"That's what I thought. One of these days, you should learn to have some guts. No one respects a coward who mutters things under their breath. Get a set of balls!" With the insult, the four goons really started laughing.

Seth whacked Gabe hard on the shoulder. "You know what I'm saying?"

Asher jumped from his father's side, "Leave him alone!"

"Ahh. Finally, someone from Lorrick's lineage with a backbone. Asher, you're too young to understand now, but trust me when you get older, you'll learn that Chosen need to stick together. The strongest of the Chosen shall lead and protect people with the Sickness, like Keegan and Cade, as long as they know their place. With that fighting spirit of yours, who knows! If you are indeed Chosen, maybe you'll even grow to be stronger than me. Although, I doubt it." Seth rubbed Asher's hair into a mess. Asher pushed Seth's hand away. Everyone laughed, especially Seth, who then noticed the box of fruits and vegetables.

"Well, well, what do we have here?" Seth walked into the kitchen, followed by his friends, Samuel, Lorrick, and Joshua. Seth dug through the box, inspecting and smelling various items. He threw a piece of fruit to each of his three friends and grabbed a fuzzy ripe peach for himself. His eyes went wide as the fruit's juicy meat melted in his mouth.

"Samuel, you've truly outdone yourself. But, don't think I'm a fool; there's a bunch of stuff in here that I've never seen before and are *not* in the crops. You have another garden somewhere in this Commune. I know you do. You'd be wise to share this information with me freely, or we'll have to do things the hard way. Remember, I have eyes and ears everywhere in Caulfield."

"Those items are difficult to grow and don't have a high yield," Samuel explained. "I'm passing them out in sequential order because there is not enough to provide to everyone yet. You'll see your stipend with the next yield. You get the same portion as everyone else. Just because you can't tell the difference between a peach and a pomegranate doesn't mean that I have some secret stash." Samuel hid a smile.

"I don't understand you, Samuel," Seth said. "Sure, the Sickness got you from the waist down, but you're the best farmer we've known. Your upper body is strong, and people flock to you. You know I'm willing to look past your deformities should you choose to become one of my team. You would be a valuable asset. And, you'd be glad you did, as someday soon I'll be running this place. You'll be grateful to be one of my comrades."

"I'm already part of a team: Lorrick's team." Samuel said, as he put his arm around his adopted father. "Should

Caulfield come under the tragic circumstance of your rule, it wouldn't matter what team I was on; you'll still need me to tend our farm." Samuel let go of his dad and rested his hand on the box, next to Seth. "Besides, it's not like you share power with anyone. You're going to treat me as if I'm beneath you no matter what team I'm on."

Seth's chest heaved deep, intense breaths. His face became as red as the fire that flowed through his veins. "Someday, Samuel, you'll be sorry. Today, you're right: I still need you to tend to the farm. But that's not going to last forever. Someday, someone with more skill than you, maybe even your *new brother*, will take your place and be smart enough to join me. He'll reap the reward of being one of my loyal servants, while you wallow in discontent with all the others infected with the Sickness. If you even live that long." Seth turned to his comrades and nodded at the box full of food.

"Take the box. These people don't deserve to indulge themselves, especially when the person who provided these goods is fool enough to reject my offer."

Something snapped inside of Joshua. "You're not taking that box from this house," Joshua said in an even tone as he placed himself between Darin and the box of food, glancing in the other room at Belinda. Seth came at Joshua instantly, his eyes wild with a jolt of adrenaline. Joshua's arms shook and his heart raced the closer Seth came. Seth nudged Darin out of the way and got directly in Joshua's face.

"It looks like the new Wilton family member needs to learn a lesson, to be taught how to show some respect. I'm not even going to give you the chance to get out of the way. This is going to be pain you'll never forget."

Seth made a fist, cocked his arm back, ready to knock Joshua out cold. Joshua didn't know what to do aside from wince and brace for impact.

With his eyes nearly shut, he could still see enough to witness Samuel stick out his hand and catch Seth's punch. The collision sounded like two pieces of solid wood smashing together, the crack loud and startling. But it was Samuel catching Seth's punch in midair that had Joshua awestruck. Seth pulled his hand back while Samuel stepped in front of Joshua. Relief washed over him.

Without saying a word, his face even redder then before, Seth threw another punch, this time directed at Samuel's face. Like the last punch, Samuel caught Seth's fist, their clutched hands shaking from the impact. Seth balled up his free hand and threw another punch, only to be caught by Samuel's free hand. The sight was extraordinary: both of Seth's fists, shaking in Samuel's hands. Samuel appeared composed as he absorbed Seth's punches without seeming to exert an ounce of energy.

"Are you really going to test my strength and resolve?" Seth said through his gritted teeth.

Samuel calmly responded. "I can do this all night if you like."

With that, Seth pulled back both hands and threw a right uppercut towards Samuel's chin. This time, instead of catching the punch, Samuel evaded the blow and Seth's fist caught nothing but air. The force exerted caused Seth to lose his balance and stumble. Samuel wasn't afraid. Instead, he just looked at Seth with regret.

Seth stood, reared back, and threw one more punch at Samuel, a right hook. Like the uppercut, Samuel shifted his torso, and Seth's punch missed its target. With the miss and the momentum of his swing, Seth twisted hard to his left but kept his balance. As he spun, Seth whipped out his left leg in a violent sweeping motion, catching Samuel off guard. The kick landed on both of Samuel's legs and he toppled over. Seth crawled onto Samuel's chest and used his right leg to pin down Samuel's left arm. Then Seth took his left hand and held down Samuel's right arm. Despite his attempts, Samuel could not jar himself loose.

"If only your legs were as strong as your upper body, Samuel. I'm going to enjoy this." Seth began raining down punches on Samuel's face. Lorrick tried to step in but was held back by Darin, Keegan and Cade.

Darin began shouting, "Kill him, Seth! Beat him to his death and I'll tell everyone it was in self-defense!"

Joshua, meanwhile, stood frozen in fear, his feet stuck in place, like they were small tree trunks rooted to the floor. He placed his hand over his mouth and did nothing as Samuel took on the beating that was meant for him. Within seconds, the blood started flowing. Everyone from the other room came running in from the noise. Gabe interceded and helped Lorrick break free of the others. Lorrick and Gabe then jumped on top of Seth, pulling him off Samuel.

Seth stood and adjusted his shirt and hair. "Do you understand how things work now?" he asked, glancing at Joshua.

"I grow tired of the disrespect from people that are clearly beneath me." Seth continued. "You all know Caulfield deserves better than what the current Council has to offer. When I rule this Commune, those who do not respect me will have lessons every day, like the one Samuel just received. Then, when everyone knows their place and a proper rank has been established, Chosen will finally propel humanity toward victory over Grey Dawn."

Seth motioned to the rest of his gang that it was time to leave. As they walked out, Seth, bringing up the rear, stopped and turned his attention to Lorrick. "Suffice it to say, the actions of your family tonight, specifically that of assaulting one of Caulfield's security, will result in a red circle. You have been advised." Seth turned and left, slamming the door behind him.

Lorrick, Mariam, Adin and Gabe helped Samuel to his feet and wiped the blood from his face.

"It's not as bad as it looks, guys," Samuel said. "Honestly, I'm fine. No big deal."

"What happened?" Mariam demanded. "What did you do to provoke Seth?"

Joshua didn't hesitate. "It was my fault. Samuel didn't do anything. I tried standing up to Seth and Samuel stepped in to protect me."

"Don't be ridiculous, Joshua," Samuel responded. "You did nothing wrong. Unfortunately, this is par for the course with Seth and his gang."

"It's never led to you having a bloody face!" Mariam exclaimed. "Come on, let's get you upstairs and cleaned up."

As Mariam, Lorrick, Adin and Asher headed upstairs with Samuel, Mariam gave Joshua a hard, disapproving stare. Ian and Belinda exchanged an awkward glance, offered their apologies to Gabe, and quickly exited the Wilton home. Without saying a word to Joshua, Gabe began cleaning up the mess that was left from the wake of Seth's visit.

The feeling of fortune Joshua experienced at dinner completely vanished. It was replaced with deep guilt over the beating Samuel received. The fact that Belinda was present to witness Joshua's cowardice only made him feel worse. But the worst part was the fear that Joshua experienced with the thought of Seth ruling Caulfield one day. Perhaps deciding to stay in Caulfield hadn't been the right decision after all.

## ❧ 15 ❧

## LAW OF THE RED CIRCLES

By the time Joshua got up the next morning, Samuel had already left to tend the farm. The rest of the family was home, but they were quiet and evasive, not speaking of the previous night's events. Whenever Joshua made eye contact with anyone, that person would just turn away and go on with their business. The guilt weighed heavily on Joshua. He wished he could go back in time, keep his damned mouth shut. Maybe then Seth would have just left, and the previous evening's violence would have been avoided.

Joshua crossed to the window facing the street outside of the house and noticed some people walking by. When they passed, they'd cover their mouths in shock. Then, he saw some kids across the street, playing in the field, pointing at his newly adopted home, and carrying on dramatically. He wondered what everyone was looking at causing such a reaction.

Joshua opened the front door and examined it but found nothing. He walked outside, and when he turned around, he saw what the commotion was over. A bright, solid red circle, the size of a large orange, had been painted onto the exterior wall of the home, just to the left of the doorframe. Joshua was positive it wasn't there the day before. Lorrick came to the front door from inside, and when he saw Joshua staring back at the house, he dropped his head and slowly strolled outside.

"You're probably wondering what that red circle is all about," Lorrick said.

"I remember Seth saying something about a red circle last night, right before he left. Is this what he was talking about?"

"Unfortunately, it is."

"What does it mean?"

"Years back, just before Samuel joined our Commune, Caulfield was in a horrible place. Our numbers were drastically down, and the crops were dying. People were starving to death. In their desperation, some began going to the crops late at night to steal whatever food they could gather. This threw our meager rations completely off balance. We couldn't get the proper nutrients to all of Caulfield's citizens. Our Commune was on the brink of anarchy.

"In a desperate act, our Council enacted the Law of the Red Circles. The law stated that a red circle would be painted on the doorway of any family whose member broke any of Caulfield's laws. If there was an accusation made by a Caulfield citizen against another citizen, the matter would go before the Council for trial before a red circle could be given. However, in situations where it was a member of the security team that made the accusation, a trial would be waived, as our security are sworn to convey and uphold the truth at all times."

Lorrick sighed and stared up at the red circle. "Samuel arrived when all hope was nearly lost and he saved our crops, saved all of Caulfield. Things went back to normal thereafter. It's been years since a family's been branded with a red circle. That's why everyone who passes is so astonished. It's something we're not accustomed to seeing now, that's all."

"So, what happens to a family that gets a red circle?"

"Nothing happens after one red circle, or even two red circles, for that matter..." Lorrick paused for a few seconds before continuing, "but, if a family receives three red circles, then..." Lorrick stopped.

"Then what?" Josh asked.

"Then one of the family members would be...publicly hung, with the family that received the circles deciding who. If the family can't reach a consensus within twenty-four hours of receiving the third red circle, then the Head of Security makes the decision for them."

Joshua was beside himself. "Does that mean if, on three separate occasions, Seth arbitrarily claims that a random citizen stole food from the farm, then without any other evidence, that citizen's family would get three red circles and they would have to decide which one of their family members would be publicly hung? What kind of sense does that make?"

"I know it's extreme, but remember the law was enacted at a time when Caulfield was ripping apart at the seams and Seth was just a boy, not Head of Security. Our citizens demanded people follow the rules, especially when it came to the food supply. We tried securing the farm and our food storage, but with limited resources, we couldn't keep the crops and harvest under lock and key twenty-four hours a day. We had no alternative but to try and scare people into doing the right thing. The thought was that assigning a red circle to the family, instead of to the individual breaking the law, would result in individual households helping to make sure that their family members followed the law."

"Did it work?" Joshua asked.

"It did. It worked well. In fact, only one person ever pushed the envelope to test our resolve in enforcing the Law of the Red Circles. The family couldn't decide who was going to be hung, so our Head of Security at the time selected the oldest member of the family. Once the public witnessed the hanging, no one ever stole food again. I don't believe a red circle was ever given after that first and only hanging. Until today, that is..."

"Oh my God, Lorrick. I'm so sorry. This is all my fault."

"It's okay, Joshua. It's not our third red circle or even our second. It's our first. Seth is just flexing his muscle because he's upset that you're living with us and he wants you to fall in line. He's always been difficult to deal with, but last night was the first-time things ever got physical. The reality is the Law of the Red Circles no longer needs to be part of Caulfield and should be abolished. This event is a perfect opportunity for me to broach the subject with the Council."

Lorrick put his arm around Joshua and turned him around to face the field across the street, with Hopkins Court in the distance.

"When you really think about it," Lorrick continued, "you've done us a favor. I'm going to get the wheels in motion to have the law abolished. I should be able to get the support I need, and Seth will have one less thing to hang over everyone's head. In the long run, this is a good thing, Joshua. Honestly. Don't worry about it."

Lorrick had a fantastic way of turning a negative into a positive. Still, Joshua wondered if the Council would really eliminate the law and if Lorrick really thought this was a good thing or if he was just trying to make Joshua feel better. Joshua looked out at the children playing in the field and thanked God that it was only the family's first red circle.

## ※ 16 ※

## ACCLIMATION

Joshua did more listening than talking in the days that followed. He was still weak and not fully recovered from the road. His routine consisted of waking up to the patter of footsteps and banter between his new family members. Joshua shared a room with Samuel, but he was always gone, off to the farm by the time Joshua had awoken. Lorrick and Gabe were usually gone early as well. Mariam was always in the kitchen, cooking up something with an inviting aroma. Joshua ate whatever Mariam gave him, their conversation just a few words, at best. While he would never say anything, Joshua noticed his portions were smaller than everyone else's. Adin was usually at Mariam's side, assisting in the kitchen. Asher spent his days at school with other kids his age.

Joshua tried his best to fit in with the routine and forget about the red circle, but it was difficult. It bothered him knowing that the red circle was there for everyone to see when they walked past the house; a red circle that came to exist because of his big mouth. Still, Lorrick, Samuel, and Gabe encouraged Joshua every day and did their best to make him feel part of the family. Even Adin and little Asher began to warm up, while Mariam remained cold and uninviting.

Ian and Belinda stopped by frequently, and Joshua always made sure to show his face whenever the twins were around. Despite the embarrassment of what took place the first night they met, Joshua took any chance he could to get to be in Belinda's presence. He stumbled all over himself and couldn't put two words together around her, but he never passed up a chance to interact with her, nonetheless.

Unfortunately, just as frequently as Ian and Belinda visited, so did Seth and his band of misfits, Darin, Keegan, and Cade. The four men were an inseparable sum of evil. After the beating that Samuel took on account of Joshua, he wouldn't say a word to Seth or his gang. Seth made sure to rub it in Joshua's face—his sudden change of demeanor since their first encounter. Even with the ribbings, Joshua remained silent. The rest of the family seemed to be past the violence that occurred between Seth and Samuel. Not Joshua. He grew more afraid of Seth each day and avoided him as much as possible.

One morning, Joshua was up early enough for the whole family to have breakfast together, except for Samuel, of course. Lorrick focused the conversation on Joshua's past.

"Joshua," Lorrick started, "we've all been so consumed with allowing you space to get acclimated to the family. You really haven't said much about yourself. Is there anything you'd like to share about where you're from or your travels?"

Joshua glanced at Lorrick and then back down at his food. "I don't know. I'm just glad I'm here, I guess. I thought I was going to die out there on Route 23."

"We're glad you're here too. It's a miracle you made it this far. I'm sure it's hard to talk about, but I need to ask: what did you witness out there on the road?"

Joshua thought back to the nightmare of the barren

wasteland, which became his mother's grave, and nearly his, as well.

"Nothing." Joshua said flatly. "Besides Leon and his gang, there was nobody out there. I didn't see a single soul. It was just...empty."

"What about Columbus, Ohio? You must have passed through Columbus. What did you see there?"

"Are you talking about the place with all the tall buildings that touched the sky?"

"I suppose so, but I can't say for sure. Weren't there signposts for Columbus, Ohio?"

"I passed many signposts, but I have no idea what they said...I can't read," Joshua said humbly.

Gabe and Adin couldn't hide their surprised expressions. Lorrick, on the other hand, remained composed.

"I didn't know that," Lorrick said softly. "We'll have to address that right away. You would like to learn how to read and write, wouldn't you?"

Joshua looked at the anticipating faces around the table, with Asher excitingly nodding his head up and down. The prospect felt like a waste of time and Joshua wanted to politely decline, but he felt an enormous amount of pressure with everyone expecting an affirmative answer. Joshua looked down and played with his food. "I don't know. I've gotten this far without knowing how. I know a good amount about farming and I'm sure I could help Samuel with Caulfield's crops, earn my keep that way."

Lorrick put his utensil down and raised an eyebrow. "Joshua, understand that if I place you with Samuel, you would be more than just a laborer at our farm. We already have enough farmhands tending our crops. You'd be expected to become his apprentice and do what he does, which requires more than just physical labor; it requires reading and writing. Plus, every child born in Caulfield learns how to read and write. You'd be the only one here who didn't know how. I can't emphasize enough how strongly I feel that you should learn how to read and write." Lorrick stared hard at his adopted son.

Joshua looked up at the watching faces for a brief second before going back down to his plate. Something inside him told him it was what he needed to do, but he fought his intuition. He so badly wanted to decline, but the pressure with everyone looking overtook the fear of having to learn something new. "Okay. That's fine. If you teach me, I'll learn."

Lorrick took in a deep breath. "Excellent. I won't be your instructor, though. Doriel is our Head Educator here in Caulfield and the oldest member of the Council. I'll speak with him, and either he will be your teacher, or, he'll assign someone else. That said, I will certainly help you in the evenings with questions and homework," Lorrick said reassuringly.

"Okay," Joshua said, hardly louder than a whisper.

After a few moments of awkward silence, Gabe chimed in, "What about other family members, Joshua? Besides your mom, did you have other family back at your Commune?"

Despite being asked about other family members aside from his mother, Joshua's mind filled with visions of her. When they lived at Hartland, she had always been present in Joshua's life. Whether it was a hug, an encouraging word, or just lending an ear, she always made Joshua feel safe and secure, without being overbearing. She was tough, but she wasn't afraid to laugh or cry with her son. She took in his pain, his joys, his struggles, and his triumphs, and shared each moment, each emotion, without judgment or reservation. Through her voice and her actions, Joshua knew, without question, that she unconditionally loved him, despite her stern nature. He thought of the morning he woke to discover her not breathing. His eyes filled with tears and he couldn't swallow. He couldn't say a word, and everyone knew it.

"Dad..." Adin said, feeling sorry for Joshua.

Lorrick responded and put his hand on Joshua's shoulder, "Rest easy, Joshua. We all know you've been through a lot. We've all lost people we loved. I think we've had enough conversation this morning. Let's just finish up and get on with the day. We can discuss those subjects later if you care to. We've got loads of time to share our stories, good and bad. Does that sound all right?"

Joshua wiped away a single tear that fell down his right cheek. "Yeah, that sounds good. I'm sorry, it's just—"

"No need to apologize or explain anything," Lorrick said. "We've all been there. Let's drop it for now. We can talk another time."

## ❦ 17 ❦

## SUNDAY

When Joshua came downstairs the next morning, the entire family was already awake. Mariam and Gabe were in the kitchen preparing breakfast, while Lorrick was seated in the living room with Samuel, who had been gone every other day that week when Joshua awoke. The delicious Sunday morning meal that Mariam was creating wafted through the house. She might not have been as welcoming to Joshua as the rest of the family, but she sure knew how to cook.

"Good morning, Joshua," Samuel said, as Asher and Adin ran by, playing a game of tag.

"Guys, please stop running," Lorrick said as his two youngest children darted through bodies. "You know that drives your mother crazy, and I'd like to enjoy this day."

"Okay, Dad," Asher said, as he continued running at full speed into the other room.

"God bless 'em," Lorrick whispered under his breath as he turned to Joshua. "How did you sleep?"

"Good, thanks." Joshua answered, stretching his arms

wide. "I'm not quite one hundred percent, but definitely feeling better every day."

"Well, you're definitely looking better," Samuel interjected. "I mean, you'll never look as good as Gabe, but you've made strides since your arrival."

"I heard that," Gabe called out from the kitchen.

While he laughed, Joshua noticed Samuel's injuries from the altercation with Seth had healed remarkably well. "You look great, Samuel," Joshua said. "I can't believe how quickly you healed. I once took an inadvertent elbow to the face messing around with a friend at Hartland and I had a black eye for weeks. If I didn't know any better, I'd never guess you had been in a fight just days ago."

"Never mind Samuel's healing abilities and his terrible sense of humor," Lorrick continued, "in all seriousness, Joshua, you do look better. Sunday is the one day of the week where residents of Caulfield can do as they please. I usually spend an hour in the morning at our prayer center, reflecting on the past week. I was there this morning and ran into Doriel. I told him we need to get you up to speed with your literacy. I want you to meet him, so I asked him to stop by after breakfast. Does that work for you?"

"Yeah, that sounds good. I'd like to meet him."

"As you should!" Gabe replied, as he walked into the room. "Doriel is one of the greatest minds in all of Caulfield, in all the world, for that matter. If you don't believe me, you can ask him yourself and he'll tell you. You will never meet Doriel's equal."

Mariam agreed with laughter from the adjoining kitchen.

"All right, all right," Lorrick said, rolling his eyes, "we all know that Doriel can be a little...intense. And self-righteous. But he is our oldest resident and you cannot deny his mind is still as sharp as a tack and he gets the job done. Cut Doriel a little slack, would you guys? And don't prejudice Joshua's perception of the man before the two even meet."

"Sorry, Dad. You know me; I'm just messing around," Gabe said with a smile.

"It's all right. Joshua, what do you feel like doing after meeting Doriel?"

"I don't know."

"You could hang out with me and a couple of my friends," Gabe offered. "We usually meet up at Meigs Field, across the street, play a game or two, hang out and talk. You are welcome to join. I know some of the other kids are anxious to meet you."

Joshua knew he needed to get out of the house more and start meeting people, but he still felt awkward, like an outsider. Or, even worse, he felt like he was an exhibit, on display, for all of Caulfield to examine. He was about to say something, anything to get him out of having to spend the day with Gabe when Samuel interjected.

"Gabe, it's probably still too soon for Joshua to be playing games. You guys are not exactly gentle, and he's still not one hundred percent recovered. You will have all the time in the world to introduce Joshua to your friends. He hasn't even been with us for a week."

Samuel turned to Joshua. "How about you and I hang out today? I was just about to take a quick stroll around the facility before breakfast. Come with me and I'll give you a quick tour of some select spots. Then later, maybe we can try some meditation."

"Meditation? What's that?" Joshua asked.

"Meditation is a form of focusing your thoughts and your energy. Humans practiced it long before the Paper Era. It helps you become more patient and keeps you in the moment, so you're not as worried about the future. It gives you a better perspective on life's problems, affording you greater acceptance of those things in life that you can't control. I find it helps me with so many facets of my life, so I take any chance I can get to meditate. Don't get me wrong: I still have problems just like everyone else, so it's not some magical cure-all that makes everything perfect. Take one look at my legs and you know this to be true."

"I don't get it, but Samuel swears by it," Gabe responded.

Samuel shook his head in agreement. "Anyone can meditate. If you can breathe, you can meditate. I think you'd enjoy it. Now, let's go for that quick walk."

"Yeah, sure. That all sounds fine," Joshua answered.

Joshua put on his shoes and the two headed out. He hadn't been out much since being introduced to his new family and living situation. The second they walked out the door, Joshua noticed a group of kids playing across the street in Meigs Field. One of the them noticed Joshua with Samuel, pointed in their direction, and all the other kids stopped in their tracks and stared. Joshua felt his anxiety kick in, knowing he was going to be the focus of everyone's attention.

Once at the street, Joshua and Samuel took a left and headed east on Elders Row. Joshua purposefully walked with his head down, at a much deeper angle than usual. He didn't want anyone to see him. He thought maybe this walk wasn't such a good idea after all.

"It's okay," Samuel said, "I know this is going to be difficult. I went through the same thing when I arrived, so I know exactly how you feel. Everyone wants to know who you are and how you ended up here. More than that, they want to know what's out there. Remember, these people have never seen the world outside of these walls. Once you've gotten to know them, though, their curiosity will fade, and before you know it, you'll be just another face of Caulfield. I know it seems far away, but that time will be here before you know it. Try not to worry too much."

Joshua nodded in agreement, but he was still nervous.

"Should we run into anyone who's overly curious," Samuel continued, "I will be my normal self and introduce you. But I'll keep it short and will keep the conversation focused on me. You won't have to do any talking. A smile and a simple 'hello' will do and I'll take it from there."

Again, Joshua nodded, as the two made a right at Halsted Street and headed south. The boys in Meigs Field, now to their right, continued to stare. Joshua and Samuel approached a dirt road on their left where lots of people were milling about at the Twin Towers main entrances, adjacent to the dirt road.

"Let's head this way, down Schubert Avenue. It's the quickest way to the crops. I'd like to show you where I spend my days." As they headed down the dirt road, Samuel addressed those that walked by, regardless of who they were, keeping his promise to Joshua of keeping it short, easing the new resident's nerves. Between pleasantries, Samuel labeled the buildings.

"I'm sure Lorrick already told you about the Twin Towers on our left. Approximately a quarter of our residents live there. Just ahead on our left, east of the Twin Towers, are Caulfield's two water towers. You can see, in front of the water towers is a small office building with a covered front porch. Anything relating to the water towers can be found in that office.

"To our right, the first building here is Burling Lab; a chemical laboratory where we make all our medicines and other stuff. The slightly larger building to its right is Clements Kitchen, where we store all our food. The last and largest building of the three on our right is Warner Hall. That's where they make all our clothing and manufacture other materials. And the green mess straight ahead where the road ends, that's where I work."

Joshua was too overcome to say anything. He just looked at the buildings and tried his best to avoid eye contact with anyone they encountered. As they approached the crops, Joshua focused his vision to make out what was growing, but he had no idea what it was. All he could see was green.

Samuel turned to a man passing them. "Good morning, Mr. Rochford. The sunlight is coming through strong today, wouldn't you agree?" The man muttered something indistinguishable in response and Samuel turned back to Joshua. "Mr. Rochford isn't much for words. He's one of our grumpier residents. Those are the ones you really have to shower with kindness."

Joshua and Samuel reached the end of the road, where another dirt road intersected. To their left, the road was a dead end into the east water tower. To the right, the dirt road ran along the entire length of Warner Hall before it turned into a paved road. Joshua estimated Warner Hall was a good three to four hundred feet long. They rounded the corner of the building and turned right, where they ran into some slick mud.

"We just turned onto Clark Street and there has always been a problem where these two dirt roads meet," Samuel mentioned. "Apparently there used to be a natural stream that ran through here at this corner of Warner Hall. It was filled in, but it's still always muddy. And when it rains, you really have to be careful. I've sunk so deep, I've nearly lost a shoe or two in the past."

On their left, whatever it was that was growing was thriving, but even inspecting the crop up close, Joshua had no idea what it was.

"They are soybeans," Samuel said, "used to make our biodiesel and other concoctions. We have two major planting periods. In the spring, usually late March through early May, we'll plant these guys, corn, peppers, potatoes, eggplant, peanuts, cantaloupe, cotton, tomatoes, and other warm season crops. In the fall, usually late July to early September, we'll plant our cool season crops, such as broccoli, cabbage, cauliflower, collards, kale, onions, carrots, spinach, and lettuce. Spring plants are harvested just before the fall planting, and fall plants are harvested in November and December. January and February, we spend our days working on the equipment, preparing whatever we can for the year ahead. We also map out our planting, as we rotate the crops every year to keep the soil's nutrients balanced."

Joshua was amazed. "We rotated our crops at Hartland, but we didn't have nearly the variety of produce that you have here."

Samuel could see the intimidated look on Joshua's face. "Please don't worry about any of this, Joshua. I'm just giving you a tour, that's all. I'm not going to quiz you about what crops are planted in the spring versus the fall."

Joshua breathed a sigh of relief. "Thanks."

"Don't sweat it. We'll keep walking forward to where the road becomes paved and head to the Watchtower. You're going to love what I have to show you."

About one hundred feet before reaching the pavement, Joshua noticed a long, dirt driveway to his left, dividing the crops in half, with a garage door at the end that appeared to be attached to the largest building in Caulfield, sitting along the east wall, surrounded by the various goodies Samuel had just mentioned. Joshua knew this was the same four story building he saw from the infirmaries north window.

"What's that building in the middle of the crops?" Joshua asked.

"That's where I maintain all the equipment for our farm. I'll show that to you another day when we have more time."

Where Clark Street finally gave way to pavement, another intersecting road ran to their right, also paved, showing the back side of Warner Hall. Samuel pointed in that direction. "This street here is Wrightwood Avenue. If we went that way, it would run into a t-intersection with Halsted Street at Hopkins Court where we could turn right and head straight back home or turn left, and head toward the solar panels and Gold Castle. This building here, on our right, across from Warner Hall, is known as the Hyde Center. That's where all of the administrative matters are handled. Classrooms for the children, Caulfield's court room, and our library are all housed in that building."

Joshua nodded politely and tried to hide how over-whelming it was to take it all in. Once they reached the south end of Clark Street, Joshua could see the infirmary a good two hundred feet to his left. Directly in front of them were the shops that Joshua recognized from when he was first being walked through Caulfield. Samuel led them to their right and continued with his tour.

"Here's where you passed out when you had first arrived and were being marched to the Hyde Center. This stretch is called Deming Place. You remember this road?"

"I do," Joshua said. "And, I remember seeing you. You were just a few feet ahead of me when I went down, except..."

"Except what?"

"You weren't wearing any shoes."

"Not bad, for a guy who was out cold from pure exhaustion on this very street not that long ago. You're right, I wasn't wearing shoes. Being the Head Farmer, I need a good pair of boots to protect my feet, but I wear through the soles fast. I only have one pair, so when they need to be re-soled, they go to Warner Hall. That's where they were the day you came to Caulfield. You're going to need a shoe upgrade your-self; I'm shocked that you made it here with those things," Samuel said, pointing at Joshua's feet. "We'll get you better foot protection once you've completed your course with Doriel and are ready to be put to work."

Samuel and Joshua ran into several more people on their way to the Watchtower, ranging drastically in age and appearance, most with some form of the Sickness. They even ran into Keegan and Cade which revealed something truly extraordinary about Samuel: it didn't matter who he was talking to, Samuel knew each person they encountered by name and addressed them in a warm and inviting tone. To say Samuel was friendly was an understatement; he gave off a sense of acceptance and comfort that was unlike anything Joshua had ever known.

They turned left at Orchard Lane, between Mistrik Manor and Gold Castle, and approached the main entrance of the Commune. The Watchtower was bigger than Joshua remembered. With a door at the ground level and ascending stairs wrapped around the outside of its square walls, the watchtower was easily four stories high. Near the top, the stairs reached a wrap-around balcony where a guard overlooked the grounds. The walls turned to glass above the balcony, so anyone inside the top room could see out in every direction.

Samuel started up the stairs and motioned Joshua to follow. When they reached the balcony, Samuel addressed the guard with the same friendly demeanor he'd used all day.

"Hey, John. How's it going?" Samuel asked.

"Hi, Samuel. I figured I'd see you here, given the amount of sunlight this morning. You're not the first one. Your buddy has been up top there for at least an hour. I haven't heard a single peep from him, but I know he's still there, as I haven't left my post and haven't seen him since he walked up."

Samuel replied with a wave and entered the tower's top room. Inside was another set of stairs, in the middle of the room, ascending like a corkscrew up to the roof. Samuel led the way up the stairs with Joshua following close behind. At the top, Samuel turned the knob on a hatch that opened outward, revealing the grey sky.

"Whoa," Joshua said under his breath when he came through the hatch a few feet from where Andrew was sitting. There were trees as far as the eye could see. There were some buildings and a small residential area, but otherwise, the landscape was filled with the brown and green of dead and living trees surrounding Caulfield.

Joshua turned to Andrew and Samuel. "This is the coolest thing I've ever seen."

Samuel and Andrew smiled and chuckled as they watched Joshua take in the unobstructed view.

"I figured you'd like it up here," Samuel said.

Joshua pointed to a large building to the east, outside of Caulfield. "What's that building over there?"

"It was some sort of factory during the Paper Era," Andrew answered. "From what I understand, Caulfield acquired many useful items from that factory. Not only did Caulfield luck out with all the inventory, but some of the structure, itself, provided materials we needed."

Joshua turned around and pointed west. "And that little grouping of houses?"

"The remains of the small town of Alto, Georgia," Samuel answered. "Most of the staff that worked at Caulfield during the Paper Era lived in that little community. Now, it's deserted like the factory on the other side. Or, I should say, we believe it's deserted. The truth is no one has been to either the factory or those houses for decades. For all we know, Leon and his followers could be living there."

The thought of Leon gave Joshua an uneasy feeling. Andrew sensed Joshua's tension and changed the subject. "This is one of the clearest days I can remember. Definitely a good night for some stargazing."

"Absolutely," Samuel said. "Let's get out here tonight for sure. I'll grab the tunes." Samuel turned to Joshua. "What do you say, Joshua? You want to hang out here tonight for a bit?"

"Sure," Joshua said, although, in truth, he didn't really see what the excitement was with looking at stars. He had looked up at the night sky now and then but didn't understand the fascination with the few visible stars. But he didn't want to pass up spending time with Samuel.

"Awesome," Samuel said with his reassuring smile. The three men stood on top of the roof for a few minutes longer, feeling the wind in their faces, before Samuel interrupted the silence. "Well, we better head back for breakfast. You don't want to be late for your meeting with Doriel!"

"Doriel?" Andrew said with a look of slight concern.

"Yeah. Lorrick asked Doriel to help Joshua get up to speed with reading and writing, and Doriel was gracious enough to accept."

"Ohhhhh," Andrew said slowly. "Good luck with that, Joshua. You're going to need it."

## 18

### DORIEL

The morning's breakfast was even better than usual. Joshua had no idea what he was eating, but he knew it made his taste buds flare and his belly content. He was thankful for the meal, thankful to be alive. Soon, the empty dishes were collected, and the entire family was lending a hand with cleaning up the kitchen when there was a knock at the door.

"That must be Doriel," Lorrick said with a raised eye.

Yet no one moved. After several seconds, there was another loud knock.

"Don't everybody get up at once," Lorrick said sarcastically, crossing to the door. "Joshua, come with me."

Lorrick cast a look of disbelief to everyone as he headed for the front door, Joshua following close behind. Once at the door, Lorrick paused, tucked in his shirt, fixed his hair, and stood up as straight as possible. With his hand on the doorknob, he closed his eyes and took a deep breath. As he turned the knob, Lorrick's eyes flew open and he forced a smile onto his face.

"Doriel. How are you, kind sir? Thank you for stopping by

this morning. Please, come in." Lorrick sounded much more formal than usual.

"Good morning, Head Council," Doriel said as he entered the home. "It is my pleasure to be welcomed into your home this morning." Doriel studied Lorrick, taking in everything from his shoes up to his hair. "Still wearing the informal attire that you wore this morning at the Prayer Center, I see."

Lorrick wore a simple navy-blue t-shirt with a pair of worn jeans, a brown rope belt, and slip-on shoes with rubber soles. Doriel, on the other hand, wore a white collared shirt with a formal black jacket, black pants and black shoes. The jacket was worn, and the shoes had nearly disintegrated, but it was the most formal attire Joshua had ever seen, none-theless. A bright yellow tie that looked like it was glowing against the black jacket completed Doriel's outfit. Matching the tie, in the coat's lapel, sat a freshly picked sunflower.

"Yeah," Lorrick said as he flattened his shirt, "I'm so used to being informal on Sundays, I just threw this on this morning and forgot to put on something more formal for your visit. It's a good thing we've known each other for so long or you might have received the wrong impression. I'm very grateful you're here, and I know Joshua is as well." Lorrick extended his arm toward Joshua, who stood just a few feet from his adopted father.

Doriel's eyes darted to Joshua, then back to Lorrick. "Of course. This is a meeting of friends after all." Doriel walked toward his new student with an extended hand. "Joshua, it is a pleasure to meet you."

Joshua took Doriel's hand and was taken aback. It felt like the man was trying to crush every bone in his palm and fingers. Though old and wrinkled, Doriel showed no signs of the Sickness and Joshua felt like his hand was being squeezed in a vice.

"Joshua," Doriel said with a surprised expression, "I

thought you were recovered from your journey, but I must have been mistaken. Are you not well? What kind of a hand-shake is this?"

Joshua had no idea what to say or do, so he looked to Lorrick, hoping he'd answer. Doriel squeezed Joshua's hand harder, getting his attention once again.

"When you shake another man's hand, you need to shake it with a firm grip. That's the only proper way."

Joshua obliged and gripped tighter.

"Come now, Joshua, you have recovered, haven't you? You can shake my hand harder than that, yes?"

Joshua squeezed Doriel's hand as hard as he possibly could.

"Joshua, I'm disappointed. I thought you were Chosen. Surely you can do better than this?"

The anger began to take hold of Joshua. He continued to squeeze as hard as he possibly could. He couldn't understand why Doriel continued to antagonize him. Not only that, but Joshua was sure that Doriel was squeezing even harder. The pain in Joshua's hand crept up into his wrist and forearm. A man he was meeting for the first time was crushing his fingers —a man who was going to be his teacher and mentor.

As the pain increased, so did Joshua's anger. Rage swelled up inside him, pumping adrenaline through his veins. Joshua squeezed Doriel's hand even harder. With it, Joshua's body began to tremble and his whole head burned a bulging, deep red.

"That's more like it," Doriel said, slow and easy.

"All right, all right. Doriel, that's enough already. Come on." Lorrick put his hand on Doriel's arm to pull him away.

Doriel let go, and as soon as Joshua's hand was free, he shook it out and rubbed it with his other hand. Doriel didn't flinch, acting as if he had just finished taking a leisurely stroll.

"We need to strengthen you up, Joshua. We can't have our

Chosen residents of Caulfield showing any signs of weakness." Doriel paused for a second before continuing. "Do you not know that those who run in a race all run, but only one receives the prize? Run in such a way that you may win!" Doriel turned to Lorrick with a look of expectation.

"First Corinthians, chapter nine, verse twenty-four," Lorrick said.

"Excellent, Lorrick."

"Don't you want to complete the message with verse twenty-five: Everyone who competes in the games exercises self-control in all things. So they do it to obtain a perishable wreath, but we an imperishable."

"Semantics, Lorrick. The Bible commands us to run to win the race! That's exactly what all Chosen should do. Joshua needs to build his body to be strong."

"Please don't concern yourself with his physical strength," Lorrick said. "We are taking care of Joshua and will make sure he's good and physically healthy. You're here to help build his mind, not his brawn. We got the other area covered, believe me."

Doriel studied Lorrick with a raised eyebrow. "Well, of course, I trust you wouldn't let a Chosen be a weakling. You would never let the gift of a Chosen randomly appearing at our doorstep go to waste." Doriel turned to Joshua and slapped his shoulder rather forcefully. "You are in good hands. Before you know it, you'll be as strong as steel. And with my help, your mind will be sharp. I must warn you I demand nothing less than excellence from my students. It will be a struggle, but how can there be progress without struggle? It wouldn't be worth the time and effort if it weren't a challenge. Are you ready for this challenge?"

Joshua immediately looked at Lorrick with a worried expression. Joshua wished he could take back his agreement to become literate. He didn't want to spend another second with Doriel, let alone spend the next several months with the man. Joshua hoped Lorrick would see the expression on his face and tell Doriel that, on second thought, they were going to forego Joshua's classes. Instead, Lorrick looked into Joshua's eyes and gave a slight affirmative nod.

Joshua drooped his shoulders and looked down at the ground. "Yeah. Sure. I guess."

"This is unacceptable!" Doriel exclaimed. "You always look someone in the eye when you are speaking to them. Moreover, when you are presented with a challenge, you must rise to that challenge and meet whatever lies ahead of you with confidence. You are *Chosen*. You are *special*. The survival of our race depends on you. How can you lead us from the brink of humanity's extinction, if you cannot properly read and write? How can you be a leader without looking someone in the eye, and shaking their hand firmly? Now, I'm going to ask you again. Are you ready for this challenge?"

Anger coursed through Joshua's chest once again. He had just met this man, and already he despised him. Joshua looked Doriel in the eye and with every ounce of hatred he could gather, sternly said, "Yes, sir, I am ready for the challenge."

A smile widened on Doriel's face projecting arrogant victory. "Much better. See? Doesn't that feel better to address me properly, with the strength and confidence that all leaders must possess? You may not like me, but you will respect me, and you will come to understand why I demand nothing but the best from you. One day, you will be grateful for my tutelage."

Joshua didn't say a word. He just continued to look Doriel in the eyes, wishing he could punch the old man right in the mouth.

Samuel appeared from the next room and put his arm around Joshua. "Good morning, Doriel. I see you've met my new brother. I'm sure you will find that he's exceptionally bright and will be one of your best students."

"We shall see. Only time will tell," Doriel said, glaring at Joshua. Doriel turned back to Lorrick. "Well, I must be off. The demands of a Council member are never-ending, as you well know, Head Council. I have several more meetings today and cannot be late." Doriel turned back to Joshua and extended his hand. "Joshua, I will see you tomorrow, first thing in the morning. Please be sure to get a good night's sleep. I want your mind fresh when we begin our lesson."

Joshua took Doriel's hand and, without thinking twice, pretended it was Doriel's neck and squeezed it with all his might.

"Excellent," Doriel said, the conceited smirk again on his face. "You may turn out to be worth something to Caulfield after all."

## ❦ 19 ❧

## THE TWO WOLVES

"Don't worry about him," Samuel said after Doriel left. "He's more bark than bite. Come on, let's head upstairs." The two jaunted up the steps and headed straight for their room. Samuel closed the door behind them as Joshua plopped down on his bed.

"Can I ask you something?" Joshua said. "How come Doriel never shook your hand or looked you in the eye when you were talking to him? Is there some kind of bad blood between the two of you?"

Samuel shook his head side and side and sighed as he plopped down on his bed, opposite Joshua. "You have to remember that Doriel is from another generation. Not only is he Caulfield's oldest resident, he's Chosen. And you personally experienced how strong the man still is today. When Doriel was young, there was such an emphasis put on the importance of being Chosen, that it distorted his view on the value of the people around him. He thinks that those with the Sickness are beneath him. That's why he acts the way he does, not just with me, but with everyone infected. He's simply a product of his environment."

"Doesn't that make you mad? Doesn't he understand that he and the rest of Caulfield's Chosen would all be dead right now if it wasn't for you and your farming skills? Just because someone has the Sickness, it doesn't mean they are worthless. Just because he's Chosen, it doesn't mean he has to treat you like you're expendable, like you don't matter."

"If there is one thing I have learned in this life, it is that no one is more important than anyone else. We are all born of the same Creator and we all have equal worth, Chosen or otherwise. I live each day trying my best to treat all of those around me with kindness and respect, regardless of who they are, what they believe, or how they treat me. We are all connected. You might not believe it, or you might not understand it, but it's true."

"Why even bother with Doriel?" Joshua argued. "Your being nice to him isn't going to change the way he treats you or views others with the Sickness."

"What good would it do for me to harbor ill will towards those that shun me or treat me poorly? Would having feelings of hatred and anger put me in a better position? Would it make me a better person? Or, would it put them in a worse position? Would it make them sorry, or make them think twice, for treating someone poorly? Of course not. Far from it. It would be like drinking poison and hoping that it affects the other person instead of me. Hate begets hate. If I were to feed that desire, it would create a vicious cycle of animosity and fear. I want to be a part of the solution, not part of the problem."

"But you do feel anger, don't you?" Joshua asked as he clinched his right hand into a fist. "When someone hurts you, don't you want to hurt them back?"

"Of course, but when that feeling comes, I stop and remind myself that anger and hatred is not the answer. I push myself not just to turn the other cheek, but also to try and truly forgive the person who has wronged me. There is no doubt in my mind that we are all one and our Creator loves the person that wronged me, just as much as me. I'm not saying it's easy. Lorrick told me when I first arrived at Caulfield, 'The right thing to do is usually the hardest thing to do.' Don't give in to hate. Stay patient and rise above the anger."

Joshua turned his head down at his hand, released his fist, and studied his open palm before responding.

"That's why you didn't hit Seth the other night, despite how badly he provoked you. You stayed patient and rose above the anger."

"That's exactly right. The easiest thing for me to do that night would have been to hit him back. It would have been so easy for me to throw a punch. But that's not why I'm here, and that's certainly not what a loving Creator wants us to do. Nothing would give Seth greater satisfaction than to see me embrace the anger and lash out at him. But nothing would bring greater sorrow to God's heart to have me give in to the hate and take a swing."

"I don't know how you do it," Joshua confessed, shaking his head. "I didn't do anything that night to try to stop Seth because I feared what he might do to me. But you weren't afraid of him. You had no fear and you didn't strike back. I don't know how you did *either* of those things."

"In this life, there is love, and then there is everything else. The more you embrace the philosophy that we are all connected, the easier it becomes to sidestep all the pitfalls that take you away from what binds us. I speak from experience."

Samuel stood from the bed and took a book from the shelf.

"When I first arrived here, feeling all the same things that you are experiencing right now, Lorrick shared a story with me, written by Caulfield's first Head Council." Samuel opened the book and settled on a page. "A grandfather, old and wise, once told his young grandson, 'There is a terrible fight inside of me between two wolves. One is evil—angry, envious, greedy, arrogant, resentful, and hateful. The other wolf is good—joyous, peaceful, hopeful, kind, benevolent, generous, and compassionate. This same fight goes on inside of you. In fact, this same fight goes on inside of everyone.' The grandson thought about it for a minute and then asked, 'Which wolf will win?' The grandfather simply said, 'The one that you feed.'"

Samuel closed the book and put it back on the shelf. The two remained quiet for a few seconds before Joshua responded. "I like that story."

"Me too," Samuel said, sitting back down on his bed. "I think we've had enough ethical discussion for the day, huh? Let's meditate. I know it's going to feel weird at first but trust me. Focusing your thoughts and your energy is like feeding that good wolf inside you. With practice, you'll become more patient and more observant of those around you. It'll be easier for you to take a step back and recognize negative emotions when they come to the surface. There are many benefits to meditating. All you need to know how to do is breathe."

## ❧ 20 ❧

## CONNECTED

"You want me to sit here, close my eyes, focus on an imaginary point in front me, and repeat a word like 'peace' or 'love' or whatever?" Joshua asked with disbelief. "And when a thought comes to my mind, you want me to push it away? Even if a thought comes every few seconds? I just keep doing that over and over? Samuel, I don't get it."

"I know it sounds weird but trust me. And, when you say your word, you don't have to say it at a fast pace, like you're racing, trying to see how many times you can say the word 'peace' in sixty seconds. Breathe in, evenly and deeply, and don't worry about your word. Then, when you breathe out, do so again, evenly, slowly. Say your word with your exhale. Repeat.

"I know it sounds corny, and it feels strange at first. But like anything in life, with practice you'll get better at it and be able to keep thoughts at bay for longer periods of time. And, when you're able to slow your thoughts and focus your mind on that singularity, you will find peace. Don't get me wrong, you're still going to have problems, but they won't seem as dire as they would otherwise. Let's start out with ten minutes."

Joshua agreed, reluctantly, and tried meditating for ten minutes. Within a matter of seconds, the first thought came to his mind: Belinda. He pushed it away, concentrating harder on the imaginary focal point in front of him, keeping his breathing even, deep, and slow. His mind wandered off again, this time to a memory of Leon and Carol, wondering what fate awaited her after she freed him. Again, he caught himself and focused his energy on his breathing and his word—light.

After a grueling ten minutes, Joshua didn't have the heart to tell Samuel that meditation was the stupidest thing man had ever created. Instead, he lied and told his brother it wasn't that bad. He even went on to say he would try it every day for a month, even though he never wanted to do it again.

Samuel didn't push the issue or discuss it any further. Instead, he and Joshua went back downstairs. With no other commitments, aside from meeting Andrew that night for star gazing, Joshua and Samuel spent the rest of the day hanging out with the family. Much to his dismay, the conversation kept coming back to Joshua's impending first day of school with Doriel. Joshua cursed at himself for agreeing to become literate.

"I haven't even started this frigging class and already I can't wait until it's over," Joshua complained. "With all due respect, Doriel is about as much fun to be around as Seth. The sooner I'm finished with Doriel's instruction, the better."

"It makes sense that he reminds you of Seth," Adin said. "He was Doriel's ward until a year ago or so. Imagine living in that house!"

Asher made a face like he just ate a bitter worm.

"Seth was Doriel's ward?" Joshua asked.

"He was," Lorrick interjected. "Seth's father and Doriel were extremely tight, best of friends. When Seth was nine, he lost both of his parents within weeks of each other. First, his mother unexpectedly passed from heart failure and then he lost his father, who suffered a brain aneurism. Seth moved in with Doriel just a few houses down from here, where he stayed until he turned seventeen and moved out. Now he lives on his own in Mistrik Manor with the rest of the Chosen."

"Well, that explains quite a bit." Joshua said under his breath.

"So, count your blessings," Samuel said. "Imagine the fun you'd have if you had to *live* with Doriel at the same time as taking his class."

Everyone in the room laughed, except for Joshua.

That evening, after helping clean up the dinner mess, Samuel and Joshua headed out to the watchtower to meet Andrew. On the way, they took a small detour to grab something from Samuel's workshop that would allow them to listen to music while counting the stars. As they approached the dirt road entrance to the crops, with vegetation on both sides and the four-story, mammoth building with the built-out garage straight ahead, Joshua paused to take in the massiveness of it all.

"I still can't believe the size of this place."

"It is pretty intense, huh? You get used to it after a while."

"We grew plenty of things at Hartland, but nothing like this. This is easily four or five times the size."

"It's a ton of work, but there's such a tremendous sense of satisfaction every harvest, when you get to see and touch the results of that hard work. I don't have to tell you; you know what I'm talking about. Come on, the boombox we need for our music is right inside the garage. Follow me."

Joshua followed Samuel through the crops toward the large garage. As they walked, Joshua realized he didn't know what Samuel was talking about. Work at the farm in Hartland was nothing but work. He had never stopped to appreciate the fruits of his labor at harvest.

Joshua turned to the deep green and other colors surrounding him and admired the health of the crops. Everything looked so alive and vibrant. The best crop at Hartland that Joshua could remember, didn't come close to what Samuel was producing. He had to resist the urge to stop and stare.

They came to a large garage door, wide enough to fit two cars, with a regular-sized doorway to the right. Samuel reached into the opening of his shirt and pulled at a chain, eventually taking the chain off. A silver key hung from the necklace along with a small silver-white cross. "Our portable music is right inside," Samuel said.

Joshua's heart beat fast with excitement and curiosity as he entered Samuel's workshop. He was about to see where Samuel spent so much of his time.

"How'd you become such a great farmer? What's your secret?" Joshua asked as he followed Samuel into the dark.

"People forget that the food, plants, and flowers we grow are living, breathing things made up of energy, just like humans. And, just like humans, that energy can be invigorated with care or disintegrated with neglect. When a flower is nurtured by its keeper and by its pollinating bees, the flower's positive energy is reinforced. It's more than just giving it soil, nutrients and water. The secret is love, Joshua. Just like everything else in life. The answer is love."

"At Hartland, we approached farming in a different way. It wasn't about reinforcing positive energy. It was about science."

"Energy is science, Joshua. You just don't understand it

yet. You haven't been taught the nature of the light source that gives all of life its energy. Most haven't. Most have been taught that it's all about hard science: what you can touch, what you can see, what you can measure. Anything outside of that realm is considered irrational or ridiculous. Trust me when I tell you that something greater than our five senses exists, and it is what sustains us. It is us. I have a feeling we will all come to know and utilize the science of spirit soon enough."

Samuel's words inspired Joshua. "I would love to work with you on the farm someday."

"I'm sure you'd be a marvelous apprentice. Thoughts become things, Joshua. Have the courage and fortitude to act on your ideas and dreams, and you will end up exactly where you are supposed to be."

The opportunity to work with Samuel at the farm intrigued Joshua. Spending time with his new brother was always a joy. To spend every day with him, surrounded with all the life and color of Caulfield's crops would be unbelievable. Ironically, the same possibility brought Joshua worry. It was the size of the farm that was intimidating. And, he wasn't familiar with most of the foods, plants, or flowers that Joshua grew. Joshua's head and shoulders sank at the realization of how much he didn't know and would have to learn.

Samuel hit a light switch and the lights on the ceiling began to glow, revealing a vast space like a warehouse. As Joshua scanned the rows upon rows and the shelves upon shelves filled with tools of different shapes and sizes, his worry doubled. If he was going to be Samuel's apprentice, learning the names and properties of the plants and flowers outside was going to be the easy part. The toughest job was going to be inside these walls, learning how to use and maintain these tools.

Joshua tried to calm himself down by concentrating on

the beauty thriving outside the garage and how thrilling it would be to spend each day under Samuel's tutelage. Joshua shook his head to gain some perspective. He was getting ahead of himself. First, he had to learn how to read and write, and who knew how long that would take. Only after that would he be assigned a role within Caulfield, and he had no idea where Lorrick was going to put him.

Joshua followed Samuel across the length of the closed garage door to a long table, five to six feet deep, that ran the length of the wall. The wall itself had three, stacked shelves littered mostly with tools and other devices. Closest to the garage door, the bottom two shelves were filled with books, manuals, and papers of every kind. Joshua didn't know what any of the words said, but he guessed they dealt with tending to the farm and the machines used in maintaining the crops.

On the top shelf rested a device that looked like a black piece of tree trunk laying on its side, approximately four feet long and twelve inches in diameter, with a smaller silver gadget that was docked inside it. Joshua had never seen anything like it. Samuel grabbed a handle at the top of the apparatus and, with his free hand, unplugged it from a nearby outlet.

"You've probably never seen anything like this before. You'll see when we get to the rooftop: this boombox is a Godsend. It came with the job of Head Farmer. The hours of physical labor are long and strenuous, but I get to play music of my liking from this thing which makes the time go by faster. It's also portable, so I usually bring it with me while stargazing. Sometimes I even bring it home for an evening or a weekend. You're going to love it."

Joshua looked at it with curiosity. "In the Commune I'm from, there was one individual who had this instrument called a flute that looked like a long metal stick. She would blow into it and a wondrous sound would fill the air. I loved listening to her play. And when I was a child..." Joshua paused for a moment to compose himself. As time brought healing to Joshua with the passing of his mother, the sadness that came with the thought of her occasionally caught him off guard. "... my mom...would sing to me. That's the only music I've ever known."

Samuel put his hand on Joshua's shoulder. "It's ok to still be sad. Trust me when I tell you that those memories will eventually bring you a smile instead of a tear. For now, you have much to look forward to; you have no idea what types of music you're about to experience. This device has over ten thousand songs. We could literally play one song after the next for over ten days straight and you wouldn't repeat a single song. The sounds and words you will hear from this device will stir every emotion inside of you. The gift of music cannot be overstated."

Joshua smiled in anticipation.

Once they got to the tower, Samuel chatted up the guard on duty before heading to the rooftop and greeting Andrew with a handshake and a warm embrace.

"You weren't kidding. The stars are out tonight. What a view from up here," Joshua said with his head up, his chin pointed toward the sky.

"Not a bad night at all," Andrew said, staring in the same direction. "There's got to be at least two or three dozen visible stars out this evening. Some nights, you can't see a single thing. This is one of the better nights for stargazing."

"I don't think we're breaking the record for most stars tonight," Samuel replied, "but we'll count them up as we always do, regardless."

Samuel plugged the boombox into a nearby outlet and music poured out of the contraption. Joshua's ears took in the strange sound. Both Andrew and Samuel chuckled kindly at the expression on Joshua's face. The rhythmic vibrations filled the space around them, astonishing Joshua. The music was soon joined with lyrics:

I see through your eyes
You breathe with my lungs
I strain with your ear to make out
The words your mother sung
I bless with your hand
You pray on my knees
It's my blood in your veins
And your heart is beating in me
Finally when will it be enough
To find there's no them
There is only us

"I see through your eyes?" Joshua asked.

"This song is called 'Only Us,' by a band named Thrice. They have the best lyrics," Samuel said. "Every person on this planet is connected to the other in a much deeper manner than we realize. With everyone fighting for their own survival in Grey Dawn and terrified of the Sickness, it's incredibly easy for all of us to be selfish and self-centered. If one person's survival comes at the cost of another's death, so be it, especially if the one who survives is Chosen. But in reality, all life is intertwined and sacred, Sickness or Chosen. No one life is worth more than another."

Samuel paused, as though waiting to see if Joshua had anything to say in response.

"But this band," Joshua eventually replied, "and this song, this is from the Paper Era. How did they know anything about the daily struggle of Grey Dawn?"

"They didn't know Grey Dawn," Andrew answered, "but they knew struggle."

"Joshua," Samuel continued, "humans' inability to see

beyond the individual wants and desires of the one has been a struggle since mankind's first recorded history. People have been separated into classes based on their wealth, sex, religion, race or culture since the dawn of time. Fortunately, spread throughout history, there are those who reminded us that we all have worth, no matter the circumstance. Religious leaders, like Buddha, Jesus of Nazareth, and Muhammad. Spiritual leaders, such as Leo Tolstoy, Susan B. Anthony and Mahatma Gandhi. They preached philosophies of peace and unity, while living lives of compassion and kindness, promoting equality for all, not just a select few. Have you heard any of these names?

"Yeah," Joshua unceremoniously answered. "I mean, we had a preacher in Hartland who was always telling us the story of Christ, how he was born to the Virgin Mary, how he performed miracles, how he rose from the dead and was mankind's savior." Joshua looked down, shrugged his shoulders, and continued. "I don't know how I really feel about all that. I mean, am I really supposed to believe that he was born of a virgin? That he performed miracles and rose from the dead? Those things are hard enough to believe and accept as it is. To say he's mankind's savior is the hardest part to believe, cause if so, he didn't do a very good job with Grey Dawn and the Sickness."

"I understand your frustration," Samuel said, "but don't let those details divert you from Christ's most important message: to love and treat others as he loved. All of those names that I just mentioned, they treated everyone, regardless of who they were, with love and compassion. These leaders knew that their actions spoke louder then words, which is why they put everyone above them and loved all, equally. They hoped we would all see the message of love and unity and follow in those footsteps. I pray every day that the spirit of love fills my soul, so I too will treat others as I would want to be treated."

"Samuel and I believe it goes farther than that," Andrew interjected. "Not only are people intertwined, but all of God's creations are intertwined. It doesn't stop with humans. All living things are connected and part of the whole. All life on this planet and in the Universe is linked in a profound and spiritual way. All of existence is one. All of existence is God." Andrew looked up at the stars. "We have to love and respect all life, all of God's creations, not just the life on this planet."

Joshua turned to Samuel. "Do you think there is other life out there, in space?"

"I don't think there's other life in the universe, I *know* there's other life in the universe. I know you can't see it now with the way our atmosphere is today, but you should see the pictures of the night sky during the Paper Era. They are magnificent. Before Grey Dawn, the night sky was inundated with stars. Scientists at that time estimated that there were ten to the twenty-fourth suns in the Universe. Think about that number! That's a one with twenty-four zeros after it." Samuel walked over and touched the handrail facing north. "That's what we've marked here, on this ledge, to remind us of all that we cannot see."

Joshua stood next to Samuel and traced his hand over the marking. The number was barely visible, but he could see it, and he could certainly feel the edges of the marking. It read:

1,000,000,000,000,000,000,000,000

Samuel smiled. "We are just one of multiple planets orbiting one star. Think of all the life that exists on this planet alone. Creation does not end here. That would be so shortsighted to think that life began and ended here on Earth. With that estimated number of stars in the Universe, and with our Creator's majesty, we are not alone in the universe."

They laid on their backs, looked up at the stars, and listened to music soothingly coming from the boombox. As the melodies filled the air, Andrew, Samuel, and Joshua counted the speckles of light scattered across the sky. Together, they counted thirty-four stars. The record was fifty-one.

## ✿ 21 ✿

## LESSONS

Joshua awoke the next morning excited. With Samuel in his life, Joshua felt a sense of serenity he hadn't felt since losing his mom. Samuel made him feel safe, made him want to be a better person. Joshua was sure his illiteracy was the only thing holding him back from being appointed to work with Samuel daily at the farm. Learning how to read and write was going to be tough, but it was going to be worth it when Lorrick finally placed Joshua with Samuel.

Joshua threw on some clothes and headed downstairs. To his surprise, the only ones up were Mariam and Lorrick.

"Good morning, Joshua," Lorrick said with slight astonishment. "It appears Samuel must be rubbing off on you. Everybody else is still asleep. You getting up this early wouldn't have anything to do with wanting to be placed with Samuel to work at the crops, would it?"

Before Joshua could respond, Mariam interrupted. "Lor, the boy can't even read. Why don't we get him to the point where he's literate like the rest of us before we entertain crowning him the next farming king of Caulfield."

Lorrick turned to Mariam, his eyebrows scrunched. "No one is crowning anyone the next farming king. I'm just excited for Joshua to join the community and become a contributing member of our Commune. Doriel will have him reading and writing before we know it, and then we'll all get to see what talents Joshua will bring to Caulfield, regardless of where he's placed. Right, Joshua?"

Joshua wanted to give an enthusiastic response, but Mariam's tone and the mention of Doriel's name brought a knot to Joshua's stomach. Even with the real possibility of eventually being placed with Samuel, Joshua still had to get through Doriel, and the first day of lessons had arrived. Joshua forced a smile and gave Lorrick an awkward thumbs up.

It wasn't too much longer before the other kids were up, and the smell of Mariam's breakfast took over the whole first floor. The meal was fantastic, as always, and Joshua was thankful once again to have a full stomach. After breakfast, the family helped clean up the mess, as was normally expected before attending to their respective duties.

"Are you ready?" Lorrick asked Joshua as Lorrick grabbed a few things and made his way to the front door.

"Yeah," Joshua said, standing in the doorway between the living room and the kitchen, not moving a muscle. "I mean, I don't know. Is there anything I need to bring?"

"No, no, we'll supply you with the materials. What I mean is, are you ready, mentally, to begin this adventure with Doriel?"

"Oh, right." Joshua's eyes danced around the room, avoiding Lorrick. "Doriel is kind of intense, but I know that if I want to be an asset to Caulfield, I need to learn how to read and write, so, yeah, I'm ready." Yet, Joshua remained frozen in the doorway.

"Good." Lorrick said while opening the door. He turned, holding the screen door for Joshua, who finally got the hint.

As the two made their way south on Halsted Street towards the Hyde Center, Lorrick tried to calm Joshua's nerves. "You are going to be fine. Doriel is intense, that's true, but he can get you where you need to be faster than anyone else. I have plans for you, Joshua, so the sooner you're literate, the better. This makes Doriel our best option."

Joshua could feel his anxiety rise as they turned left onto Wrightwood Avenue. "Any last-minute advice?"

"Over the years of interacting with Doriel, I have found it's best to say as little as possible when conversing with him. Also, Doriel will share many of his random thoughts and ideas with you, without invitation, that have little, if anything, to do with the lesson. When he does, just nod in agreement. Don't fall into the trap of arguing with him. Just let him think he's the smartest person on Earth and that he is never wrong, and you'll be out of there before you know it."

Joshua knew it made sense and told Lorrick the same as they approached the main entrance of the Hyde Center.

The Commune was alive with activity. The number of people mulling around far exceeded what Joshua experienced the previous day when he went for his quick facility tour with Samuel. As Lorrick and Joshua wove through the residents, everyone stopped and stared at Joshua. Some said hello to Lorrick and he gave a quick hello back, but Joshua did not say a single word. He just wanted to get to Doriel's class and get this whole literacy thing over with.

Joshua followed Lorrick through the double door main entrance of the Hyde Center. A small lobby gave way to three hallways: one to the left, one to the right and one straight ahead. Lorrick and Joshua proceeded straight ahead, where doors appeared on both sides of the hall every thirty feet or so. At the hallway's end, there was another intersecting hallway, and Lorrick and Joshua turned right. There were signposts, but they were useless to Joshua.

"We've only turned once and I'm already lost." Joshua said.

"Learning your way around this building will be a challenge at first. The good news is there are only two floors: the main floor and the basement. The bad news is each floor is immense, approximately fifty thousand square feet in size, each, with lots of rooms and hallways. It can feel like a maze at times, but signs are posted throughout, and you can always ask someone if you get lost. But, don't worry, I won't leave you on your own until you get adjusted."

It was far bigger than anything they had at Hartland. Joshua cringed at the thought of getting lost, so he stayed close to Lorrick's side from the moment they entered the building.

After another few minutes of walking and turning down other hallways, Lorrick and Joshua eventually entered an office where two women, around fifty years old, sat at respective desks going over paperwork. One of the ladies had Sickness on her left hand. The other did not have any Sickness, at least, not from what Joshua could see.

"Good morning, ladies. This is Caulfield's newest resident, Joshua Barratt. As I mentioned last week, Joshua will be receiving instruction from Doriel for the next five or six months. Joshua, these are the head administrators for the Council, Ellen Cummins and Marie Covatta."

"Hello, dear," Ellen said. "It's nice to meet you."

"Hi, Joshua, and welcome," Marie said. "If you ever need anything at all, you come straight to us and we'll help you out."

Joshua thanked them both and followed Lorrick through the office and into another doorway at the back of the room. With organized piles of paper stacked on the desk, the floor, and all the shelves, Lorrick's office felt crowded and Joshua tried his best not to disturb anything.

"Whoa, I don't think I've ever seen this much paper in one place," Joshua said, wide-eyed. "Do you have to read all of this?"

"I do, and I have," Lorrick replied. "One of the perks of being Head Council." Joshua couldn't tell if Lorrick was being serious or sarcastic. "Most are old petitions previously brought before me. Their issues have been long resolved, but I keep the materials just in case I need to revisit anything."

"Why would you revisit an issue that's already been resolved?"

"The issue could come up again. I want the Council to be consistent in our rulings. Plus, it's a constant reminder that those who don't learn from mistakes are doomed to repeat them." Lorrick pulled a few things from his pockets and placed them on the desk before grabbing a sheet of paper off a shelf. "Come on. We don't want to be late for your first class."

Lorrick and Joshua headed to the stairwell and proceeded to the basement. The first door to their left was closed, but Joshua could tell from the cracks around the edges of the door that the light inside was on. Lorrick turned to Joshua before knocking. "Remember, his bark is worse than his bite. When he starts going off on tangents, just nod your head and act like whatever he's telling you is interesting and you agree with him, regardless of whether it's interesting or you agree with it. He's Caulfield's most effective teacher, so while his methods might be frustrating, anyone else would take twice as long, so stay patient. The material will seem overwhelming, but you will get through it. Remember, you'll have my help at home, along with the rest of the family, with questions and homework."

"Okay. I'm ready," Joshua said, already agreeing to something regardless of whether he actually agreed.

Lorrick knocked on the door. Joshua heard footsteps on

the other side approach before the door opened with a slow creak. "Good morning, Head Council." Doriel said in an arrogant tone as he extended his hand to Lorrick. After the two shook hands, Doriel turned to Joshua. "And, good morning to you, Joshua." Doriel extended his hand once again, this time to Joshua, who knew exactly what was expected of him. Immediately upon embracing the handshake, Joshua squeezed as hard as he possibly could, as if his life depended on it. After the painful experience, Doriel instructed Joshua to sit down at a small desk adjacent to a much larger desk belonging to Doriel.

Lorrick and Doriel exchanged a few more words as Joshua took a seat at his desk. Joshua's mouth grew dry and the palms of his hands began to sweat. Doriel left Lorrick's side, sat down at the large desk next to Joshua, and looked at him straight in the eye. Joshua wanted nothing more than to turn away and avert Doriel's gaze. Yet, from Doriel's visit the preceding day, Joshua knew the importance of eye contact, so he ignored his instincts and matched Doriel's intense stare. Lorrick watched from the doorway.

"Before we begin," Doriel said with a loud and deep voice, "we need to go over my ground rules so you know exactly how things will take place in this classroom over the next few months. First, I expect and demand your maximum effort and concentration. You are here to learn, not daydream. Second, I expect and demand that you follow my direction without pause or question. I am the teacher, you are the student. Never forget your place in our relationship. A student is not above the teacher." Doriel turned to Lorrick with a look of expectation.

"Luke, chapter six, verse forty. You forgot the rest of the verse: but everyone, when he has been fully trained, will be like his teacher," Lorrick said.

"Maybe someday, with hard work and strict discipline,

Joshua will become just like his teacher, but today and for the foreseeable future, he is the student." Doriel turned back to Joshua. "Third, I expect all homework and other assignments to be completed fully and on time. We have a rigorous schedule to follow, and I have other duties that are more important than this one. Therefore, should you disobey any of my rules, you can go somewhere else, as I will not allow you to waste my time. Do you understand?"

Joshua continued looking Doriel in the eye. "Yes, sir."

"The only reason I have agreed to accept Lorrick's request that I personally teach you is due to the circumstance that you are Chosen, as I am, and as Lorrick is. We are the last hope for humanity. We are special. Do you know how I got my name?"

Joshua wondered what that had to do with anything. A quick glance at Lorrick and Joshua remembered some sage advice.

"No, sir, I do not," Joshua said, pretending to be interested.

"My grandfather, a Chosen, was named Dorance. He was a great man who was instrumental in establishing Caulfield and making it the safe haven that it is today. The name 'Dorance' means, 'dark and handsome.' His son, my father, was named Daniel. He was also Chosen and continued my grandfather's legacy as one of the greatest men to live in Caulfield. The name 'Daniel' means, 'God is my judge.' When I was born, my father hoped that I would be better than both he and his father in my importance to humanity's survival, so he combined the two names together, taking the D, O, and R from Dorance and the I, E, and L from Daniel, creating Doriel."

"Interesting," Joshua replied, again following Lorrick's advice.

"A great responsibility falls upon me as an heir to this line of great, male Chosen leaders," Doriel continued. "Accordingly, I give one hundred percent effort in everything I do. I was Head Council of Caulfield for nearly three decades before giving the seat to Lorrick, willingly, so I could spend the short remainder of my years teaching the youth of Caulfield. They are the future and need to be shaped accordingly."

"I see." Joshua said, rather impressed with his ability to feign interest.

"As a male Chosen, Joshua, you have the same duty to lead humanity, and you must do so properly. If we are to survive as a race, we need discipline and strength. You must be firm and you must be consistent. It matters not what others think of you. The only thing that matters is being a tireless leader and never showing fear or weakness. Do you know what the name Joshua means?"

"No, sir, I do not."

"I didn't think so. The name Joshua means 'God is gracious, God is my savior.' If you are to be a savior to the people of Caulfield and an instrument of God's grace, then you must learn discipline and strength. You must learn to be firm and consistent. As Chosen, you are a member of the most important class of people left on Earth. Without Chosen genes, the Sickness would wipe out all of humanity. Without Chosen genes, we would be lost forever. Do you understand? Do you realize how important you and the rest of Caulfield's Chosen are? Do you appreciate the level of dedication expected of you to lead this race out of Grey Dawn?"

Joshua was numb. It was all too much to take in. If he was expected to lead humanity out of Grey Dawn, then humanity was going to be disappointed. Instead of voicing any concerns or raising any challenges to Doriel's statement, Joshua fell back on Lorrick's guidance.

"Yes, sir, I do." Joshua said, lying just as much to himself as he was to Doriel.

"Proverbs, chapter 22, verse 6 states, 'train up a child in the way he should go, even when he grows older he will not abandon it.' Now, let's start you off the way you should go because if you are going to lead humanity into prosperity, you must know how to read and write."

## 🦋 22 🦋

## BODY AND MIND

The next several months of instruction from Doriel were painstaking for Joshua. Doriel demanded nothing but perfection. At first, Joshua thought he could deal with the demand by studying with avid diligence. He figured his effort would pull him through. He was wrong. Joshua soon realized he could never meet Doriel's expectations, as they were not only unrealistic, but they were continuously changing. One day, Doriel demanded doing something a certain way. The next day, it was reversed. When Joshua made a mistake or couldn't follow the deranged logic, Doriel would raise his voice and scream in Joshua's face: "Are you really that stupid? How can you be such an idiot? Don't you listen to a word I say?" Joshua would hold back tears and do his best to concentrate, even though his thoughts were scattered because of Doriel's constant verbal and mental abuse.

When Joshua got home, he would run to his room to release all his anger and negative emotion, sometimes with tears, but just as often with punching whatever was nearby. Once he regained his composure, he would tackle his homework. The only thing more plentiful than Doriel's yelling insults were the assignments, taking three, sometimes four hours, each night to be completed. Joshua would work on whatever he could understand on his own and would save things he didn't understand for after dinner help with Lorrick, Gabe or Adin. Once his homework was finished, he would spend his evenings with Samuel, venting the frustration of dealing with Doriel.

"You know what he told me today?" Joshua said to Samuel one night four months into his lessons. "He told me I was worthless. I got an answer wrong and he slammed his instruction book on the desk and told me that I would never amount to anything and that he was wasting his time and energy on me. Then the crazy old man threw the book against the opposite wall and made *me* go pick it up and find the page we were on. I can't take his cruelty any longer. I hate him. I hate the man with every fiber of my being!" Joshua's eyes filled with tears, his breath short and stuttered.

"Joshua, close your eyes and take one deep and full breath after the other. Try and concentrate on your breathing and letting go of all the negative thoughts and hatred of Doriel. Concentrate on your breathing just like we do when we meditate."

Joshua followed Samuel's advice and took one deep breath after the next. Within half a minute, Joshua was much calmer, his appearance noticeably different. He was getting back to where he needed to be. Samuel seized the opportunity.

"Now, keep your eyes closed and your breathing even while I explain a couple things to you. I want you to keep an open mind, no matter how foolish or impractical the things I'm about to tell you might seem. Just listen to me as a brother, knowing I would never lie to you or steer you in the wrong direction."

Joshua nodded, keeping his eyes closed and his breathing even.

Samuel calmly began. "We are all products of our environment. When our bodies and minds are developing as children, we learn how to communicate with others by the way our parents and those in our household communicate with us and with each other. I have heard from several reliable and credible sources that Doriel's home as a child was filled with physical, verbal, and mental abuse. His father demanded perfection. When Doriel wasn't perfect, his father would scream at him, mentally abuse him and physically punish him. Doriel's father did this believing that the abuse would make his son stronger and force his son to push himself harder than he realized he could push himself."

Joshua continued listening with his eyes closed. He pictured Doriel as a small boy being tormented by his father.

"I don't know how Doriel made it through his father's vicious upbringing," Samuel continued. "What I do know is that as Doriel grew towards adulthood, that abusive attitude and mindset became his core, and ultimately shaped him into the adult he is today. On a subconscious level, Doriel might not like who he is or what he's become, but it's all he has ever known. Now he understands this abusive mentality to be a form of motivation. It's a twisted form of motivation, but motivation, nonetheless. Ultimately, Doriel is trying to get the best out of you. He wants you to take the constant criticism and belittling as a challenge, wherein you reach deep down within yourself to give more than you thought possible to prove him wrong. He wants you to do whatever it takes to show him that you *are* worth something and that you are *not* an idiot or a waste of time."

Joshua opened his eyes and looked at Samuel. The rage that coursed through Joshua moments ago was gone. It was replaced with concern for the young, scared and battered Doriel being raised by an abusive father during Grey Dawn.

"Thanks Samuel," Joshua said. "I never thought I'd feel

bad for Doriel, but no one deserves to be treated this way. I wish he knew that his negative motivation doesn't work on me. His hurtful and malicious remarks make me want to give up, not push myself. If it wasn't for you, there's no way I'd make it through this ordeal. I'd eventually believe that I was worthless and a waste of time. I felt that way on Route 23 and I almost gave up. I don't ever want to feel that way again."

"Fortunately, you're not his son and once this class is over, you won't have to endure anymore of Doriel's abuse. Regrettably, not all of us are so lucky." Samuel looked at Joshua, waiting.

"Seth..." Joshua whispered, thinking of a nine-year-old boy losing both of his parents, and then being raised by Doriel, living with his warped idea of negative motivation every single day. Joshua's heart broke for the little boys that were Doriel and Seth, who both suffered so much pain. "I don't want to turn into Doriel. I don't want to abuse my children the same way Doriel abuses me, the same way Seth is going to abuse his children someday."

"And you *won't*, Joshua. You're in a unique position. You're the only one I have ever known who has the pleasure of being under Doriel's direct and individual tutelage. All his other students receive his instruction in a group setting. Being in a group alleviates some of the pressure, as Doriel can only concentrate his efforts on one student at a time. Plus, a bond forms between the students, allowing them to rely on each other to get through Doriel's cruelty. You, on the other hand, have no other students to hide behind or bond with. This makes the lesson that much harder for you. But, remember, it's only a lesson via a teacher-student relationship. You are not his offspring and you do not live with him. Once you are literate, you will no longer be his sole pupil, and the relationship will end, for all practical purposes."

Joshua's head sunk as Samuel's words reminded Joshua

that the class was not yet over, and he still had to bear more of Doriel's teaching.

"You're almost there," Samuel continued. "The end of Doriel's class is within sight and will soon be over. Furthermore, when it is over and when you look back on this time with Doriel, you must *forgive* him for the way he treated you. Even if he doesn't ask for forgiveness."

## ✤ 23 ✤

# THE LIBRARY

Joshua's final exam for Doriel's class was just weeks away. If he passed with a grade of seventy-five percent or higher, he would be finished with the torture of being under Doriel's one-on-one instruction. When Doriel went into one of his tirades, Joshua would try and imagine Doriel as a little boy, receiving the same abuse from his father. While this practice kept Joshua from having crying outbursts of rage once at home, it didn't change the fact that Joshua did not like his teacher. In fact, the tremendous dislike Joshua had for Doriel further motivated him to study. He was pushing himself in ways that he previously didn't think possible. Joshua pushed himself not to prove Doriel wrong, but instead to get away from the man. If Joshua failed the final, he would have to repeat the *entire* class. The thought of having to spend an additional six months with Doriel was the extremist of motivations. Joshua was going to do whatever it took to pass that exam.

In the six months that had passed, Joshua was now at the point where he needed little help from Lorrick, Gabe or Adin. To get away from the ruckus at home, Joshua began regularly studying at the library on his own. One Sunday afternoon, Joshua asked Lorrick and Adin if they would go with him to help in the one area that was really causing trouble: The Bible. Joshua's family never turned him down when it came to help with his studies, and soon the three of them were in a study room at the library reviewing Doriel's lessons.

"This is where I'm going to fail. I know it," Joshua said.

"Trust me," Adin said, firmly, "if you use the flashcards I gave you, I promise you will pass the final. Those are the *same* flashcards I used when I was taking the *same* final, given by the *same* man. I passed that final, and you will too, if you use them. It's not like Doriel is going to suddenly test you on different passages from the Bible. The passages he references with you today are the same ones he used when I was his student and the same ones he used when Gabe was his student. Use the flashcards and you'll pass the exam."

"I don't understand why I have to memorize passages from the Bible anyway. There are plenty of other ways to test my ability to read and write."

"I agree," Lorrick replied, "but Doriel does things the same way they were done when he and I were in school. Before the famine, this was a place of strict religious adherence and education. Today, while most of Caulfield's residents find little to no use for spirituality or the Prayer Center, when Doriel and I were growing up, knowing and following Christianity was the number one priority. Doriel is stuck in that same headspace today."

"But why make me memorize these specific passages: 1 Timothy 2:11-14 'A woman must quietly receive instruction with entire submissiveness. But I do not allow a woman to teach or to exercise authority over a man, but to remain quiet. For it was Adam who was first created, and then Eve. And it was not Adam who was deceived, but the woman was deceived and became a wrongdoer.' And Romans 1:27 'and likewise the men, too, abandoned natural relations with women and burned in their desire toward one another, males with males committing shameful acts and receiving in their own persons the due penalty of their error.' And the scariest one yet, Nahum 1:2 'A jealous and avenging God is the Lord; the Lord is avenging and wrathful. The Lord takes vengeance on His adversaries, and He reserves wrath for His enemies.'"

Joshua's complexion turned white and his eyes went wide. He readjusted his seat before continuing.

"Am I supposed to believe that women are beneath men and should be silenced? That gay people deserve to be punished? And if I don't believe in these things, that God will hate me and have vengeance upon me?" Joshua asked.

"You already know the answer to those rhetorical questions." Adin said.

"Fear is a powerful emotion," Lorrick interjected, "easily stirred in humans, and Doriel likes to control through fear. He would rather be feared than loved. Plus, as a heterosexual Chosen male, these passages are self-serving, and he doesn't want anyone questioning his rule or authority. Don't let his handpicked Bible verses scare you. Instead, concentrate on the passages in the Bible that promote love, patience, and kindness."

"But none of those passages are required memorization under Doriel," Joshua complained.

"Then just do what I did and memorize what you have to for the final and forget about it." Adin said. "Once you pass this test, you never have to think about those passages again."

"She's right," Lorrick said. "God is not some man, sitting on a throne, controlling everyone and everything through fear. Life's Creator is beyond the pettiness of jealousy, vengeance and wrath. God is love. *That* is what you need to remember. 1 Corinthians 13:4-8 'Love is patient, love is kind, it is not jealous; love does not brag, it is not arrogant. It does not act disgracefully, it does not seek its own benefit; it is not provoked, does not keep an account of a wrong suffered, it does not rejoice in unrighteousness, but rejoices with the truth; it keeps every confidence, it believes all things, hopes all things, endures all things.'

"Live your life with love, Joshua. Do not live in fear. Fear traps your spirit; love sets it free."

## ❧ 24 ❧

## FARMERS

An hour after completing his exam, Joshua received confirmation that he had passed Doriel's final with a grade of eighty-eight percent. It had been half-a-year since his first lesson, and now Joshua was reading and writing on his own, at a proficient level. And, best yet, his individual lessons with Doriel had come to an end. Still, the encouragement and reminders provided by Samuel and Lorrick over those six months reminded Joshua that he had to forgive Doriel. Every night, as Joshua lay in bed, thinking of the things in his life that he was grateful for, he would say a prayer for Doriel and his wellbeing.

Now that Joshua was fully healed and literate, he needed to become a contributor to Caulfield. Lorrick saw a special connection between his two adopted sons and decided that Joshua would become Samuel's apprentice. The bond between them was strong, and Joshua loved spending time with his older brother, so when Lorrick told Joshua the news, he lit up with joy. Not that he had any burning desire to wake up before dawn and leave the house before anyone else was even up, but the idea of being with Samuel in a working capacity appealed to Joshua. Samuel had an inherent way of making others feel at ease and accepted, and Joshua had come to cherish this feeling. Joshua knew that the more time he had with Samuel, the better.

On the morning of his first day on the job, Joshua awoke to a gentle nudge. He stretched his arms out and then rubbed his eyes, followed by a yawn to get some extra oxygen. Joshua sat up and looked out the window. Through the sky's grey haze, he could see the outline of a full moon low on the horizon that gave off enough light to see that Samuel was fully dressed and ready to go.

"Rise and shine," Samuel said in a whisper. "Are you ready to learn the ways of Caulfield's Head Farmer so you and I can trade places and I can sleep in like the rest of these lazy bums?" The smile of Samuel's face was a mile long. "Come on, little brother, let's get going. It's best to get out there before the sun comes up, while there is still moisture in the air."

Joshua begrudgingly got out of bed and slipped on his clothes. Within minutes, the two left their home to begin Joshua's first day of work.

As they left the house, Samuel threw Joshua an apple. He took a bite, and the sharp crunch against his teeth, followed by the sweet and tangy juice of the fruit on his tongue, captured him.

"Wow," Joshua said with a full mouth, making his words nearly unintelligible. "If you can make me half the farmer that you are, I'll be amazed. There hasn't been one thing that I've eaten here that hasn't been outstanding."

"Thanks. You are going to be great too. There's one thing, though, that you might want to address right away because it's known to make for a terrible farmer."

Joshua swallowed his large bite of apple. "What's that?"

"Don't talk with your mouth full of food. You could grow the most amazing, mouthwatering apples in the world, but the minute people see what's going on in that mouth of yours, you won't be able to get rid of that apple if it's the last piece of grub in Caulfield."

Joshua gave an embarrassed laugh and apologized. When they got to the crops, Samuel walked Joshua through the rows of various plants, herbs, fruits, and vegetables. They seemed to be endless and everywhere. As Samuel named each, Joshua repeated the name in his head five times. He tried hard to concentrate on Samuel's instruction while ignoring the temptation to just stand and stare at the vegetation in front of him with awe.

"You've already eaten all of the foods I grow here, but what so many people don't realize is that it's just as important to grow flowers, plants, and herbs with medicinal qualities. This row contains broadleaf plantain, which is a brilliant poultice for drawing out insect venom. It also has anti-inflammatory agents. On this side, we have wild impatiens, which have extraordinary healing properties for itches, rashes, and other skin irritations. We also grow yellowroot, used for stomachaches and mouth sores. In the next row over, we have sassafras to make into a tea that helps build up the body's natural immunity." A few bees flew overhead, dipping from flower to flower.

"Plants used to draw out insect venom?" Joshua asked in a dumbfounded tone. Worry shot through the new apprentice thinking of all he needed to learn to grow and maintain these unfamiliar plants and flowers. The worry doubled at the thought of properly extracting the healing agents from these items. Joshua thought becoming Samuel's apprentice might have been the worst decision Lorrick ever made.

Samuel turned to Joshua with a look of compassion. "Don't worry. I know this is overwhelming right now. No one expects you to be able to take my place tomorrow or the day after tomorrow. We'll go over everything slowly, step by step, and before you know it, you'll know this stuff just as well as I do. Plus, I have over four-dozen farm hands that work with me. They can help you get familiar with our system if I'm indisposed. You are going to be better than fine; you are going to be spectacular." Joshua closed his mouth and took a dry swallow before nodding in agreement.

Once Samuel identified all the different fruits, vegetables, plants and flowers, he summarized the differences in farming techniques, the seasons in which certain crops were planted and harvested, and what made each crop thrive. Samuel knew everything by memory, not consulting a single book or written instrument while providing the information.

Samuel and Joshua made their way to the garage entrance. The last time Joshua was there, he dreamed of becoming Samuel's apprentice. Now that he officially carried that title, though, he was worried by the reality that following in the footsteps of such an amazing man and farmer was going to be daunting, to say the least.

In the back of his mind, Joshua also worried about the secret garden, or whatever it was that Seth was so obsessed over. If Samuel really was keeping this secret place behind Seth's back, Joshua figured he would soon know about it as Samuel's apprentice. Assuming Samuel shared its location, Joshua would have the additional burden of continuing to hide it from Seth and his group of bullies. And, if this place did exist, it raised ethical concerns as it would mean that Samuel has lied, and continues to lie, about its existence.

Joshua couldn't understand why Samuel would maintain such a secret garden in the first place. Joshua began feeling emotions of anger and disbelief toward Samuel for lying to him, to Seth, to everyone, about this place. It was too much to take in. Between the task of learning to farm and the thought that he was going to have to hide this secret garden from Seth, Joshua felt lightheaded and sick to his stomach.

"Breathe deeply," Samuel said as if reading Joshua's mind. "In through your nose, out through your mouth. Nice and even. Close your eyes if you have to and concentrate on any peaceful thought that comes to your mind."

Joshua closed his eyes and thought of his mom standing in that wonderfully peaceful place that Joshua dreamt of when he was on the road. He took several deep breaths and his heartbeat slowed. He became so lost in the thought he didn't even notice when Samuel opened the door and turned the inside lights on.

When Joshua opened his eyes, the vast space lay before him, tools in every direction. It was going to take years before he was going to be comfortable standing in front of such a sight.

Samuel placed a hand on Joshua's shoulder. "Remember, this is your first day and we are in no hurry. I know this is a lot to take in. Over time, I'm going to show you how to use all this equipment and how to tend to the crops. I'll be right by your side as you take each step. I promise, you will be fine. Trust me."

Joshua let out a deep sigh and concentrated on Samuel's promise. "Thanks. I believe you. Just know that I'm holding you to that promise. The only reason I have any faith at all that I can learn this stuff is because you're going to help me."

"And, that's exactly what I'm going to do." Samuel said.

Without taking another breath, Samuel began identifying the tools and explaining how they were used. Joshua tried paying attention, but the task in front of him was so prodigious that whatever Samuel said went in one ear and out the other. Joshua was sure there was no way he was ever going to learn about all this equipment and how to use it.

For a third time that morning, it was like Samuel read Joshua's mind. "I think that's enough talk for this morning. Here, let's grab a few items we can use outside, I'll turn on some music, and we'll head out to the crops and truly get this day underway with some physical activity."

Samuel handed Joshua a rake, which felt like a hundred pounds but weighed no more than five, and the two headed for the crops. As Joshua passed the shelf holding all the books on farming, botany, and horticulture, he noticed several books by someone named Luther Burbank. Joshua paused and pulled one down.

"Do you know Luther Burbank?" Samuel asked.

"No, I've never heard of him."

"He's one of the greatest botanists that ever lived. I owe much of my success to his teachings. I think you'll enjoy his works, his ideas, and even his philosophies. You can read anything you want, anytime."

Samuel reached for his boombox and turned its power on. Just like the night on the watchtower rooftop, waves of music vibrated from the speakers into the open air around them. Samuel watched Joshua's face as the song filled the garage.

To what end do we
Proceed so boldly
If all we are is
Chemical reactions
And what world have you
So deftly sold me
If you reduce me
If I have no soul to touch
No heart to love
No evil to rise up above
No angels and no ghosts
No real victories to toast
If you believe that this is true
Then I must ask
To what end do you proceed

Joshua couldn't believe what he was hearing. The music was loud and had such force that it took him by surprise. He wasn't sure if he enjoyed it or hated it. It was certainly like nothing he'd ever heard.

Samuel turned a dial on the device to lower the volume. "Sorry, buddy. I know on the guard tower we listened to some fairly mellow songs. When I'm out in the field working, I like a higher tempo, so I play stuff that's a little harder, a little more upbeat to keep my body moving. And I play it loud, so I can still hear it outside. You okay listening to music?"

"Of course. I'm not messing with your routine in any way. If you usually listen to heavier music while working outside, then we're listening to heavier music while working outside. It's just that I've never heard anything like this before. It's not like the songs we listened to while star gazing. I really liked that one song 'Only Us,' and what was the name of that other song? I think it was 'Open Water.'"

Samuel laughed.

"What's so funny?"

"The song that was just playing was written and performed by the same band that wrote and recorded 'Only Us' and 'Open Water.'"

"Really? They were so different."

"I know, when I first started listening to Thrice, I admit it took a while to like some of their heavier stuff. It's an acquired taste. But now I love it. Their music and lyrics are the cream of the crop, no pun intended."

As the two men gathered a few more things before heading outside, Joshua scanned the garage and noticed the back wall wasn't a wall, but a large, two-car garage door, just like the one at the front of the garage. It was closed with no handle he could see.

"What's back there, behind that garage door?" Joshua asked.

"Oh, that's just the connection to the main building, known as the Wheaton Armory. That garage door existed before this outer garage was built. There's a large warehouse on the other side filled with random junk. Then it's mostly just hallways and small rooms, stuff like that. This garage had already been added when I got to Caulfield. We no longer need the rest of the Armory to do this job."

"Has it always been closed?"

"Apparently, the entire building was once utilized by Caulfield. During the Paper Era, it contained vehicles, weapons and prisoners, with administrative offices to keep track of things. At Grey Dawn, it was converted to house our citizens, although they still used the warehouse to maintain the armored buses. Once they stopped sending out search parties and the population began to decline, they considered sealing it off because of its size and energy consumption. I guess the Council was right in the middle of deciding whether to shut it down when someone was assaulted in one of the rooms. That was enough for the Council to formally close it. They kept this garage space open, though, to store and maintain all the crop tools, and sealed that garage door between the two structures."

Samuel put his hand on Joshua's shoulder. "Who knows? Maybe once you learn how to grow all these foods and plants, Caulfield's population will grow to a point where we will have so many residents the Council will have no choice but to re-open Wheaton Armory again."

"I don't know about that. But, it's a nice thought," Joshua said.

"Oh," Samuel said. "I almost forgot. If you're going to be a farmer, you need better foot protection; you need a real pair of shoes. You can't be wearing those...whatever the heck those things are."

"Hey, watch it! These things got me all the way from Hartland to Caulfield."

"That's fine, and you can keep them if you want, but you can't work in those things. There's a pair of appropriate shoes, with laces and everything, under the shelf to the left." Samuel pointed to a shelf in the corner. "Get those on and we'll finally get this day started."

Joshua slipped on the shoes, which were a touch big, but they worked. They definitely offered more support and protection than his homemade pair of shoes from Hartland.

As they approached the crops, the first signs of dawn broke on the horizon. It was still grey but was noticeably lighter than it had been when they entered the garage. The air was cool, but refreshing, and being in Samuel's presence calmed Joshua. For the first time since joining Caulfield, he felt fully content and knew that he was, indeed, exactly where he belonged.

## 🏵 25 🏵

# ANDREW

Joshua learned something new from Samuel and his staff every day and was quickly becoming acclimated to Caulfield's farm, produce, and equipment. The routine came easy: Monday through Thursday, Samuel and Joshua would tend to the fields with the farm hands, doing whatever was needed to make sure Caulfield had enough to eat. These were the hardest workdays. Saturday, they would clean and maintain their equipment and meet with Lorrick to discuss concerns relating to the crops. Sunday was their day off, although Samuel would sometimes go to work for an hour or two just before dinner. Joshua offered to help, but Samuel would always turn him down.

That left Friday, Joshua's favorite day, when they distributed food to all of Caulfield. Folks lined up with check-lists in hand, and Joshua passed out each resident's ration for the week. Now that his novelty had worn off, Joshua enjoyed speaking to the residents. It was a nice way to transition into the weekend.

There were also home deliveries to those in Caulfield who couldn't come to the farm because of the Sickness or general illness. Twice a week, on Monday and Thursday, Joshua and Samuel made deliveries over their lunch hour. Samuel gathered sacks of food and, using a pushcart to carry the goods, they would make their way around Caulfield to drop off packages.

The more time Samuel and Joshua spent together, the more impressed Joshua became with Samuel's abilities. Whatever Samuel touched produced an amazing yield. The fruits and vegetables were healthy and tasteful. The flowers and plants were vibrant and radiating. Joshua knew he still had much to learn to reach Samuel's farming status.

Farming techniques and operations aside, the bond between the adopted brothers continued to flourish. Aside from William at Hartland, Samuel evolved into the father figure Joshua never had, actively listening and caring about Joshua's life. Ironically, Joshua knew nothing about Samuel's life before Caulfield. According to Samuel, when he appeared at the gates of Caulfield, something happened that caused a severe case of amnesia, so Samuel's life before arriving appeared to be a blank slate.

One day, as they were returning to the crops from dropping off a ration of food to a particularly sick family, Samuel surprised Joshua with a detour. "I know you've seen it, and weren't all that impressed, but let's quickly stop at the Prayer Center. I'd like to say a prayer for the family we just visited."

Samuel led Joshua to the front entrance of Caulfield and the guard tower. He'd been up to the rooftop many times, but never found much interest in the Prayer Center on the first floor.

Inside was a small room, maybe thirty square feet, with strange religious symbols covering the walls. For Joshua, the most distinguishable symbol was the cross which he was familiar with from his former Commune. However, the remaining symbols were a mystery to him. The rest of the room was empty, aside from a few chairs, and Andrew, who knelt in front of one of the chairs, deep in prayer.

Joshua appreciated Andrew's benevolent nature, and the two were developing a good friendship of their own, but Joshua had a hard time looking at him. Both of his hands and arms, his neck and head, basically everything from the waist up, showed one of the worst cases of Sickness Joshua could remember. He felt a tinge of shame every time he failed to look Andrew in the eyes when they spoke. Joshua knew it was the character of the person that mattered, and Andrew was one of the kindest people at Caulfield, but the Sickness in Andrew was so severe. Joshua tried his best to ignore it, but often couldn't help it.

Joshua and Samuel stood in silence for a moment in the open doorway until Andrew noticed them. "Samuel! Joshua! How are you, my friends?" Andrew said as he stood up to greet them.

Samuel turned to Joshua. "I thought we'd stop by and say a quick prayer for the Clement family. We just came from delivering their rations and they are all terribly ill."

"I'll be sure to say a prayer for them as well." Andrew turned to Joshua. "I understand you're learning the fine arts of agriculture and horticulture. And Samuel tells me you've even been reading some Luther Burbank material as well. Word around Caulfield is you're a natural and already exceeding expectations at this early stage of your apprenticeship."

"I'm doing my best, but it's going to take me a while to get to Samuel's elite farming status."

Andrew nodded in agreement. "There is no doubt that his farming skills are truly exceptional. Samuel always shrugs it off, in his modest manner, but it's true. People said that the lack of sunlight had caused the crops to die, but Samuel said that it was just the way the crops were being tended to and that the amount of sunlight was ample despite being filtered. Samuel turned out to be a gift from God."

"He certainly has a gift," Joshua said as he looked at Samuel. "Although, I am not sure that Samuel or his talents are necessarily gifts from God."

"Really. Where would you say the gift is from?" Andrew asked.

"I don't know. Maybe he's just a good farmer."

"Ahh," Andrew said. "Do you not believe in something greater? Call it whatever you want: God, Yahweh, Allah, Brahman. What you call it is irrelevant. Do you not believe?"

"I'm not sure what I believe. At my former Commune, which was smaller than Caulfield, people either didn't believe in God or they were Christian."

"Which were you: a non-believer or a Christian?" Andrew said.

"Me? I mean, my mom was born a Christian, but we really didn't talk about it, and I didn't give it much thought. There was one guy who was always saying, 'Jesus said this, Jesus did that. Jesus is Lord. Worship him and praise Jesus or the devil will get you.' Whenever I ran into him, I would keep my mouth shut and get away as quickly as possible."

"What are your thoughts on Jesus?" Samuel asked.

"I don't know." Joshua answered, wiping some sweat from his forehead. "I like his message of peace and love and treating other people the way you want to be treated. But I have difficulty with some of the other stuff. It's hard for me to believe that God came down from the sky and miraculously made Mary pregnant. It's hard for me to believe that he rose from the dead. Most of all, the thing that really doesn't sit right with me is the idea that if I don't believe all of those things, then I automatically go to hell to suffer for all of eternity."

Samuel and Andrew gave each other a side glance, but remained silent, waiting for Joshua to continue.

"Plus, in my Commune, there was way more suffering and depression than there is here in Caulfield. And, as good as we have it here, it pales in comparison to the Paper Era. If Jesus is God and loves us so much, why would he take away the Paper Era? Why would he leave us with Grey Dawn and the Sickness? If I loved someone, I would never do that to them. Objectively, it doesn't make a whole lot of sense to believe in God, given these circumstances."

"While I understand your point," Samuel said, "there is a danger in keeping a tally of what's good versus bad in your life to determine the existence of God."

Joshua scrunched his brows. "Why is that?"

"Think about it. You left your Commune on foot, where you faced and survived the elements for weeks on end. You ran into a gang of savages, and yet, someone in that same gang gave their own life to set you free. You made it all the way to Caulfield, where you were nursed back to health and adopted by a family that took you in. Now, you have learned how to read and write and are learning to be a farmer of a wide range of crops. Your new life here is allowing you to be someone who can give back to those around you. And that's not even mentioning the fact that you're Chosen."

"So what? Because of all these positives in my life, I'm supposed to believe in God?" Joshua asked.

Samuel paused for just a moment before answering. "That's my point. There are just as many positives in your life, as there are negatives. This holds true for everyone, no matter what their situation. Having a good life versus a bad life is a matter of individual perception. Just because you might perceive your life as good doesn't automatically mean that God exists, and vice versa. God either exists or doesn't exist."

"So, what do you guys believe? Do you believe in God?"

"Absolutely, we do," Andrew said, without a moment's pause. "I am a practicing Hindu."

"Hindu?" Joshua asked.

"Hindus are followers of Hinduism, which speaks to me, personally. In a nutshell, Hinduism believes that all living creatures have a soul, which are all part of a supreme soul. Each soul goes through a continuous cycle of life, death, and reincarnation. The goal is to achieve 'mokhsa,' or salvation, which ends the cycle of rebirths to become part of the absolute soul."

"So, you don't believe that Jesus was the Son of God?"

"I believe we are all children of God. You see all these symbols on the walls? These are the symbols of the major religions that were practiced around the world before Grey Dawn. Hinduism, Buddhism, Judaism, Christianity, and Islam. All beliefs in God are welcome here."

"I thought Christianity was it," Joshua said. "You either believed in Jesus or you didn't. The citizens of my old Commune didn't know about any of these other religions. At least, not that I'm aware of." Joshua turned to Samuel. "What do you believe?"

"Before I answer, I have a question for you," Samuel responded. "You've been here for quite some time now, and we have spent a lot of time together. Would your opinion of me change depending on my answer?"

"No way." Joshua quickly answered. "You treat everyone in Caulfield with genuine kindness. You're even nice to that monster Seth. If anything, I admire you to such a degree that, whatever your opinion is, I would respect it."

"Thank you, Joshua," Samuel said. "The answer to your question is that I believe in something greater: God, Creator, Source. Like Andrew said, it doesn't matter what you call it. I believe this with all my heart, and I will never waiver in that belief."

"But, of all these religions that you mentioned," Joshua continued, "how do you know which one is the correct one?"

"Andrew and I have discussed this on many occasions," Samuel said. "We agree that it doesn't matter because whatever you call God and however you know God is a personal choice, as is your relationship with God. No one should make those decisions for you. It's not about a correct religion, Joshua, it's about spirituality. When it comes to Spirit, we are all one with the one who is all."

Joshua raised an eyebrow and gave a quizzical look.

"If you look at the religions symbolized on these walls," Samuel continued, "and you study their teachings, you find that they all share one common core belief: The Golden Rule. Specifically, they preach of treating others the way you want to be treated. Treat everyone with love, because every single person, Chosen or otherwise, Christian or Buddhist, is just as deserving of love as everyone else."

Joshua brought his hand to his face and briefly pinched his lower lip before responding. "Doesn't it bother you that there's no way to know for sure if God exists? Moreover, doesn't it bother you that the majority of Caulfield doesn't care about God or spirituality? I mean, look at this room. It's tiny! If more of the people of Caulfield agreed with you, do you think your Prayer Center would have been relegated to such a small space?"

"The fact that Samuel and I are in the spiritual minority doesn't bother us," Andrew answered.

"When I arrived here," Samuel interjected, "the Prayer Center was in another building and was much bigger. But people used your same reasoning and questioned the existence of God because of Grey Dawn and the Sickness, and most lost their faith. They wanted the Prayer Center space to be used for other purposes, so Andrew and I moved it here. We don't hold it against anyone. Free will is a gift from our Creator. We were not made to obey God like a robot. We just pray that those who have lost their faith, find it once again."

"What about Seth?" Joshua asked, determined to find a flaw in the argument. "Do you pray for someone like Seth?"

"Absolutely," Andrew said, again without hesitation.

"Think of what you learned from your class with Doriel," Samuel added. "And, I'm not talking about the reading and the writing."

Joshua folded his arms and sighed. "I don't know. I can see why someone would believe in living a life of love and having hope that things will turn out for the best, but praying for Seth is something else altogether. He's cruel, conceited, arrogant, and narcissistic. If God does exist, why our Creator would make someone like him Chosen, I will never understand. It's just one more argument against the existence of God."

Joshua looked up at the ceiling before turning back to his friends, pointing his finger.

"Besides, you two still haven't told me what proof you have to establish the existence of God in the first place. How do you *know* God exists?"

"When I look at everything around me," Samuel answered, "good or bad, when I think of the complexity of all life, all existence, how it's all interconnected and how we have barely scratched the surface of understanding it, I can't help but think there is something greater. Plus, if you really want to hear something that will blow your mind and cast aside any doubts, talk to..."

"Well, well. Look what we have here," Seth interrupted through the open doorway. "Another gathering of Caulfield's religious devotees. And there's a new member to the group this time. Joshua, I'm disappointed. I had hoped you'd have better sense than to join these two in the Prayer Center."

"Good morning, Seth," Andrew said with a friendly tone. "We were just talking about you and praying for your well-being. How are things today?"

"Don't patronize me, Andrew. You wouldn't think it possible, but that face of yours can get even uglier than it already is if you don't watch yourself."

"I...I don't think he's patronizing you," Joshua said with a stutter. "We really were just talking about how Andrew and Samuel pray for everyone in Caulfield...including you. I think he's serious when he asked how things are going today."

Seth laughed. "Well, isn't that sweet. You fools believing in some God is an absolute joke. Look at you. Andrew deformed from the waist up, Samuel from the waist down. What do they have to offer anyone? Aside from Samuel's farming skills, you two are absolutely worthless to Caulfield. Just more mouths to feed. The people of Caulfield are beginning to wake up. Moving this ridiculous Prayer Center to the watchtower is proof that our Commune realized counting on God is irrational. Love doesn't get things done to survive Grey Dawn. Chosen do."

Seth entered the Prayer Center and put his arm around Joshua, addressing him personally, but speaking loud enough for Samuel and Andrew to hear.

"There are two absolutes you can count on in life, Joshua: The Chosen and the Sickness. I say it's a good thing that Samuel and Andrew pray for me because I'm everyone's last hope. Pretty soon, they're not only going to be praying for me, but they are going to be praying to me. I am Chosen, I am the strongest that Caulfield has to offer, I am the smartest that Caulfield has to offer, and I alone embody the last hope for our race—not some God that you cannot see or touch. I'm the closest thing to a God anyone will ever know. Most in

Caulfield already realize this truth, and soon, everyone will know it. It's only a matter of time before I'm Head of the Council and ruling this Commune."

"No one ever said you were a modest man, Seth," Andrew replied. Seth ignored Andrew keeping his attention on Joshua.

"Joshua, the sooner you become my ally, the better off you will be in the future. I've heard how far you've come in a short time under Samuel. Soon, you will have learned everything you can from this buffoon, and his presence will be just as meaningless as Andrew's. As a Chosen and as Caulfield's future Head Farmer, you will see that these people need us, our direction, our leadership. They need someone strong to bring them to a place where humanity can thrive once again. You need to put this God garbage behind you so Chosen like you and I can lift Caulfield to its zenith. Lorrick is the only reason that I'm not on the Council already, and he's growing old and weak. His time is nearly finished, and my time is nearly upon us."

Seth grinned as he patted Joshua on the back, turned and walked away. Andrew, Samuel, and Joshua stood there in silence until finally Samuel spoke.

"God has already forgiven Seth, for he does not know what he speaks. We need to keep those prayers coming for Seth and hope he eventually finds the grace of God. A Caulfield ruled by Seth would be catastrophic for everyone—especially those suffering from the Sickness."

## 26

### INSURANCE

The following Saturday was one of the greyer mornings Joshua could remember. It started out just like every other Saturday morning over the past weeks of being Samuel's apprentice—the two brothers had been up since before dawn and the list of tools and machinery to clean and maintain was long. As they brought the garage to life, Joshua instinctively reached for the boombox when it surprisingly turned on by itself, scaring Joshua half to death. Samuel laughed.

"Sorry about that. I shouldn't laugh, but the look on your face..." Samuel laughed some more. Joshua smiled, and eventually had a few chuckles himself before Samuel continued. "I should have warned you, the boombox is so old it sometimes acts funny, turning on and off by itself. Probably a short somewhere, but I'm not going to mess with it. Not a huge deal."

The morning took another unique turn after the two finished with their early morning routine. Samuel made a quick scan of the outside area and said, "Are you ready for a little surprise? You know what it is, don't you?"

"I'm ready for whatever, but I have no idea what you're talking about." Joshua was lying. He wondered if Samuel could sense the sarcasm in his voice. Samuel must be referring to the secret garden, but Joshua hoped he was wrong. If Samuel really kept a secret garden, Joshua did not want to know anything about it. That way, Joshua could insist he had no idea about it when Seth eventually pressed him for information. Joshua knew it was only a matter of time.

Up to this point, Samuel never mentioned anything about a secret garden. He would sometimes disappear for an hour or so, but they were both so busy, Joshua never thought anything of it. The idea of Samuel spending this time at some secret location seemed ridiculous. Regardless, Joshua knew he had to keep any anxiety about such a place to himself. If Samuel did have something to hide, he would only tell Joshua if it was absolutely necessary. There was no need to question Samuel's judgment.

"Trust me, you'll dig it. Come on, follow me," Samuel said.

The two men walked to the back of the garage. On one end, the side wall bumped out, creating a small, enclosed area, seven feet square, with a storage bin where they kept small, recycled parts, like screws, nuts and bolts. They also kept the home delivery cart in the enclosure. On the opposite wall of the enclosure, to Joshua's amazement, Samuel reached for a small rectangular box, to the right of the back garage door. Joshua had never noticed it before. The face of the box lifted, revealing a number pad with a large button at the bottom that read "Enter." Sam pushed six numbers: 0, 4, 0, 7, 0, 0, and then the "Enter" button. The garage door lifted from the ground and began to creep open, exposing an even larger space than the one they were standing in. Random stuff was littered everywhere. Parts of engines, gears, belts, pistons, valves, hoses, clamps, and more were scattered about the clutter. It made the equipment strewn around their everyday garage look sparse by comparison.

"I thought you said we didn't need any of the random junk that was behind this door," Joshua said in shock.

"I said there was junk back here, but whether or not we ever need it remains to be seen."

"Man, I thought you were going to show me the freaking secret garden Seth won't shut up about. I'm relieved that it's random car parts instead."

"I'm saving the secret garden for later," Sam said sarcastically. "For now, I want you to enjoy the vast amount of treasures that can be found in this place. There are some cool things from the Paper Era that I bet you've never seen. You have to get back there to see for yourself."

Aside from the car parts, the huge warehouse was filled with other assorted items. Workbenches spread out along the perimeter of the room that held multiple types of machinery and tools. In the center, there was a large bus painted grey that had other modifications. And in the back corner, a tarp covered something that appeared to be the same size as the bus in the center of the warehouse.

"Whoa!" Joshua exclaimed as he approached the bus in the middle of the room. "What is that thing?"

"Back before our time, when Grey Dawn first arrived, the people here quickly realized they were going to need to go out and find supplies. They took whatever materials they had and used them to fortify the buses on the premises. Then, a special team would use the buses to go out, gather up supplies, and bring them back. This place is where they fortified and maintained those buses. Most people in Caulfield don't even know this stuff is here."

"How come there's only one bus left?"

"There are actually two," Samuel said and pointed to the corner with the tarp-covered object. "There's a second bus under that drop cloth. As for all the other buses, unfortunately, these gathering missions were treacherous. At the onset, gathering parties not returning to Caulfield were the minority. However, over time, missing parties soon became the norm. I guess they got picked off, one by one. These two buses here are all that's left. Again, this was many years ago, well before our time."

"So, they stopped making supply runs? Is that why they have this area closed off now?"

"I guess after they were down to two buses, the Council decided the supply runs weren't worth risking any more Caulfield lives. It was just too dangerous. There was so much fear of what was going on outside these walls. Once they stopped making runs, this building became all but abandoned, until that assault that I told you about, resulting in the building being officially closed. After they locked up this place up for good, it became a thing of the past."

The two walked around the warehouse as Samuel continued. "Not long after I was appointed the Head Farmer, Lorrick brought me here and told me the history I just shared with you."

"Lorrick brought you here? Why would he do that?"

"Lorrick is a planner and prepares for situations well in advance of an actual need. He saw that I had a gift for farming and maintaining equipment. The man is incredibly perceptive. He also learns from his experiences. You already know that when I arrived at Caulfield, the crops were dying, the population was decreasing, and the people had lost their faith. After stabilizing the crops, Lorrick wanted me to help him prepare for the worst-case scenario. We came here, and I began working with him sporadically. He knew a good deal about maintaining and fixing these buses and I learned a lot from him, as well as from the various manuals that we have here."

Joshua turned with Samuel with surprise. "You mean these buses actually work?"

"They do. Over the past five years or so, we have gotten both buses to run. We haven't been able to fortify the one under the drop cloth, though. This one here has the wheels and lower half fully armored and protected. I'll get to the windows eventually. And this bus here is a manual transmission, versus the covered bus, which is automatic. I'll show you how to operate both. Then, it's just a matter of finishing up the fortification on this bus and starting the fortification on the other. I figured you could help me." Samuel put his hand on the metal plates that covered the driver's side of the bus.

"You want me to help you fortify these buses?"

"Exactly. It doesn't look great, but we're not concerned with looks. Each bus just needs to be as safe and durable as possible."

"Why? What's the worst-case scenario?" Joshua asked.

"I asked Lorrick the same question when we started working on this project. Today, you and I might be frightened at the idea of Seth taking over the Council and the harm he would cause Caulfield. But Lorrick, he *lived* through this place nearly tearing itself apart. He has no delusions when it comes to the harsh reality of Grey Dawn. If it nearly happened once, it could happen again. If Caulfield were ever on the brink of destruction, we'd have a legitimate shot to leave this place and escape the danger."

"Leave Caulfield?" Joshua said.

"Again, this is worst-case scenario. After barely surviving the famine, Lorrick understandably was worried about the future. Getting these buses in operating order was an insurance policy. You shouldn't find that so surprising. Look at you and your mom, for example. Born and raised in Hartland, knowing nothing else, but fleeing, on foot no less, because of what lay in store over the horizon. Your mother knew the risk of leaving Hartland was great. But the risk of staying was greater. I'm sure if your mom had a choice between leaving on foot or leaving in a well-armored vehicle, she would choose the latter."

Joshua stood in silence, staring at the armored bus in front of him. "I get what you're saying, it's just...I've been out there. The only thing out there is Leon and his gang of savages. Even if we had to leave Caulfield, where would we go? I don't know if I would choose Leon and the unknown that lays outside Caulfield's walls over any kind of chaos happening inside these walls."

"Let's pray we never have to make that choice, and this is an insurance policy that remains nothing more than an insurance policy. Let's pray that the grace of the Golden Rule finds its way to Seth's heart. If not, let's pray that he never comes to power."

## 27

## HOME DELIVERY

"I have a suggestion," Samuel said one morning on their way to the farm. "I think you should start making home deliveries on your own."

Up to that point in their working relationship, Joshua mostly assisted with preparing and pushing the cart, while Samuel handled the delivery of the goods to each resident. Joshua stayed with the cart the whole time, though. He'd never made the deliveries on his own.

"You definitely know your way around here now, and I think you'll enjoy getting to know some residents of Caulfield that you haven't really interacted with yet. The truth is, I could use the extra time to get some things done around the farm, and there's no need for both of us to continue making deliveries. Besides, you're finally starting to develop some muscles. You can't go back to having those scrawny little arms that you had when you started this job." Samuel broke into a light laugh. "If you quit pushing that cart around, you'll lose that little bit of muscle you've gained, and then you'll never get Belinda to notice you." Samuel's light laugh turned into a hearty one.

Joshua just rolled his eyes.

That next Friday, Joshua gathered the materials that he needed and began the route of his first solo delivery run. He purposely arranged for Rachel Organa to be his last stop. Ms. Organa was well known and liked in Caulfield, especially by Samuel. Boisterous and friendly, she would talk to anyone willing to listen. She claimed to be ninety-three, one of the oldest residents, but no one was checking the records to verify. Joshua had plenty left to do back at the garage upon completing his deliveries, so he needed to make his delivery to Ms. Organa a quick one, if she'd let him.

"Oh! Come in! Please, come in," she said, opening the door at Joshua's knock.

"Hi, Ms. Organa. I'm Joshua, Samuel's assistant. We've met before once or twice. I have your delivery for you." Joshua walked into her residence, arms full of groceries.

"Don't be silly! I know who you are, plain as day. Here, put the groceries down on my kitchen table, just around the corner to your left. Then come back in here so we can visit."

As Joshua made his way into Rachel's kitchen, the amazing smell of fresh baked bread and a flavorful tomato soup filled his nostrils. He had expected it to smell like the infirmary. But Ms. Organa's kitchen didn't smell like that at all. She was clearly a good cook and must have just made these delicious smelling provisions. His mouth watered as he made his way back into Ms. Organa's living room.

"My Samuel told me that you'd be making deliveries starting this week. Samuel and I are very close, and he's told me all about you. He thinks you're doing a great job with the crops. He says you're a quick study and have an excellent work ethic."

"Thank you, Ms. Organa. I've been so fortunate being adopted by the Wilton family and getting to work with Samuel. Not just because of his farming skills, which are second to none, but more so because he's such a positive and encouraging person. Most people light up when they are around him and enjoy his company. Most people."

"You don't need to beat around the bush with me, young man. That creep Seth has been jealous of Samuel ever since he came to Caulfield. I don't know why Seth has it out for Samuel. Perhaps it's Samuel's innate curiosity and love for spirituality, while Seth is all about the tangible aspects of life. Then again, maybe certain people just don't get along."

Joshua nodded. "Yeah, we ran into Seth the other day at the Prayer Center, and the two of them and Andrew got into a debate about God. I honestly don't know who's crazier: Andrew and Samuel with their fifteen different religions, or Seth, believing that he's the closest thing to God we will ever know."

"I know exactly what you mean. Religion can be very confusing and ultimately manifest into a very dangerous practice when dogma replaces reason. You must remember Joshua, separate cultures in humankind's early existence created these different ideas of what and who God was to them based on what they believed to be true at that time. These cultures would defend those beliefs rigorously, even if they were later discovered to be erroneous."

"What do you mean, erroneous?"

"Take our solar system, for example. As we stand here, right now, it feels as if the ground and the earth are stationary, and we are upon it, staying still when at rest. Yet, the earth is spinning round on its axis at one thousand miles per hour. Even more miraculous, at the same time as the earth spins on its axis, our planet is revolving around the sun at sixty-seven thousand miles per hour!"

"I never knew," Joshua said, stunned. "I mean, I knew the earth spun on its axis, creating night and day, and I knew it spun around the sun creating the seasons, but I never knew it was moving so fast."

"Think about those early civilizations, Joshua. They only knew what they felt: being stationary. Hence, passages in the Old Testament stating that 'the world is firmly established, it will not be moved,' and 'God established the earth upon its foundations, so that it will not totter.' Early mankind thought the earth was still, at the center of the solar system, and incorporated this belief into their religious concepts and scriptures."

"Ok, so they got it wrong. Big deal. Couldn't they easily fix it?"

"If you examine our history, it is a big deal. When it became apparent to scientists, like Nicolaus Copernicus and Galileo Galilei, that the sun was at the center of our solar system, with our earth spinning around it dogma ruled over reason, and most of the population believed in the principle that these biblical passages were authoritative and incontrovertibly true. To argue or suggest that it was the earth rotating around the sun was considered heresy and punishable by death."

Joshua was flabbergasted. The thought of killing a scientist whose discovery clashed with a religious principle seemed ludicrous. "They didn't actually kill these scientists that you mention, did they?"

"Copernicus died of natural causes shortly after his publication stating that the earth traveled around the sun, so he never had to suffer through an inquisition. But Galileo was not so fortunate. He studied the movement of our solar system and published his findings, arguing that Copernicus was correct. The leaders of the Christian religion conducted a trial to determine if Galileo was guilty of heresy, not once, but twice. After the first trial, he was found guilty and was forbidden to hold or defend his beliefs, all because of a religious scripture written by man before man had the technology to study the solar system."

"Why was there a second trial? What happened?" Joshua asked.

"Galileo refused to obey the order from the first trial. He continued to hold and teach his beliefs, so he was tried a second time. Again, the leaders of the Christian religion held that Galileo was guilty of heresy, and he was placed under house arrest until his death. The Christian leaders of the time were so sure of their religious principles and scripture that they refused to consider that the solar system moved in ways that were being proven by observation and scientific study. Galileo spent the final nine years of his life imprisoned, with the publication of his works being forbidden."

"That's terrible," Joshua said.

"Throughout history, not just Christian religious leaders, but the leaders of every major world religion have discriminated against, imprisoned, tortured, and even killed people who held beliefs contrary to their specific religious teachings." Rachel looked away from Joshua and out a window, as if in a daydream. "That's the travesty of fanatic religious belief: it allows dogma to rule over love, and people become willing to harm others in the name of God. It took the leaders of the Christian religion three hundred years before they acknowledged their mistake with Galileo and cleared his name. Do you think three hundred years is a bit long to fix it?"

"It is," Joshua responded. "That's an awfully long time."

"During the Paper Era, religious zealots of separate countries were so undeniably convinced that their religion was the true religion, that each faction killed for it, again, in God's name. Unimaginable to think that this religious tension played a role in the rise of Grey Dawn."

"Rise of Grey Dawn? What are you talking about? I thought we didn't know how Grey Dawn came to be."

Rachel gave Joshua a look of confusion. "You don't know how the Paper Era ended?"

"In the Commune where I was born and raised, there was only speculation. Our records did not contain that information. All we knew for sure was that the sky went grey and the technology of the Paper Era failed."

After a few awkward seconds, Rachel continued. "I had no idea. I just figured everyone knew. I shouldn't have made that assumption." She took a deep breath. "This is a bit complicated, but I am going to try and explain this to you as simply as possible. Please, sit down for a minute."

Joshua obliged. Rachel sat down next to him.

"The Commune you came from, how was it powered?"

"Hartland did not have electricity like we have here in Caulfield. We made wood fires for heat and cooking. That was our only form of power. We also made and used candles to help see in the dark."

"The power from solar panels and biofuel that we use at Caulfield are only a couple forms of energy that people learned how to harness during the Paper Era. At that time, the most prevalent form of energy came from the use and burning of a fossil fuel known as crude oil, which is a nonrenewable resource. A nonrenewable resource has a finite amount, meaning once it's all used up, it's gone forever. Crude oil is a thick, black liquid found deep underneath the earth's outer layer." Rachel stood up quickly, putting her hand on Joshua's shoulder. "Let me get something from another room before I go any further," she said before running off and appearing a minute later with a globe in her hand.

"Have you ever seen one of these?" Rachel asked.

"Yes, we had one in my old Commune."

"Good. Right now, we are approximately here." Rachel pointed to a spot on the southeast corner of the United States of America landmass. "During the Paper Era, the vast majority of crude oil came from here, in an area of the world generally known as the Middle East," Rachel pointed to a landmass on the opposite side of the globe, labeled Saudi Arabia. Joshua studied the globe, comparing the sizes of the countries Ms. Organa described and their geographic locations.

"After many years, Paper Era scientists discovered that the extraction and use of crude oil, along with other fossil fuels, like coal and natural gas, was destroying our environment. Burning fossil fuels released carbon dioxide into the air, warming our atmosphere, thereby causing our delicate climate to become unstable."

"I don't understand. How did this cause Grey Dawn?" Joshua asked.

"The burning of fossil fuels was just part of the problem. At the same time, the world's population was growing at the fastest rate in human history. To feed these large masses, humans tilled their fields to grow food and sprayed their crops with insecticides to keep insects and other organisms from eating the produce. Over decades, the practice of tilling the land and using insecticides resulted in the soil losing its nutrients and becoming eroded. This compounded the problem."

Joshua didn't follow. "How so?"

"Healthy soil naturally absorbs carbon from the air, helping to keep carbon amounts balanced. However, eroded soil cannot absorb carbon, so we were creating more carbon dioxide while at the same time taking away the ability for the gas to be absorbed by the earth. The planet eventually got so warm that large ice masses near the earth's poles melted, warming the ocean and killing countless numbers of fish and sea life, while frozen land in those regions thawed, releasing methane, a gas even deadlier than carbon dioxide. Our ancestors were destroying the planet and slowly killing themselves in the process."

"If they knew it was happening, why didn't they stop?" Joshua asked in a worried tone.

"For numerous reasons. Some people were making so much money in the fossil fuel industry, they attacked the scientists, claiming their findings were unfounded and inaccurate, thereby causing portions of society to distrust the scientists and not believe in global warming. For others, the use of these non-renewable fuels and insecticides was so prevalent, so commonplace, and the immediate harm was so subtle, that most people just shrugged their shoulders and ignored the problem.

"Whatever the case, the extraction and burning of fossil fuels continued, the earth's soil continued to erode with tilling and insecticide use, and the world's population continued to exponentially grow. Eventually, with the environment in turmoil, our world experienced a famine unlike anything in mankind's history, with the worst famine taking place in the Middle East. Those countries fell into a deep poverty and their people died by the tens of thousands, causing severe social unrest and breakdown."

Rachel stopped for a moment and stared off into nothing once again.

"Ms. Organa?" Joshua asked, gaining her attention.

Rachel had difficulty continuing. "The situation was dire, affecting every nation, resulting in all the world powers getting involved, taking sides and pointing blame. A starving world with a devastated environment was primed for war. All it needed was a spark, and that spark was found in that same place we were just discussing: Religion. With tensions at all-time highs, religious tolerance turned into religious extremism. It was radical religious fanatics, interpreting their religious scripture as justification under God to do whatever they needed to do to survive, even engage in violence, which brought us Grey Dawn."

"How?" Joshua demanded impatiently. "How did it lead to Grey Dawn?"

"The immense and extreme weaponry of the Paper Era must have been more powerful than we can imagine. We don't know who struck first, but missiles carrying bottom quark bombs were launched and detonated by the thousands. These weapons of mass destruction killed billions across the globe instantly. Worse still, the damage already caused to our environment during the Paper Era acted as a catalyst, turning the event even more cataclysmic, if that were even possible. These events wiped out nearly all of mankind and filled the sky with a permanent cloud. This is what gave us Grey Dawn."

Joshua looked down at the ground, too shocked to say anything.

Rachel started up again, quickly, sensing the shock in Joshua from hearing this news. "I'm sorry I had to be the one to tell you all this, my dear. I know this is all very hard to hear and accept, but we need to learn from our history and our mistakes. People who do not learn from their mistakes are doomed to repeat them."

## ❧ 28 ❧

# THE COUNCIL

Joshua worried more about the future of Caulfield after his encounter with Seth at the Prayer Center and Ms. Organa's revelation of Grey Dawn's origin. During his food deliveries and distributions, he would subtly ask residents their thoughts on the future of Caulfield and Seth potentially joining the Council of Elders. Of all these residents, Mr. Lenrod was always the most informed on the latest gossip.

"My last customer of the day." Joshua said and gathered Mr. Lenrod's weekly ration. "It's nice to see you again, sir. What's the latest news in Caulfield?"

"The latest rumors are the most sensational since your arrival. It appears the Council is so eager to have Seth Blackmore as a member they are considering adding another seat to the panel. This is obviously major news. Never in my lifetime would I expect the Elders to go from nine to ten seats."

"What? That can't be true." Joshua said.

"I only tell you what I've heard, my boy. But, trust me, my source is reliable."

"Why would they want Seth? Everyone knows the guy reeks of arrogance."

"There is no arguing that point. Our entire Commune knows about his conceited nature. But he's strong and exhibits a confidence and intensity that appeals to many residents. The average age of the Council is fifty-four, and only three of the nine members are Chosen. People want someone young, Chosen, and ambitious to lead. They believe this will bring them a sense of security."

"They should find their security in Lorrick. Thank God he's around to prevent such a travesty from happening."

"He might not have a choice. If the matter goes to the Council and five members vote in its favor, Lorrick will have to allow it. Not to mention that Lorrick's health appears to be a concern. Apparently, he doesn't look himself and has developed a cough? Have you noticed anything?"

"No, not at all," Joshua lied. Lorrick had developed a cough over the last couple weeks but kept shrugging it off like it was nothing.

"Curious..." Mr. Lenrod waited for Joshua to elaborate, but he was not taking the bait.

"Anything else?" Joshua asked.

"Yes," Mr. Lenrod said, enjoying the opportunity to chitchat. "There's talk that the solar panels may be in worse shape than we realize. Surely, you've noticed the power flickering on and off recently like the rest of us?"

"I have."

"The last of the replacement panels were installed years ago. Residents are worried that the panels are failing and it's only a matter of time before the Council limits our power usage. We need both our generators and solar panels to power our Commune. If we lose one, we're in trouble."

"I'll take power issues over Seth being on the Council any day. We got by fine at my former Commune without power."

"And then we'll be coming to you for advice, young man. How are things with you, anyway? You seem to be on top of your game. Everyone knows what a fine job you're doing as Samuel's understudy."

"Thank you. Yeah, my confidence with all the different farming has grown tremendously. Samuel is an amazing teacher. He's taught me so much, and I'm feeling more and more comfortable in my position."

"I can see that." Mr. Lenrod inspected his ration. "You serve Caulfield well. Until next time, take good care of yourself."

Joshua didn't want to mention it, but his gained experience in his farming responsibilities was bittersweet. While Samuel trusted Joshua to handle things on his own, the indirect consequence was that Samuel spent more time away from the crops. He would say he was going to tend to the bees or work on reinforcing the buses and disappear for hours. They still spent a great deal of time together, but it had decreased.

Lorrick's health also concerned Joshua. With Lorrick being in his early seventies and people noticing his cough, it must have been worse than Joshua and the rest of his family thought. Lorrick was getting plenty of nutrition, and they were also producing various herbal remedies to assist with his health. Still, he was beginning to look sickly and weak. No one was used to seeing him in that condition.

Of everyone in the family, Adin was the most concerned. That night, Joshua heard Adin tending to their father. It sounded like she needed assistance, so Joshua got up. Adin had just given Lorrick a dose of a strong cough syrup made from honey, ginger, thyme, and marshmallow root when Joshua entered the room. The syrup also contained melatonin derived from the feverfew plant, lavender, and valerian root, to help with sleep.

"My God!" Lorrick complained, not able to hide his feelings on the syrup's taste. "Don't they have something to help with the flavor? It's torture drinking that concoction."

"Dad, I love you, but I couldn't care less what it tastes like. That cough of yours is what's torture. It's not only keeping you from getting any sleep, but everyone else in the family is up as well. You know this stuff works, so just keep the fact that it tastes like garbage to yourself."

Joshua fixed Lorrick's pillows while Adin helped Lorrick drink orange juice to chase down the syrup. He laid down, thanking Adin and Joshua for their help, and gave a small cough to clear his throat. Within seconds, he was fast asleep. Joshua took a seat next to his adopted sister.

"You okay?" he asked quietly.

Adin glanced at Joshua, then turned back to her father and sighed. "I'm worried. This cough isn't going away. The syrup and other medicines we give him help treat the symptoms, but they aren't curing the cause of the illness."

Joshua didn't say anything. He just looked at Lorrick along with Adin.

"Can I ask you something?" She said to him. "This whole time you've been here as part of our family, you've never really talked about the details of your mom's passing. I know she was sick and died on Route 23, but what actually happened? Was it...like this?"

Adin was on the edge of her seat, anxious for an answer. Initially, Joshua was going to deflect, as he always did when the topic of his mother came up. But when he looked at Adin, he couldn't do it. She wanted to know what they were dealing with and Joshua had to tell her what happened with his mom, so she'd be best informed.

"Everything went so quickly with my mom," Joshua started, looking away from Adin. "It's tough to break it down. She was fine when we first got on the road. We were pushing it in terms of pace, walking fourteen, fifteen, sometimes sixteen hours a day. We had been on Route 23 for maybe two weeks or so when I first noticed a small cough she developed. It was mostly in the mornings when we were first getting up and moving. She'd blow it off, saying it was nothing."

Joshua felt the tears welling up. Adin took his hand while Joshua continued avoiding eye contact.

"A week after that, her lungs got worse. She would wake up coughing and it would continue throughout the day. By the end of the fourth week, she was in terrible shape. She would have violent coughing fits, especially at night. Our pace declined drastically. We would have to stop every five minutes for her to rest. Her eyes were droopy. She wasn't eating anything; I mean nothing. She'd only drink water."

Joshua stopped for a second, the first couple of tears leaving his eyes. He wiped his cheeks with his shoulders before he continued, still looking anywhere but in Adin's eyes.

"By that time..." Joshua shook his head, he couldn't control it; tears ran freely down his face. "I knew...I knew she was going to die." Joshua stopped to gain his composure and Adin took the opportunity to interject.

"Joshua, it's ok, we don't have to..."

"No," Joshua said, "I want you to know what happened. She couldn't walk anymore. She could barely talk. She had a raging fever. Her whole body was soaked with sweat all the time. Her breathing was labored. It was a struggle for her just to keep her eyes open. She begged me to move on without her. I told her there was no way I was leaving her. I just sat next to her...there was nothing I could do. We had no one else to help us. I felt so..."

Joshua pulled his hand from Adin and covered his face with both hands, crying hard. Adin scooted her chair over and put her arm around him.

"I'm sorry, Joshua. Please. You don't have to tell me anymore."

Joshua swiped at his tears. "No, it's important you hear this. When she finally understood that I was not leaving her side, she made me promise her that no matter what happened, I would continue on Route 23. She made me swear to her that I would never give up."

"That's good, Joshua, that means—"

"That's not all, Adin. Listen to me, please!" Joshua exclaimed, for the first time, looking Adin directly in the eyes. "After she died, I continued on Route 23 for what felt like an eternity. I was angry, hungry, tired, scared, and desperately lonely. Watching my mother die on the road, I was sure my fate would be...the same as hers."

Joshua's tears had stopped. His face was still wet, but his sadness had transformed into something else. The change in his demeanor caught Adin off guard.

"Depression," Joshua continued, now stern in his delivery. "Depression coursed through my soul and consumed me to the point where I was going to take my own life. Suicide seemed so simple, so easy. It was a friend that I was going to fully embrace, even if it meant breaking a promise to my mom that I swore to keep."

Joshua stood from his seat and walked a few feet away from Adin, pulling a handkerchief from his pocket to wipe his nose and face. She stood up with him and took his free hand, pulling him around to face her.

"But you obviously didn't take your own life," she whispered. "What made you change your mind?"

Joshua looked down at their joined hands, suddenly shy again. "I had a dream I was with my mom. It was the most lucid, vivid dream I've ever had. It felt so real; it felt more real than this. She filled me with her love, and it reminded me of my promise. She told me that she was always with me and asked me to never lose hope."

Adin smiled. "You know that was her, right? That was her spirit encouraging you to push onward because she knew you were going to end up here. She knew you still had lots of life to live. You know that?"

Joshua wiped his nose and face again. "Yeah, I know it. It's easy to forget. But sitting here, telling you what happened, it reminds me that it really was her, and she's still with me." He smiled. "Thanks for having me tell the story so I could be reminded. I needed that."

Adin smiled back. "Thanks for sharing. It means a lot to me." Adin turned back to her father, her smile dissolving into worry.

"Come on," Joshua said, pulling Adin. "Morning is going to be here before we know it. We both need some rest. Lorrick is going to be okay. You'll see. They have great medicine here, and he's under good care. He's going to turn around."

Despite the surety in his voice, there was a part of Joshua that felt bad saying this to Adin. She was no fool. Lorrick was getting worse.

In the nights that followed, there were many occasions where Joshua and Adin would be awoken in the middle of the night to Lorrick's violent coughing. After tending to him the best they could, they would sit by his side. Sometimes they would chat, other times, they would sit in silence.

Joshua never said anything on the subject, but on the really bad nights, he was filled with dread. If Lorrick passed away, not only would they lose a father, but Caulfield would lose its greatest leader. Making matters worse, if he died a position would be open for Seth on the Council. Not just any position, but the Head Council position. Was the Council so scared of

Grey Dawn and the Sickness that they would appoint Seth as Head Council if Lorrick died? Surely, they wouldn't do such a thing. If they appointed him as an Elder, they would have someone else with more experience serve as Head Council. Joshua assured himself that's what made the most sense.

He wanted to share these thoughts with Adin but didn't want to make matters worse by putting more worry on her. Whenever the thought of Seth popped into Joshua's head, he bit his tongue and kept it to himself. Little did he know, Adin was doing the exact same thing, but for a completely different reason.

## ✣ 29 ✣

## ADIN'S BURDEN

One damp, Monday morning, after a couple hours of outside labor cultivating the crops, Samuel informed Joshua he was going to tend to the bees for a while and perhaps take care of a few other matters. Joshua thought nothing of it and continued with his work. Eventually, Joshua headed back into the garage and realized they never turned on the music that morning. He reached for the boombox, but to his astonishment, it was missing. After a moment, Joshua recalled that they had brought the device back home with them Saturday evening. He didn't think Samuel had it with him that morning when they returned to work, but he wanted to be sure, so Joshua went around to the rear of the building, by the apiary, to confirm with Samuel.

To Joshua's surprise, Samuel was nowhere the be found. Normally, once they arrived at the farm, Joshua and Samuel would not return home until it was time for dinner. However, it was just over a five-minute walk, each way, if Joshua moved with some urgency, and the thought of having no music the rest of the day didn't appeal to him. So, Joshua decided to run home and retrieve the musical companion.

When Joshua entered his home, it was unusually quiet. He was not used to the stillness, given the number of people in the family living in such small quarters. He walked through the living room into the kitchen where, to his shock, he found Seth and Mariam sitting at the kitchen table talking in low voices.

"Joshua!" Mariam exclaimed, standing up. "What are you doing here? Shouldn't you be attending to the farm?"

"Yeah...but Samuel and I brought the boombox home this past weekend and we forgot it this morning. I'm just going to grab it real quick. I'll only be here for a moment."

Seth stood up from the table and approached Joshua. "Good to see you carrying out your duty to Caulfield. By now, Samuel must have taught you nearly everything he knows. I've heard from several farm hands that you are self-sufficient, and Samuel no longer watches over you. You realize, Joshua, that things are turning out just as I told you. A Chosen will soon be our Head Farmer, and Samuel will be dispensable."

"Whatever Seth." Joshua said.

Seth turned his nose up to Joshua and gave him a concentrated look. "You and Samuel have grown very close during your apprenticeship. Surely he has shown you the location of his secret garden." Seth let out a long breath. "This doesn't need to be difficult, Joshua. Why don't you share the location with me?"

Joshua shrugged his shoulders. "It's just like Samuel keeps telling you: there is no secret garden. There are only the main crops to the north and south to the garage. That's it. If there was a secret garden, you're right, he would have shown me its location by now. Or, you would have found it by now, given that we're locked inside this Commune, where there are only so many places to hide things. Not only has Samuel never shown me any kind of secret garden, he hasn't even discussed it. I swear, Seth, he hasn't shown or discussed anything with me relating to this place you are so obsessed with."

Seth gave a quick, sarcastic laugh. "That's what I thought. Soon you'll need to make a very serious decision. You will need to determine where your loyalties lie. Caulfield is on the cusp of a new era and new leadership. I am confident that the next time I ask, you will show me the location of the secret garden."

Seth turned to Mariam. "We'll continue our conversation another time." With that, he left, slamming the door behind him.

"Everything okay?" Joshua asked Mariam.

"Fine," Mariam said as she turned away from him, headed for the stove. Maybe Joshua was seeing things, but he swore he saw a tear roll down Mariam's cheek before she turned around.

"Okay. Just making sure. I was surprised to see Seth here alone, talking to you. I was just concerned. As long as everything is okay..."

"I said it's fine," Mariam said sharply with her back to Joshua. She began tending to some items that were in front of her for that evening's dinner. Joshua got the hint. He turned around and went upstairs.

Mariam heard Joshua rummaging through his room. A minute later, she heard him leave through the front door.

Mariam sighed and continued preparing the vegetables in front of her. Within seconds, a couple of tears were visibly running down her face. She stopped working to wipe her tears and gain her composure. A minute later, Adin appeared from one of the bedrooms on the main floor. She walked into the kitchen where her mother was standing. Adin was visibly shaking, and her face showed that she had been crying hard. Her hair and clothes were disheveled, and both of her cheeks were rosy red. The two stood there in silence as they began to hear the sound of raindrops outside tapping on the kitchen window. Adin stared out into the grey, looking at the rain, silent. Her mother walked over to her and put her hand on her shoulder.

"Please don't touch me," Adin said in a low voice, pulling away from her mother.

"Sweetheart, it's going to be okay."

"You don't understand," Adin said, beginning to cry again. "You don't understand what he's like..."

"Shhh. Honey, calm down. It's over now."

"It's not over now! He'll be back. And when he comes back, we'll go through this same routine again, like we always do. I don't know, Mom. I don't know if I can do this any longer. Maybe we made a mistake. Maybe this is the wrong decision."

"Adin, we've talked about this, over and over. We all have our burden to bear. The world is a tough and harsh place. Your father is not well and he's getting worse. I don't have to remind you of this fact. I honestly don't know if he's going to recover. Regardless, it's only a matter of time before Seth is on the Council. Once he's a member of the Elders, he's going to rule Caulfield. We would be ignorant to think otherwise.

"He is Chosen. You are Chosen. What he says is true: if humanity has any hope of surviving, we are going to need the offspring of Chosen. He is the strongest male in our Commune. I don't like it any more than you do. And, if I could take your place, so you would not have to endure what you're going through, I would do it in a heartbeat. But I can't."

"I know you can't take my place, Mom. I just don't know if this is the right decision. Look at you and Dad. You're both Chosen, but Gabe still has the Sickness."

"I gave birth to five children, Adin. Five! And of those five, Gabe was the only one to get the Sickness. Other women in this Commune would give their lives just to have *one* Chosen child!"

"I know. You're right. I just don't know if I can get through this."

"You must get through it, honey. You must, and you *will* get through it, not just for yourself, but for everyone at Caulfield, for the entire human race. Plus, if you were to conceive one of Seth's offspring, you would assure yourself security in Caulfield's future. With such news, I'm sure your father would pair you with Seth immediately. Or, Seth will make the pairing himself, if he's already on the Council by that time.

"Please understand, you'll be taken care of and tended to better than anyone else. You'll live in a home, like ours, not some apartment converted out of two or three old jail cells. Most importantly, you'll sit at the right hand of Caulfield's leader; you'll have some say, behind closed doors, about how things move forward. I'm so sorry sweetheart. I know it's not fair, but you know it's our best option. In the end, this will provide you with the best life possible in our future Commune."

Adin took some deep breaths while Mariam wiped away Adin's last tears.

"I know. I know." Adin said, as she sat down and gathered herself. "It's just...I don't know if this is the right way to go about this...and Seth...he can be so...mean. Sometimes, when it's just the two of us, he's nice...but other times...I don't know if I *want* to be paired with him..."

"I know sweetheart, I know." Mariam said, sitting down next to her daughter and holding her hands. "But no one is perfect. Seth will be a good partner who will protect you and your family. You will see. When you get down, think about your favorite things. Think about your family and friends. Try and get those bad thoughts out of your mind and try not to worry. Remember you're strong, and you can get through it. For the both of us."

With Adin's tears finally subsided, the mother and daughter sat together at the kitchen table, holding hands and staring out the window into the rain. They didn't say another word.

## ❦ 30 ❧

## SETTING A TRAP

**I**an and Belinda had finished their busy workdays and sat down to eat their dinner.

"Do you think we should visit Lorrick tonight?" Ian asked. "It's been nearly a week since we last saw him."

"We probably should, even though everyone is saying he's still very ill. I don't want him to feel obligated to stay up to visit with us."

"Let's go first thing after we're done eating. If he is resting, we will make it a quick visit. Mariam must be beside herself."

"I hate to think about what would happen if Lorrick doesn't make it. He's been Head Council for so long. His loss would be—" Belinda took in a deep breath and continued. "What do you think would happen?"

"I don't know. Seth is so vocal about being the leader of Caulfield. He'd probably petition the Council to take Lorrick's place before they even buried the body. The real question is whether the Council is as afraid of Seth as everyone else. And, if they are afraid, is it to such an extreme degree that they'd appoint him Head Council from the start."

Ian sat still for a moment and put his fork down before continuing.

"What are we talking about anyway? We're acting like Lorrick is already gone. We don't know what's going to happen to him. We need to stop."

"Remember what Lorrick looked like the last time we saw him?" Belinda asked. "Whatever he has is not going away. Don't get me wrong, Ian, he's been wonderful to us since Mom and Dad died. But there's no use in denying the truth. Unless he makes a miraculous comeback, he's going to die, and we both know that Seth is going to take his place as Head of the Council."

"I'm not delusional, Belinda. I just hate talking about everything like Lorrick is already gone. He's not gone. We don't know what the future holds."

"I understand, but we have to think about our options, given the circumstances. Ultimately, you are right, we don't know what is going to happen. I don't see any harm in discussing what we need to do to prepare for whatever future awaits us."

"Belinda—"

Ian was interrupted by a loud bang at the door. The twins looked at each other with concern, knowing who it was without having to say a word. Ian, begrudgingly, opened the door to find Seth, Darin, Keegan, and Cade. Seth merely gave a look to Ian, and obeying the unspoken command, Ian stepped aside and gestured for Seth to come in.

Before entering, Seth turned to his three comrades. "Darin, come with me. Keegan, Cade, wait here." Seth and Darin walked into the house and Ian closed the door behind them. Belinda walked into the room where the three men were standing.

"Belinda, I'm glad you're joining us, as what I have to discuss concerns you," Seth said as he eyed Belinda from head to toe. "We're all aware of what kind of condition Lorrick is in. For all we know, he could be dead at this very moment. While I cannot mention names, I have been assured that once he dies, I will be appointed as Head of the Council. I know how close you both are to the Wilton family, especially Samuel. That's why I am here. When I am ruler of Caulfield, I will expect everyone to obey my orders. There can be no leniency. You know as well as I that Samuel maintains a secret crop and refuses to acknowledge its existence or disclose its location. This infuriates me to my very core. All of the food that is grown in Caulfield belongs to our *citizens*, not him. Samuel's deception to the very people he's sworn to serve will no longer be tolerated."

"I understand your concern, Seth," Ian said, "but neither Belinda nor I know where Samuel keeps his secret garden."

"I know, Ian. Unlike Samuel, you and Belinda are honest people. Besides, the two of you would have no way of knowing. But you can help me. The only thing I want more than a rule abiding Caulfield, with me as Head Council, is to know the location of Samuel's secret garden, so our people can see Samuel for who he really is. If this occurs when I am Head Council, I will have no choice but to use Samuel as a harsh example of what happens if you put your own needs before the needs of our people. On the other hand, if I'm provided with the location of the secret garden before I'm Head Council, Samuel's punishment would be much less severe, I'm sure."

Seth looked at Ian and then Belinda, expecting one of them to say something.

"Ian already told you, and he meant it," Belinda pleaded, "we are not aware of the location of Samuel's secret garden. If either of us knew, we would tell you."

"I know you don't know where it is, Belinda, but I'm sure you can find out. With Joshua now in the picture, we have a unique opportunity. Everyone knows how close Samuel and Joshua have become. They spend their days working together and their nights under the same roof. Samuel will soon reveal the secret garden's location to Joshua, if he hasn't done so already. Samuel will never tell me the location...but Joshua will."

Seth broke out into a mischievous smile. Ian and Belinda looked at each other in worry and confusion.

"What does this have to do with either of us?" Ian asked.

"I've already tried on several occasions to get Joshua to fess up, but his loyalty to Samuel is too strong. And there's only one thing that's more obvious than Joshua's loyalty to Samuel." Seth turned to Belinda and slowly looked her up and down, once again. "He is so completely awed by your beauty that I'm willing to bet he would do anything to have it all to himself."

"What? You think if I give myself to Joshua, he'll tell me the location of this place? A place we're not even sure exists?" Belinda shook, distraught at Seth's suggestion.

"No, my dear. I think that if Joshua *believes* he has a chance to be with you, just a chance, he will do whatever he needs to do to make it happen." Seth walked around the room, addressing the twins simultaneously.

"If Belinda convinces Joshua that she wants a secret place to go where no one will discover the two of them together, he will take her to this secret location. He will not be able to resist the temptation. He will lead us directly to Samuel's secret garden, willingly." Seth turned back and made eye contact with Belinda. "You won't need to have sex with Joshua. Not even close. I would never allow that to happen. You just need to make him *believe* that you want to be alone with him, somewhere private, where no one can find you."

Then Seth turned to Ian. "In the meantime, you'll be in

Joshua's ear, convincing him that Belinda is desperately in love with him and that her advances are true."

The twins looked at each other and then back at Seth. Ian sat down and rubbed the stubble above his upper lip in thought. Belinda remained standing, still upset, but outwardly relieved at hearing the totality of Seth's plan.

"So, let's say Belinda does this and your plan works, and Joshua leads you to Samuel's secret Garden, what happens then?" Ian asked.

"I'm sure the Council would have no choice but to remove Samuel from his position, if he didn't resign first. Maybe he'd get another slap on the wrist of some kind. Whatever his punishment, it would be minuscule compared to what I would do to him if this discovery were made while I was Head Council. I know Samuel means a great deal to both of you and you'd rather see his punishment handed down from Lorrick. Aside from that fact, once I'm Head of the Council, I will not have forgotten what you did for me and will appoint one of you to be on the Council, accordingly."

"What happens if we do this and there is no secret garden?" Belinda asked

"Belinda, I wouldn't ask you to do this if I wasn't sure there was a secret garden. Alas, hypothetically, if there were no secret garden, I would deliver the same guarantees: Samuel would avoid any merciless treatment at my direction, and one of you would be appointed to the Council."

Ian stood and approached his guest. "May I speak to Belinda alone for a moment, please?"

"Of course. Darin and I will wait outside. I'll give you a few minutes to decide, although you would be idiots to refuse my request." Seth and Darin walked themselves out. Once the door was closed, Belinda spoke first.

"I don't know, Ian. How long has Joshua been here? One year? In that time, I have not made a single advance toward him. I've been friendly, but if I had any interest, I would have given him a sign by now. He's going to know something is up."

"I don't think he will. Seth is right. He loses all his composure when you enter the room. He'll be too excited at the idea of you wanting him to stop and wonder why it took so long for it to happen. Besides, even if he does question why you're suddenly interested, he's not going to care enough to hesitate. He's certainly not going to think that you're trying to find the location of a secret garden. Seth very well may be chasing a ghost."

"You see some of the unique stuff that shows up now and again. I think he might have a secret garden somewhere. I just don't know why Seth cares so much about it."

"Seth wants to be in control of everything and everyone. It's not about the food or the resources. It's about the fact that Samuel is doing something behind Seth's back, outside of his control, which is driving him crazy."

"What's the downside if we do this, besides me having to pretend to be attracted to Joshua? We give Seth the location of the garden, which is really nothing, and in return, we save Samuel from any trouble, and one of us gets appointed to the Council. We give up nothing, and, in return, we assure both of our needs being met for the rest of our lives. Seth is right. We can't turn this deal down." Belinda looked intently at her brother.

After a long pause, he spoke up. "Tell him we'll do it."

## ❧ 31 ❧

## AN EXTRA HAND

Maybe Joshua was losing his mind, but he swore he kept catching Belinda staring and smiling at him. When it happened, he'd convince himself that it surely must be in his head, nothing more than wishful thinking. Still, just the mere possibility of Belinda having any interest in him made Joshua's heart burst. It also gave him confidence. For the first time since arriving at Caulfield, Joshua was able to form whole sentences when speaking to her. Whenever they spoke, Joshua would inwardly beam with pride at not being a bumbling idiot in her presence.

One night at dinner, as the family discussed the events of the day, Lorrick surprised everyone with an unexpected announcement. "Belinda stopped by the Hyde Center today and asked if she could lend an extra hand with the crops. Apparently, work is thin at the Warner Hall, and she knows Samuel and Joshua are up to their ears at the farm. She thought maybe she could help by delivering food, allowing for Joshua and Samuel to concentrate on other matters." Lorrick smirked at Joshua. "What do you think? Would you like Belinda to help you with distributing food?"

Joshua tried to play it off like he was indifferent to the possibility of working with Belinda, but his reaction was a dead giveaway. "Belinda? Help? Distribute Food? Good. Sure. Yeah. I mean, I could use a hand...with stuff, you know, around...the place."

"What a surprise," Gabe said, "Joshua doesn't mind Belinda giving him a hand at work. I can't believe it." Everyone at the table busted out laughing; everyone except Samuel.

Lorrick turned towards the other side of the table. "Samuel, what do you think? Would you be all right with this arrangement?"

Samuel glanced at Joshua, "Ahh...I don't know...I think she's best off staying at Warner Hall, helping out with clothing and stuff."

"What?" Joshua exclaimed; his expression filled with disbelief. Everyone else laughed.

"I'm just messing with you, Joshua," Samuel said, giggling. "You know I have no problem with Belinda helping at the farm. I really like the idea of someone else taking care of delivering food so Joshua and I could concentrate on other matters. I just have one question."

"What's that?" Mariam asked.

"Why, all of a sudden, does Belinda want to help with the crops? Seems a bit peculiar to me. We all know she's had it easy at Warner Hall for years and that she could take on additional responsibilities. I thought she liked having little to do. Why, suddenly, does she feel like she needs more work?"

Joshua immediately sat up straight in his seat and got defensive. "Are you serious? Is that really so peculiar that someone in Caulfield wants to try something new? Maybe she's bored and just wants to find something to help pass the time. Maybe she realizes how important the crops are and she wants to learn about them. Did you ever think of that?"

The mood at the table had shifted from lighthearted teasing into tense confrontation. Samuel intended to calm the situation. "Please don't get upset, Joshua. I was just thinking out loud, that's all. If she wants to help, and Lorrick is fine with the arrangement, I'm not going to turn her away."

Joshua looked at the faces around the table and slowly slouched back down into a regular sitting position.

"Sorry, Samuel." Joshua said softly. "I didn't mean to get all crazy."

"I know, Joshua. It's ok. Belinda can give us a hand, no problem."

"Very well," Lorrick said, "we'll have Belinda assist you in deliveries on a part-time basis, effective immediately."

Joshua pulled his head up and couldn't help it. His smile was, without question, the biggest smile anyone had seen on his face since he joined the Commune. His cheeks burned bright red, and his eyes lit up. Lorrick, on the other hand, gave a few hard coughs and didn't look so good.

"I'll let Belinda know first thing in the morning," Lorrick said, getting up as if it hurt him to talk. "She can report to you, Samuel, on delivery mornings. I believe the day after tomorrow is a delivery day, so expect her then. Now, if you'll excuse me, I'm going to get some rest."

## ❧ 32 ❧

# EUPATORIUM PERFOLIATUM

As far as Joshua was concerned, Belinda's first day couldn't arrive soon enough. He couldn't get over how lucky he was that they were going to work together. On the morning of Belinda's first day, Joshua had a bounce to his step on the walk to work.

"I'm so excited, Samuel! Today's going to be an amazing day."

"Wow, you can't even hide it. You might as well stick a sign on the front of your shirt that reads, 'sucker in love.' Actually, that would be a severe understatement. It should read something more like, 'Belinda's love slave.' You think she'd like you wearing a shirt like that?"

"Come on, man. Don't pretend like she's not the most gorgeous person you have ever seen. You know this is true."

"Okay, she's pretty. Some even say she's the most attractive woman in Caulfield. I just get the feeling from the way she acts, and the things she says, that she's all about Belinda. When she engages in a conversation, the topic usually is about her or comes back around to her. I understand that nobody is perfect, and she's been through a lot like everyone else. I just hope she'll start looking outward, thinking about others, versus inward, thinking about only herself."

"Maybe you're right, and one day she'll become a little more selfless. But on this day, I'm not worried about it. On this day, the most beautiful woman in Caulfield will be making deliveries with *me,* and I'm going to love every second of it."

"All right, lover boy," Samuel said with a laugh. "Just don't forget that she has to do more than just look good. She's helping with deliveries, and, once she's up to speed, she's going to be making them herself so you and I can concentrate on other pressing matters."

"Yeah, of course. Just let me enjoy the little bit of time I'm going to have training her before we get to that point."

Joshua and Samuel made their way into the garage and began the morning like any other workday. The work was physically and mentally challenging, as always, making the time go by quickly. Before he knew it, Belinda stood in the doorway of the garage, wearing skintight clothing that accentuated her curves. It took all of Joshua's willpower to keep his eyes above her neck. She had a yellow carnation pinned in her hair, and while the color was different, this was the same flower Joshua dreamt of when he was on the road. He took it as a good sign.

"Hi, guys. I'm here. Reporting for duty!" She looked directly at Joshua, who tried to keep it cool but was obviously on the verge of turning into a blubbering mess.

"Hey!" Joshua said as he took an excited step toward Belinda, not realizing that a rake lay in his path. Joshua's foot found the handle and caused him to trip. Somehow, he didn't fall over, but the commotion caused both Belinda and Samuel to laugh out loud. He didn't want Belinda to think he was a fool, but he considered her laughter a success. He didn't care what caused her to laugh; as long as she was laughing, Joshua was good with it.

"Come on in," Joshua said, waving her into the garage. "I have everything ready to go for our deliveries this morning. I figure we'll make an easy run today, get you used to the route. Then, once you get familiar with the actual deliveries, I can show you the prep work. That's the most boring part, but it's easy. I think you'll like the work, and I know our residents will enjoy you bringing their rations."

"Thanks, Joshua," Belinda said with a flirtatious smile. "That's very sweet of you." She walked over to Joshua and put her hand on his arm.

Joshua was so nervous he could barely breathe. "Yeah, sure. Great. Right this way. I'll ... show you the cart and my delivery chart." Joshua led her to the little enclosure at the back of the garage.

Music was playing as usual, and as the two made their way past Samuel, the song 'Silhouette' By Thrice rang out.

The look on Belinda's face went from flirtatious to straight disgust. "Oh my God, what is this music? It's so... aggressive and...terrible."

"Oh, don't worry about that. We have the iPod on shuffle and there's plenty of other music that's not nearly as heavy. This is Samuel's favorite band, Thrice. You get used to it. When I first heard it, I questioned it too, but it's grown on me. Now, I dig it."

"There is no way I will ever like that music," Belinda said.

Samuel rolled his eyes and said, under his breath, "I'm sure the guys in Thrice are all broke up about it."

"What was that?" Belinda asked.

Joshua interrupted. "Oh, Samuel's always saying wise-cracks. He's only playing."

Belinda gave Samuel a dirty look, then turned back to

Joshua, where the dirty look transformed back into the flirtatious smile from when she first arrived.

Joshua and Belinda grabbed the cart and were on their way. At each stop, Joshua showed Belinda the clipboard and matched that delivery to the goods being dropped off. Belinda needed to understand that they weren't just bringing food. They were also delivering specific herbs and other natural elixirs that Samuel had developed over the years. These natural medicines helped citizens with any ailment, from upset stomachs to fevers.

As they made their way along the route, Belinda laughed at all of Joshua's jokes, no matter how corny or stupid they were. She also accompanied him to the door of each delivery. Many of the individuals invited them inside for a couple minutes of small talk. Everything was going wonderfully, better than Joshua could have imagined, until they arrived at Andrew's door.

Belinda became cold and rigid. "I didn't know Andrew was on the delivery route. I'm not going up to his door. No way."

"Normally, he isn't, but he's been sick, so we're dropping off some things for him. Why? What's the problem?"

"Don't you know about Andrew?"

"Know what about Andrew?"

"That he's...not right."

"What are you talking about? Is this about him being a follower of the Hindu religion?"

"No, that's not what I'm referring to, although that is another problem with the man. No, what I'm referring to is much worse."

"Belinda, I'm sorry, I have no idea what you're talking about."

"I'm sure you know that in the Bible it says that it's a sin for a man to lay with another man, and Andrew is...one of those..."

"Andrew is gay?"

"Yes, and you look at any passage in the Bible dealing with the subject and you'll see that being a gay person is a sin against God. Andrew is a sinner, and I refuse to associate with someone like him. He should thank his lucky stars that he's a resident of Caulfield. If it wasn't for Samuel, Andrew wouldn't even be here."

"I'm sorry, but once again, I don't follow you."

"When the Council first established the rules of Caulfield, they realized that humankind had come into this predicament because man had turned his back on God. The Sickness was a result of God's wrath for failing to live by his rules. If we were going to survive the Sickness, our Chosen were going to have to procreate. This meant men lying *only* with women, the way it should be. Therefore, the Elders decided in their wisdom to forbid gay persons within the walls of Caulfield. If you were discovered to be gay, you were expelled from the Commune."

"Caulfield has laws against being gay? That can't be true."

"It's true. And Andrew admitted freely, to anyone and everyone, that he was gay. Naturally, the Elders were alerted, and they were about to throw Andrew out until Samuel stopped them."

"Samuel stopped them? How?"

"Samuel had become such good friends with Andrew that he threatened to join Andrew and leave Caulfield, and if they forced him to stay, he vowed he would never again tend to the crops. The Elders knew he wasn't bluffing. If Andrew went, Samuel would refuse to maintain the farm. The Elders couldn't afford to let such a thing happen, so they made an exception with Andrew and he was allowed to stay."

"I can't believe neither of them ever told me about any of this."

"Well, it's true." Belinda stuck her nose in the air. "So, you can do whatever you need to do, drop off whatever you need to drop off, but there's no way I'm going up to that man's door." Belinda crossed her arms, her feet set in the ground like they were encased in concrete.

Joshua couldn't care less that Andrew was gay but wondered why he and Samuel had never said anything about it. That issue would have to wait, as Joshua's immediate priority was getting things back on track with Belinda. They were having such a good day, until this happened.

"It's okay," Joshua said. "I'll drop off Andrew's rations. You can stay here. No problem."

Joshua grabbed a small bag filled with various items and headed towards Andrew's residence. Belinda didn't move a muscle. Joshua knocked on Andrew's door, but after several minutes, there was no response. He pressed his ear against the door and listened for any kind of sound but heard nothing. He knocked again, this time harder, and said with a loud voice, "Andrew, you in there? Everything okay?"

There was still no answer. Joshua knocked again, even harder, "ANDREW?"

The door opened slowly, revealing a very sick and emaciated Andrew. His face, normally full of color, was pale, his hair slick with sweat and matted to his head. He had a blanket wrapped around his body. Joshua, at a loss for words, just stood there.

Finally, with a weak voice, Andrew said, "Joshua. Thanks for the rations. I'd invite you in, but as you can see, I've caught a nasty cold and I don't want to get you sick. Why don't you put that stuff down by your feet, in between us, and I'll get it."

"No problem," Joshua said as he lowered the bag down. "What happened? How long have you been ill?"

"Four or five days now. Been brutal. Hard to get out of bed. Samuel stopped by yesterday, told me he'd include some Eupatorium Perfoliatum with this delivery." Andrew knelt down, picked up the bag, and began rummaging through it.

"Eupa...what?" Joshua asked.

"Eupatorium Perfoliatum. We call it 'Eupa,' so you already got it. It's a special flower used to create a tonic that helps the body fight off colds and flus, that sort of thing. Samuel began making it years ago, from one of Burbank's books."

Andrew found what he was looking for and pulled it up, showing the small brown vial to Joshua.

"Here it is. Eupa. A miraculous antidote for fever, chills, aches, and pains. Horrible after taste but you feel so much better after taking it that you don't care. Please remind Samuel that this flu is going around and he needs to make as much as possible. We're going to need more."

"No problem," Andrew said. "I'll remind him."

Andrew looked over Joshua's shoulder and saw Belinda standing in her incensed, arms crossed pose. "What's Belinda doing?"

"Oh, yeah...she's working with me now," Joshua said, looking back at Belinda. "Today's her first day. She's going to help with deliveries so I can concentrate on other duties." Joshua turned back to Andrew, "Our whole Commune leans so heavily on Samuel, this should help take some of the pressure off."

"It's going to be difficult for Belinda to deliver my rations if she refuses to come to my door, don't you think?" Andrew asked sarcastically.

Joshua didn't know how to react. "Uh, yeah, she's...I don't know. We'll figure something out."

"Let me guess. She doesn't want to come up here because

I'm gay." Andrew looked away for a second before continuing with his thought. "Some things never change."

Joshua, once again, was at a loss for words. "Uh, I don't know. I guess she's...I don't know."

"It's okay. You don't have to explain yourself or defend Belinda. I've dealt with this behavior ever since I decided to stop living a lie." Andrew's tone was reassuring, despite his flu.

"Thanks, Andrew. I...I didn't know. How come you never told me?"

Andrew looked surprised. "Would it have made any difference to you had you known I was gay? Would you have treated me differently?"

"No," Joshua said without thinking. "Not at all. It's just... why wouldn't you just tell me?"

"It's not that I was hiding the fact from you. It just never came up. The truth is, it came as quite a shock to many of the residents here when I came out. People demanded I be exiled. Samuel stood up for me, and it only added to the turmoil. They began demanding that *both* of us be banished. Without Samuel, the radical residents of Caulfield knew they were doomed, but they wanted us out anyway. You see the irony there?"

"Absolutely. If Samuel had been banished, they would have ended their own lives by following their own, man-enacted law."

"Precisely," Andrew said, pointing his finger at his friend. "They wanted to kick me out, but they knew they couldn't, so they made me the one gay exception. Still, it caused many hard feelings internally. Lorrick advised us to let the dust settle. Samuel and I followed Lorrick's advice. Soon enough, most saw me for the kind-hearted, hard-working contributor to our Commune that I am and realized my sexuality had nothing to do with it. Then, there's folks like Belinda."

"I get it. I'm glad you are here. Caulfield wouldn't be the same without you. Now, get back to resting and nursing that nasty cold, and I'll finish up my run."

"Thanks. And, again, please don't forget to tell Samuel about the extra Eupa."

Joshua promised he wouldn't forget and headed back to Belinda, who was still standing with her arms crossed. As he got closer, Belinda tapped her right foot out, like she was in a hurry and upset that he'd taken so long. Joshua smiled nervously at Belinda.

"Sorry that took so long. Andrew is really sick, along with a bunch of other people, and he wanted to make sure I delivered an important message to Samuel."

"Whatever," Belinda said with a huff. "I saw that sinner looking at me and motioning towards me. I know you two were talking about me. I couldn't care less. I'd just expect more from you, Joshua. You really need to reexamine the people you associate with. You want to make sure you're on the right side."

Joshua had no desire to discuss the issue any further. He couldn't believe she was taking such a hard stance on such a trivial matter. If it were anyone else besides Belinda, Joshua probably would have turned this opportunity into a debate. Instead, he wanted to get past it as quickly as possible.

"Let's get this route done and we can get on with our respective days." He said.

Belinda and Joshua completed their final deliveries and were soon back at the garage. Joshua wanted to confirm with Samuel that he'd risked his life to keep Andrew in Caulfield, but he didn't want to bring up Andrew in front of Belinda. He would have to wait until he was alone with his brother to discuss Andrew's story.

Joshua and Belinda searched the crops and the garage, but Samuel couldn't be found anywhere. That wasn't unusual, as

Samuel sometimes disappeared. But still, Samuel knew that Joshua and Belinda would be back from their route, so where had he wandered off to?

"Well, I think that's it for today. I'm not sure what else Samuel would want to cover this morning, so I'll relieve you of duties," Joshua said. "You did really well! Thanks for your help! Will I see you in three days for another round of deliveries?"

Belinda held Joshua's gaze. "Thank you. I really enjoyed spending time with you. You will definitely see me in three days, if not sooner."

She wrapped her arms around Joshua and gave him a long, strong, steady hug. Her touch and smell enveloped him, making him lose himself. He was mesmerized.

Somehow, even though Belinda's aura had ripped away his ability to make sense of what was happening, Joshua raised his arms and wrapped them around Belinda, like they had a mind of their own. He could feel her ribs expanding with each breath. Joshua's knees must have locked in place, otherwise, he would have collapsed straight to the ground.

Belinda pulled away and gave Joshua a kiss on his cheek. Belinda saw the state she had put him in and gave a small laugh. She put her right hand on his cheek and rubbed her thumb against his cheekbone.

"I hope you don't mind that I gave you that kiss. Was that okay?"

It took Joshua a couple of seconds to snap out of his trance. "Huh? Oh, yeah. Of course."

"So, you're not mad?"

"Mad? Mad? I'm the exact opposite of mad! I'm ecstatic! I think you are amazing. I think you are...the most beautiful woman I've ever seen."

Belinda smiled. "We have to be careful, Joshua. I really like you too, but you know how things are around here. In my mind, it's a foregone conclusion that the Council is going to pair me with Seth; it is just a matter of time and everyone knows it. We could get in a lot of trouble if anyone were ever to find out about our feelings for each other. Do you understand what I'm telling you?"

"Yeah, I understand."

"Good. Then we can continue to see each other and allow our relationship to...evolve. We just have to keep this as our little secret." Belinda took the yellow carnation out of her hair and handed it to him. Then, she took his right hand and walked backward, away from Joshua, causing their arms to slowly extend upward.

"I'll see you soon, Joshua," Belinda said as she let his hand go and turned to exit the garage. Joshua stood there in shock, holding the carnation. As she made it past the crops and began to turn right on Clark Street, she looked back and waved one last time, with a smile. As she rounded the corner, Joshua waved back and smiled too, but Belinda was already out of sight.

Joshua stood there, wondering if what had just happened was a dream. *Belinda kissed me*, Josh kept repeating in his head. *Belinda kissed me*! Joshua jumped up and down with uncontrollable joy. He laughed and shouted, "Yes! Yes!" over and over in a state of complete euphoria.

Joshua made his way out of the garage and towards the crops, not knowing what to do with himself, when he finally saw Samuel coming from the far end of the back of the building. The space containing the apiary was nothing more than five or six feet of gravel between the back wall of the Armory and the east wall surrounding the Commune. It made sense to keep the apiary at that location because it was isolated, and they didn't need anyone getting stung. Samuel didn't spend a ton of time back there, but it was enough that it didn't seem strange to see him coming from that direction.

"Hey, Samuel!" Joshua said, all giddy. "What's going on?"

"You're in a tremendous mood," Samuel said, one eyebrow raised. "I take it your deliveries with Belinda went well?"

"They sure did. She's going to be great. We only have one small, tiny problem." Joshua adjusted is shirt collar. "We're going to have to figure out a way for her to deliver Andrew's rations without any interaction between the two of them while he's ill."

"Why is that?"

Joshua didn't want to ruin the moment by getting into an ethical discussion about Belinda's opinion. Joshua decided he would put everything as delicately as possible, even if it meant avoiding the issue. "Oh, well, you know...people can sometimes be kind of strict about things. Belinda takes every word of the Bible quite literally, and since the Bible says specific things about...you know...men not...laying...with other men...and that sort of thing."

"I see. Yeah, that Belinda is something else. She's a real rule follower, that one."

Joshua couldn't tell if Samuel was being sarcastic or making a serious statement.

Samuel knew his apprentice didn't want to talk about it. "It shouldn't be an issue," Samuel continued. "We'll have Andrew back to health in a couple of days. By the time Belinda is making deliveries on her own, Andrew won't be on the delivery route. What's that you have in your hand? Is that the carnation Belinda had in her hair earlier?"

"It is. Crazy right?" Joshua looked down at the flower, relieved they were moving onto the next subject. "I can't believe she gave it to me. You remember that dream I told you about when I was on Route 23, the one with my mom? Well, this is the same type of flower that was in the dream. That's got to be a good sign, right? Maybe I should give her a flower in return?"

"You better be careful. Remember, the Council pairs all Chosen, so it's not up to you. Plus, I hate to be the bearer of bad news, but the color of a carnation changes its meaning dramatically. I remember you said the color of the carnation in the dream you had of your mom was pink. I also remember telling you that it's no coincidence, as a pink carnation symbolizes a mother's love. On the other hand, a yellow carnation symbolizes rejection, or that you cannot be with someone. You better do your homework first, if you plan on giving her a flower in return. You don't want to send the wrong message."

Joshua looked down at the carnation, disappointed. "I wonder if she knew the yellow color meant rejection. Damn. Well, what's the coolest, most exotic flower that you know? I want to give her something special, something unique."

"The most exotic flower that I know is a blue water lily. It's the only flower that rises up from under water and blooms on the water's surface. At night, it closes, only to reopen again the next morning. However, you wouldn't want to give one to Belinda. Besides the fact that there are none around here, they symbolize reincarnation and the eternal cycle of life and death that the soul experiences. A red rose would be more appropriate for the message you're trying to get across, as it symbolizes a deep emotion of love, longing, and desire. But I don't like it, Joshua; I think it's really a bad idea, given the circumstances."

"You're right. I probably shouldn't give her any flowers. But it is tempting," Joshua said as he whistled his way back into the garage to finish the day. Samuel was clearly worried, but Joshua was too love blind to see it, his thoughts fixed on Belinda and their next encounter.

## ❧ 33 ❧

## FULL DISCLOSURE

That evening, Joshua's good mood continued. Everyone knew it was because of his time with Belinda, but nobody asked. Joshua also kept from sharing the day's events with everyone, even Samuel, despite how badly he wanted to tell his best friend that Belinda had kissed him. Joshua still couldn't believe it. She kissed him. Just the thought of it sent Joshua into a smiling frenzy.

His elation continued through the night, making it hard for him to get any rest. He kept thinking about Belinda. He couldn't wait to see her again. He pictured their next time working together and was absolutely determined to kiss her, if the opportunity presented itself.

There was not a shred of doubt in his mind. He was going to kiss her. If he could be alone with her.

Joshua knew that finding some privacy was going to present a problem. Whatever he did, he couldn't get caught. The idea of Seth finding out what's going on with Belinda sent a chill of raw fear down Joshua's spine. He couldn't care less about the Council; it was Seth that scared Joshua to his core. He was going to have to be extra careful. Take every precaution. If they were both careful, they were going to be fine.

Finally, a restless night of tossing and turning came to an end when Samuel shook Joshua awake.

"Hey, let's get moving a little earlier than usual today. I have a few things that need to be addressed that will take us out of our usual routine."

"Okay," Joshua said with a yawn. Despite the lack of sleep, he was still ready to face the day, especially knowing that he'd see Belinda again soon.

As they approached the garage, Samuel altered his course, walking south of the garage, towards the back of the Armory and Samuel's apiary. It was the same place Samuel came from yesterday. Joshua stopped at the garage door, confused, and pointed in the direction of their usual route. "Aren't we going..."

Samuel shook his head no. "Follow me. You'll see why in a minute."

Joshua picked up his pace until he was directly behind Samuel, who now led Joshua to the rear of the Armory, toward the graveled pathway between the Armory and the east wall. As they turned left around the corner, Joshua realized how seldom anyone else was ever back there, with the exception of Samuel.

The sound of the stones crunching under their feet seemed loud and abrasive. The Wheaton Armory's four stories stood tall to their left, with the east wall of the Commune towering on the right, running the length of the building. At the midway point stood Samuel's apiary. It was large, at least six feet in height, with its two ends touching the armory wall and the east wall, respectively. There was no way around it if one approached from the other side. The bees were quiet, as expected for that time of morning, but a few whizzed Samuel and Joshua.

Along the outside of the building were four large venting fans, five to six feet in diameter, with two at the ground level and the others three stories up. Large grills protected the rusted fan blades. Joshua figured they must have been for ventilation of the Wheaton Armory back when it was in use. Samuel walked right past the first fan and approached the second, reaching around to the right side of the fan's grill. Joshua couldn't see what Samuel was handling or doing, but there must have been some sort of fastener or clasp, because Joshua heard a clank of metal on metal, like Samuel had released a latch. Samuel pulled on the right side of the grill, and the whole face of the fan, including the grill and the fan blades, opened. Joshua stood awestruck, confused, not ready for this.

When the fan's face opened approximately a foot, Samuel stopped and whispered, "Why don't you get on my right side before I open this hatch any further." Without a word, Joshua scurried around to Samuel's right as he continued opening the hatch. A small light flickered on inside the awaiting tunnel. Joshua was sure there was no light a moment ago. There must be some type of mechanism that turns the light on once the fan's face opened to a certain degree.

Given how old and rusted the fan blades and grill were, Joshua figured the hinge would wail and moan when being opened, like an old, heavy, creaky door. But it was dead silent. If Joshua's eyes were closed, he would have no idea what was happening.

Finally, with the fan's face opened wide enough for the two of them, they entered the dimly lit tunnel. Samuel went in first and Joshua followed. Once inside, the light showed how the face of the fan was on a large hinge and bolted to the inside of the tunnel.

Again, speaking in a quiet tone, Samuel asked Joshua to close the opening. The inside of the door had a small handle, which allowed Joshua to close the fan's face completely. The hinge must be heavily lubricated because the fan blade and grill were heavy and difficult to pull shut, but, again, didn't make a sound as Joshua closed it.

Joshua turned back around to see that the tunnel narrowed down towards the ground. If they were going to proceed any further, they were going to have to crawl through the air vent. As if reading Joshua's mind, Samuel said, "We're going to have to get on our hands and knees to crawl through the vent from here."

Joshua dropped to his hands and knees and followed Samuel through the tunnel just a few feet forward before it made a sharp, ninety degree turn to the right. Once around the corner, the tunnel stretched the length of the building, with intervals of light shining through slits in the metal. Samuel crawled to the first recess of light. Through one of the slits, his face reflected strips of light. He pushed on the vent, which opened yet another hatch on a hinge. Samuel crawled through that vent and Joshua followed.

Getting to his feet, Joshua looked around. To his right was a long hallway with an endless wall to the right and a row of jail bars, separated by walls approximately every thirty feet, to the left.

"Come on. This way." Samuel headed the other way, to their left, where, after five feet or so, the hallway made a ninety-degree right turn. Around the bend were offices, about the same size of the cells they had just seen. Samuel made his way down the hall and finally started sharing where they were.

"I believe I've told you that the Armory was used for housing weapons and other equipment, while also serving as an administration building, when the prison was in operation during the Paper Era. Then, when Caulfield was transformed from a prison into our Commune, there were suddenly over six thousand residents, which was more than they had rooms to accommodate. So, they converted many of the offices upstairs into sleeping quarters. Desks were moved or pushed into a corner, and mattresses were brought in, so everyone had a place to sleep."

Samuel came to a door to his right, and opened it, revealing another hallway. This time, the hallway was nothing more than a thirty-foot long passageway that led to another door at the end. There were no rooms or windows on either side. Samuel made his way through the new hallway, towards the opposite door. Joshua remained right behind Samuel as he continued with his explanation.

"However, when I got here, there were just over two thousand people remaining in Caulfield. Hard to believe, but our population had shrunk to a third of its original size due to the Sickness and starvation. At that point, this building had been closed for years. The only thing still in use was our main garage. That's how it was until Lorrick and I made what I'm about to show you, which no one else is aware of."

Samuel had reached the door at the end of the hallway and opened it, revealing a courtyard filled with an abundance of life. There were plants, flowers, fruits, leaves, and vines, in every direction. Colors of every variety, with hues that Joshua had only imagined, filled his vision. At the heart of the courtyard stood an apple tree, complete with bright, full, and ripe red apples hanging from the branches of the tree, in bunches. On the ground, there were concrete pavers, creating pathways that snaked through the garden, all converging to a circle that encompassed the very outskirts of the apple tree.

Samuel's secret garden. Seth wasn't crazy after all.

Joshua stared at the plush foliage while Samuel made his way along one of the paths. The beauty of the garden captured Joshua. It was such a stark contrast to the greyness around him. The garden's colors and shapes filled Joshua with reverence beyond comparison, the life emanating from the garden enveloping his heart with peace and comfort.

For the first time in his life, Joshua could feel the grace of God and God's connection with all creation.

"I know you're in shock," Samuel said, twisting through the path without looking back, "and you may even be angry, but I need you to listen to me for a minute, without any prejudice."

Joshua didn't answer. He just stood there and basked in the garden's beauty.

"You've already heard what Caulfield was like when I arrived. I know it's hard to comprehend, today, because our bellies are full, and we've grown content in our comforts. But you have to trust me when I tell you that starvation leads to madness. Our citizens were so desperate that most were ready to kill if it meant their survival. They would do whatever it took, if it meant their starving child's survival. Insanity loomed and anarchy was a breath away. A spark was all that was needed for Caulfield to destroy itself."

Joshua nodded his head, but he wasn't listening; he was too mesmerized by the garden.

"Joshua, listen to me!"

Joshua jumped at Samuel's demand. "Sorry. I'm listening. Caulfield was on the verge of destruction..."

"That's right. But with my abilities, the farm made a quick, and, some might say, miraculous recovery. The wickedness on the threshold of erupting was held at bay. Sanity and reason prevailed. Still, the lesson was not lost on Lorrick and two other members on the Council at the time. Together, they decided there needed to be a backup plan should Caulfield ever find itself in that place again.

"The Armory had been closed for some time, but this select group knew about this courtyard. They realized they could grow a second, secret crop, not in the public's eye, so that people could survive if a ravenous mob ever pillaged our main crops. So, guided by Lorrick, they made the secret entrance into the ventilation system, and I began creating this place. We swore each other to secrecy, knowing that the sustained existence of this secret garden depended on its autonomy."

Samuel reached the center of the garden and began inspecting and picking apples off the tree.

Joshua's head slowly bowed toward the ground. His mouth hung partially open as he realized the burden that was now on him. "You mean I'm the fifth person, in all of Caulfield, that knows about this place?" He asked.

"That's correct. However, the other two Council members that helped establish this place with Lorrick have since passed away. You, Lorrick, and I are the only living residents of Caulfield that know about this garden."

"That can't be," Joshua said. "Seth knows about this place. He must know. He's obsessed with it. One of the others must have told him."

"While it's true that Seth has somehow been informed of this place, he doesn't know for sure that it exists. My guess is he either overheard others discussing it or was flat out told by one of the two now deceased. I know I never told him, and Lorrick would never have disclosed the secret. I didn't know the other two well, so it's possible one of them said something to Seth on their deathbed."

"This is crazy. Seth is not going to leave this alone. He's going to threaten me with my life if we don't tell him."

"Listen to me, Joshua. Seth doesn't actually know about this place and he certainly doesn't know its location. He doesn't even know that a courtyard exists within Wheaton Armory. What's more important, though, is that Seth never, ever, gets confirmation of this place. With Seth making his move to join and eventually control the Council, he would use it to guarantee his own survival. This garden was not built to assure one man survives, but as an insurance policy for all of Caulfield."

Joshua knew Samuel was right, so he pushed the fear of Seth aside for a moment to collect his thoughts as Samuel made his way back towards Joshua, a bundle of apples in hand.

"Why are you suddenly showing me this place?" Joshua said, still working the puzzle pieces. "Why, after a year, are you finally telling me?"

"I first thought about telling you when Lorrick's health began declining. Lorrick hasn't been to this garden in months. The reality is, he's going to die someday, just like all of us. But if Lorrick's health continues to decline at its current rate, his passing will come sooner rather than later. Upon his death, I would be the only living person in Caulfield that knew about this place. What if something were to happen to me? I can't be the only one with this knowledge; there must be at least one other person."

Again, Joshua knew Samuel was right. The two began placing the apples in a cloth bag as Samuel continued.

"And now we've had this influenza hit Caulfield. There are so many sick people, there's no way I could make enough Eupa for everyone without using some of the yield from this garden. Plus, Eupa, in and of itself, doesn't make the entire medicine. It's the main ingredient, but you have to extract certain things from the flower and then add in other ingredients, like apples, to help activate the serum. It also helps with the taste. A child would never take Eupa without the help of the apple to mask the bitter flavor.

"That's why I brought you here today. You need to know the full extent of the resources we have. You also need to learn how to make the Eupa medicine, as I need your help to make more. It all made sense."

Joshua couldn't help thinking of Seth again, and worry crept across his brow. "I know you said not to worry, but Seth keeps interrogating me about this place. Until now, it's been easy to say I didn't know about it because I honestly didn't know about it. Now what?"

"You just tell him you don't know. He's believed you thus far, he'll believe you moving forward. Joshua, I cannot stress this enough: this secret has to remain between you and me. I will eventually tell Lorrick that you know, but in the meantime, please keep this place, and this secret, between us. Of all the rules and regulations, of all the things that go on here in Caulfield, this request takes top priority. Do you understand? Seth cannot find out about this place, no matter what happens."

Joshua felt sick to his stomach. Somehow, he was going to have to keep his cool the next time Seth bullied him about the secret garden. Samuel asked him to keep a promise, though, and Joshua knew he had to keep that promise.

"Okay, I won't tell anyone about this place or its location. You can trust me. What about Lorrick? Can I tell Lorrick that you showed me this place?"

"No. Someone could overhear your conversation, and, at this point, it might not look good that Lorrick helped create this place. When we made this garden, it made sense. But now that Caulfield is properly nourished and the main crops are plentiful, others might misunderstand why this garden was created. Someone could twist the truth and accuse Lorrick of conspiring, behind the backs of the citizens of Caulfield, to create this place for his own resource. We know nothing could be further from the truth. But with Lorrick holding the highest office in Caulfield, he needs to be free of any ties to this place."

"I get it. Don't worry. I won't tell anyone. Our secret is safe."

## ❧ 34 ❧

### CONFIRMATION

S eth pounded on the door. It took longer than he liked for it to finally open.

"Oh, hi, Seth. I didn't know it was you," Ian said awkwardly.

"I won't hold it against you," Seth said as he pushed past Ian and into the residence. Ian closed the door behind him and yelled for his sister. The two men took a seat in the living room. The patter of shuffling feet from above was immediate. Within seconds, Belinda barreled into the living room. Seth looked her up and down with a slow eye, as usual.

"Belinda, you are simply gorgeous," Seth said, rising out of his chair to greet the new arrival. "You are going to make an amazing bride for me someday."

Belinda hugged him. "Oh, Seth, go on. I love it when you tell me how beautiful I am. But don't you dare forget to flatter me on my smarts as well. I'm more than just a pretty face, you know."

"Indeed. Adam and Eve have nothing on us. You and I, my dear, are going to singlehandedly save humanity. Just don't go taking an apple from a snake and try to feed it to me. I won't make the same mistake Adam made. And if you fall for the temptation, I won't go down with you."

"Don't be silly, Seth. I know to stay away from apples and snakes. I can resist temptation from anything or anyone, besides you, of course."

"That's my girl. Speaking of temptation, I trust things with Joshua are progressing nicely. I know you've been appointed to be an assistant with ration delivery. I'm sure the enticement of your beauty is working its magic as we anticipated?"

"Absolutely. He's believing everything exactly as you said he would. I had to hug him and kiss him on the cheek the other day. It was so gross. But he was putty in my hands. I promise you if there really is a secret garden, and Joshua knows its location, he'll be taking me there within a few days. I might have to do the unthinkable and actually kiss him on the lips, but once I do, it will be the nail in his coffin."

"I knew I could count on you. Obviously, do your best to get the location of the garden without having to kiss him. That said if you do have to kiss him, just close your eyes and pretend it's me."

"That's exactly what I plan on doing. In fact, when I hugged him and kissed him on his cheek, I pretended it was you. It was the only way I could get myself to do it. Joshua is the exact opposite of you. He's unattractive, in every possible way. I mean, look at him. He's got no real muscles, with his scraggly brown hair and that big space between his two front teeth."

Seth laughed. "I know, but he's going to be our Head Farmer once the location of the secret garden is revealed and Samuel is relieved of his duties. He might be unattractive, but once this is all over, he's going to be necessary for our survival. Plus, he is Chosen, after all. Don't worry. I will have him under my control, so do your job now and then pay no attention to him once it's done."

"Of course, Seth."

"Perfect, now if you'll excuse me, I have some other matters to attend to."

Once Seth was gone and the siblings were alone, Ian gave a concerned look to Belinda.

"What's your problem?" Belinda said with an annoyed tone.

"Nothing. It's just, we've gotten to know Joshua since he's been here, and he seems like a good kid. And Samuel is like a brother to us. What does Seth mean when he says that Samuel will be 'relieved of his duties?' This just doesn't feel right. I think we may have made a mistake."

"Ian, get a grip. It's not like Seth is going to kill Samuel or banish him. If Samuel is hiding something from us, then I don't blame Seth for being upset. Whatever minor punishment Samuel gets will be deserved, as far as I'm concerned. Plus, you heard Seth. His plans include Joshua, so it's not like he's really in any kind of danger either. Besides, you're not the one that's going to have to convince Joshua that you like him. If there's anyone that should be protesting this plan, it's me. But what are we supposed to do? Tell him no? Tell him we won't help him? Come on, Ian, you're smarter than that."

Ian firmed up and nodded his head to his sister. "You're right. This is what we must do, and it will be over soon enough. Thanks for setting me straight."

"You're welcome. I'll need some reciprocal support from you before I go to help Joshua with deliveries tomorrow. God, I hope I don't have to kiss him."

## ❧ 35 ❧

## KEEPING A SECRET

Joshua had the same extra bounce in his step on their way to the farm the next morning. His smile stretched ear to ear. Samuel pretended not to notice.

"Will Belinda be joining you again today for another ration delivery?" Samuel asked.

"That's the plan," Joshua said, glowing. "I need to make sure she knows exactly what she's doing before we send her off on her own. It might take another three or four weeks of shadowing me before she's familiar with what she's supposed to do."

Samuel rolled his eyes.

"What?" Joshua said with a chuckle. He continued, trying to be serious, but he couldn't hide his smile. "I'm serious. You don't want her screwing up rations. We have a very precise system to make sure people get exactly what they are supposed to get. You can't just expect her to know what's going on overnight. It's going to take some time."

"Whatever, Joshua. You can't even make that argument with a straight face. I'm not going to fight you. You want the time with Belinda, I'm not going to hold you back. Just remember that you still have to get your work done, which means working later than usual on days when you're training Belinda."

"I know. It's all good. I'll work late if I must. You know I will."

"And, the secret that I shared with you the other day, that stays between you and me, right? Nobody else can know."

Joshua couldn't believe Samuel thought he had to remind him of the importance of this secret. "Of course. That goes without saying. It stays between you and me."

A couple of hours later, Belinda reported for duty as scheduled. Samuel took one look at her and rolled his eyes for the second time that day. She wore skintight pants with a loose shirt that somehow exposed her stomach and cleavage all at the same time. Her wavy, thick hair fell past her shoulders, and you could tell she had spent a considerable amount of time preparing it. The icing on the cake was the lipstick she wore made from beeswax and crushed flowers. Her lips glistened in a way that screamed, "Kiss me." Joshua had never seen her in clothes like that before and had never seen her lips so accentuated.

"Reporting for duty!" she said while clasping her hands and pushing her arms together, causing her cleavage to announce itself even more.

It took every ounce of will power within Joshua to keep his eyes from drifting down. "Hey! All right. Let's get our stuff together and get our deliveries started."

As they prepared for their route, Joshua noticed Belinda's once casual and random looks and touches had turned into full-fledged, outright flirtation. Anytime and every time there was a chance for Belinda to put her hands on Joshua or be close to him, she did it. Instead of just passing him whatever he asked for, she'd push herself into him as she handed him the item. When speaking, she touched him on his chest, his arms, his shoulders, even when it wasn't necessary.

And it didn't matter what he said or how he said it, to Belinda, Joshua was the funniest and most interesting man in Caulfield. When the conversation turned serious, she rubbed his back and consoled him in the most nurturing way. No matter what it was that they were discussing, Belinda found a way to touch Joshua, and he ate up every ounce of it.

Despite all the flirting, the two did have a job to do. Joshua was in the middle of impressing Belinda with a seemingly hilarious story about Gabe when Samuel interrupted them.

"Hey guys, I know you're having fun and all, really enjoying each other's company, but there's a lot of work that needs to get done, so can we maybe speed up this process a bit?"

"Sorry, Samuel," Joshua said. "We're just getting the last bit of supplies. We'll be on our route momentarily."

Joshua turned his back on Samuel and made a funny face toward Belinda. She laughed, and dropped her head, covering her mouth with her hand like she was embarrassed.

Belinda and Joshua continued their playful and enticing banter the entire delivery route. Her conduct was so over the top at times, there were brief moments when Joshua wondered if her behavior was a little peculiar. Then, he would concentrate on her beauty and push the thought aside. Joshua decided he'd rather be infatuated with every touch, every giggle, and every wink. He was the happiest he'd been in his entire life.

When they finished their route and returned to the garage, Samuel was nowhere to be found and the music was off.

"Where do you think he went?" Belinda asked.

Joshua knew exactly where Samuel was, but he acted none

the wiser. "I'm not sure. But, knowing Samuel, he probably went back to the house to fetch something. Or, maybe he decided to take a little break. With the music off he's definitely not anywhere near here. That's how you know if he's around."

Joshua pulled the delivery cart to the nook in the back of the garage where it was always stored, and Belinda followed. When he turned around, Belinda was right there, maybe a foot or two away from him. No one could see them from this vantage point without walking into the garage. They were finally alone, at last.

"You know, Joshua, I've been thinking about you non-stop since the last time we were together." Belinda crept slowly closer. "I've been thinking about how handsome you are." Belinda put her right hand on Joshua's chest. "Have you been thinking about me?"

"Oh my God, non-stop. You're amazing. You...take my breath away."

"Did you enjoy holding me close to you?" Belinda asked, coming closer to Joshua still, putting her other hand around the back of his neck.

"Very much."

"Did you enjoy my kiss?"

"Yes, I enjoyed it very—"

Before Joshua could finish, Belinda leaned in and kissed him hard on the lips. He closed his eyes and let his instincts take over. It was the most incredible feeling. His entire body went on autopilot, his hands on her waist, pulling her in tighter, his heart was pounding in his chest. He became lost in ecstasy, pulling her in tighter still, wrapping his arms around her back, wanting her body pressed against his. Suddenly, her hands found his chest and she pushed him away.

"What?" he said, shocked. "What's the matter? Are you ok?"

"Joshua, we can't do this. We have to stop. What if someone were to find us? Do you realize what would happen?"

"No one is going to find us. Samuel isn't here. We're safe."

Belinda smiled and leaned in once again. The two started right where they left off. All his senses were in overload. He wanted her so badly at that moment that it consumed him entirely.

She was the beginning and the end. She was everything.

Belinda ran her fingers through his hair and pressed her body harder against his. They kissed more deeply, more passionately. He thought he was going to explode. His thoughts became completely absorbed with nothing but her.

She pulled her head back again, but this time, she didn't push him away, keeping her body firmly against his, her arms wrapped around his shoulders.

"We have to stop. I want you so bad. I want *all* of you, but we must stop. Someone could be around the corner. If we get caught, we'd be in serious trouble, a world of trouble. I want to keep going so bad, but we can't. We have to stop. Unless ... Is there anywhere we can go where you can guarantee that we'll be alone? Is there somewhere that no one else could find us?"

Joshua leaned in and whispered, "Can you keep a secret?"

## 36

### BEYOND THE PINES

Joshua awoke with vigor. It was Saturday. He went to sleep the night before feeling ashamed of himself, having told Belinda to meet him at the apiary first thing after breakfast on Sunday morning. He didn't tell her about the secret passage into the Armory, but that's precisely where he was going to take her.

He felt terrible about betraying Samuel, but after a night of dreaming about Belinda, he convinced himself it was no big deal. Taking her to the Armory on a Sunday morning was perfect. Samuel would be meditating for at least an hour, so he would be occupied. Lorrick hadn't been there in months, and it wasn't like Lorrick was suddenly going to go in his current condition. Plus, Joshua wasn't going there just to show her the garden. He was going there so they could be alone; it had nothing to do with the garden. Joshua trusted Belinda. Her passion was undoubtedly sincere. Not to mention that she had plenty of reason to keep things secret. She would be in just as much trouble if anyone knew she was having a physical relationship with Joshua. He had thought it through, and everything was going to be fine. He was sure of it.

That Saturday was like most days. Joshua and Samuel worked on the maintenance of farming tools and extracted some valuable nutrients from plants and flowers. Work seemed fine but Samuel was acting a little strange. No one else would notice, but to Joshua, the slightest difference in Samuel was perceptible. Whatever was bothering Samuel, Joshua was sure it had nothing to do with him telling Belinda to meet him the next day. Joshua convinced himself that Samuel acting strange so soon after Joshua had decided he was going to show Belinda the secret passage was nothing more than a coincidence. Maybe it was Lorrick's failing health bothering Samuel.

As they prepared to close the garage for the evening, Samuel made a suggestion.

"I made plans to have dinner with Andrew tonight. You want to meet me at the watchtower rooftop afterward? I think tonight might be a decent night to see some stars."

"Absolutely. That sounds like a plan. I'll see you there."

"Do me a favor and grab the boombox on your way there," Samuel requested. Joshua confirmed he would do exactly that.

Dinner that night was wonderful, as always. The meal consisted of something involving eggplant. Whatever it was, it was delightful and left Joshua feeling peaceful. His thoughts turned to Belinda, of course. What was it going to be like to be alone with her for the first time, not having to worry about someone catching them? How far were they going to go? His mind raced, and his heart soared. Sitting on the rooftop with Samuel would help calm Joshua's nerves and get his mind off his impending date.

When he got to the tower with boombox in hand, Joshua didn't even bother selecting any other artist but Thrice. He knew Samuel would make the request as soon as he got there. Whoever owned this iPod during the Paper Era loved Thrice just as much as Samuel did. Joshua found a playlist fit for stargazing, with soothing songs perfect for setting a relaxed atmosphere to sit back and stare into the cosmos. The second song had just started when Samuel appeared.

"Nice choice," he said when he heard the music.

"I figured you'd like it. How was dinner?"

"No one in Caulfield cooks as well as mom does, but Andrew is a close second. The food was excellent, and we had a nice visit. He has a way of helping me see a different perspective when things are troubling me. He's an incredible man and friend."

"Troubling you?" Joshua asked. "I knew something was up! What's wrong?"

Samuel turned his gaze on Joshua and remained silent for a second before shrugging his shoulders and gazing up at the stars. "Oh, just the usual stuff. Making sure I have everything in order with the crops and equipment. I'm worried we don't have enough Eupa to go around for the current flu making its way around. I think we should make some more on Monday."

"We made plenty of Eupa. I even think we'll have some left over. Still, if it will make you feel better, we'll make some more on Monday."

"Let's do that. This influenza is nasty. Besides, I'll have you make it completely on your own; I will do nothing but oversee. That way I'll know for sure you have the process memorized."

Joshua chuckled. "Why are you so worried about me memorizing the process of making Eupa? It's not like either of us is going anywhere any time soon. We have the rest of our lives for you to make sure I have the recipe and technique remembered."

Samuel was silent once again before turning his eyes

slowly back towards the sky. "There are two things in this life that I am sure of: love is the answer and tomorrow is promised to no one. We never know how things are going to turn out, Joshua. We can spend our entire lives planning every minute, every detail, anticipating every angle to control the outcome of any given situation, and it would be a worthless venture. Life has its own agenda; we are just along for the ride. If I were to fall over and die, right now, there would be nothing either one of us could do about it."

"Geez, what's the matter with you? Are you sick or some-thing? I've never heard you talk like this before. What are you trying to do, scare me?"

"I'm sorry, Joshua."

"Are you sick?"

"No, I'm not sick. I'm just trying to prove a point that you never know what's going to happen in the future, and I'd feel better knowing you've memorized the process of making Eupa, that's all."

"Weren't you just telling me that no matter how much you try and plan for something that it's pointless because you never know what's going to happen? You, my friend, are trying to control the future with me memorizing how to make Eupa, and if I'm following your logic, this is a futile exercise."

Samuel shook his head and huffed, "You're right. You are absolutely right. Life has its own agenda. If something happens to me and you haven't memorized how to make Eupa, you and the rest of Caulfield will have to figure it out for yourselves."

Joshua sat there for a minute staring at his adopted brother, who was staring up at the sky. He waited for Samuel to look back at him, but that was apparently not going to happen anytime soon. Joshua couldn't hold it in any longer. "What's the matter with you? You're freaking me out. You haven't been yourself all day, and now you invite me up here to make sure I've memorized how to make Eupa in case you die? Tell me the truth."

"I'm sorry," Samuel said calmly, continuing to gaze into the cosmos. "I don't mean to freak you out. And I'm sorry if I was acting weird today. I poked my head into Lorrick's room this morning before leaving for work, and his condition is getting worse. The stuff he was saying wasn't making much sense. It's hard for me to think about losing Lorrick. He's been an amazing father and mentor. He's one of the best men I've ever known. I know the natural cycle of life is one of birth and death, and I know when he leaves his physical body, he will be leaving it for a much better place. Still, it's hard, and it's been weighing on my mind."

Samuel finally turned to Joshua, "I'm not sick, aside from the general Sickness that rules the lower half of my body. I'm just dealing with the fact that we are all mortal and every single one of us will leave this life one day, some sooner than others."

"It's okay," Joshua said. "Sorry for freaking out on you. I promise I have memorized the Eupa process, but we'll do it again on Monday so you can see for yourself that I got it."

Samuel agreed, and the two sat together, listening to the music. Joshua knew there was something wrong with Samuel beside Lorrick, but he wasn't going to push it. Whatever it was, it would be dealt with in time. Joshua reminded himself that they weren't going anywhere. As he thought about his impending date with Belinda, he felt another jolt of guilt running through his plan to bring Belinda to the Armory. He tried to forget about it and concentrated on the song playing, 'Beyond the Pines.' As he listened to the lyrics, he thought about Samuel and hoped his melancholy mood would wear off soon. Joshua couldn't picture his life without his best friend.

Somewhere down the way, there's a hidden place that anyone
That all of us could find
But all our maps have failed, so venture through the veil and
realize
These roads are intertwined
Far beyond those walls, gleaming black and white
Further than our false schemes of wrong and right
Is a field where we can walk
Leaving all our names behind
I will meet you there, beyond the pines
Templed in twilight or dawn
The light and easy air
Tracing the lines on our palms
Somewhere down the road there's a place that we can go
Where everyone and everything's divine
And when we're all awake
We can finally make an end of these divisions in our mind
And I will meet you there – don't go to sleep
Our souls and feet both bare – with grass beneath
Oaths we needn't swear are vast and deep
Our breath will be our prayer – alone – complete
I will meet you there

## ❧ 37 ☙

# A PLACE TO BE ALONE

The morning of Joshua's date, the family went about their usual routine. Mariam made an excellent breakfast for the family to share. Asher and Adin ran around. Lorrick tried to join everyone for breakfast but was too weak, so Mariam made him a plate and Samuel, Gabe, and Joshua helped feed him. Lorrick took a few bites and swallows, which gave the family some peace. Joshua thought about what Samuel had said the previous night, about the cycle of life and how we will all pass on from this life, some sooner than others. Joshua hoped Lorrick would make a miraculous comeback, but with each passing day, that hope faded.

Once breakfast was cleaned up, Samuel went upstairs to meditate. As soon as Samuel closed the door, Joshua told everyone else there was something he needed to attend to at the crops and set out to meet Belinda.

As Joshua approached the crops, he scanned the area and was happy to see that there was no one in sight. He cupped his hand in front of his mouth and huffed a few times, checking his breath. He approached the back of the Armory with his heart pounding in his chest. He was nervous, excited, thrilled, and terrified all at the same time.

As he rounded the corner, he found Belinda there waiting for him. She leaned back against the very fan they would soon be entering. As he drew near, Belinda pushed herself off the wall and opened her arms, inviting Joshua in for a hug. They embraced for a few seconds before Belinda pushed him gently away.

"I thought you had a place where we could meet? You know this isn't going to work. I mean, first, anyone can come back here at any time. Second, there are bees whizzing back and forth, all over the place. I'd prefer not to get stung. Last but not least, are we really supposed to relax and get comfortable on this gravel?"

"Shhh," Joshua whispered. "Keep your voice down and follow me. We'll soon be totally alone and will be able to speak as loud as we want. For now, let's keep it down."

Belinda said nothing further as Joshua reached for the latch and opened the fan to Belinda's astonishment. They climbed in, with Joshua leading the way, and crawled through the venting system.

"Welcome to the Wheaton Armory," Joshua said as he closed the vent and stood in the adjoining hallway.

"I've never been in here before," Belinda said, turning her head in every direction. "It's kind of spooky. I don't know, Joshua. I kind of get the creeps in here. It's eerie, don't you think?"

Belinda's reaction and tone carried more unease than awe. Joshua had hoped that once they'd entered the building, she'd be all over him. Instead, she balled up, clearly not impressed.

Joshua had to think fast. He had to make this more exciting.

"No, no, this place isn't eerie at all. You're just feeling that way because we're in an empty hallway, that's all. Let's go up to one of the rooms on the top floor. There's more light up there, and then I can also show you something that's going to be so cool, especially from such a high vantage point."

Before she could reply, Joshua grabbed her hand and led her around the corner and to the stairwell. They walked up to the fourth floor and peeked into each room until they finally came across what looked to be an office of some sort. The back wall of the room had a large window facing the center courtyard. There was a desk to the left of the window and a couch directly opposite the desk.

Joshua pulled Belinda into the room and went straight for the window. The garden had an even more enchanted quality from above, the shapes and colors from the various fruits, vegetables, and flowers iridescent. The life from the garden's treasures emanated waves of joy and delight. Once again, one look was all it took to know that there was more to life than just the harsh reality of Grey Dawn, a testament that God was all-encompassing and loved all creation unconditionally. It was breathtaking.

Belinda did a double-take before finally breaking the silence with a long and measured, "Whoa."

"See," Joshua said with a smile. "This place isn't spooky at all. It's the exact opposite. It's amazing! Isn't it?"

"I had no idea. This can't be..."

"It is! I was pretty taken aback when I first saw it too."

"When did you first discover this place?"

"Samuel just showed it to me for the first time the other day. This building was shut down years ago. Samuel and Lorrick created this garden as a back-up plan, just in case Caulfield ever went into another draught. With Lorrick's health declining, Samuel brought me here so he wouldn't be the only one left alive who knew of its existence. Samuel swore me to secrecy, but I knew I could trust you to keep it a secret."

Joshua turned to Belinda and leaned in to kiss her. Instead of leaning in, though, Belinda backed up, and pressed her hands against Joshua's chest, pushing him away from her.

"What's wrong?" he said.

"You and Samuel are wrong for so many reasons."

Belinda ran back into the hallway and shouted, "We're in here! Up on the fourth floor! Hurry!"

Joshua, utterly confused, tried yelling over her, "What's the matter with you? What are you doing?" but she just continued shouting.

Joshua grabbed at her arms, but she pushed him away again. Seconds later, Joshua heard the pounding of running footsteps in the hallway. Joshua yelled to her again just as Seth and his squad of goons came around the corner. Belinda stopped shouting.

Seth smiled. "Well, hello, Joshua."

## ❦ 38 ❧

### SETH'S VISION

J oshua just stood there with his jaw dropped as far as his face would allow it. His eyes darted between Belinda and Seth.

"Come now, Joshua, don't act so surprised," Seth continued. "When Belinda let us know you wanted to meet her at the apiary, we staked out the perfect hiding spot within the crops to keep an eye on you. Besides, did you honestly think for a second that Caulfield's most beautiful female, a Chosen female, would have any desire to be with the likes of you? Surely you are smarter than that."

Everyone laughed, except Joshua. Seth sauntered over to the window while Belinda and Darin leaned against the desk. Keegan and Cade stayed in the doorway like two guards on watch, negating any type of escape for Joshua. Not that it would make any difference. Even if he did get away, he had already led Seth straight to Samuel's secret garden. There was nothing he could do now to correct this. He wanted to curl up into a ball and die.

Seth looked out of the window and let out a long whistle. "Wow! Look at that garden. Amazing! What's even more

250

amazing is how selfish Samuel is for keeping all this resource from the citizens of Caulfield. He should be ashamed of himself."

Joshua finally snapped out of it. "Keeping all of this resource from the citizens of Caulfield? Seth, every single resource in that garden is used for the residents of Caulfield. Samuel doesn't keep anything for himself. The only reason this is here is because of what occurred when Caulfield was on the brink of starvation when Samuel arrived."

"Why do you continue to be so naïve? Caulfield's yield has been bountiful for years. There's no need to maintain something like this any longer. And there's certainly no need to keep it a secret. Whatever caused the issue with Caulfield's crops in the past has come and gone. No, Joshua, I refuse to be as gullible as you. Samuel had only his interest in mind with this place.

"But don't you worry. Your help in unveiling the location of this garden could not have come at a more opportune time. You see, I have just been informed that the Council has finally decided to increase the maximum number of Council members. The formal announcement will be made tomorrow wherein the Elders will be increased from nine to ten seats, with me as the new member of their faction."

"You lie," Joshua said.

"You will see tomorrow. Once I am a formal member of the Council, I will put rules into effect that will set us on the path that we should have been on years ago. We have been at the mercy of Samuel for long enough. I've seen how you have studied and mastered Samuel's farming techniques. I have also been keeping tabs on you from other sources. You, my fine, simple friend, have made Samuel expendable with the knowledge and experience that you have gained.

"The first thing I am going to do is remove Samuel from his position as Caulfield's Head Farmer. You will be taking his place and should be excited about the promotion. Samuel, well, he will be punished in some way for maintaining this treasure behind Caulfield's back. The truth is he could never be trusted from the start, showing up out of nowhere, claiming to not remember where he came from. Absurd. He's been a thorn in my side from the first day of his arrival. Now, I can expose him to everyone for the fraud that he is. With me on the Council and you tending our crops, I will oversee everything you do with our Commune's most vital resource.

"Removing Samuel as Head Farmer would be a monumental mistake," Joshua said.

"I am sick and tired of his autonomy," Seth hissed. "Caulfield needs someone in charge of the farm who can be monitored and controlled. I will not have another incident like this, where someone is hiding a resource, because of a greedy and selfish individual. You, Joshua, you are going to be under my thumb. I am going to keep you on a very short leash."

"You're crazy," Joshua said. "If you remove Samuel, the crops have no future."

"I am the future!" Seth shouted, jumping just inches from Joshua's face. "The present regime is dying. I don't mean to be crass, and you have my sympathies, as I know how hard it must be for you to accept that Lorrick won't be with us but for a few more weeks, maybe less. The fact is his death is going to necessitate a new Head Council. I've already been assured by the same sitting Council members that have created my seat that I will be appointed the position of Head Council upon Lorrick's death. Once the position is mine, I will quickly make the leadership changes we need to make Caulfield grand again. I will appoint Darin to the open Council spot that I just vacated."

"Darin?" Belinda protested.

"Don't worry," Seth said, turning to Belinda. "I will honor

my side of our agreement, and either you or Ian will be the next Council appointee, following Darin."

"You can't do that!" Joshua screamed. "You can't just appoint whoever you want to the Council! You'll never get the support you need!"

"Under normal circumstances, I might agree with you, Joshua. However, I've been warning the Council, both publicly and privately, that Samuel could not be trusted. Now, you have given me the credibility I needed to prove what a lying, selfish, untrustworthy individual Samuel is. Once the Council are made aware of the resource he's been hiding, they will realize I've been correct from the start and will have no choice but to adopt my recommendations. Samuel will be cast aside, where he belongs."

"Did someone say my name?"

Samuel appeared between Keegan and Cade. Belinda let out a loud gasp, while Cade was so startled, he noticeably flinched.

Seth, on the other hand, acted with swift and precise movement. With his left arm, he grabbed Joshua and pulled him in close. With his right arm, Seth reached behind his back and, from his belt, exposed a knife.

Samuel took an impulsive step toward Seth and Joshua, only to be held back by Keegan on one side and Cade on the other. Seth's laugh matched the sadistic look in his eyes.

"How nice of you to join us, Samuel. We were just admiring what an amazing job you've done with this secluded garden. You have truly outdone yourself. It's a shame you had to betray all of Caulfield by keeping this place for your own selfish benefit all these years. This will undoubtedly result in your resignation as Head Farmer, at the bare minimum. You can also trust that it will result in a second red circle for your family. I will thoroughly enjoy the numerous punishments you will receive for lying to me and all of my fellow citizens about this place."

"Seth," Samuel said with an even and calm voice, "you need to put the knife away. Whatever wrong you think I've done, Joshua has nothing to do with it. Please, be reasonable. Put the knife down and we can all go straight to the Council, allow our wisest advisors to address this situation."

Seth's grip on Joshua tightened, and instead of putting the knife down, Seth pulled the knife up, and placed it flush against Joshua's neck. "Samuel, you fool. Clearly, you weren't standing there long enough to hear what's going on with the Council."

"I heard every word. I heard how you strong-armed the Council into adding a seat, and how you intend on taking the Head Council's role upon Lorrick's death. I heard how you intend on pushing me aside so you can control Joshua's running of the farm."

"And that's not all I intend on doing. I've saved the best announcement for last. Once I am Head Council, I will ensure Caulfield's rise from this pitiful state by giving this Commune the strongest Chosen offspring possible. Every single Chosen female of Caulfield will belong to me. It will be *my* seed that will bloom the next generation of Chosen to rule over the people."

Samuel looked at Seth with abhorrence. "The citizens of Caulfield will never allow such a thing to happen."

"The citizens of Caulfield have already given their blessing, including the wife of our current Head Council, your mother, Mariam."

"What are you talking about?" Samuel asked, his abhorrence turning into concern.

"Mariam has always known that the best chance humanity has of surviving and outlasting the Sickness is if my seed is used to impregnate as many of Caulfield's Chosen females as possible. That's why she and I agreed we should put the plan in place, now, starting with Adin. And our planning and intuition have paid off. As we speak, a Chosen child is forming in the womb of your sister; she's carrying my offspring. Adin's baby will be the first of dozens of my Chosen children in our Commune. The beginning of Caulfield's ascent has officially begun. Congratulations, Uncle Samuel."

## ❧ 39 ❧

## THE UNTHINKABLE

Samuel threw Keegan and Cade off each arm like rag dolls and darted straight at Seth. With one rapid and cohesive movement, Seth threw Joshua and the knife aside and shuffled his feet, angling his lower body sideways to receive Samuel's blow. Just as the two men were about to collide, Seth reached out, grabbed Samuel, and used all of his speed to throw him in the same direction he was charging.

The momentum from the throw doubled Samuel's inertia and he headed straight for the window behind Seth. The window was no match for the sturdiness of Samuel's rigid frame. On contact, the glass shattered into a million tiny pieces. Samuel's feet lifted off the floor as his torso began to go out and over the window's edge.

Seth let go of his nemesis, intending to let Samuel fall to his bloody death. With Samuel's upper body now outside the window, he made one last, flailing motion and grabbed hold of Seth's shirt collar. Seth grabbed Samuel's arm and tried to yank it free, but Samuel held on with a vice-like grip. Seth tried using his right foot as a brace, but it was no use; the momentum was too strong and Samuels's grip too tight. Gravity took over once the rest of Samuel's body hung out the window, and Seth followed, headfirst.

In an instant, they were both gone.

To Joshua, the entire event happened in slow motion. When the realization hit him that Samuel and Seth just fell out of a four-story window, Joshua broke into a cold sweat, and the room began moving in waves. Belinda's screams, which were ear piercing at first, slowly faded out to silence. The room went black. With a thud, Joshua hit the floor.

When Joshua regained consciousness, his vision was fuzzy, and he couldn't remember where he was or what was going on. He could sense commotion all around him, people shouting and running. He tried to shake it off and focus his eyesight. The silhouette in front of him was...Belinda...yes, it was Belinda. Someone stood at the window, looking down. There were tiny bits of glass all over the floor. Whoever was at the window was shouting down to people on the ground floor. Various voices from below shouted back.

"They're not breathing!"

"There's blood everywhere!"

"Oh my God! They're dead! They are both dead!"

When he heard the word 'dead' a second time, Joshua remembered where he was and what he had just witnessed. He wished he had never remembered. Darin, who was standing at the window, turned to Joshua, who was still on the ground, now sitting up. The look on Darin's face was beyond rage. It was the deepest anger, overshadowed only by the lust for vengeance. Darin took slow steps toward Joshua and then quickened his pace. Joshua sat frozen in shock.

"This is all your fault!" Darin screamed as he grabbed Joshua by his shirt collar and pushed him against the front of the couch. "You did this! You killed them both!" Darin reared his fist back, meaning to punch Joshua right in the face. He closed his eyes and squinted, preparing for impact.

"Stop it!" Belinda screamed, startling both Joshua and Darin. "Hasn't there been enough violence already? Please, just stop!"

With his clenched fist hung in midair, Darin turned back to Joshua and looked him hard in the eyes. Darin brought his face down, inches from Joshua's nose.

"This is your fault," Darin said through gritted teeth. "You are the reason Seth is dead, and I will spend my entire life making sure you pay for this debt. Wherever you go, I will follow, and I will have my vengeance."

Darin let go of Joshua and ran out of the room. Belinda didn't move; she just stood there crying. Joshua slowly got to his feet. He stared at the empty window and the shattered glass on the floor. He could hear Keegan and Cade screaming below about getting help. Joshua put his head down as the memory of Samuel and Seth falling from the window came flooding back. He felt like he was choking as tears gathered in his eyes. He took one step toward the window, then another, the broken glass crunching under his feet.

As he drew closer to the window, the rows of windows on the other side of the courtyard appeared, one floor at a time in his periphery. First the fourth floor, even with him, then the third, second, first, and finally the garden. He kept his gaze at the bottom of the window as the apple tree came into sight. When he finally reached the window's edge, he looked straight down, his vision blurry with tears. He blinked hard, and the tears gushed out, streaming down his cheeks.

When he opened his eyes again, he saw the lifeless bodies of Samuel and Seth on the garden floor.

Seth laid face down with a pool of blood next to his head, and his right leg completely bent upward. Samuel laid face up, with so much blood coming from his eyes, nose, and face, he was nearly unrecognizable.

Joshua fell to the floor a second time, but this time he remained conscious. This time he curled himself up into a ball and wailed.

## ❧ 40 ❧

## DARIN'S RAGE

J oshua sat at his table with Belinda next to him. To their left, Darin, Keegan, and Cade sat at their own table. In front of them were all nine members of the Council, including a very sick Lorrick. Lorrick's eyes were bloodshot red, and his face glowed with fever. Somehow, though, he sat there with the rest of the Council. Behind Joshua, the room burst with as many of Caulfield's citizens as the room could hold, packed tight into every corner. There was a very low murmur through the crowd. Lorrick banged a gavel, and the room went dead silent.

"This hearing has been called to order to determine the facts surrounding the deaths of Samuel Wilton and Seth Blackmore. Upon its conclusion, this Council shall deliberate to determine if any of the parties have violated Caulfield laws and shall administer punishments accordingly. The five of you were all present at the time of the incident. You will each be given a chance to speak. You will not interrupt each other. If it is not your turn to speak, you will remain completely silent. If a member of this Council interrupts you while you are speaking, you will pause your testimony and answer that question before proceeding. I am going to remind you all that you have sworn before this Council, and before God, to tell the truth, the whole truth, and nothing but the truth. We will start with you, Mr. Brown. Please proceed with your recollection of how Samuel and Seth came to their deaths."

Darin stood and started his testimony. "For years, Seth suspected that Samuel was maintaining his own secret crop, for his own personal benefit, behind the backs of the citizens of Caulfield. Seth refused to live with this injustice, and he assumed if anyone besides Samuel knew about this place, it would be Joshua. Seth also knew that Joshua was attracted to Belinda, so Belinda agreed to act as Seth's agent to try and find out if Joshua knew where this secret crop was located. It turned out he did know and agreed to take her there. Belinda informed Seth, who then followed Belinda and Joshua to the garden. Keegan, Cade, and I accompanied Seth as a security measure, and as witnesses, in case the events of this incident ended up before this Council. When we confronted Joshua and told him we were taking this matter to the authorities, he somehow alerted Samuel, who suddenly appeared. Seth—"

"What do you mean that Joshua alerted Samuel?" one of the Council members asked. "How did Joshua alert Samuel?"

"I don't know. All I know is Seth was explaining that it wasn't right that they kept this resource to themselves when suddenly Samuel appeared."

Another Council member interjected. "So, you actually don't know how it came to be that Samuel joined you?"

"That is correct. I don't know how he knew we were there. I know that Seth, Keegan, Cade, Belinda, and myself never said anything to Samuel. Therefore, since Joshua is the only one left, I just assumed it must have been him who alerted Samuel of our presence."

"Please continue."

"As I was saying, when Samuel appeared, Seth told Samuel that it was not acceptable to be maintaining and using this resource for himself when the whole of Caulfield could benefit from this place. After Seth made the announcement, Samuel charged. Seth happened to be standing right in front of a window. When Samuel hit Seth, the force pushed them both backward. Upon hitting the window, it shattered, and they fell to their deaths."

A female member of the Council spoke up. "So, when they went out the window, Seth went first, with his back towards the window, and Samuel went second, facing the window?"

Darin turned to Keegan and Cade for a split second, and then back to the Council member. "Yes, ma'am, that is correct."

"Keegan Stone," another Council member said, "you are next, please tell us your recollection of the event."

"What Darin said is exactly how it happened. I don't have anything to add to his statement."

"Mr. Stone," the Council member continued, "did you inform Samuel that you would be confronting Joshua that morning in the Armory?"

"No, sir. I did not."

"Very well. Mr. Cade Grissom, do you have anything to add to Darin's testimony?"

"No, sir, I do not have anything to add. What Darin said is how it happened."

"Mr. Grissom, did you inform Samuel that you would be confronting Joshua that morning?"

"No, sir, I did not."

"Mr. Barratt, please proceed with your testimony."

Joshua stood up from his seat. His heart pounded,

partially from nerves and partially from anger at Darin's testimony. Joshua was so mad and nervous that he didn't know where to start, so he just stood there for a few seconds.

"Mr. Barratt, please proceed with your testimony," one of the Council members said impatiently.

"Most of what Darin said is false. It is true that Samuel was maintaining a secret crop. However, he was not doing so for his own benefit. He used the yield from the garden to benefit all of Caulfield. He also maintained this garden as insurance in case the main crops failed again.

"And Belinda didn't ask me to show her the garden; she tricked me. She told me she was attracted to me and wanted to be alone with me. She asked me to take her somewhere no one could find us. That's why I took her to the Armory. It's the worst mistake I've ever made in my entire life."

"Mr. Barratt, please just stick to the facts. We don't need side commentary."

"Sorry. Like I was saying, Belinda tricked me into showing her the secret passage into the Armory. Once we got inside and up to the fourth floor, she started screaming for Seth. Seconds later, Seth, Darin, Keegan, and Cade appeared. That's when Seth told us he was going to be on the Council. He said the Elders were adding a tenth seat, just for him, and he was going to punish Samuel for maintaining the garden. That's when Samuel arrived."

Joshua went quiet when he said Samuel's name. He fought back the tears. He didn't want to cry in front of all these people.

A Council member interrupted. "Did you tell Samuel that you were taking Belinda to the Armory that day?"

"Absolutely not. I was keeping it a secret from him—from everyone, I thought."

"Then how did he know you were there?"

"I have no idea. He just appeared. And, as soon as he did, Seth grabbed hold of me and pulled out a knife. When that happened, Keegan and Cade grabbed Samuel on each arm. Seth started talking again about how he was going to rule Caulfield."

Joshua paused and looked back into the crowd, finding Adin staring back at him. Joshua and Adin had bonded since Lorrick became ill and had become even closer since Samuel's death. Joshua told her that he knew about her pregnancy, that it was Seth's child.

As she stared back at Joshua, a terrified expression came over her face. What would the Council and citizens of Caulfield do if they were informed at a public hearing that Adin was pregnant with Seth's child? A child conceived out of wedlock and outside of a pairing selected by the Council? Adin, without saying a word, was begging Joshua not to say anything about the baby.

"Mr. Barratt, please continue," a Council member said. But Joshua just stood there, staring back at Adin.

Finally, Lorrick spoke. "Joshua, what happened next?"

Joshua turned back to the Council. "Samuel tried to reason with Seth and asked him to lower the knife. But he didn't. Instead, he put the knife to my throat!"

A unified gasp came from the crowd, followed by lower murmurs. Lorrick banged on the gavel once again, quieting the spectators. Joshua continued, "That's when Samuel threw Keegan and Cade aside and charged Seth. But he was only trying to protect me, because, like I said, Seth had a knife to my throat."

Another Council member spoke up. "Mr. Barratt, I'm sure you're already aware of the fact that the area was thoroughly searched, and no knife was found."

"One of Seth's cronies must have grabbed it before anyone else got there. I swear on my life, Seth had a knife to my throat. And Samuel didn't smash Seth through the window. He did charge Seth, that is true, but Seth grabbed Samuel and threw him toward the window. That's what broke the window. The only reason Seth went over was because, when Samuel was falling, he reached out trying to grab anything to stop himself. Samuel ended up grabbing Seth, but only to save himself. He wasn't trying to pull Seth out of the window with him."

More whispers came from the public but went silent without Lorrick having to bang the gavel a third time.

"Don't you understand what I'm telling you?" Joshua continued. "Seth threw Samuel out of the window. Samuel's death was intentional! Seth's death was unintentional! Don't you understand?"

"That's enough, Mr. Barratt," an elderly man on the Council said. "Ms. Belinda Lillith, what is your recollection of the event in question?"

Belinda stood, looked at Joshua, then at Darin, Keegan, and Cade, and then back to the Council. "It's...like Darin says. I don't have anything to add, except...I don't think Samuel intentionally pushed Seth into the window. I think that was an accident. We all knew Samuel. He would never intentionally hurt anyone."

Darin jumped up. "Obviously, we didn't know Samuel. He was maintaining and hiding this resource from all the citizens of Caulfield!"

With Darin's exclamation, the crowd erupted into a large roar, making an unpleasant sound that clashed against itself. Half of the crowd booed, while the other half cheered. Lorrick banged his gavel on his table again to bring the clattering and horrible crowd noise to a halt.

"Enough!" Lorrick shouted.

After the crowd settled, Lorrick continued. "This Council has heard all of the eyewitness testimony. We will convene over the course of the following weeks to determine what laws have been violated, if any, and the resulting proper course of action. Until we have made our ruling, it is vital that the Commune of Caulfield continue to operate and perform all its duties. We must remain fully functional. Therefore, until further notice, Darin Brown will now act as the Head of Security, with Keegan Stone and Cade Grissom as part of his department. Belinda Lillith will return to Warner Hall full time. Joshua Barratt will act as Head Farmer. Mr. Barratt will maintain and use the courtyard garden for our Commune. Whether that resource was being used for all of Caulfield in the past has no relevance to the fact that it will now, and forever, be maintained for all of Caulfield.

"It is also true that our Council was going to announce the addition of a tenth seat to our panel. And, that seat was going to be occupied by Seth Blackmore."

A large, uniform huff rose from the crowd.

"Given Mr. Blackmore's untimely passing," Lorrick continued over the noise, "this Council will also determine if we will honor the additional seat, and, if so, to whom it will be appointed. This hearing is adjourned."

Expressions of shock and concern mixed with footsteps shuffling and bodies stirring once the Elders had left the room. Joshua sat for a moment with his head down, wondering if the Council was going to punish him for what had happened. Belinda was long gone by the time Joshua finally stood up. Darin and his crew mixed in with the moving crowd.

Joshua turned around and noticed one lone set of eyes on him: Adin.

She stood like everyone else but wasn't moving, instead, just staring at Joshua. He stared back, wondering what she was thinking, waiting for her to do something. Bodies passed between their gaze, breaking their line of sight in sporadic flashes. Then, Adin mouthed two words to Joshua that he understood immediately: "Thank you."

Joshua nodded his head and continued to stare as Adin mixed in with the rest of the masses. Until that moment, Joshua had never realized how pretty Adin was.

## ❧ 41 ❧

## LORRICK'S ADMISSION

Nearly all of Caulfield gathered again, just a few days after the hearing, at Caulfield's cemetery in the farthest southwest corner of the Commune, next to the power station. Andrew presided over the ceremony. He included stories of Samuel's friendly and loving nature, and his dedication to keep Caulfield's citizens nourished and healthy. Andrew also shared Seth's visions of a strong and prosperous Caulfield, where all its citizens, one day, would be fully immune from the Sickness. He somehow accomplished this without making Seth sound like the arrogant man that he was.

As the ceremony proceeded, Joshua's thoughts filled of Samuel. There were no words to describe how much he missed his best friend. Other people in Caulfield would say things like, "it will get better," and "time heals all wounds," but, at that moment, he felt like his heart, his very soul, had been ripped out of his chest and would never return. It was the same feeling he had when he left his mother behind on Route 23. Joshua kept asking himself the same question, over and over: why is this happening to me *again*?

As the wrapped bodies were lowered into the ground, Joshua's despondency morphed into hatred. He watched as Samuel and Seth were buried together and couldn't stand the extreme inequality of it. Seth didn't deserve to be buried with someone as kind and caring as Samuel. Why should Seth be given the same respect, the same appreciation as Samuel? More than that, it was Seth's fault they were both dead. If it weren't for Seth, none of this would have happened. If it weren't for Seth, Samuel would still be alive.

As they shoveled the dirt onto the two buried bodies, Joshua grew enraged. He would give anything, even his own life, if he could go back in time and make certain that Seth was never born.

As the service ended, something dawned on Joshua that he hadn't noticed until that moment. Lorrick and Darin weren't there. Lorrick was too ill to attend. But Darin was fine. Keegan and Cade were there, making Darin's absence even stranger. Joshua wondered where Caulfield's new head of security could be that was so important, he missed the burial of his best friend, the man who never should have existed in the first place.

As the crowd dispersed, Joshua waited for Andrew and the two of them headed back towards the center of Caulfield together, both physically and mentally exhausted. Joshua had to get back to work, even though he had no idea how he was going to fill the shoes of Caulfield's greatest farmer.

"It's hard to believe that he's gone," Andrew said. "I know you're going to miss him just as much as I will."

Joshua didn't say anything back. He didn't want to. If he went down that path, it would just be more tears.

"As difficult as this is for you and me," Andrew continued, "Samuel is counting on both of us to forge ahead. He's counting on you to keep the crops going, keep Caulfield's citizen's belly's full and medicine's stocked. He's counting on me to tend to our sick residents and remind our Commune that not everything is black and white, and we need to accept all things in life, even if they make us uncomfortable. I know it's overwhelming to think about it, but these are things he would want us to do, expect us to do."

"I know. It's just that—I don't know if I can do it. I don't know if I can keep the crops as healthy and vibrant as Samuel did. I don't know if I can make the medicines like Samuel did. Not alone."

"Joshua, you are never alone, even when you feel like you are the last soul on Earth. You have a path in front of you, and there are two ways you can walk down that path: in faith or in fear. How you decide to walk that path will directly affect the outcome of the journey. If you walk in fear, every success will be a fluke, while every failure will be hard evidence that you can't do it, and that you never should have even tried in the first place. This pattern will continue until you ultimately fail.

"On the other hand, if you walk that path in faith, every failure will be a minor setback, while every success will be a living testament that you can do it, and that you never should have doubted yourself in the first place. This pattern will continue until you ultimately succeed. Every journey, every life, is filled with successes and failures. How your journey, your life, ultimately turns out will depend on your mindset as you walk that path, as you live that life. Walk in faith, Joshua, don't walk in fear."

"You sound like..." Joshua was going say his mom, but he couldn't without being reminded of how both his mother and Samuel had been taken from him, so he stopped himself and gathered his composure. "Thanks...for the encouragement. That makes a lot of sense. I'm just scared, and I miss Samuel. I miss him terribly."

"I do too, and everyone is scared in life, one way or

another, but not everyone is brave enough to admit it. It's okay. You will be okay. One day at a time. Let's get through this day, and we can worry about tomorrow, tomorrow."

"I'm so grateful for your friendship, Andrew. Especially now."

"The feelings are mutual, my friend. We will get through this together."

The two men walked back at a leisurely pace, often stopping to talk to other residents, and finally parted ways just before they reached Elder's Row. As Joshua approached his front door, something was amiss. When he had left that morning, he took note of the one red circle outside his family's front door. It was a daily reminder of the trouble he caused his family on the very first night he joined them. Now, as he stood there facing that same doorway, there was not one red circle, but two.

Anger coursed through his veins. Did he earn a second red circle for his family? Or, was this for Samuel and the secret garden? Either way, it made Joshua sick to his stomach. Instead of going to see Seth buried, Darin took the time to paint a second red circle on his family's door. This madness had to stop.

Joshua would go to Lorrick. If Lorrick was strong enough to preside over the hearing just a few days ago, then he was strong enough to get the Council to abolish the Law of the Red Circles.

As Joshua reached for the doorknob, he heard a low rumbling and felt a vibration. He stopped and turned around to locate its origin. The sound and vibration intensified. It was all around him. Everything was shaking. Then, as quickly as it had started, it stopped. Mystified, Joshua grabbed the handle and rushed into the house.

"Did you guys feel—"

"There you are!" Mariam jumped out of her seat. "We've

been desperate for you to return!" Mariam had stayed home to care for Lorrick, who had been bedridden since the hearing. "Lorrick is so weak he can barely talk. He's been asking for you since you left for the funeral. He says he needs to speak with you, and *only* you. He's delirious. He's not making any sense. Would you please get in there and settle him down? He's not going to make it through the night if he keeps up like this."

Joshua beelined straight for Lorrick, knocking and opening the door without waiting for a response. Lorrick had his eyes closed. Gabe, who sat at his father's side, gently put his hand on Lorrick's arm.

"Dad. You wanted to see Joshua. He's here."

Joshua came to Gabe's side, and Lorrick opened his eyes.

"Yes," Lorrick said weakly. "Good. Joshua, please sit down. Gabe, please, leave us for a moment."

Gabe glanced at Joshua with grave concern before getting up and leaving, closing the door behind him. Joshua took a seat. He could tell that his adopted father was at death's door.

"Joshua, I've been...hesitant to discuss Samuel with you since his passing. But now, I believe...I have no choice. I am dying, Joshua. I need to know...when Samuel showed you the secret garden, what did he tell you?"

"He told me that the two of you built the garden as a backup plan, in case the main crops ever failed again, and people started stealing food."

"Is that all?"

"Yeah, pretty much. He said that you and he were the only ones that knew of its existence, but he wanted me to know because he was concerned with your health, and if anything happened to him, the garden would be lost forever."

"What about...his gift?" Lorrick asked.

"His gift? I don't understand."

"Did he tell you...how he brought our crops back?"

"He showed me his various farming techniques. He taught me how to tend the soil and look for certain characteristics to determine the health of any given crop if that's what you mean."

Lorrick closed his eyes and mumbled something to himself.

"What's that? I couldn't hear you."

Lorrick kept his eyes closed, but spoke louder, which was still barely a whisper. "When Samuel came to Caulfield, he was young, younger than you. When I brought him to the crops, I did so just to keep an eye on him while I worked. Caulfield was dying...our crops...dying...I did not know why. That's when I saw...I saw a miracle." Lorrick shook his head, reliving the memory.

Joshua's eyes went wide. "What was it, Lorrick? What did you see?"

"I was looking at a nearly dead stalk of corn. I was on one knee...Samuel was standing next to me when I saw Samuel touch the stalk. Before my very eyes, the stalk of corn went from light brown to dark green. I opened the husk and inside the corn was healthy, when seconds before...wilted, rotting."

"I don't—"

"I swear to you. I witnessed this miracle. Samuel tried to explain, but I never understood. He said he could alter the vibrational energy of the corn, or any living thing, for that matter, somehow raise the vibration, therein manipulating the atoms to make healthy. He also—"

Lorrick broke out into a violent cough and couldn't catch his breath. Joshua found some water on the nightstand and raised Lorrick's lips for a drink. The coughing fit stopped, but Lorrick's breathing was labored and weak.

Joshua sat on the edge of his chair, inches from Lorrick's face. "He also, what?"

"He also could communicate, telepathically, and could read people's thoughts—"

"Lorrick, this is all impossible."

"I swear on my life. He claimed we all could...we all have the same gift. We just don't know...how to use it." Lorrick stopped, too weak to speak any further.

"It's okay, Lorrick. I'm here. Take a break. Just breathe. Easily. Take a few breaths and continue when you can."

After a minute, Lorrick continued. "Samuel said we all have the ability to do the things he did. We just need to learn, to train our minds, operate on a higher vibrational frequency."

"Lorrick, if Samuel could do these things, why didn't you inform the Council? Why were you the only one to know?"

"Samuel swore me to secrecy. If others knew, they would treat him...like a God. He made me swear, and I was so desperate, I swore the oath."

"I can't believe it," Joshua said.

"There's more." Lorrick was barely audible. Joshua moved closer, his ear an inch from Lorrick's mouth. "Samuel tried to teach me. I struggled. But I kept a journal of his lessons. Beware of danger, Samuel warned. Once learned...could use to destroy life, cause harm to...atoms...and control people's... thoughts...telepath..." Lorrick was fading.

Joshua got in close to Lorrick's face. "Lorrick. Lorrick! Where is the journal?"

"The journal is...in..." Lorrick moved his mouth for a moment longer, but no words escaped his lips. Then, with one final breath, Lorrick died.

## ℀ 42 ℀

## ADMITTING THE TRUTH

"No. No! Lorrick? Please don't. Lorrick?" Joshua started crying, shaking his adopted father's lifeless body.

Gabe burst into the room, followed by Mariam, Adin, and finally, Asher. Gabe pushed Joshua aside.

"Dad! Dad!" Gabe screamed. He started pounding on his chest. Mariam covered her mouth and started crying. Adin held her little brother, covering his face. After a few minutes, Gabe stopped, exhausted, and turned to Joshua.

"What did you do to him?"

"I didn't do anything. He was talking to me. That's all."

Adin let go of Asher and walked over to her brother, putting her hand on his arm. "Gabe, Dad has been sick for a long time. You know that. We knew this day was coming. This isn't Joshua's fault."

"What was he so desperate to tell you, anyway?" Mariam asked.

Joshua looked around the room. He didn't know where to start. "I…I don't know. I could barely hear him. He was saying things that didn't make any sense."

"Like what? What was he saying?" Gabe demanded.

"He said that Samuel had powers. That he could make anything grow just by touching it. Then he also said Samuel could communicate telepathically and read people's minds."

The rest of the room sat in silence, staring at Joshua incredulously.

"See!" Joshua exclaimed. "I told you he wasn't making any sense."

Gabe shook his head. "You expect me to believe that my father, our father, said those things to you?"

"You can believe whatever you want to believe. All I know is Lorrick said Samuel had these powers and that anyone could learn how to have these powers. Samuel tried to teach him."

"Oh my God, Joshua, stop it!" Mariam screamed. She grabbed Asher and stormed out of the room, with both of them sobbing. Mariam mumbled something about contacting the rest of the Council, but her words were garbled.

Gabe covered his father's face with a blanket. With tears running down his face, he stood and sternly turned to Joshua.

"You never speak to anyone of what my father said to you. He will die a respected and loved citizen of Caulfield. I'm not going to have his memory, or his reputation, tarnished by a bunch of nonsense. Do you understand me, Joshua? Not a single word."

"I swear, Gabe," Josh responded, "I swear I won't tell another soul."

Gabe left the room, mumbling under his breath. With only Adin left, Joshua looked down at Lorrick's covered body and came to the horrifying realization that Lorrick died on the same day Samuel was buried. Joshua was too numb to cry.

"Why don't they believe me, Adin? What did I do wrong?"

Adin came closer and gripped Joshua's arms. "Everyone is

just scared. Dad had started saying all kinds of things that didn't make sense, mumbling about the energy in the universe, that there was no wrong and right, that everything happens for a reason. At times, we would find him talking to the air like someone was there. This morning he started having a conversation with Hannah and Alessia. They've been dead for years. He's been back and forth between consciousness and unconsciousness. The majority of what he was saying made no sense. He sounded like a mad man. We all knew he was going to die. No one is blaming you, Joshua. Our family has been through so much, with losing Samuel and now Dad. You're just an easy target, that's all."

Joshua nodded in agreement as his numbness gave way to tears. Adin pulled him close and hugged him firmly. Joshua hugged Adin back, and the two cried in unison.

## ✽ 43 ✾

## SAVING SETH'S VISION

Joshua did his best to get on with life, but it seemed virtually impossible after burying Lorrick so soon after Samuel. He knew his grieving would have to yield to the priority of the farm. It was up to Joshua, now, to keep the crops healthy and keep the people of Caulfield nourished. He didn't need Andrew to remind him that it is what Samuel and Lorrick would have expected of him. Joshua wanted to give up, but for those others in Caulfield whose survival depended on him, Joshua pushed through the sorrow of losing his best friend and his adopted father and worked the crops. He reminded himself of this fact as he walked up to the garage each morning, knowing that his day of working the fields would be just one of many without Samuel.

One morning, when he got to the front of the garage, Joshua reached for the chain around his neck that previously belonged to Samuel, with the lone, silver key and the small silver cross, a reminder of how Samuel lived every day, asking Spirit to fill his heart with love and patience. Joshua turned on the lights and headed toward the boombox. He knew what band he was going to be listening to exclusively for the foreseeable future.

With so much to do, the day did go by quickly, despite the occasional crying fits. That evening when Joshua got home, he was famished, but still didn't have much of an appetite. He walked into the kitchen where Adin was making dinner. She had become a good cook in her own right, but she was still no match for Mariam. Since Lorrick's passing, though, Mariam hadn't cooked a single thing.

"Hey, Joshua," Adin said, "How'd it go today?"

"It pretty much sucked. I got some stuff done, but I had to stop every ten minutes because I couldn't see with the tears in my eyes."

"I know the feeling. I think my ten-minute alarm just went off."

Adin turned to Joshua with tears in her eyes, and a forced smile on her face. Joshua put his arm around Adin's shoulder and told her it was going to be ok.

"What can I do to help get this meal prepared?" Joshua asked.

Adin smiled, this time for real, and had Joshua cut up a few things. Footsteps pounded above their heads, then down the stairs and into the kitchen. It was Gabe. Unlike Adin, who had swollen eyes from crying, Gabe looked fresh and resolute. He looked so composed that Joshua couldn't help but stare.

"You okay?" Gabe asked, giving Joshua a funny look.

"Yeah, no. I mean, I'm okay, I guess. I didn't mean to stare. You just look so...at ease."

"Looks can be deceiving." Gabe answered, playing with the bracelet around his wrist. "I'm trying like hell to be a source of inspiration for Mom. She's been inconsolable since Dad died. She barely gets out of bed. Barely says two words. I'm worried. I figure I better have the appearance of a pillar of strength, so she knows she has someone to lean on. I don't know what else I can do."

"That's all you can do," Adin said.

"I just hope she snaps out of it sooner rather than later. Having her in this state just makes matters worse. Speaking of making matters worse, did you guys hear what Darin is currently doing?"

"No," Joshua said, "What now?"

"He's going around Caulfield asking residents to sign a petition he is calling 'Save Seth's Vision.' The Petition demands that the Council expedite their ruling on the case of Samuel and Seth's deaths and appoint Darin as Head Council."

"What?" Adin said.

"I know. It's crazy but true. I ran into Darin earlier today. He's telling people that moments before Seth was murdered, he shared a vision of how Caulfield was going to rise above the Sickness and how he was going to lead humanity to a place even greater than the Paper Era. Now Darin is vowing that he's going to fulfill Seth's dream, in his honor. Darin is telling everyone that failure is not an option, that he'll do whatever it takes to make Seth's vision a reality."

"And I thought this day couldn't get any worse," Joshua said, rolling his eyes.

"Doesn't Darin have to be on the Council first, before being appointed Head Council?" Adin asked.

"That has been the pattern since Caulfield's inception, but the law does not make it a specific prerequisite. Technically, the Council can appoint anyone as Head Council, as long as that person is a citizen of Caulfield. Everyone knows that the Elders already agreed to have an additional seat created, specifically to allow for Seth to join the Council. Darin is taking it a step further and claiming that the Elders were also in agreement to appoint Seth as Head Council, upon

Lorrick's imminent passing. Then, they were going to appoint Darin to occupy the newly vacant seat. Darin is arguing that the Council should do the right thing and appoint him as Head Council."

"What about Council Campbell? Dad always said she was the best-qualified candidate to be the next appointed Head Council. What about her?" Adin asked.

"I hate to admit it, but the fact is Caulfield has never had a female appointed as Head Council. If Darin is telling the truth, and a majority of the Elders had already agreed to appoint Seth as Head Council when Dad died, Council Campbell never even had a chance. Fear can be a huge motivator, and everyone is so afraid of the Sickness they can't help but be drawn to someone with an apparent immunity and a 'take no prisoners' mentality. People might not have liked Seth, but they were willing to look past his brash manner because he brought a sense of security. Now that Seth has died, people are going to be even more frightened. Darin is playing his cards perfectly. He's feeding into people's fear, while at the same time continuing to draw on the memory of Seth. Since Seth can't be our next Head Council, Darin is arguing he's the next closest thing. If I had to guess, I'd bet that Darin will be our new Head Council within a few weeks, maybe less."

Joshua felt like he was going to be sick. The nightmare he'd been living for the last couple of weeks just kept getting worse.

## ⚜ 44 ⚜

## EVERYTHING BELONGS

The following days were some of the worst Joshua had experienced in Caulfield. Everyone was talking about Darin becoming the next Head Council. Plus, some of the citizens who had been very friendly to Joshua, had suddenly began avoiding him. Folks like Mr. Lenrod were always good for a quick chat. But since the hearing, Mr. Lenrod had avoided Joshua at every turn. He wondered if it had to do with a possible punishment coming down. He wondered if people actually believed that Samuel was using the resource of the secret garden all to himself, and Joshua was, therefore, also to blame, via guilt by association.

Joshua did his best to forget about the worries and keep his mind on his work. Still, with the loss of Samuel and Lorrick, combined with Darin's petition and possible punishments coming down in the near future, Joshua sunk into a deep depression. Passing the two red circles on his family's door every day made things worse. He wondered why any God would make people like Seth and Darin. He wondered why any God allowed someone like Samuel to die young.

Joshua also worried about his family and, especially, about Adin and her baby. Adin had become the only reason why Joshua was even trying anymore. The responsibility he'd previously felt toward Caulfield, knowing his mom, Samuel, and Lorrick would expect him to carry on, was fading.

Joshua needed to keep Adin and her baby safe. If only they could leave Caulfield.

A week after they buried Lorrick, Joshua went to the watchtower. It had become a pattern, the watchtower offering an escape. Joshua would look up at the handful of stars, listen to music, and think about his mom, Samuel, and Lorrick. This night, to Joshua's pleasant surprise, Andrew decided to join him.

"I stopped by your place to see you, and Adin said you'd be here," Andrew said as he sat down next to Joshua. "She said you've been coming here every night for at least a week now."

"Yeah. I'm having a hard time. Coming here relaxes me. Although..."

"Although, what?"

"Although coming here reminds me of Samuel. I miss him so much. Maybe coming here makes it worse. I don't know. I'm in a bad place."

"I understand." Andrew glanced at the boombox. "Maybe when you come here you should try listening to something besides Thrice," he said with a smile.

"What are you saying? That I'm a glutton for punishment?" Joshua gave a little laugh. "You're right. Maybe I should just keep it on random play for a while."

Andrew laughed back. "That's a good thought."

"I have another thought," Joshua said firmly. "You like to discuss the nature of God. If there even is a God, why does God allow people like Seth and Darin to exist? And, why does

God allow someone like Samuel to die young? I know you believe, without question, that something greater exists, but if that's true, I can't understand why people like Darin are alive while people like Samuel are dead. It makes no logical sense."

Andrew looked at Joshua but did not answer the question. Instead, the two sat silently while a song played in the background. It was another one of Samuel's favorites. Andrew's ears perked up, and he nudged Joshua, "Listen to this song."

> There's a darkness that is brighter than our light
> There's a danger, love, to holding on so tight
> I'm finally seeing I've been seeing this all wrong
> I'm finally seeing now that everything belongs
> There's a shadow that believes in fits and starts
> And it's the paradox that feeds the famished heart
> I'm finally seeing how the spaces make the song
> I'm finally seeing now that everything belongs
> There's a web and every thread ties you to me
> And we are here and now, the future's yet to be
> I'm finally seeing that our weakness makes us strong
> And everything belongs

When the song ended, Andrew spoke up. "I love that song. It reminds me of a Buddhist philosophy known as 'Indra's Net.' Imagine that all of existence is a multidimensional spider's web covered with dewdrops. If you look closely at one dewdrop, you'd see it contains the reflections of all the other dewdrops. And, in each reflected dewdrop, you continue to see the reflections of the reflections of all the other dewdrops. This goes on for infinity.

"That's what life is, Joshua. Every living thing in the universe is connected. What we label as good, bad, smart, dumb, important, trivial, gay, straight, Chosen, and Sickness are all linked together as one. Every single living thing in God's universe is part of God. This means that no one, no single life, has more worth or more value than another. Everyone carries the same amount of importance in the eyes of our maker."

"That's bullshit," Joshua contested.

"I understand your frustration. It's easy to get caught in the trap of thinking that certain individuals are more deserving than others to live. Be cautious, my friend. If you get caught in that trap, you become the very thing that you despise. Everything belongs, Joshua. That's why the most important thing in life is love. I know you resent Seth and Darin, but you can't harbor disdain for them. You have to forgive them, realize that God loves them, just as much as you, and move forward with your life with peace in your heart."

"They don't deserve to be forgiven, Andrew. More than that, they don't *want* to be forgiven. All they want is power. All they want is control. All they want is to put you down so that they can feel bigger than you, more important than you. How am I supposed to love them? Seth *killed* Samuel. I'm supposed to forgive him for killing my brother, my mentor, my best friend? Plus, there's other stuff that Seth did that I can't get into with you right now, but, trust me, it's just as horrible."

"I never said it was going to be easy. Just take it a day at a time. When you feel that urge to hate, take a step back, take a deep breath, and let it go."

"Andrew, I'll never forgive Seth, that's just a fact, so you can forget it. As far as Darin goes, he hasn't killed or raped anyone that I'm aware of, but there's no way I'm ever going to love the guy or want to hang out with him. I'll tell you that right now."

"No one said you have to hang out with him. Just don't

give in to hate. If that means you need to avoid him for a little while, I don't see anything wrong with some Darin absence in your life."

The idea of not having Darin in his life, in any measure, appealed to Joshua. "Now that sounds more like it," he said. "The absence of Darin in my life. That sounds downright spectacular."

Andrew gave Joshua a funny look.

"I'm not saying I wish the guy had never been born, like I feel towards Seth," Joshua continued. "I'm just saying that if Darin belongs just like everyone else, I don't want to be around the guy. Ever."

"I hate to break it to you, buddy, but the only way you're going to do that is to leave Caulfield, and I don't think that's happening any time soon."

"It's still nice to think about a life without Darin." Joshua sat silently for a bit before continuing. "What do you think? You ever think we'll beat the Sickness and get out of Caulfield?"

Andrew looked up at the sky. "It's hard to say. The Elders have been pairing for so long, but our Chosen numbers continue to decline."

"What if you could leave *before* we beat the Sickness. Would you?"

Andrew didn't hesitate. "No. Caulfield is my home. Besides, if I were to leave, who would be Caulfield's token gay person?"

They both laughed.

"Seriously, though, Caulfield is my home. Even if I had the chance to leave, I wouldn't. Not if I had a choice. Why do you ask, Joshua? Are you planning to make a break for it?"

"Nah. Even if I was, it's not like I could get out of here alive. This place is sealed up pretty tight." Joshua thought about life with Darin as Head Council and the hell he would create. "On the other hand, if Darin gets appointed Head Council, it might be worth the gamble. Death sounds better than a Caulfield run by Darin."

## ❧ 45 ❧

## NO FURTHER DELAY

J oshua tried his best to keep up with his daily routine. He decided to take Andrew's advice and lay off the Thrice for a while. Still, there was no way he was going to stop listening to them, so he compromised with himself to just let the music play on random shuffle.

It had only been a few weeks since Samuel's passing. As far as the crops went, in that short amount of time, Joshua had already become slightly concerned. It was barely noticeable, but any person who worked the fields every day saw that the vegetation wasn't quite as lush as it had been a month ago. He was going to have to keep a close watch on their condition. On the other hand, the secret garden, now referred to as the courtyard garden, continued to thrive. Joshua couldn't understand it.

In a shocking move, the Council appointed a young apprentice to Joshua named Dolon. Joshua figured he'd get an apprentice eventually, but Dolon was an odd choice, as he had no farming background whatsoever. His previous position was as an administrative assistant to the Elders. Joshua couldn't understand why the Council would assign an apprentice to him when there were so many other issues to address, like issuing a ruling on Samuel and Seth's deaths or announcing the appointment of the next Head Council. Whatever was going on, Joshua didn't trust it one bit. Dolon's appointment was not made on a whim.

The more Joshua thought about a Caulfield without Samuel and Lorrick, with a potential punishment coming down on his family, with Darin as Head Council, the more he thought about Andrew's question: are you planning to make a break for it?

If he did attempt to break out, he'd need at least one other person to leave with him. He already knew Andrew wouldn't go. Gabe wouldn't go with the condition Mariam was in. Adin wouldn't go because she'd never leave Asher, not to mention her pregnancy. He could go alone if he became desperate, but that didn't appeal to him. Whatever he was going to do, he needed to make up his mind quickly. The longer he stayed, the more likely it was that he would never leave.

One morning, Dolon and Joshua loaded up the cart for deliveries to those special few in Caulfield. Joshua looked forward to seeing Rachel. She always had a way of cheering him up. The music played loudly, as usual, and as the two young men made the finishing touches on the cart, the lyrics from the boombox caught Joshua's attention.

There was a time when I tried to hold the ocean in my fists
When I mistook the language for the light
There was a tightness that gripped my soul
and bubbled at my wrists
And choked me within inches of my life
But now I'm letting go and I can finally breathe, I can finally breathe
And my hands are open, reaching out

I'm learning how to live with doubt
I'm learning how to lean into the grey
'Cause I've had enough of black and white
I'll find another way and I will lean into the grey

Now that the music had been put on random selection, the number of Thrice songs drastically decreased. But every time a Thrice song came on, Samuel came to mind. Sometimes Joshua knew what the lyrics meant. But certain songs, like this one, he wasn't sure. What did it mean to 'lean into the grey?' Did it have something to do with Grey Dawn? This music was made well before Grey Dawn existed, so it must mean something else, but Joshua had to get moving, so he put the question to the back of his mind and turned his attention to the task at hand.

He took his usual route while Dolon stayed behind to address other matters. The interaction between Joshua and the people receiving deliveries had turned somber since Samuel's passing. Everyone was feeling his loss. On top of that, everyone knew how close Joshua was to Samuel. The 'I'm sorries' people had previously said during his deliveries had now turned into an awkward silence. Not to mention that there was still the very real possibility that Joshua was going to be punished by the Council. Everyone on his delivery route had turned weird with Joshua. Everyone, that is, except Rachel. She shared in the sadness of Samuel's passing but found a way to keep things positive.

Fortunately, Rachel was always his last customer on his route, so Joshua could stay a little longer. He was nearly to her residence when he passed the Prayer Center with its door wide open. Doriel sat inside, a stern and intense look on his face. Joshua hoped he could get by without drawing Doriel's attention, but the cart was loud.

"Hello, Joshua," Doriel said as he came to the doorway

with one eyebrow up, ready to inspect and criticize Joshua's response. "Good to see you performing your duties and moving forward after Samuel's death."

"Hello," Joshua said as he continued pushing his cart forward, not planning to stop.

With one eyebrow still up, Doriel continued. "It's important that we all continue to perform our duties, despite the unexpected and early loss of our greatest leader and our finest farmer. Fortunately, Seth is experiencing the countless joys of God's Kingdom in Heaven, and Darin has picked up the leadership torch rather admirably in his absence. As for Samuel, well, we're fortunate to have you fill his shoes, but there's no use in wasting your time pondering over his eternal damnation."

Joshua stopped in his tracks and dropped the cart from his hands with a loud thud. Rachel's delivery somehow did not fall out of the cart, despite landing so violently. "What did you say?" Joshua asked, gritting his teeth.

"Now, now, no need to get all worked up," Doriel said with a wave of his hand. "It's certainly not your fault that Samuel chose an eternity in hell. He had his chance and was well aware of the consequences. Even I, myself, personally warned Samuel on dozens of occasions of what could happen, but he wasn't as fortunate as those of us, like Seth, who recognized and accepted that Jesus is the one and only way to God's kingdom. There is nothing any of us can do for him. The choice was his, and he chose to never accept Christ as his savior."

Joshua couldn't believe the words coming from Doriel's mouth. "You really believe that Seth is in Heaven and Samuel is in *hell*?"

"It's not a matter of belief, Joshua, it's a matter of fact. The Bible clearly states that Jesus is the light and the way to God, and only through him will any of us ever make it to

Heaven. I don't make up the rules. Seth was baptized and confirmed in the name of Christ. Samuel, on the other hand, was never baptized and never confirmed. I showed him the passages in the Bible indicating that only through Christ could he attain God's ultimate treasure, but he ignored the scripture. Now, he's paying the price. 'The fear of the Lord is the beginning of wisdom.' Proverbs chapter 9, verse 10."

Joshua was beside himself. "I was in that very Prayer Center when I heard Seth, with my own ears, talk about how the belief in God was foolish and a waste of time. I was there when he said that the closest thing to God any of us would ever know was him, not Jesus. Seth was the cruelest, most condescending and controlling man I've ever met. If there was anyone who deserves an entirety in hell, it's Seth!"

"It's true that Seth could be patronizing at times, but you must understand the pressure he put on himself to be a powerful leader. He knew that everyone was counting on him and there was no room for weakness. He had to crush any perceived weakness in him so the Commune would have security in a strong Head Council."

"That didn't give him the right to treat other people so poorly." Joshua answered.

"How others perceived him matters not, as long as they knew who was in charge. Let them hate, so long as they fear. You might have heard that Seth came under my ward when he was just eight years old. In those early days, Seth would often cry to me, about the pain of losing his parents, about not being sure if he could lead us out of Grey Dawn. I put an end to that nonsense quickly.

"Furthermore, I witnessed his baptism and confirmation myself, he confessed his sins regularly to me, and he trusted in Jesus to get him to Heaven. He had to lead our Commune with the firmness and consistency required of any respectable leader. I admit sometimes he got carried away, but he knew it and admitted it to me. I never said he was perfect, but he made the right choice when it came to religion. Have you been baptized and confirmed as a follower of Christ? Don't make the same mistake as Samuel."

"Make the same mistake that Samuel made?' Joshua said. "Samuel was the kindest, most considerate person I have ever known. He treated *everyone* with love and respect. It didn't matter to him if you were Chosen or not, had the Sickness or not, believed in Christ or Allah or no God at all. He treated everyone with the same inviting and caring nature, always making those around him feel important and included. If there is anyone on this Earth that lived a life mirroring the life of Christ, it was Samuel. If Heaven exists, I have no doubt that Samuel is there, not Seth."

"Joshua, there is no use in arguing the point. The truth is there, in *writing*, in the Bible. It's as plain as black and white: Isaiah, Chapter 64, Paragraph 6, 'For all of us have become like one who is unclean, And all our righteous deeds are like a filthy garment; And all of us wither like a leaf, And our wrongdoings, like the wind, take us away.' You see? When we are born, we are born with sin. Unless you believe in Christ to take away that sin, all your kind and generous acts are nothing but filthy rags. Believe and accept that Christ is your savior and receive the gift of eternal life, or don't. It's as simple as that. Christ, himself, said he was the *only* way to our Heavenly Father. Go through him, or don't go at all."

Joshua was too angry to respond, and Doriel knew he had the better of him.

"Alas," Doriel said, "we are wasting our breath. The rules are the rules, and there's no point in going on any further if you are going to choose to ignore the written word of God. You best get back to your duties. And, while you're at it, think long and hard about whether you are with Christ or against him."

Joshua picked up his cart and started on his path again without responding. He couldn't say another word; he was too mad to speak. Doriel had a way of getting under Joshua's skin like no one else. Joshua tried Samuel's breathing techniques to calm his anger and frustration, closing his eyes and taking three deep, controlled breaths. He immediately started to calm down.

In that moment, he realized things were never going to change in Caulfield. Doriel was always going to make Joshua miserable. Darin would soon be on the Council, maybe even Head Council. Caulfield would become a place of absolutes, a place where the people in authority and their rules were more important than love. It was time to leave. He'd made up his mind. During the next rainstorm, he was breaking out of Caulfield, dead or alive.

## ❧ 46 ❧

## THE GREY

Joshua mulled over the details of his escape as he rolled the cart up to Rachel's residence. He gathered her delivery and knocked on the door. It took her longer than usual to answer. He put his ear to the door and listened for any noise, but there was only silence. He knocked again, this time louder. A few seconds later, the door creaked open. Joshua was beside himself. One look and he knew, without a doubt, that Rachel was extremely ill. Her eyes were all puffy and filled with water, her nose a bright shade of red while her face was as white as paste. Somehow, she still had a smile on her face.

"Hey," Joshua said, "I have your rations. It's not the greatest stuff ever grown, as I'm having a bit of an issue with the crops right now. Still, I do have some Eupa for you. You better take some."

"It's fine. You're fine. Come in, but don't come too close. As you can tell, I caught whatever has been going around, and I don't want to give it to you."

Joshua went to the kitchen while Rachel shuffled to a

chair on the other side of the room. After he put the goods down in the kitchen, he made his way back to the front room. Joshua didn't want to say anything, but Rachel really looked like she was in terrible shape.

"How long have you been sick?" he asked.

"Oh, I don't know. I've been feeling lousy for a couple of weeks or so. I look worse than I feel," Rachel said with a forced smile.

"Have you gone to see Mary? She'd take great care of you."

"No, not yet. I'll go in a couple of days if I don't start to feel better. But what's Mary going to do for an old lady like me? I've made it this many years; I like my odds that I'll recover from this cold. Grey Dawn hasn't slowed me down. Besides, I've lived long enough, and I know what's on the other side. When my time comes, I'm going to have no problem leaving this place behind."

"You know what's on the other side?"

"Of course, I do. Haven't I told you about the time when I died?"

Joshua made a face letting Rachel know that he wasn't going to be fooled. "What? Come on. You're messing with me."

"Joshua, I'm serious. I'm not messing with you in the slightest. When I was a teenager, I caught some type of flu, pneumonia, something. My parents and I didn't realize how bad it was. We went to bed one evening, and when my mother checked on me in the middle of the night, she discovered that I was burning with fever. They took me to the infirmary immediately. I was so sick..." Rachel paused for a moment and shook her head, "I was delirious, in and out of consciousness. I barely remember going to the infirmary."

Joshua realized Rachel was not pulling his leg. She was sincere. She was telling him the truth.

"What happened when you got to the medical unit?"

"I remember being on a stretcher, people moving frantically around me. I couldn't see them, but I could hear the commotion all around me, feel the intensity in the air. Everyone was scared. But I was terrified. And so weak. I was holding on the best I could, trying to stay conscious, but I just got to a point where I couldn't hold on any longer. I had to let go. I knew I was going to die.

"The next thing I knew, I was no longer on the stretcher. Instead, I was up against the ceiling, watching everyone below me rush around, yelling instructions at each other. At the same time, I realized that I was no longer in pain, no longer sick with fever and congestion. In fact, I had never felt better in my entire life. I felt invigorated, like my five senses had been multiplied by a thousand.

"As I watched everyone running around, I suddenly realized that the body everyone was working on was my body. It sounds weird to say this, but it seemed perfectly natural to me, normal, in my exalted frame of mind, to be looking down from above on my own body. I wasn't alarmed in the slightest and instead felt at total peace. I was more content than I had ever been in my entire life. I did not want for a single thing."

Rachel went silent for a minute, staring off into the distance, finally wiping her sore nose with a handkerchief.

"Then what?" Joshua said, not able to contain his excitement. "What happened next?"

Rachel snapped out of her trance. "I became aware of a presence off to the side, drawing my attention, a single pinpoint of light that began pulling me toward it. It enveloped me, enveloped my entire being. The light was unconditional love, unrestricted peace, impeccable harmony. I realized I knew this place, that I had been in this place before, and that the life I had experienced in Caulfield was nothing more than an illusion, an opportunity for my spirit to grow and experience the wonder of God's creation. I realized every spirit is born of the Source and I was back in its presence. Think of the most love, the most joy you have ever experienced in this life, and multiply it by a million, and you still don't come close to the way you feel when you are reunited with Spirit. I was home."

"That's astounding," Joshua said.

"There's more. I was approached by the silhouettes of three beings of light. The light emitting from them held more love, more feelings of intense joy than I can describe. A choir of angels sung in the distance, an orchestra of voices and sounds I've never known on this earth, praising God and frolicking through my spirit and all of eternity. The silhouettes in front of me showed me my life. Everything that ever happened, every word I ever spoke and emotion I ever felt, was reviewed in an instant. Then, they told me, not with spoken words, but with thought, that I was home, but that I had to go back, as there were other things I still had to accomplish with my life. I didn't want to go. I begged them to let me stay, but it wasn't a choice. Before they sent me back, they assured me they would be with me, in spirit, for the entire duration of my life, even if I couldn't see or hear them.

"I felt like I began falling backward, like someone had pushed me off a ledge, and then I slammed back into my body through the top of my skull. The commotion around me blared once again; people screamed that I had been resuscitated, that I had been saved. Pain coursed through my body with the labor of each breath, mucous rattling as my lungs expanded and contracted. The fever and sweat poured over my head, saturating my body."

"That sounds terrible," Joshua said.

"I didn't want to open my eyes. I kept them closed,

praying that I would go back to where I was. I prayed harder than I ever had my entire life. However, with each passing second, I became more certain I was going nowhere. I was back in my body and it was going to be the remainder of my lifetime before I was back in Heaven and one with our Creator again."

Rachel was so sincere in her telling of the memory that Joshua had to believe her. But he still had to ask some questions.

"Are you sure it wasn't a dream or some type of, I don't know...hallucination or something?"

"I know what I experienced, Joshua. When I was on the spirit side, with God, I was more alive than I've ever been. Dreams are fuzzy and distorted. This...this was more real than anything I've ever known."

Joshua pressed on. "But how do you know you were in Heaven? What I mean is, shouldn't you have been judged first? Shouldn't you have been examined or something to make sure that you accepted Christ as your lord and savior or something?"

Rachel smiled. "Joshua, don't think of God as a domineering parent, waiting to punish or reward you, as its child, upon reaching the spirit side. God does not judge, does not punish, and does not separate us, sending some to Heaven and others to Hell, depending on the religion we chose while on earth. The various religions are nothing more then various cultures trying to comprehend the incomprehensible. The Source is so complex, so beyond human understanding, that no culture, no society, could ever capture the essence of our Creator and reduce it to written rules and regulations. It would be like trying to hold all of the waters of the ocean within your fist.

"Try to think of God as an encouraging partner. All living

things are born from the Source. We have only forgotten this truth during this life. When our body dies and our soul reunites with our Creator, we remember we are all a part of the same eternal oneness, bound by one thing and one thing alone: absolute unconditional love. We are *all* a part of it. God is love and unity, not judgment and separation."

"But what if you're a terrible person, like Doriel," Joshua said, "or the way that Seth was before he died? They don't deserve to be in Heaven."

"All spirits originate from the Source, to experience God's creation and majesty, and to grow and mature in the process. All souls return to the Source upon the body's death, Seth and Doriel included. Try not to categorize a person's life as good or bad. There is just life. Furthermore, even if you do categorize, there is no one on Earth that is good all the time or bad all the time. Life is not black and white, life is grey, all life. Individual souls are darker or lighter shades of grey, sure, but even the evilest person has some goodness in them and vice versa."

Joshua sat silently for a moment. "That just doesn't seem fair to think that Samuel and Seth are in the same place."

Rachel gently asked, "what has got you so concerned about Heaven and Hell, and who goes where?"

Joshua was surprised by her question. "On the way over here, I ran into Doriel in the Prayer Center. He started telling me how Seth is in Heaven, but Samuel is in Hell because he was never baptized and confirmed. It didn't matter that Samuel was the kindest person we've all ever known. He's going to Hell because Christ said that he was the only way to the Heavenly Father."

Rachel leaned forward. "Joshua, when Samuel was alive, and you came to him when you were upset with the way Doriel or Seth had treated you, what would he suggest you do?"

It didn't take long for Joshua to answer. "He always told me to turn the other cheek. He would do his best to calm me down and then remind me to forgive them. He never spoke poorly about them or anyone. He would...pray for them."

"Would you say that he expressed love toward them?"

"Yes, I would. Samuel expressed love towards everyone."

Rachel smiled. "Don't get caught up in the absolutes and the man-made requirements as to what God is and what Christ means to mankind. God is love. Period. When Christ said that he was the only way to the Heavenly Father, he wasn't saying, 'Believe I'm the Son of God or you'll be damned for eternity.' He was saying, 'Do in your life as I have done in mine; love your fellow man as I have loved you; forgive your fellow man as I have forgiven you.' Finding God through Christ means living a Christ-like life, in the name of unconditional love, which is exactly what Samuel did."

"That's *exactly* what I told Doriel. I told him that Samuel lived a life that mirrored Jesus, and that Samuel deserved to be in Heaven more than anyone!"

"Joshua, please understand, a soul doesn't go to Heaven because it *deserves* to go there. The soul goes to Heaven because that's where the soul *came* from. And while God doesn't judge you, each soul comes to understand the feelings that it caused others to experience during its lifetime. In that life review I was telling you about, when you relive each moment in your life, you feel, physically and emotionally, what it was like to be on the receiving end of those actions. The soul steps into the shoes of the other and feels the pain it caused when it was cruel, just as it feels the joy it provided when being kind. The soul is not judged for those actions but is simply allowed to comprehend how it made others feel."

Joshua nodded his head. He still didn't know what to believe because what Rachel said didn't make a whole lot of common sense. Rachel spoke from her heart, with little to no filter, so there was no reason for her to lie. But Seth in Heaven just seemed unfair, and he couldn't get past the idea of everyone going there. If you live life hurting others, there must be *some* price to pay. The life he'd known was black and white, with hard and fast rules, and the enforcement of those rules with punishments was going to be even graver when Darin took control of Caulfield. Joshua's thoughts shifted to the fact that he had to get out of this Commune before it was too late.

Thinking of his escape in Rachel's presence reminded him that he would be leaving her behind if he followed through with his plan. The thought of it broke his heart, and Rachel could tell.

"What's the matter?" Rachel asked. "Are you still having issues with what I experienced?"

"No," Joshua replied. "That's not it at all."

"Well, what is it, dear? I can tell something else is on your mind, but I can't help if you don't share it with me."

"It's just...well..." Joshua was scared to ask her. He looked down at the floor. "Have you ever thought about, maybe, I don't know, maybe leaving Caulfield?" Joshua looked back up at her, his eyes wide.

Rachel smiled. "Why do you ask. Are you thinking about making a break for it?"

Joshua immediately went on the defensive. "No! It's just—"

"I'm just teasing you," she said with a wave. "The answer to your question is no; I don't think about leaving Caulfield. I'm old and my time in this life here is coming to a close. With Darin taking control, I would strongly consider it if I were younger. But to leave when I'm in this condition? No. It doesn't make sense. Caulfield has been my home my entire life, and it is also going to be my grave."

Joshua wanted to hug her but resisted the urge.

"But I will tell you this. If I were going to make a getaway, I'd do it at night, and I'd wear all black. I'd also do it in a rainstorm. I don't need to remind you of how violent and deafening they can be. The cover of night with dark clothing is perfect to hide your body, while the cover of rain hides your sounds. And I'd bring a raincoat," Rachel said with a wink.

## 🕃 47 🕃

### THE PLAN

W hen Joshua got back to his house, the whole family sat in the front room, looking apprehensive.

"What's up?" Joshua asked.

Gabe glanced around before speaking. "Council Campbell secretly informed me that it's only a matter of days until Darin is appointed as Head Council. I shared the news with Mom, and she and Adin let me in on the secret of Adin's pregnancy with Seth's baby. A secret that you were apparently aware of, Joshua?"

"I'm sorry I didn't say anything. It wasn't my place."

"We can deal with those issues later. Right now, we have much more pressing matters on our hands. The fact is pregnancy out of wedlock is forbidden in Caulfield. Seth might have had grand plans to change or avoid this law when he was Head Council, but he's dead and gone, and the pregnancy law still stands. In a month or two, Adin's pregnancy is going to start showing. Once that happens, there's going to be a third Red Circle on our front door for sure."

"I agree with you that a third Red Circle is coming,"

Joshua replied. "Darin knows about Adin's pregnancy, but hasn't gone public with it yet. I'm not sure why he's waiting, but it doesn't matter. If it's Adin's pregnancy or my involvement with Seth and Samuel's deaths, either way, it appears our family will be dealing with another Red Circle in the near future."

Joshua looked around at each face in the room. Everyone appeared numb trying to comprehend one of them dying from public hanging. Joshua closed his eyes and thought of his mom, telling him to never lose hope. He wondered what Samuel and Lorrick would do if they were in such a situation. He prayed for their guidance before continuing.

"Lorrick and Samuel spent the past ten years making contingency plans for something unforeseen. None of us could have known that we'd be sitting here without them, contemplating receiving a third Red Circle and Darin being appointed Head Council. Maybe this is exactly what they were afraid of and planning for." Joshua waited for someone else to say it, but his comment was met with silence.

In a calm, matter-of-fact tone, Joshua said, "We have to leave Caulfield."

"What do you mean?" Mariam snapped.

"I've been thinking about it for a while now. We must load up the armored bus in the inner garage with as much food as it can hold. Then, during the next rainstorm, we leave in the middle of the night. It's the only way we're all going to survive."

"Are you senseless?" Mariam asked. "How are we going to make it past the guard tower? There's someone stationed at the double gate every minute! Even if we made it out, where in the hell would we go?"

Joshua tried to remain calm. "We don't know what will happen out there. But we do know what will happen if we stay: one of us is going to die. I made it all the way from

Hartland on foot with nothing but a backpack. If I made it that far on my own, we will find some place outside of these walls where we all can live and not have Darin as our dictator. If we don't find a place, we'll make one."

"You must be crazy," Mariam said.

"I don't know, Joshua," Adin said. "I'm scared. What about my baby? What if something goes wrong?"

"If we stay here, one of us is going to die!" Joshua said.

"Stop with this nonsense!" Mariam screamed.

"He's right," Gabe interjected. "Mom, with Darin as Head Council, he's going to make an example of us. He's going to use either Adin's pregnancy or Joshua's involvement with the accident as justification for a third Red Circle. There's no way we can select one of us to die, so Darin will select for us, flex his muscle. It won't be Adin because she's pregnant with Seth's child. It won't be Asher cause he's too young. As much as Darin hates Joshua, he's Head Farmer. It's going to be you or me, Mom."

"On the other hand," Joshua continued, "If we leave in the next couple of days, we all live, assuming we can get out. Mariam, you had five children via natural childbirth. You can help with Adin's delivery when the time comes."

"Even if we agreed to leave, how would we ever escape Caulfield?" Adin asked.

"Like I said," Joshua answered, "Over the next forty-eight hours, we bring as much food and supplies as we can to the bus. Then, during a storm under nightfall, we make our way to the bus. Gabe can approach the guard on duty at the main tower, tell him that one of the Elders needs to see the guard immediately for an emergency, and Gabe has been sent to relay the message and relieve the guard of his duty. Once the guard is gone, we'll have a small window of time to get out.

"Gabe will wait at the tower for our arrival. The noise from the bus will surely wake many residents, so our timing has to be perfect. As soon as Gabe sees us coming, he'll start opening the inner gate. Once the bus is past the first gate and inside the vestibule, we will have to wait for the inside gate to fully close before Gabe can open the outside gate. While the outside gate is opening, I'll climb on top of the bus and throw Gabe some rope. He'll climb down from the tower and join us. By the time the outer gates are fully opened, Gabe will be in the bus, and we can make our escape. I know it's risky, but it should work and it's the best chance we have of keeping our family together and safe."

"I can't believe we're having this discussion," Mariam said, her voice a growl.

Gabe ignored his mom and continued from where Joshua had let off. "Our timing has to be spot on like Joshua said. Once the other guards realize we're escaping, we have to assume that they will open fire. I'm thinking worst-case scenario." Gabe turned to Mariam. "Mom. Do you really want to stay and die or see me die?"

"Of course not!"

"One of those two things will happen if we stay."

"If we leave, where are we going to *go*?" Mariam asked.

"Joshua, do you think we could go back to Hartland?" Adin asked.

Joshua bit his lip and sighed. "I don't know. I don't know if they will allow us in. And, even if they do, I don't know if we'd want to go there."

Adin took the opportunity to address something that had always been on her mind. "Joshua, you never explained to us why you and your mom left Hartland. What happened that made you two leave?"

Joshua dropped his head, closed his eyes and rubbed his temple, reflecting back on Hartland. "Our numbers were alarmingly low, and our leaders couldn't figure out how the Sickness was being spread. According to my mom, they planned a more radical approach and were going to separate all Chosen from the rest of the Commune. Face-to-face contact between the two groups would be forbidden. Not only that, but once a Chosen woman was no longer able to have children, she would be removed from the Chosen group and sent to live with the other group. My mom could no longer bear children, so the two of us would have been separated for good. We would have never seen each other again. There was no way she was going to let that happen. She tried to convince them to change their minds and have everyone leave Hartland together, as a Commune, in search of other Communes and a cure for the Sickness. But she was unsuccessful, so we fled."

"Did the separation of the Chosen work?" Gabe asked.

"I have no idea. My mom and I left before they separated anyone. For all I know it could have worked. Or it could have failed. All I know for sure is, if we go to Hartland, Adin, Asher, and I would be grouped with the Chosen, while Gabe and Mom would be grouped with the rest."

Mariam got up from her seat and left the room without saying another word.

"Okay, so we don't go to Hartland," Gabe said, looking in the direction where she had just left. "It doesn't change the fact that we have to get the hell out of here as quickly as possible. Mom knows we have no choice. She'll agree to go. She knows it's our only chance for the whole family to survive and stay together. I'll talk to her alone."

Over the course of the next day, Gabe and Joshua took turns bringing all sorts of equipment to their armored vehicle. Joshua loaded the bus whenever he could get away from Dolon, who acted more and more like a spy than an apprentice, and Gabe loaded while on guard duty, walking the premises.

That evening, Joshua accompanied Gabe to get a spare

tire onto the old, rusted rack on top of the bus. When they returned home, they found Mariam crying in the kitchen with Ian and Belinda. Belinda gave Joshua a disgusted look, and Ian was clearly in full-on concentration mode.

"What's going on?" Gabe asked. "Isn't it a little late for a visit?"

"I'm sorry, Gabe," Mariam mumbled, whipping away tears. "I know I told you I'd go, but I'm just not one hundred percent sure that we should be going. And, if we do leave, Belinda and Ian are like family, like my own children. I had to tell them so they could decide for themselves if they wanted to come along."

Joshua didn't say a word. He was in shock that Mariam told Belinda.

"I can't believe you were going to leave us behind," Belinda said to Gabe. "I would have *never* done that to you."

Gabe knew how to handle Belinda. "Easy now. I knew Mom was going to say something to you, and on the off chance she didn't, I was going to give you two the option to join us. But don't get all high and mighty about loyalty. You might have everyone else in Caulfield fooled, but I know you too well and know you played Joshua to get on Seth's good side. You can deny it or not, I don't really care, but you know you played him, and you know I'd never leave without you and Ian so lose the drama."

"*What?*" Belinda shouted.

"He's right," Ian interjected. "Belinda, please. We've all done things that we're ashamed of and pointing fingers doesn't do anyone any good." Ian sighed through his nose, running a hand across his face. "The idea of Darin ruling Caulfield is not a pleasant one. You can say what you want about Seth, but at least with Seth you knew where you stood. Darin is like a wild dog, and now that he's the biggest dog, I'm afraid of what he can do. He's ruthless and full of malice.

If what Council Campbell says is true, then we need to escape with Mariam and the rest of our family."

Joshua stormed out of the room, went straight for the stairs, and jaunting up to the second floor. Gabe gave chase and followed Joshua into his bedroom.

"What's up?" Gabe asked.

Joshua erupted. "I can't believe we're going to bring Belinda!" He wanted to make sure he was loud enough, so Belinda could hear every word he said. "She deliberately lied to me to get me to play into Seth's little trick. She's the reason that Samuel is dead!"

"You have to calm down. Screaming your head off and blaming other people is not going to bring him back. I don't trust her any more than you do, but the fact is, adding Ian and Belinda to the group makes sense. Ian is extremely resourceful, and I don't think he ever had it out for you or anybody else. While it does appear that he was in on the deception, or, at the very least, aware of it, he's not a bad guy at heart and wants no part of Darin being Caulfield's Head Council. Once we're on the road, trust me, we'll be glad that Ian is along for the journey."

"Fine. Ian can come. But Belinda can stay here."

"I know you hate her, but you cannot ignore the fact that she's been through a lot too and has been like a part of our family since well before you got here. She made a mistake, I get it, but we all make mistakes. Plus, at the risk of sounding like some of the others here in Caulfield, humanity is losing the war against the Sickness and Belinda is Chosen. If we leave here without her, we're not only leaving behind a family member, but we'd be out there with one, exactly, one Chosen female in our group. If we leave here with Belinda, we have two. That doubles our odds of survival, doubles our odds that we can bear children that are immune to the Sickness. We're protecting our family while thinking about our reality after we've made it past these walls. Do you understand what I'm saying?"

Josh wanted to rage some more, but he couldn't, as everything Gabe was saying made perfect sense.

"I understand what you're saying, but I don't trust her one iota. However, given the circumstance, I guess we really don't have a choice. You're right: she's part of this family and she doubles our likelihood of survival." Joshua sat down, looked around the room, up at the ceiling, and back at Gabe. "Besides, I think to myself, 'what would Samuel do?' and I know he'd bring her. Lying bitch and all, he'd bring her."

"You're right. He would," Gabe said with a laugh. "So, let's get passed this and continue with our plans." Gabe paused for a second. "You know, it just occurred to me, with Ian coming, we can use him as a lookout. I'll get the guard to leave the tower. We'll station Ian between us and I'll signal to Ian when we're clear so he can signal to you. You'll get the bus moving and we'll be on our way. Now, we just have to wait for a stormy night."

## ❦ 48 ❦

## TIME TO EXECUTE

A night of violent storms finally arrived. The sonic booms of thunder, flashes of lightning, and constant spatter of pounding raindrops made for an eerie atmosphere, but it was perfect for their escape. Joshua sat in his room, going over the plan repeatedly, each time getting more nervous, to the point where he thought he was going to be sick.

Gabe stuck his head in. "Belinda and Ian just got here. We're all ready to go." Gabe's gaze darted to the sweat dripping down Joshua's forehead. "You okay?"

"I didn't think I'd be this nervous when it finally came time to do this thing. I'm a wreck." Joshua got up and ran his fingers through his messy hair. He had to get moving, yet he just stood there, looking at Gabe.

"Come on," Gabe said forcefully. "It's time to put this plan into action and get the hell out of here. We know what this place is turning into. This isn't home anymore with Dad and Samuel gone and Darin lined up to take charge."

Joshua nodded. "You're right. Let's get this done so we can find a better life."

He could barely feel his legs underneath him, but they moved, and he and Gabe joined the rest of the family in the living room, which was lit by nothing more than a single candle. With Belinda and Ian there, all seven heads that were going to make the break were accounted for.

The rain was heavy and consistent. In his head, Joshua knew it was a perfect night to flee Caulfield, but he couldn't get his nerves off the edge. He kept thinking about what would happen if the escape failed, what Darin would do to him and to the others who were foolish enough to go along with his plan.

"Let's review the plan," Gabe said. "Everyone but Ian and I will get to the bus quickly and quietly. Remember to walk in a single file and keep your heads down. No one will be out at this time of night, especially in this weather, but keep your heads down anyway. If anyone sees you and says something, just ignore them and keep walking. Ian, you'll leave right behind them and station yourself on the roof of Mistrik Manor where we marked. I'll head straight for the tower. Once the guard has left, I'll signal to Ian from the east window. Mom, you wait on Clark Street at the crop entry. After I've given the signal, Ian, you relay the signal back to Mom and get down to the corner of Clark and Deming. When you see that signal, Mom, get to the garage and bus as quickly as possible. We'll have maybe ten minutes before the guard is back. Not much time, but it's plenty if we do this properly."

Joshua took over. "As soon as Mom is on the bus, I'll hit the gas and pick up Ian on the way to the tower. Gabe will keep an eye out to the north for the bus. When he sees it, he'll open the inner gate and when the bus is between the inner and outer gate, he'll close the inner gate and open the outer gate. Once that outer gate starts to open, Ian will climb up to the bus's roof and throw the rope to Gabe. Gabe, as soon as you secure that rope, get your butt down to the bus quick and we're out of here."

"Everybody got it?" Gabe asked.

Everyone either nodded or made an undistinguishable grunt—everyone, that is, except Joshua, who stared at Gabe. Joshua thought once again of what Darin would do to them all if the plan failed. Joshua could tell from the look on Gabe's face that he seemed to know what Joshua was thinking. Gabe looked at Joshua straight in the eyes and said with confidence, "Let's go."

As they walked out into the rain, one by one, the cool air and wet raindrops made everyone start shivering. When the party went east on Schubert to head towards the crops, Gabe and Ian continued south on Halsted, toward Mistrik Manor and the tower.

The group of five going east, led by Mariam, walked on the muddy road in a single file. Asher was next, followed by Adin, then Belinda, and finally Joshua. The first few hundred feet went by uneventfully. With each step, Joshua felt a little more at ease. He knew that the most dangerous part of this plan was right now: the five of them walking passed the Twin Towers in the middle of the night in a rainstorm. It was too suspicious to explain away. If they got to the bus without notice, the first and most difficult hurdle would be passed. Up to that point, it couldn't have gone any smoother.

As the group approached the northeast corner of Warner Hall, they found that the rain had saturated the ground to a point where it was difficult to walk. Mariam tried her best to lead everyone around the groups of large puddles, but it was useless. With each step, the ground gave way and mud oozed out from under their shoes in every direction, causing a distinct "squish" with each step, followed by a suction between the muddy ground and their shoes that made a second noise like pulling a suction cup from smooth glass.

PUCK. They became a loud chorus of ten feet, one after the other, back and forth, squish-PUCK-squish-PUCK. Not only was it noisy, but it slowed the group down tremendously. Despite the cold night air and chilly wet rain, Joshua could feel his temperature rising. They were going to be caught if this kept up.

As they maneuvered through the mud, Joshua thought of the ironic possibility of Ian and Gabe executing their half of the plan so perfectly, that it would be too fast for the rest of them slowed by the terrain. If Gabe got rid of the guard before they even got to the bus, it could mean the tower guard getting back too soon, with the escape failing without even really getting started.

Mariam led the group around the final turn to go south on Clark, which was the muddiest section yet. Each of the four in front of Joshua had a difficult time getting through it. When it was Joshua's turn, he sunk lower than usual into the mud, each step laborious. Instead of simply spreading around the base of his foot when it hit the ground, the mud came up around his foot and he sank deeper into the earth.

On the final step before reaching the corner, his left foot sank above his ankle. He tried to pull his leg up, but his foot was stuck. He reached out to his right and leaned against the outside wall of Warner Hall for balance. He pulled on his leg with his left hand for additional force, he kept his other hand against the wall for leverage. Just as frustration started to set in, his left leg shot up violently as his foot came free. Immediately, he knew something was wrong. He looked down to find his foot free, but his shoe still stuck in the mud.

He began to panic. He couldn't leave Caulfield barefoot. He'd need that shoe if he was going to survive outside these walls. He had to get it back. Joshua stuck his left hand deep into the mud and felt the slippery shoe. He tried to get a hold of the toe, but the ooze made it impossible to grab. Several times, he grabbed hold and pulled, but before making any progress, he would lose his grip and his hand would come up empty.

He swore under his breath. He couldn't believe, of all things to slow him down, of all things to foil the escape from Caulfield, it was a shoe stuck in mud that was going to do him in. His panic morphed into plain defeat. The escape had failed.

"Grab it by its laces," Joshua heard mixed into the sound of the pouring rain.

Joshua took a second to understand what he'd just heard. He thought it must have been Belinda speaking, but it was unquestionably a male voice. Or was it? He must be mistaken. Joshua looked up at the corner of the building just a couple feet in front of him, expecting to see Belinda, but no one was there. It couldn't be possible. The sound of millions of raindrops might have made it more difficult to hear, but he heard it. He knows he heard it. Someone was talking to him.

The voice rang out again, only louder. "Grab it by its laces!" The sound came from his left. Joshua turned towards the voice, and there, standing just beyond the edge of the muddy ground on the small, covered porch of the water towers' office, was Andrew.

"Grab it by its laces, Joshua," Andrew said calmly, confidently. "You should be able to get a hold of a lace and pull it free."

Joshua snapped out of it and stuck his hand down into the wet mud again. Once he was on the shoe, he felt around it until he found the distinct texture of a shoelace. He wrapped his fingers around the lace and pulled.

The lace came away from the shoe an inch or two until the lace was finally taut. Suddenly, the lace dug into the crease of his fingers at his big knuckles and the shoe would not budge. Searing pain shot through his fingers, but he was not going to stop until he had the shoe or until the lace broke, whichever came first. He continued pulling, with every ounce of energy he had, until the shoe finally started to give way. He shoved his other hand into the mud and grabbed the lace with both hands. What came free looked like an oblong ball of mud with string attached to it.

A sense of relief washed over Joshua. He stood up to thank Andrew, but he was no longer standing on the porch. He was gone just as quickly as he had appeared. Joshua's mind wondered for a second what Andrew was doing there and if he knew what they were doing. But the thought lasted only a second as Joshua didn't have time to ponder any questions. Both he and his shoe were free from the mud pit. He needed to catch up with the rest of the group. They must have realized by now that Joshua wasn't with them.

He wiped the mud from the outside of his shoe and scooped out more that had gathered inside. With one last squish, he put it on and ran around the corner, trying to make up for lost time and get to the garage entrance as quickly as he could.

At the entrance to the crops, Mariam was waiting for Ian's signal while the others had already entered the garage.

"What the hell happened?" Mariam said, rounding on him. "We get here, turn around, and you are nowhere to be found. Another few seconds and I was going to have to double back and try and find you! What happened?"

"I got stuck in the mud. Then my shoe got stuck in the mud and I couldn't get it out. It's okay. I made it. We all made it, and no one saw us." Joshua left out the part about Andrew. The disclosure would only worry Mariam, even though Andrew was not a threat.

"Well, you better get on that bus with the others while I wait for Ian's signal. Quickly."

Joshua made his way to the back of the Armory garage

and boarded the bus as quietly as he could, explaining to the others what had just happened with his shoe and the mud. Joshua took his seat sat at the wheel and kept the door open so he could hear what was going on inside the garage. From his vantage point, he had a clear view of Mariam and the garage door, so he would know when it was time to start the loud engine.

He went over maneuvering the stick shift in his hand a few times and felt the clutch with his left foot. Joshua hadn't driven a stick shift, but he'd gone over everything with Samuel a few times before he died. "Listen to the engine," he said to himself, several times. He tried to stay calm, convincing himself that he knew everything he needed to know about driving their getaway vehicle.

His thoughts turned from Samuel's lessons to Samuel, himself. Joshua missed his friend and found himself asking the same question he'd been asking himself ever since Samuel passed: Why did he have to die? He wished Samuel could be there with them for this escape. Everyone would feel so much better, so much safer, if Samuel were there at that very moment.

Suddenly, Thrice blared from the outer garage. Joshua looked at Belinda quizzically. Was he hearing things? No, he wasn't, because Belinda shot back the same look to Joshua—she heard the music too. The music got louder, and Joshua could hear the lyrics as plain as day:

> The tyranny of deterioration
> It worries me that it's all just a waste of time
> Taking one step forward, two steps back
> Still I believe there's a thread through the thorns
> And I believe that there's somewhere it's warm
> And I believe that it's ever bright beyond this black
> So keep holding on to hope without assurance

Holding on to a memory of light

It was one of Samuel's favorite songs, 'The Long Defeat.' But no one was in the outer garage to have turned on the boombox. Mariam was outside, at the end of the pathway, waiting for the signal from Ian. Belinda, Adin, and Asher were on the bus with Joshua. There was no one else there. The boombox couldn't be playing, but there it was. The song rang louder still with the chorus, and the tears began to swell in Joshua's eyes as the image of Samuel materialized in Joshua's head.

> But will the morning come?
> For all I know we'll never see the sun
> But together we'll fight the long defeat

The lyrics hit Joshua hard as he tried to swallow but couldn't. Not only were visions of Samuel flooding his mind, but he also thought of Lorrick and his mom. It was too much for Joshua to try and comprehend as the second verse began to play.

Belinda began shouting at Joshua, "Turn that damn thing off!"

Joshua ignored her and continued listening to the music.

> The suffering that I see all around
> It's enough to keep me crashing down until I
> I lie wrecked and reeling from these falls
> Still I believe there's a word in the wire
> And I believe there's a way through the fire
> And I believe there's a joy that blooms beyond these walls

Just as the last word from that second chorus rang out through the garage, Joshua jumped up and bee-lined for the boombox. He couldn't believe that he was about to leave it behind. He startled Mariam, who was running back toward the bus with her arms waving frantically.

"What are you doing? Ian gave the signal! We have to go!" she screamed at Joshua.

Joshua pulled the boombox's plug from the wall, grabbed its handle, and ran back to the bus, closing the door behind him and Miriam. With the pathway to freedom directly in front of him, it was time for Joshua to put his driving skills to the test.

## ❧ 49 ❧

## THE GATE

"Let's go!" Mariam shouted as she whacked Joshua hard on the shoulder as she ran past him. Sprinkles of cold water splattered onto his face, invigorating him. He pushed his left foot down hard against the clutch as he turned the key in the ignition. The engine kicked with a reverberation that made the whole bus shake. After a few seconds, the engine turned over and the bus spit black smoke from its exhaust.

Joshua looked in the top mirror to make sure everyone was seated, and then turned the lights on and released the emergency brake, moving the stick shift into first gear. He pressed down on the gas, emitting more black smoke into the garage, and slowly lifted his left foot to gently release the clutch. With a high-pitched squeal from somewhere underneath the bus, the wheels turned, and the bus headed toward the dark rain ahead.

The engine roared louder, reminding Joshua he needed to switch into second gear. He did so, releasing the clutch and pressing the gas once again, but he didn't give it quite enough gas and the bus jerked with a large hiccup. Joshua pushed harder on the gas and the engine smoothed out, with the bus continuing to move forward and gaining speed.

As he pulled out of the garage and drove the crops' short pathway to Clark Street, the rain started pouring down on the exposed bus. The sound of the rain pounding hard on the metal roof was distracting enough, but it paled in comparison to the blurred view ahead. He knew one of the instruments before him would activate the windshield wipers, but he didn't know which one. He would have to deal with the blurry glass for now.

Joshua prepared for his first turn as the bus approached Clark Street. "Hold on!" Joshua shouted before yanking the wheel hard to his left. The bus reacted as expected, and all four passengers were thrown to their right. Adin and Asher, sitting on the left side of the bus, found themselves on the ground in the middle isle, while Belinda and Mariam were smashed up against the windows on the bus's right side.

The adrenaline running through Joshua's veins made him forget that he was turning on to the unpaved portion of Clark Street. The entire bus slid to the right on the slick mud, with the back end coming around like a whip.

Joshua had to gain control of the bus or it was going to spin out.

Whether it was instinct or divine intervention, Joshua jerked the wheel hard to the right while pressing down on the accelerator. He could feel the bus correcting itself. He was not going to spin out after all, but he came into contact with the paved portion of Clark Street with the bus at an angle. The sudden shift from mud to wet pavement made the back end of the bus skip, causing all the passengers and the cargo to bounce up and down.

Joshua keep his foot on the gas and the engine boomed, reminding him that he had to switch gears. Again, he lifted his foot off the gas while hitting the clutch and switched into third gear. Once again, as he reapplied his foot to the accelerator, he didn't give it enough, and the engine puttered until Joshua gave it enough gas to be satisfied.

"I thought you knew how to drive this thing!" Belinda screamed. Joshua ignored her concentrating on the next turn, a right, onto Deming Place, which was approaching quickly. As the turn loomed near, Joshua panicked, not remembering how to down shift. He didn't want to kill the engine, so he just kept his foot on the gas, making a wide right turn, with the passengers again being thrown in the back, this time to everyone's left.

"Joshua! Look out!" Adin shouted as the bus rammed through one of the wooden beams supporting the overhang of the front porch where the various shops for Caulfield were located. Then the bus ran through a second and finally a third before the small porch roof came crashing down behind the bus. Everyone bounced around in their seats and on the floor, hanging on to whatever they could find around them. Joshua knew he couldn't stop and revved the engine further, steering the bus back into the middle of the road.

"Don't forget Ian!" Mariam shouted. Joshua slammed on the brake and the clutch at the same time. He opened the door, and Ian ran on board, soaked to the bone.

"What the hell was that?" Ian shouted. "All of Caulfield heard you crash! We need to move *now*!"

Joshua didn't need Ian to tell him that they likely woke up a good amount of Caulfield's residents. At this point, it didn't matter. He had one more left turn to make, one hundred feet away, then it was another hundred feet to the gate and Gabe at the guard station. They were almost free.

Joshua threw the shift into first gear, hit the gas, and was on the move again. As he approached his final turn, he slowed the bus down somewhat, but never took it out of gear. He whipped the wheel hard to his left. With the bus going at a slower speed and most of the mud washed from the tires, the bus held better traction around this corner. However, Joshua failed to make the turn wide enough to avoid Mistrik Manor on his left. The driver's side end of the bus hit the building with a thud, followed by the sound of metal scraping against concrete. It was one of the most horrible sounds any of them had ever heard.

"Damn it!" Joshua shouted as they cleared the building and he straightened the wheel.

"We're almost there," Belinda shouted. "The gate and the guard tower are straight ahead! We're almost there!" The light coming from the tower blurred into the disfigured mess that was the windshield. Visibility was terrible, but at least he could make out enough in front of him to avoid any more collisions. The windows to his sides did have rain on them, but they were nowhere near as distorted to look through as the windshield.

Joshua glanced out each side of the bus. He noticed way more lights on in Gold Castle and Mistrik Manor than one would expect for the middle of the night. The commotion from his collisions must have stirred Caulfield's residents.

"People are up!" Joshua shouted as he tried to concentrate on the road in front of him.

"Who cares?" Ian responded. "We're almost at the gate! Forget about those people!"

Ian was right. The group was just a few seconds away from entering the final challenge of their escape plan.

"Gabe better open that inner gate soon! It's just ahead!" Mariam yelled.

"We can see that Mom!" Adin shouted. "Gabe will open the gate!"

On cue, the inner gate, now just yards in front of them, began to open.

"He did it! He did it! Look! He did it!" Asher said excitedly, jumping up and down in his seat.

Joshua pulled the bus into the area between the inner and outer gates. He threw the transmission into neutral and applied the emergency brake.

"Go! Go!" Joshua shouted as he opened the door to the bus.

Ian grabbed the rope from the supplies and exited the bus with it looped around his shoulder. He ran to the front of the bus, climbed on the hood, and made his way to the top of the bus. The loud stomps of Ian's feet mixed with the tapping of the raindrops were deafening inside the bus cabin.

Joshua glanced at his driver's side mirror to see the inner gate beginning to close. He knew it only took ten seconds for the gate to close, but it seemed to be barely moving. Was the rain affecting the gate's ability to close? Beyond the inner gate, Joshua could see moving lights in the distance. Caulfield was definitely awake.

The shouts of men and women behind the bus could be heard through the pouring rain.

"What the hell is going on?"

"Who is in that bus?"

"Guards! Guards!"

Joshua's heart was pounding hard in his chest. "Come on, come on," he said under his breath. He heard the distinct clink of the inner gate completely closing and turned his attention to the front. Through the rain-distorted glass, Joshua could see the outer gate opening. Ian's feet rustled above the passengers once again. Through the bus door, which was still open, Joshua heard Gabe's voice shout, "I got it!"

With a loud thump, Ian jumped off the bus roof onto the hood, startling everyone inside, and then jumped off the hood onto the wet ground. The rope swayed back and forth just outside the bus door. Gabe began climbing down. The outer gate was almost completely opened.

"We're going to make it," Joshua whispered to himself.

Ian ran up the bus steps, dripping wet once again. Joshua continued watching the rope swaying back and forth another few seconds, when, suddenly, Gabe's body hit the ground hard. He got to his feet quickly and darted up the steps, limping, also dripping wet like Ian. "Go!" Gabe screamed.

Joshua closed the bus door, disengaged the emergency brake, hit the clutch, and threw the stick shift into first gear. The shouting from the residents of Caulfield had grown. The chorus of voices inside the bus, mixed with the shouting outside and the steady rain hammering the roof had Joshua on the brink of meltdown. He tried to concentrate on the outer gate. He just needed another second to make sure he could clear it.

Joshua glanced in his side mirror to see someone running with a flashlight and a gun. It had to be one of the guards. He could vaguely hear the man shouting, "Stop!" repeatedly. The outer gate was still rolling, but it appeared to everyone that they could no longer wait for the gate to open all the way.

"Go, Joshua! Go!" Ian yelled, "Guards are coming fast!" Ian looked over his shoulder and outside the back of the bus, where there was a wealth of action.

Joshua hit the accelerator, and the bus began moving forward. He did not think he was going to clear the gate, but it opened a little further with each millisecond, so even if he hit the gate, they'd eventually be clear. With just a few feet left from crossing the threshold of the opening of the outer gate, the unthinkable happened—the gate switched directions. It was *closing*. Then, the loud horn sounded, resonating throughout Caulfield.

"What the hell is happening?" Joshua shouted.

The rest of the passengers were speechless. No one could

believe what they were seeing or hearing. There was no way Joshua was going to stop, but there was no way he was going to make it through the gate, either. As soon as the front of the bus reached the barrier of the outer gate, it made impact with the right side of the bus. The screeching sound of metal on metal made everyone cringe. Joshua kept his foot on the accelerator, moving the bus forward, the friction from the gate slowing him down and pushing the bus to the left.

Before Joshua could anticipate it, the left side of the gate slammed into the left side of the bus, the sound of metal screeching on metal coming from both sides of the bus. With a thud, everyone jolted forward, and the bus came to a hard stop. Both sides of the gate reached the side mirrors on the bus. Sticking a good twelve inches out from the body of the bus, they acted as stopgaps. Joshua had his foot on the gas, but the wheels just spun. The bus stood still, suddenly illuminated from the watch tower spotlight.

"What are you doing? Go already!" Belinda screamed.

"I can't! I'm stuck! The gate has me stuck here!" Joshua screamed back.

"Shit!" Gabe shouted as he looked out the side window and up at the guard station tower. "Erik is back!"

"Erik?" Joshua asked.

"Erik, the night tower guard, that I got rid of. He's back! I can see him in the tower!" Gabe looked at Joshua with despair. "He must be the one that reversed the gate and sounded the horn!"

Maybe if he could get the bus out and get free from the current predicament, Joshua would be able to smash through the outer gate. He'd have to back up all the way to the inner gate and gun it. He didn't know if he had enough space to get any momentum, but he had to do something.

Joshua shoved the gearshift in reverse and hit the gas. The bus inched backward, again with the awful sound of metal scraping against metal. But after just a few inches, the bus once again came to a halt. The wet ground and the force of the outer gate pressing against the bus was causing its immobility.

"What are you doing?" Mariam shouted.

"I'm trying to get the bus free from the fence, but it's stuck!" Joshua shouted back.

Joshua threw the gear back into first and hit the gas. The engine roared, but the bus went nowhere. They were jammed within the outer fence and there was no way out. It was over. Soon the rest of the guards would be there to collect Joshua and the entirety of his crew. Tears of frustration, anger, and fear flooded Joshua's eyes. He had led his family to certain suffering, maybe even death. Darin was surely going to make a hard lesson out of all of them.

Joshua turned around to look at everyone. With the tears now rolling down his face, he said the only thing he could think of.

"I'm sorry. I'm so, so sorry."

Everyone stared back at him in complete silence, too dejected to respond.

## ✯ 50 ✯

## THE AFTERMATH

"**D**on't move another inch or I will open fire!" Erik shouted from the tower. Joshua put his head down. All he could feel toward himself was hatred. He let everyone he cared about down.

With a loud bang, the bus gave a massive jolt. The outer gate began *opening* again!

Everyone looked up. What seemed impossible was happening: the outer gate was, indeed, opening. In just a few seconds, the side mirrors would be clear of the gate, and they would be free.

Joshua wiped the tears from his eyes and backed the bus up, turning the wheel to make sure his left side mirror would clear the gate post on his left. He hit the brakes and put the bus back in first gear. He just needed a few more inches.

Asher, looking up at the guard tower, pointed and said, "Look! It's Andrew!"

Everyone except Joshua crammed on the right side of the bus to get a glimpse at the tower. Just as Asher had said, there was Andrew, standing at the tower window with his torso leaning out, his right hand raised in the air, fingers fully extended, and waving at the bus with an enormous smile on his face.

Gabe laughed out, "He did it! Andrew saved—"

Before he could finish his sentence, a loud distinguishable CRACK was heard, accompanied by a flash of light in the tower behind Andrew. The passenger side of the bus was splattered with blood.

"Ahhh!" Adin screeched, covering her mouth.

Andrew's body fell from the guard tower to the ground next to the bus. It wasn't clear where Andrew had been shot, but his entire face and right shoulder were covered with blood, and he didn't appear to be breathing.

Not a second later, the outer gate stopped and was suddenly *closing* again. Gabe shouted at Joshua, "Go!"

Joshua threw the bus in gear and hit the gas. The engine boomed as the bus revved forward. Just as the side mirrors cleared the gate on both sides, a loud CLINK, CLINK, CLINK tapped along the roof of the bus, followed by three holes that began leaking water.

"Another guard from the tower is shooting at us!" Belinda shouted. "We've got to get out of here now!"

Joshua knew that it was going to be close. He switched into second gear, and the bus picked up speed just as the outer gate met the back of the bus. The terrible sound of metal on metal rang out once again. Only this time, the bus had enough momentum that it wasn't going to stop, not if Joshua kept his foot on the gas.

CLINK, CLINK, CLINK

Three more holes in the roof acted as an incentive for Joshua to keep his foot on the gas, no matter what.

The engine revved hard as Joshua threw the bus into third gear. The force of the gate pushed the bus to its left. Joshua kept his foot on the gas, and a second later, he felt the bus break free of the gate.

They were clear.

He shifted the bus into fourth gear as the passengers behind him broke out into cheers and utter relief.

"We made it!" Gabe said as he patted Joshua on the back.

Joshua glanced into his rearview mirror to watch the gate closing behind him. Was the guard pointing his rifle at the bus from the tower?

SMASH! The rear windshield window on the emergency door shattered into a thousand little pieces.

"They're still shooting at us! Everyone keep your head down!" Joshua yelled. A second shot rang out, immediately followed by another CLINK. Joshua threw the bus into fifth gear and made a hard left, with Caulfield fading in the distance.

## ❧ 51 ❧

## A SIGN OF HOPE

Three hours had barely passed since their escape before Joshua pulled over. They had driven north on Route 23 and everyone agreed they were far enough away from Caulfield to stop. With the adrenaline that had been pumping through their veins during the break, no one had initially noticed that the bullet that shattered the back window had also hit Asher's left shoulder. It was just a graze, but it took out a chunk of his arm and he was bleeding badly. They bandaged him up while they were on the move and did their best to cover the rear window and bullet holes in the roof. Once they stopped, everyone realized how exhausted they were. It was still dark, so they decided to get some sleep. Joshua and Gabe volunteered to keep watch.

Now that they were free of Caulfield, Joshua began feeling tinges of regret, but he didn't want to admit it to Gabe. Joshua knew they had to leave, but he'd forgotten how isolating the world outside of Caulfield felt. He was worried about everyone's future, especially the future of Adin's unborn baby. But most of all, he felt an enormous amount of guilt over Andrew being shot.

"Is everyone asleep?" Gabe whispered to Joshua.

Joshua looked up in his mirror showing the cabin. "Yeah," he whispered back.

"I can tell something's up with you. What's the matter?" Gabe asked.

"I feel terrible about Andrew. I wonder if he survived. I should have convinced him to come with us."

"I know what you mean, but it's not your fault that Andrew was shot. No one asked him to do what he did. He saved us on his own volition, knowing that the risks involved were dire. Be thankful for his sacrifice and the fact that he wasn't on this bus, because, had he been, we never would have made it out. Lord knows how Darin would have punished us. We need to be mindful and thankful for what Andrew did and make sure that we honor him by making our future count."

"I'm also worried about Adin and her baby."

"I know. I'm worried too. At least we're all together."

Joshua sat in silence and thought of Lorrick and Samuel.

"I swear to you, Gabe, I'm going to make this right for Adin and her child. I owe it to Lorrick to see this through. I'm going to do whatever it takes to make sure they are safe."

Gabe smiled and then winced. "I trust you will."

"How's the ankle?"

Gabe lifted the left foot onto the dash. His ankle swollen, a dark shade of purple.

"It sucks, but I'll be ok. I can move my toes. It's probably just a bad sprain."

The rain passed by morning, and the group continued their journey. Once moving, Asher was clearly in pain. The rough ride made it difficult for Asher to get comfortable. Mariam removed the bandage to examine his injury. It didn't take a genius to see that it had taken a turn for the worse. No one was an expert in diagnosing gunshot wounds, but everyone knew what the onset of an infection looked like. They needed to find another Commune.

Joshua didn't recognize any of what he was seeing. As they approached a river with a collapsed bridge, Joshua had absolutely no memory of the scene. Moreover, if the bridge were collapsed on his way to Caulfield, he never would have made it to the Commune.

Somehow, Joshua was no longer on Route 23. He must have unknowingly diverted onto another highway.

He pulled the bus over next to a small pond. Each passenger got off to look for another way over or across the river, except for Gabe, who said it was too painful to walk.

Upon walking closer to the bridge, Ian shouted, "There's another bridge off in the distance to our left. It's not far, less than a quarter mile away I'd guess, and appears to be intact. There's got to be a way to get to that bridge."

Ian climbed one of the taller trees to get a better view of the other bridge. Watching her brother struggle up the tree, Belinda lost her patience.

"This is all your fault, Joshua," Belinda complained. "We're lost, and you have no idea where we are going to go. We never should have listened to you about leaving Caulfield."

"Belinda, please," Adin responded. "You are not helping the situation. You didn't have to come on this trip. We need to stay positive, work together, not blame one another for an unforeseen hold up like a downed bridge."

While Joshua and Gabe had planned and prepared as best they could for a long voyage, neither of them had anticipated the mental challenges the whole family would have to overcome to survive. They had plenty of food, water, and fuel, but hitting this obstacle was testing everyone's morale.

Mariam and Joshua stood at the tree base waiting for Ian

to reach the top of the tree while Asher and Adin walked off to relieve themselves.

"This is pointless!" Belinda exclaimed. "What are we going to do, Joshua? This was all your idea, so what are we going to do, huh?"

Joshua could hear Gabe swearing from inside the bus. Belinda felt no guilt or gratitude about the fact that she was out of Caulfield or what it took for them escape. Instead, Belinda acted with a sense of privilege, like she was entitled to survive, no matter what the cost to others. She made the blood in Joshua's veins boil, and he feared he might say something to make a bad situation worse.

Mariam hadn't said anything, but she had given Joshua a few looks. Without saying a word, Joshua knew what Mariam was thinking: it was a mistake that they left, and it was Joshua's fault that they did so.

The weight of the family's situation and survival intensified inside of Joshua. He felt doubt begin to take over. He thought that when they broke out of the Commune, they would find a safe place to go. Maybe they'd even find the place where Samuel was from, which would save them all. But the reality was they were in a worse position now than they were before they left. Joshua's spirit was on the verge of breaking; despair started to find its way back into his heart.

Ian confirmed from the top of the tree that he couldn't see any other route to the bridge and that they had no choice but to go back from the way they came. They were going to have to find another route.

As the group rounded back up and boarded the bus, Joshua waited to be last. He insisted on doing this to be sure that everyone was accounted for. Once everyone was on, Joshua took one last look around, his mind racing, filled with all the problems that seemed to be mounting fast. He stepped up and reached for the railings, grabbing them tightly with both hands.

Just as he was about to pull himself up into the bus, a cool breeze swept across his body, captivating and seizing him. Instead of taking that next step, he eased his grip on the railings and paused to enjoy the tender, crisp air. It was brisk, with a freshness that felt new and invigorating.

Joshua tilted his head back, closed his eyes, and took in a deep breath, filling his lungs with the light air. He did this again, and a third time, and decided to take the precious seconds to center himself, to let his thoughts and troubles go and focus on the moment. The breeze was a gift, and he wanted to fully enjoy it and forget all his problems.

Once the breeze passed, Joshua opened his eyes and tightened his grip on the railings, intending to pull himself up. Just then, he noticed a change, something different. To his left and behind him, he sensed a brightness that wasn't there when he had closed his eyes. He turned his head, curious to see what had changed. What he saw, he was not prepared for. His jaw dropped. He let go of the railing and stumbled backward, just catching himself before tumbling over.

Right there, before his eyes, was the most magnificent flower he had ever seen, fully bloomed on the water's surface, near the pond's edge. The thought of a flower blooming in water seemed impossible. Yet, there it was, making its presence known to all in its vicinity.

In the next moment, a bright ray of unfiltered sunlight pierced the grey sky and shined down directly on the flower, accentuating the array of colors and textures. Its deep blue petals culminated into a center that was brilliant yellow with hints of every color Joshua could think of glistening of the tips of the flower's stamens. He didn't know what kind of a flower it was, but it didn't matter. He was utterly mesmerized by its aura and beauty, bathing in the bright sunshine. The combination of the sunlight, the water, and the flower captured Joshua. It was simply magnificent.

Ian came down the bus stairs and was instantly taken aback the moment he laid eyes on the vision in front of him.

"Oh my God. Guys, come here and look at this flower in the water! Look at the sunshine!" Ian screamed to everyone on the bus. Everyone except for Belinda, who seemed disinterested, joined them, even Gabe.

"Wow. What kind of flower is it, Joshua?" asked Asher.

"I have no idea," Joshua said, still gazing at the wonder. "I've never seen anything like it."

"I've never seen it's equal," Ian said. "I would remember seeing something this breathtaking."

Adin started crying and laughing with joy. "Look at the sunshine! It's—" She was too emotional to talk.

Joshua broke from his trance and turned to the others, "Did any of you see this, at any time, before just now?" They all shook their heads in a unanimous no.

"No one?" Again, everyone just shook their heads.

Joshua couldn't understand it. The flower was right outside of the bus. Everyone except Gabe had been off the bus for several minutes. Yet, had it not caught Joshua's fleeting glance, they all would have missed it.

Belinda finally opened a window and leaned out. "That's what we are all so amazed by? A flower? A useless, does-us-no-good flower? What is the matter with you people? We are in serious trouble here, and all you want to do is be awed by some stupid flower?"

Belinda slammed the window shut and sat back down, looking the other direction.

Instead of rage or anger at Belinda's tirade, Joshua felt the most overwhelming sense of peace. Enthralled by the vibrant blue pedals and yellow center of the flower and contemplating the impossibility of it all made the darkness occupying Joshua's heart vanish. Joshua's mind filled with the memory and spirit of Samuel, the unconditional love and warmth of his dear friend. This miraculous water flower right in front of him was the spirit of Samuel, embracing Joshua, telling him that everything was going to be all right.

Joshua hadn't felt this way since the first time he saw the secret garden. A smile broke out on his face. As the love and memory of Samuel enveloped Joshua, he became certain of one thing: he would be reunited with Samuel, whether in this lifetime or the next. This faith, this hope, this love they shared, would always be a part of Joshua, and would remain a part of him for all eternity.

## THE END

# ABOUT THE AUTHOR

The son of a nurse from the City of Chicago's south side and an immigrant from Colombia, South America, Paul was born and raised in Chicago's Lincoln Park. Today he is a civil litigation attorney and lives in Wheaton, Illinois, with his wife Rachel, and their two sons, Andrew and Sam. In his spare time, Paul is working on the second installment to The Gift of Samuel.

**f**

Made in the USA
Monee, IL
23 March 2021